Grievous Bodily Charm

BY C.P.LAMONT

Text copyright© 2024 C.P.Lamont

All Rights Reserved.

This is a work of fiction. Names, characters, businesses places events and incidents are either the products of the author's imagination or used in a fictional manner. Any resemblance to actual persons, living or dead or actual events is purely coincidental. No part of this publication may be reproduced, stored in a retrieval system or transmitted in any form or by any means including photocopying, electronic, recording or otherwise without prior written permission of the rights holder, application of which must be made through the publisher.

CHAPTER ONE

The attentive waiter returned to the table, one of the regular clientele was absent. There was no uproarious laughter this evening. One of them raised his hand and beckoned him over. No small talk was engaged, drinks were ordered, Blue Goose. The Ivy was busy for a rainy Tuesday October evening. David had an ominous feeling of doom; however, he would not be the first to raise concern. They were not children, but hardnosed financiers, on the surface anyway.

'Relax David; it was just one of those things.'

'I'm sorry I don't share your optimism. He called me on Saturday, he was frantic. He was very worried, we should all be worried, I certainly am.'

'I feel the same David, but we can't do anything about it, c'mon, let's pretend we are enjoying ourselves at least.'

David raised a smile and his glass. 'Here's to the future, good or bad.' Simon was smiling but he agreed with David, but he wouldn't say it, he was dead and it wasn't "just one of those things." They should *all* be worried about their own personal safety. But he had to go through a charade to feign confidence. Simon chortled. 'Still ever the optimist David?'

David quaffed the vodka, this was not missed by the waiter; he was the most generous of the six regulars and the most charismatic. He was not a blueblood like the others, but he had impeccable manners. However, he was very subdued tonight, he was smiling but it was synthetic. He was troubled. He had to shake himself out of this doom laden torpor. He caught the waiter's observant eyes. No communication was needed, another round of Blue Goose. The gloom lifted instantly from the table. They switched off their phones and placed them on the silver tray held by the waiter. A semblance of calm returned to the party of financiers.

David had that fleeting moment of introspection; he had come a long way from a tenement in Dunmore Street (Kirkton), in Dundee, to the hallowed address in Montague Square in Mayfair. He had pre-planned a visit to Dundee in September to take his elderly parents to an exclusive tour of the Victoria & Albert museum before it was officially opened to the public. His smile expanded naturally without any forced effort. Dundee always brought a smile to his face when the vodka flowed and tongues became less rigid, some of the six spoke about their clients; Russian Oligarchs, and their avant garde business ethics. These Russians were rank amateurs compared to the Labour Party that had hegemony over Dundee with impunity and questionable financial practices in the 1970 s and 1980s. However, that was then and this is now, millions of pounds were the prize for facilitating investment strategies.

Not one of the bluebloods could come close to David's portentous view of where technology was heading. The 'Big Bang' changed the Stock Exchange in the 1980's, Fintech (Financial Technology) chip & pin apps would be the next big thing. David had seen this, others had not. He had set up a Technology Fund to invest in various chip & pin apps, in Cambridge and Silicon Valley. four years later, he sold the patents, overnight he had accumulated £200 million as he was the majority investor. The publicity of this made him a sought after financial advisor/ investor. Whether he sought the limelight or not it was thrust upon him.

He had left school in Dundee bereft of qualifications. The majority of his peers were guided to the construction industry, Caledon Boatyard or the NCR; and the young women to the Timex factory, which was well paid. But he was different, how? He didn't know. He had stumbled into computers by complete accident. In the local newspaper he spotted a vacancy for an Information Technology apprentice with the council. That was for him, why he didn't know.

His young cousin was an aficionado of computers, he asked her to give him a rundown of buzz phrases and the elementary components of the most popular computer, the name of the next computer which was due to come on stream, and the software which would be pre-installed. The interviewer was impressed at his knowledge of where technology would be going. However, he was concerned by his lack of qualifications. What were the reasons? David was candid, he could count, subtract and spell, his teacher(s) mistakenly appraised that he was academically challenged (thick). He held no grudges against them. He surprised the interviewer by challenging him on mental arithmetic, spelling or current affairs. His gamble paid off, he was hired. And he never looked back. His parents were pleased if slightly confused, where did he attain this knowledge?

He rose to the lofty position as the I.T. Manager within five years, not bad for a technophobe, but now he was absorbing information at a voracious rate. However, the majority of his managers were only vaguely interested in the unstoppable speed of evolving technology.

In the smoking room he had read in the newspaper that the council had purchased hundreds of computers and software services which cost in excess of £2 million pounds, but for how long? The contract was a commercial secret. He made an urgent appointment with the Head of Procurement. It was very clear to him that he was unaware that the computers were an end of line purchase. David advised this was unwise without establishing the cumulative cost of the contract and that it was a very bad deal. The Head of Procurement was indifferent; the bulk of the money was coming from central government, 'what are you getting your underwear in a tangle for?'

David detected there was an odour more pungent than Hai Karate aftershave; corruption. He stopped himself from pointing out the obvious, why buy these computers when they would be obsolete in less than a year? Someone had been incentivised. 'If I can't beat them, then I'll eclipse them.' He mused. The audit team must be less than vigilant, I'll lay the breadcrumbs, if they don't follow them, and only then my plan of financial security will begin.

And so began the genesis of financial accumulation of council funds into fictitious accounts of four suppliers. An invoice for £4000 was paid into one account three months later a further £17000. It was a computer novice's dream scam; he was anything but a computer novice. He had hacked into the accounts and 'approved' the various invoices, when they were in the system and had been approved, no discrepancy would be flagged up. The money would be paid in to the various accounts automatically. It helped that the auditing department were not computer savvy. With the third- party money he established a property company in Dundee and accumulated a plethora of two bedroomed flats. Luck had not finished with him yet. He had let out a property in Grove Road, Broughty Ferry to a party of four affluent young women who were attending the Open at Carnoustie in 1999. One of them was an entrepreneur from Silicon Valley, David and Johanne were attracted to each other not only for the love of golf but their mutual obsession of financial technology. She had backing from a Wall Street financier, David could now see around corners so to speak. He diligently validated her story; after all he was from Kirkton. Not to his surprise Johanne had underplayed her hand, she was a multi-millionaire, and suddenly he felt more attracted to her for some undefined reason. He invited her out to various pubs and restaurants in Broughty Ferry during the period of the Open. Both were single, Johanne enjoyed the politeness of The Royal Arch, but enthused about the cross-section of society and the enthusiastic participants of Karaoke in the Eagle. She strongly advised him to come to Silicon Valley and observe the different paths that Wall Street was investing billions of dollars in start-ups in Silicon Valley. He was intrigued to say the least. He had an abundant amount of disposable income; would it be now or never?

He requested to take a sabbatical of three months unpaid leave from his position with Dundee City Council, to explore innovative ideas into the evolving Information Technology sector, in the cradle of computer science innovation in Silicon Valley; with the aim of bringing the IT sector back into the council's control which would save the council millions over a five year period. His request was turned down, simply because the Council's I.T. department could not function without him; damming praise indeed. He hand delivered his resignation, and with his outstanding holiday entitlements cleared his desk that evening; not before but after cancelling the invoices which were in the automated payment system.

He stayed in San Jose; Johanne's company owned an apartment block. His eyes were prised wide open, he found it embarrassing how far the UK was behind the USA in technology terms; he would not be left behind. After three months in Silicon Valley he visited hundreds of fledgling companies, he was fully immersed in the optimistic zeitgeist of the numerous start-up companies. On his last night he invited Johanne and her business manager to dinner. He had a proposal; he drew a detailed mental picture for them; that he intended to set up an investment fund to back start-ups in the financial technology sector in Silicon Valley, his view was that banking had been virtually untouched by technology, in the near distant future people that would normally visit branches would be in the minority, most banking would be done from home computers. This would save banks billions in costs. PayPal was the pioneer for money processing; however, there were other companies enhancing present software, PayPal if it wants to remain the premium brand will be compelled to buy these companies or the patents. One guy told him in the near future the masses would do their bank transactions via their mobile phones. Home computers would be virtually extinct in 10 years' time. He was a believer. Were they?

They listened intently, he was prepared to invest his own money, but he needed financial investment from Wall Street, Johanne had been down that precarious route, would she be able to open doors? This would be a joint venture. He looked at her, hoping she would break the silence; he didn't have to wait too long.

'Well, David, you certainly have not wasted a minute over here. I hear what you say, but I'm not convinced that PayPal will go on an acquisition strategy, that would be very costly, this is the year 2000, they've only be trading over a year, they won't have the money to buy similar payment processing software companies. But I will think it over. What's your take on it Bernie?'

'I'm with David, and I'll agree with you also regarding PayPal, maybe not having funds to secure various similar patents, But what is to stop another company or bank buying PayPal?'

'Wow! You really think that's possible?'

David didn't factor this in; he wished he had thought of this, he had another idea. 'What if PayPal over the next say five years bought other software companies, which is possible, as Wall Street is burning through cash, hoping to hit the jackpot, with at least one of their investments, then when PayPal have the patents, some other conglomerate or Hedge fund buy's PayPal?'

Bernie and Johanne held their forks in mid-air, fission was in the atmosphere. All her doubts were swept away; they would set up a fund with Wall Street money and buy the start-up(s) or invest in them. Then PayPal could buy their start-up, thus Wall Street get a return on their investment, and Johanne and David benefit as well.

'You should go to the golf more often in Scotland, Johanne!'

'Well your Scottish education and your charm have won us over David.'

'It certainly has, which university did you study?'

'None I'm afraid, I had help from my cousin, and I was self-taught, if that doesn't sound too arrogant. Technology is a labour of love, it never stands still. Nor do I; I have a property business in Dundee, it's doing very well. That will be the source of my funds for this venture, if everything works out.'

'That's really fascinating, sounds like the American dream, well done. And thanks to you, I've got the pitch in my head for Wall Street.' David felt proud.

'I hope they agree to back us.'

'Of course they will David; we have an excellent business relationship with them, Bernie will secure funds as soon as possible, should only be a matter of weeks.'

'Really? That soon!'

'Wall Street want to get their money in start-ups, quickly, they are afraid of missing out. I'll take care of the finance, enjoy your meal.'

'I certainly will Bernie, and thanks to you and also Johanne for the invitation to Silicon Valley, it's been an education.'

Kismet was still by his side; Wall Street poured millions of dollars into their five most promising start-up companies of which two were in the telecom sector. Then the dotcom crash arrived. Wall Street wanted out, Johanne held the gate open for them, and paid fourteen cents on the dollar, there was no negotiation. She remained calm during the madness, twenty-something multi-millionaires (on paper) were wiped out over a matter of days. Johanne picked up their stock and stock options again with as little as two cents on the dollar. David had listened to Johanne's strategy of a once in a lifetime offer, however, it was cash only, they had to move fast to relieve the panic stricken CEOs of the start- ups.

   David re-mortgaged his property portfolio and had the money transferred into her account. He never looked back. In 2001 the World Trade Centre buildings were struck by two airliners, the stock market crashed, Johanne invested. In 2002 the Telecom & Technology sector raised its head up slightly above the pessimism, Johanne invested again; she invested a large tranche of the fund in PayPal and Amazon. David read her daily market reports that she emailed to him every night when the NYSE closed. He had a mentor who showed him how to invest when others were running away from the markets, four years later, his last email came as a shock; a Wall Street fund had made cash; or cash and shares offer for the fund. Johanne was selling; she recommended he does as well; however only on a straight cash basis. His £400,000 stake was worth £12million, Johanne had negotiated with the future owners that they would pay all their costs including federal and state taxes. He emailed her immediately; he would agree to sell on her recommendation.

   His wanderlust could no longer be sated. It was time to say au revoir to Dundee, he had his accredited Financial Advisor certificate; it was time to relocate to London. 2008 was momentous; the banking crisis had caused mayhem in the economies of the Western world. Banks were not lending to each other, mortgages were very difficult to acquire; that could only mean one thing a prolonged economic recession. The London and south east property market descended into a downturn. Johanne's sage advice was lodged in his head, 'invest in blue chip companies and property in a recession.' He was taking her advice. Mayfair would recover through time; that would be his preferred area to live. No mortgage for him, with no interest from the banks it was pointless having all his money in a zero interest account. He would hedge his bets. The property he had purchased was bought in 2005 for £3,500,000; his offer of £2,400,000 was accepted on the first offer on a cash only basis. Recently completed office blocks had lost 59% of their value; signed up tenants were looking for more favourable leases. This could be his foot into the commercial market.

He had invested in a former textile factory in Salford, Manchester; he then converted the factory into forty-five spacious flats to rent. The BBC had a plan to have a bespoke Media City built there in 2007 and completed by 2011. Thousands would be employed. It was a no-brainer. While the factory was being gutted he had three offers from companies to buy him out at 300% of his original purchase; thanks, but no thanks. Ironically he had never purchased a TV licence in his adult life; you can take the boy out of Kirkton etc. He had purchased a house in Broughty Ferry for his parents who would be horrified if they knew he hadn't a TV licence.

However, time and political events move quicker than people anticipate; disappointment never alters its shape or mood. Obama was heralded to change America and transform the world into a better place, he didn't. He involved himself into the Scottish and Brexit referendums. Karma got sweet revenge, it gave the United States Donald Trump; karma is a crazy bitch.

During the Scottish Referendum he was stopped by numerous members of different nationalities at the exclusive gym in the leisure club. A minority spoke in hushed tones about conspiracies, how it would never happen, because if it did, the European Union would collapse like democratic dominoes; it would never happen. Depending who he spoke to it was a conspiracy orchestrated by the C.I.A. or KGB. He had to confess he was indifferent either way. And he was not a fan of conspiracy theories. He called his dad (who believed in political conspiracy theories) in Dundee and put forward some of the conspiracy theories; he gave him short shrift about Putin and the KGB. 'What are the Russians going to come to Scotland for...our food banks and methadone?' He was serious. Then he went on a rant regarding his least favourite socialist MSP, who hadn't had a real job in her effing life! He had to ask him what she had done now. To paraphrase, she jumped on any environmental or political event. She had spoken out about an organization that was vehemently anti-trade union and anti-Semitic at every political event, the company was a disgrace to Dundee etc. She just happened to marry the owner's son. She had not put this on any social media site, because it was a private matter. It was not on her Wikipedia page which was an anodyne mixture of her hard-left credentials. His dad opined that's why she had softened her rhetoric, she was no longer turning up for photo-opportunities, Palestine, Syria or any other war torn countries were erased. David knew she was a political chancer, but surely she couldn't have done this?

As he was based in London he wouldn't have a vote, he considered that fortunate. He still had his abode in Dundee, so he could have registered to be eligible to vote in the Scottish Referendum, but he wouldn't do it as he couldn't envisage when he would return to Dundee for any length of time.

History had shown Scotland voted No. However, the UK voted to leave the EU. Again at the gym it was the Russians who had 'fixed' the vote to leave the EU. Or maybe it was the CIA. His dad called him after the EU result, again about his least favourite socialist MSP who never had an effing job in her life, (as if he had forgotten this) 'well she was anti-EU, then she became a Remainer, obviously not related because she married into that, anti-trade union, and anti-Semitic family, her words son, not mine, if this is meant to be a democracy, why do we have List MPs, who are not elected, become MSPs if the people didn't vote for them?'

David moved the subject from politics; he was worried about his blood pressure. They spoke about the new V &A being built at the Waterfront. He was full of praise; it's going to change Dundee for the better; jobs and tourists. Did I tell you that the List MSP is trying to take credit for the V&A, we've had some chancers in Dundee, but son she is shameless.' With that praise, David ended the conversation. Tomorrow, it was his dad's birthday, when he opened his curtains; he would have a Mercedes sitting in his driveway. He would hazard a guess it wouldn't be from that effing MSP.

Everything was running smoothly in his business and personal life, until that fateful day in 2016. David had received an urgent phone call from the Merchant Bank; the UK & US Governments had suspended all financial transactions due to a breach of international financial transactions. The Merchant Bank advised him to seek other funding options.

He was onsite at the office block, it was at the fitting out stage, and it would cost £15 million to complete. Where was he going to acquire this money in the next four weeks? This £15 million had to be deposited in an escrow account to pay the various building contractors. He would have to contact his lawyer who had organised the loan. He cut short his inspection of the office block on the 23rd floor. He spoke to the site agent who was explaining to David's investors that everything was on time, and on budget. They were on the final stage, three months to fit everything out and install the office furniture and then the international bank would have their 600 staff in for training. He spoke to the investors, his father had been rushed to hospital; he had to fly up to Scotland. They understood and wished his father a speedy recovery.

He took a taxi to Canary Wharf; in the taxi he called Nigel, his secretary explained he was at a meeting, could she take a message, and he would call him back, what was his name?

'David Fisher, he has my number, I'm in a taxi on my way to his office ; and the message is the £15 million will not be coming as agreed from the Merchant Bank that he had negotiated…I hope he has not budgeted for his bonus.' He felt some semblance of calm return. His mobile rang out. 'Hi

David, I heard about the suspension of the bank's licence, I have a proposition to put to you, I'll speak to you when you arrive at my office.'

David was mystified, what did he mean a proposition? Could this be a scam to cut him out of the deal by bring in new investors to finance the £15 million, and then replace him as the majority investor? I don't think so! Or being optimistic or deluded; has he someone who can supply the last tranche of money for a fee above the market rate? Notwithstanding Nigel would be imposing an arrangement fee on the transaction, probably 3% (£450,000). Not bad for Nigel, but horrendous for him. He had no choice either way, better to lose £450,000 than his personal investment of £23 million. His property, investment portfolios and pension had all been secured on the loan. The taxi pulled up outside the office block. Time to face the music; I hope the conductor is in a good mood. Once he signed in and was giving a visitor pass to hang round his neck, he made his way to the 15th floor. He was in the elevator alone with a fevered imagination; Nigel could pull a rabbit out of the hat, hence his name 'the magician'. I hope he does. The elevator door opened, Nigel was standing waiting on him. Six ft four inches of optimism, in his late 40s but he looked much younger. 'How is your fevered imagination David?' He stepped out onto the plush carpet, and walked the twenty metres to his office. 'Fevered? Hard to believe, hard to believe my world came to a crashing halt less than thirty minutes ago.'

'I heard from a source the raid was going to happen four days ago, it's total bullshit, all a misunderstanding, it'll be sorted out in a couple of months, obviously that doesn't help you. But I have other options.'

'That's fine, are they going to cost me?'

'Quite the contrary.' He opens the door. Sitting in the far corner is a man in his late sixties. David is perplexed at this unexpected visitor, he wasn't a banker, he could guarantee that. He rises to his feet and walks towards David, with his hand outstretched. 'Pleased to meet you David, Nigel has told me all about your financial difficulty. I am Pavel Ashuvok.'

Nigel walks behind his desk and sits down, he is smiling. David sits across from him; Pavel pulls up a chair and sits beside David who is clearly uncomfortable.

'Sorry Pavel, I'm David Fisher. I assume Nigel has explained that the bank pulled their final instalment of finance in the last hour, through no fault of mine.'

'I have David, where Pavel comes from this is a common practice, it's all politics, total bullshit, which doesn't help you.'

'And where do you come from Pavel?' Russia or a former Russian state he guessed.

'Moscow, but I have been a British citizen for five years.'

Nigel exhibits to David his passport then returns it to Pavel. 'Pavel has been a client of mine for just over three years. I explained how you are a successful businessman; this project when finished will make you a rich man. However, you have had a funding difficulty with the bank; Pavel is willing to replace the bank's funding with his own; and on better financial terms. Also, because the bank broke their agreement with you and left you in financial difficulty, they are liable for any costs that you accrue in securing alternative funds; including any arrangement fee sourcing these funds.' Nigel was smiling.

'How can they pay costs, if their funds have been frozen?

'Quite simple really. They pay a punitive daily rate, which is confidential between you, I and the bank; this will blow over very shortly. So are you going to thank your prescient lawyer?'

'I'll thank you when the contract is signed and the money is deposited in the escrow account.' Nigel hands him his pen, he turns over a two page document, Pavel has previously signed and pushes the document towards David.

'Once it's signed the money will be in the escrow account in the next hour.' He was smiling, but his eyes were screaming, 'fucking sign it!' Which he duly did. Pavel had risen from his seat shook David's hand and then shook Nigel's hand, then walked out. David was left in stunned silence as he watched him glide through the door.

Nigel picked up the phone, 'bring it in now Julie, no need for the smelling salts.'

'Look this is a whirlwind; you'll have to explain everything including the 'death stare.'

Julie came into the office with a tray which held a bottle of champagne and two glasses and left it on the table. 'Thanks Julie.' They moved and sat at the table at the window.

'You obviously don't know Pavel? He is not here as a political dissident, he and Putin are good friends; he worked in the metal industry as a scientist he was the architect of modernising the Russian economy. He has £400 million in British banks, he pays his taxes, and he's not one of the undesirables that fled Russia with ill-gotten gains that he robbed from Russia. So don't worry.'

'Okay, I get that, what about the death stare that you gave me?'

'If you hadn't signed in twenty seconds, the deal was off.'

'You're kidding? And you've not told me Pavel's terms.'

'I have negotiated a much better deal; to paraphrase what's in the contract, a two page contract at that. You will not be paying the £1 million end of contract fee; he's agreed to reduce it to £250,000. Which your former Merchant Bank will be liable, now don't be shy and pour your clever lawyer some champagne.' He did as instructed, but there was still no smile on his ashen face.

'I'm still in a wee bit of shock I am not ungrateful, far from it. Seeing a two page contract unnerved me as well, I've never seen a contract on two pages.' His phone made an audible sound similar to manic laughter, Nigel was laughing. 'What age are you, what is that sound for?'

David took out the phone and touched the app. 'The £15 million is in, it's in!'

'That's good; you didn't have any doubts did you?'

'I was a wee bit sceptical; you must have arranged the money to bounce into the escrow account as soon as it hit my account?'

'I thought that would be best for everyone, but before you drink your champagne, I've booked a table for you and Pavel at Cipriani's for Thursday , there are two reasons, to get to know Pavel and to listen to him about future investment opportunities.'

'That sounds good to me, any idea what he means by future investment opportunities?'

'Drink your champagne David.'

***

Jonathon Gove looked at his watch, the car to take him to Heathrow airport should be here soon. His compact suitcase lay in the middle of the oak floor, three nights in New York lay ahead, no one from the dining cabal knew about this hastily arranged trip. But they would certainly be informed when, not if the deal was completed. No nerves or doubts entered his conscience. If everything went to plan, he would be dining in the restaurant at The Carlyle Hotel at 8pm local time. No alcohol would pass his lips until he lifted his utensils in the restaurant; his suite was on the 30th floor. He was booked on the BA flight at 14.30 and would arrive at JFK 17.30. A limo would be waiting on him when he had exited customs. Oh, how he wished his father could be here to eat his words. He was deemed to be a trader in the City however, he had more ambition, and would take the road less travelled, no leaves were on this road, only gold, however, it would be strewn with obstacles that were dangerous.

He had texted David that he was off for a romantic liaison for three nights to New York; he had to cover his absence with a plausible reason. He requested he keep this information to himself. David had replied with a smiley face. He was a man of few words unless he got angry, which was rare.

They had met at a residents meeting with the Leaseholder's proposal for the upgrade of stairwell and elevator replacement. David was the new resident in the block; he had raised concerns about the excessive costs that were involved. He suggested there had been a miscalculation. To emphasise his point he had four other quotes that were the minimum of forty percent of the Leaseholder's builder's quote. No one had challenged the Leaseholder quotes before. David had also written to the Leaseholder requesting the cost of purchasing the Leasehold of the building. David had convinced the Leaseholder to modify the quote, and consider the owners' request to buy the Leasehold. Jonathon was impressed how he managed to do this over four months, but had he achieved it by fair or foul means? The majority of overseas owners were indifferent, money was not a concern; status was. Jonathon had gone to David's flat to thank him on behalf of the permanent residential owners. He was invited in, and was immediately impressed that the alterations had been completed in such a short space of time; he had passed the various builders coming to and fro from various vans to the imposing building. From their accents they were undoubtedly Scottish. David had brought six various tradesmen down to London from Dundee that he had facilitated over the years maintaining or modernising his portfolio of properties in Dundee. He offered them £1500 a week, plus a £1000 completion bonus. They would be staying in house he had purchased twenty minutes from Mayfair. All the permits for parking, loading and unloading had been granted. When David had secured the Leasehold, he had suggested that the façade of the building would benefit from maintenance, there were no objections. An elderly couple asked David if it were possible to fix some windows in their flat, they had not been able to open them for years. The former Leaseholder did not carry out the promise to repair the windows. When the Dundee builders came down to David's flat to go over the plans in detail, David sent the joiner up and he overhauled all the sash windows in a day; David picked up the cost. The builders had earned brownie points with the elderly couple. The only problem there had been was the chap's 'curious accent.' But apart from them the joiner was deemed a happy chap.

Jonathon walked over to the window, the car was pulling up. Everything in order, he pulled on his shoes ready to vacate the flat. However, there were a series of impatient raps on his door. He showed some concern.

***

Michael Ogilvie was the elder statesmen of the six regular diners, in his sixties; he hated London, but had more antipathy for the City of London Police. The Big Bang was the catalyst for massive fraud in the City, it seemed he was the only honest former trader left, and this was not from the mouth of a narcissist. He had been employed at a long-established bank as a Financial Controller for Overseas Accounts; he was concerned about a young trader in Singapore, everyone was praising this young man, because of his burgeoning profits that were emanating every week. Michael was not convinced; he oversaw the trader's requests for more money, on paper he was making millions, but no money had been transferred to the London account from the 'profits.' He kicked his assessment with accompanying paperwork upstairs. He expected to be called up the next day; he wasn't called that day or any other day. He had copied his synopsis and his warnings for his own protection. This was a scandal that would overwhelm the bank, he had built an excellent reputation in the City, and this obvious fraud would destroy both. He resigned the following Monday. He was friendly with a financial journalist and had described his findings, the journalist passed on this information to the City of London Police. An eyebrow was never raised.

Michael set up a consultancy for financial and future tax planning (avoidance) plans. He had to acquire a discreet office in Mayfair, Canary Wharf did not appeal to him, too many young ambitious men and women. Rules were treated similar to tax; evaded or ignored. New money was coming into London from China, Russia and India. Many of the citizens of these countries that had crossed his path were ready to invest were mind-boggling, the sums were fantastic, for young individuals but more importantly they were legal.

His commission on the sums invested were stratospheric. However, some of the Russian clients wanted him to handle every aspect of their finances; investments, taxations and acquiring expensive properties. The property sector he could only recommend a third- party, this was acceptable, as long as everything went through his office. The Russian clientele did not find dealing with various professionals attractive. They wanted a one-stop service. Michael would accommodate these requests. It was additional money for nothing; as far as he was concerned. He had acquaintances who were freelance estate agents. They would secure a commission, and so would he. On the train home to Surbiton he was able to calculate his commission on the various investments; it was a most enjoyable commute, even though he was in the minority who thought this. He was a one man consultancy; he had a cardinal rule that he reluctantly breached. If he was being swamped by requests for appointments, however lucrative, he would turn them down. He circumvented his golden rule. Destiny shook her head in disbelief. His enjoyable commute to and from his office would be a distant memory. A First-Class season ticket did not adjust his endurance. He had unwittingly joined the disconsolate band of commuters. Hopefully his friend would ease his burden. The tariff would be disproportionate, but unavoidable.

***

    Simon had already ordered, his colleague's latest recommended client was ten minutes late, plus ca change. He was more comfortable in Boujis restaurant when it came to the final agreement of the contract. If any doubts were raised; which were very rare he would give the client the immediate option to cancel there and then. This was a new client who had come recommended from Michael Ogilvie, this was the third and final meeting; the contract would be signed, the copy of the contract had been perused by the client's lawyer. Everything was in order. No wrinkles were present, no need for the legal iron. £100 million would be transferred to the British Virgin Islands (BVI) a well-used tax haven from a bank in the Russian Federation. British Governments of every stripe threatened to 'tighten' up the banking system in the Autumn Statement (Budget) after the latest financial scandal. Very few changes were made. And for good reason, many former Ministers or MPs were invited onto various Boards of Banks/ Financial/Investment Companies, who coincidently operated an office in the BVI. There were much more pressing domestic matters on hand to consider.

    Michael didn't gel with the client; he thought he failed to grasp the complex financial hoops that had to be negotiated. Michael explained this was London, not Moscow. Patience was the key in London. Simon was known to circumvent certain legalities; Michael would not alter his tried, trusted and *legal procedures.*

    Simon's moral compass was set by the City; it's only illegal when you are caught. In the meantime carry on regardless. The myriad of shell companies and off shore accounts in overseas tax havens superseded any embryonic concerns. His weekly dining companions acquiesced with this indigenous view of transactions. The weekly dining at The Ivy was to catch up on completed or forthcoming business. They were all interconnected. And it was in all their interests not to upset or overcharge clients especially from Russia. They had proved in the past that they did not take any complaints to any Financial Authority Ombudsmen, they sought to rectify any misunderstanding without sending an email; they preferred sending their *customer services managers.* It saved on unnecessary paperwork, which was good for the environment. The recipient(s) would not concur with this expedient method.

    David Fisher on the other hand was reticent about courting these businessmen or oligarchs for business even though the business was perfectly legitimate, his concerns were if they had disagreements with each other, after all they were divided into two camps pro-Putin and anti-Putin; the majority were in the latter. Would their businesses be affected?

Simon sated David's concerns he had a friend in the Economic Crime Unit, if he was not happy with any particular concern, his friend would run the name through a data-base. This was news to the other dining companions. Simon had been on a four hour liquid lunch from early in the day with a client, he should not have imparted this news to his dining companions. However, it reassured them, but he was angry with himself. No one questioned him about his friend.

His client walked in, he was not alone; the client walked over to Simon, who rose from the table to greet him, the client's burly companion was obviously his personal security, who sat at a table facing the entrance of the restaurant. 'And how are you Simon, I see you have ordered.' He shook his hand and the client invited him to sit.

'I'm very well Sergei. You are keen to complete business, the paperwork is here all it needs is your signature.'

'Where are the papers, I will sign them now, I have other business that I need to complete in a very short period of time.' Simon retrieved the paperwork from the black leather briefcase which was under the table. He placed them on the table, Sergei duly signed them.

Simon examined the paperwork all was in order. His commission was £3 million, however, he had to grease four other intermediaries; that would reduce the commission by £750,000, which ironically he couldn't offset as a business expense, for various reasons, the primary reason money laundering is illegal.

**

Motcomb Street in Belgravia was changing and house price inflation was rampant due to the singular pertinent reason; the influx of Russians, and it was a torrent not a trickle. This property had changed ownership three times in fifteen months; he knew this because he had sold this property personally. No one had lived in the two bedroomed flat, the same furniture from the first sale was still in situ. He was fully aware this would be unusual in any other part of the UK, but this was *de rigueur* in Belgravia, if any area in Belgravia had an address such as Eaton Square it would be dubbed *Red Square* because of the influx of Russians that had purchased and sometimes moved in. When he first sold the flat it went for £2 million now it would be sold for the asking price of £2,750,000. He showed the potential client around, the details of energy and council tax tripped off his tongue. The deal with the Estate Agent was not complicated; he would only accompany overseas potential buyers to the properties. He would receive 1.5% of the commission. There were no hissy fits from the Estate

Agent; the property would be exclusive to his company when it was placed on the market not too far into the future.

He alighted from his BMW, Faith Healer from The Sensational Alex Harvey Band on repeat booming out from the speakers in the doors. He closed the Spotify app on the dashboard; he thought they were good; but not sensational. He had similar taste in music to his older brother, a plasterer who played The Sensational Alex Harvey Band far too often when they shared a bedroom in Dunmore Street.

Two glamorous women stepped out of the Lexus, early thirties, both puffing away on cigarettes; they each had a property schedule clutched in their manicured hands. One smiled the other didn't.

'Hello David?'

'Yes…it's a nice morning, but a little bit cold.' They threw their cigarettes onto the pavement. Hopefully none of the neighbours are at home observing this slovenly act from their windows.

'We don't have much time, I will tell you whether I want to buy or not, please lead the way.' They conversed in Russian. Ten minutes was spent viewing the flat.

'Okay David I will buy, and make sure the property is taken off the market today.'

And with that they left. He called the Estate Agent and advised that he would be receiving a written offer at the full asking price. He and David did not display any elevated emotion, they had seen this transaction played out on numerous occasions. He locked up the flat and descended the stairs, the stairwell and common landing areas desperately required redecoration and the carpets in the entrance hall and on the stairs needed replaced. He would text the Estate Agent to liaise with the Leaseholder, but only after the sale and paperwork was completed.

He was meeting Pavel at The Dorchester for dinner that evening; he had to return to his office to retrieve some paperwork that he would leave with Pavel to read at his leisure, It was a bespoke portfolio of shares that he should invest in, they were all Tech companies based in Mumbai; he had personally invested £250,000 in them eight months ago, it had grown by twelve per cent this was not a bubble. He stood on the stairs that led from the front door of the apartment block to the pristine pavement, the two cigarettes were a blemish on the pavement he descended down the stairs to the pavement and picked up the discarded cigarettes. Two workmen emerged from the builder's van across the street from his car. 'I'll take them mate… got to keep the area tidy, we get the blame for any discarded cigarettes or fast food wrappers.' He handed the stubs over to him. The builder's hand was smooth and his nails were manicured.

***

Jonathon was getting annoyed, he moved rapidly to the door, he was ready to give the driver an earful; alas that would have to be parked for the time being; as soon as he unlocked the door, it was thrown open, two men in their thirties pulled him onto the sofa.

'Jonathon, we do not have much time, your car is waiting to take you to Heathrow; here is some reading material that you will read and memorise; follow it to the letter, no mistakes or excuses. We will be in contact when you return, enjoy your stay in The Carlyle.' They had made a point which was taken on board. There would be no reminder letter. He placed the sheaf of papers into the forlorn looking suitcase; the day can only get better. He stood up and completed a heartfelt and longing 360% pirouette of his apartment. I hope to see you soon, but who can tell?

***

The 'Magician' (Nigel) had booked a table for the pre-theatre slot at The Dorchester, for two reasons, it was nearby and it was reasonably priced. A three course meal from the set menu for two and a reasonable priced bottle of wine for two would come in at less than £150. Nigel would be picking up the tab. There was method in his frugality; The Dorchester was only a leisurely ten minute stroll from his flat. He had chosen well. The Iron Duke pub in Avery Row could be his pit-stop for a nightcap. It always helped him accumulate his thoughts. He was a sporadic customer, very polite staff but knew when he wanted to talk or be left alone.

He waited in the lobby of The Dorchester it was approaching 7.00 pm, dinner was booked for 7.30pm it was a pre-Theatre dinner in The Grill an eloquent and exquisite restaurant, and the food was excellent, this was not the first time he had been here; diners would enjoy their meal and the hotel would have a taxi at the front of the hotel to whisk them to their preferred theatre. He would take Pavel as he had done in the past with other overseas clients to The Bar in The Dorchester; it had an exquisite and rebellious past clientele; today's Uber-rich, celebrities and social gadflies, couldn't lay a glove on the outrageous financiers, film stars and the flappers of the 1920's. Wild parties then went on for days with a voracious appetite for cocaine. And they talked to each other over dinner.

Pavel came into view; Nigel advised he was not teetotal. That was a positive in his eyes, as long as he kept an eye on the details, he would be happy. Pavel saw him, and strode purposely towards him with a welcoming smile. 'Good evening David, would you join me in The Bar, before we eat?'

'Of course, Pavel, have you been in The Bar before?'
'More times than I can remember, come, come, what do you drink David, whisky?'
'Blue Goose vodka no ice please.' They walked into The Bar, it was rammed David had never seen it so full. 'Over here David, I have a table reserved.' They squeeze past throngs of patrons to the table, Pavel stops the waiter and orders drinks for them; a double round. Pavel leads David to the seat at the table, there are four other seats that are unfilled, but no one tries to sit in them. The waiter places the drinks on the table. Pavel slips the waiter a £50 note. David is impressed; he has seen in the past a welter of wealthy individuals hand over the waiter or waitress a £5 note as if they were Mother Theresa. This has been a good start to the evening. He has noticed Pavel has ordered vodka as well. Pavel pushes the well-filled glass to David. 'Sip it slowly, and tell me what you think.' He raised the glass slowly to his lips and takes a slow methodical sip, it was not Blue Goose, it had a smoother taste, and it was certainly not Smirnoff either. 'It's very nice Pavel, what is the name of it?

'I thought you would like it, it is Beluga Noble it is a very good premium brand.' David knew of it but had never tasted it, and it was over £100 a bottle. Pavel was not an exponent of foreplay; he wanted to get down to business. This suited David. 'Okay David, I will get to the point, life is too short. I have a sum of money that will be sent from Moscow to Cyprus then onto a bank in the British Virgin Islands, then some of it will come to London, it will not be subjected to money laundering laws. Everything including business transactions will be done electronically by phone, tablet or laptop. This is not dirty money from Russia; I am not on any so called 'hit list' from Vladimir Putin. . So do not worry about your safety or mine.

'I knew him (Putin) from the early days in St. Petersburg, we have all stayed loyal to him, he has cleaned out the stables, under Yeltsin, oligarchs took advantage of his illness, he was an alcoholic, and they kept him on the booze. They did not want him to get well. The oligarchs formulated ruinous privatisation programmes. They borrowed money from US and UK banks and bought every industry you can think of at a heavily discounted price, thus making them billionaires. The US and UK companies would then purchase the oligarchs' shares at the real market rate. But the oil and gas sectors were privatised before Vladimir came to power. He had a crack team of forensic accountants go over the oligarchs' bank accounts, financial transactions and emails. His intuition was correct; these gangsters had robbed the Russian people. Vladimir reversed the privatisation of the oil and gas sector, namely taking them back into state ownership, and throwing the gangsters and Banksters in jail. Here in the UK you give these Banksters Knighthoods!

'I was the CEO of the forensic accountant team, we returned over £200 billion from these fraudulent privatisation schemes. Over the years I have invested my bounty that I received from the State. Now I want to invest in Western and Eastern companies, especially technology, but not Bitcoin, it is just a bubble or a Ponzi scheme. I have over $600 million to invest. I need to purchase a home in London for my family, I am a UK citizen. I am sure you have a number of questions to ask?'

David's vodka lay virtually untouched. He assumed Pavel's 'bounty' had been incentivised by the simple logic, the more you return to the State, the more money you earn, probably tax free, and a promise to let him emigrate after he had successfully repatriated hidden funds from the oligarchs' secret overseas tax havens, which the nearest was Cyprus. He had to ask about Putin, fuck this Vladimir nonsense. First he swallowed the vodka in a few avaricious gulps, complete with sound effects. Must be a big question coming up thought Pavel; he was correct.

'Pavel, I know there are various stories and newspapers that spread disinformation about, Putin, in the newspapers and on social media, they say he has £20 billion stashed away. For example, he has placed former KGB officers from St. Petersburg into financial institutions, such as banks and made them CEOs, some of them are now billionaires. And if Putin wants rid of any investigative journalists, the Russian Secret Service (FSB) contact the Russian mafia and they bump them off.' Pavel laughs out loud. He catches the waiter's eye, and signals another double round. 'David, I have read on the Internet about Putin's £20 billion, did it not cross your mind, if the so called journalists are so clever and said he has property in Spain and in Barcelona and Madrid, why can't these journalists follow the transactions to where the money ends up? I have a simpler method why doesn't *Vladimir* give me say £450 million or $600 million plus to me and I can employ an intelligent Financial Advisor say in London, to invest. Less convoluted, but more simple, don't you agree? The waiter came over with the drinks. 'David, it's your turn to tip the waiter.' David slipped the waiter £50.

He never saw this coming, he had looked online and on social media, Pavel was literally a ghost. Some snippets that he had come across said he was well-respected from western companies and the EU. A Commissioner from the EU had been quoted as saying Pavel had 'brought discipline to the chaotic privatisations under the Yeltsin regime. And he was returning the economy onto firm foundations.' The German government thought so as well, they signed up to import natural gas from the Russian Federation. Pavel was the architect of this agreement, his name wasn't on the contract but he was the catalyst. Russia had an abundance of natural gas, Germany wanted stable energy prices, which was tantamount to a stable economy.

And for all intents and purposes Germany *is* the EU. And it all came down to his internal antenna; did he believe Pavel's version of *Vladimir* or the Daily Mail's version of *Putin?* He was not prepared to come to an instant judgement; he was heavily conflicted; his head said the Daily Mail, however, his wallet sided with Pavel. No surprise there then?

He had drawn up various contracts for former clients and had the contracts sent over by courier to Nigel, who proof read them, then when it came to sign them Nigel would not come across any pernicious surprises, he went through a charade of studying them very carefully. This was not a charitable act, he (David) paid through the nasal passages for this expertise.

He agreed with a property developer that he was having a pint in Jolly's Hotel in Broughty Ferry many years ago he shared this piece of wisdom; 'plumbers and solicitors cause more problems than the *Taliban.*' He laughed at that, but over the years, he reluctantly concurred now. I wonder how he is doing?

'David, shall we go to The Grill, I'm quite peckish.'

'Sure, I am looking forward to this meal, and I am sure you will not be disappointed Pavel.'

'There is always a first time David, but I doubt it. I see you enjoy Beluga Nobel; will you now change from Blue Goose?'

. 'I certainly think it is smoother, and more potent.' They walk the short distance to The Grill and are escorted to their table in the far corner of the restaurant, many of the affluent clientele, are emptying from their tables and are making their way to their pre-ordered taxis. David has walked over this beautiful wooden floor on many occasions. If this floor could talk, shame would stalk some of the present patrons, probably unaware of their grandfathers and grandmothers exuberant behaviour... 'More cocaine anyone?' was a casual invite to dining companions in the 1920's.

The waiter smiled as he halted at their table, when they were seated, he asked if they required drinks before they order. Beluga Noble was ordered. David ordered from the set menu, as usual. Scottish salmon for starters, braised Lemon thyme chicken with seasonal vegetables. His side dish was French fries. For sweet he ordered Contemporary grapefruit tart. Pavel ordered Onion soup, followed by T-bone steak, mashed potatoes and cut green beans. No dessert. . Nigel's £150 paltry budget was still not breached. The waiter came over with the drinks, double measures. Pavel brought out the requisite £50 note and to the annoyance of a couple in view he handed it to the Polish waiter. 'Before our starters are brought to the table I will give a brief description of how things used to be done before Vladimir was elected. A man is trying to get a fake MOT certificate for his car, which will cost him 10,000 roubles say £200 for arguments sake. The man who organises the certificate takes the cash to the passport office and uses it to jump the queue for an international passport. The manager of the passport office takes the money to a professor who can help his daughter get a university place. The professor in turn takes it to a doctor to get an operation for his wife, and the doctor then hands it over at the army recruitment office so that his son can avoid conscription. The officer in charge at the recruitment office gives the money to a builder who has promised to allocate him a council flat, and the process finishes at the top of the social ladder when the regional governor gives the builder a building plot in return for the council housing block. The governor goes on to meet the President himself, and keeps his job after guaranteeing the 'right' results in the regional elections, as well as promising to fight corruption. The story finishes with the driver coming to pick up his fake MOT and is amazed when he actually gets it. 'What about all this stuff on TV?' he asks. 'The government's cracking down on corruption. How did you wangle it?' The reply? 'Well, why do you think it used to cost 10,000, and it's gone up to 15,000 now?'

'What I told you was from an article from a magazine, which has been circulated to newspapers in the West, some of it is true some claims are embellished, under Yeltsin this was a good example, under Vladimir Putin, corruption has not been eliminated but there is less. Now who in the West can hold up a mirror to their democracies and not see the reflection disfigured? Iraq, Afghanistan? Bush and Blair are Christians, I am glad I am a non-believer, the EU is corrupt, and thus in Russia we take no lessons from any country in the West. So that is the politics overview over. Now let's talk business while we enjoy our meal.'

'Sounds good to me Pavel, I know politics is a dirty business. You have given me a different perspective of Putin and Russia. Good to get down to your attitude to risk. I can acquire a home for you in Belgravia or Mayfair, obviously depending on your budget.' The waiter comes over with the starters. They fall into silence until he has completed his task.

'I prefer Belgravia there are fewer Russian exiles with blemished characters. My budget is up to £15million.'

'You shouldn't have any difficulty in purchasing a house. I will send you some of the properties that are suitable, if you can view them and give your opinion that would be most welcome.' David had a list of properties that were not on the open market, however, if there were a buyer on a strictly cash basis with the minimum of paperwork, then the buyer would own the property within four weeks. Notwithstanding David would receive an additional commission from the Estate Agent. This was evolving into a business transaction that he had not previously encountered. Was Pavel really laundering Putin's money or was he just making a point that the story of Putin's alleged wealth was misinformation? London was now the *de facto* money-laundering capital of the world. If Putin *was* laundering ill-gotten gains, this was the city to do it, and the ideal emissary would be Pavel. Who was he to be the moral judge to arbitrate which funds from Russia were tainted and which were legitimate? He never asked beyond the legal requirement where the funds originated.

However, his primal instinct was making him nauseous if it was not that it must be the Beluga Nobel. He had been advising Russian clients for approaching three years about investment strategies; some just deposited the money into his company's account and only required an update every three months. It was very clear to him, what the clients' long-term plans were; to require a luxurious home, and keep their disposable income in tax havens which could be easily accessed from London. The demographic in London had changed over the last decade; the oil sheiks were no longer the Uber-rich; Russians were in the ascendency, and they were not discreet with their wealth. Some were obviously the *nouveau-riche*, lacking in further education and manners, but their money compensated for these archaic deficiencies.

***

In Leicester Square in London at the Moon under the Stars pub, John Armstrong has been served at the bar; he makes his way through the crowd to the table where his colleague is jealously guarding the table, from disappointed tourists. Her coat is placed on the empty seat, and she is asked the same monotonous question, 'excuse me is someone sitting there? And she wearily replies. 'Yes, he is at the bar, getting the drinks.' Then the Smart arse emerged, dressed in a Smart suit, white shirt, and grey tie, tanned and in his late thirties. 'He must have gone to the toilet to snort some cocaine?'

'Probably…you're still not getting the seat, so do one!' Then she put her ID casually in full view on the table. 'Has your boyfriend stood you up then?' He is looking at the ID, and then turns his back on her. 'There you go Edwina, has anyone told you that's a shit name?' He places the pint of cider in front of her.

'My mum was a fan of curries what's your excuse?'

'Who has wound you up then?'

'The beautiful chap with his back to us, but I'm okay, he thought I was keeping your seat for an invisible friend. But never mind that what do you think of my theory?'

'Anything is possible, but not someone from the MLIU (Money Laundering Investigation Unit) and you need proof Edwina, I don't need to tell you that, and if you are wrong it's back to checking invoices for you Edwina Collins, have you thought about that?'

'I think about that all the time, but when I have all the intelligence, I'll lay it all out for you, and then we will take it to the Anti-Corruption Unit.'

'No, no, singular; *you* not *we*. I don't trust them.'

'Jealous of them?'

'You must be kidding, I'll help but as for taking the proof you are on your own, I don't want to be isolated when or if the backlash kicks off, I'm quite selfish that way.'

'Really? You selfish, you do yourself down.'

'I can't disagree. Sometimes I let my feminine side show.'

'Now you're a sexist and selfish at least my skin colour doesn't bother you'.

'Asian people don't bother me, but white men who use skin-care products do.'

'This conversation is going awry, what's the latest while I was away?'

'So how was your holiday then?'

'Holiday! Minus twenty-five in St. Petersburg, uneventful thank God, but I got a good feel of the place, the former ambassador was really helpful, he told me tales that I promised not to repeat, so don't ask ever okay?'

'Not interested, and anyway he was probably bullshitting you, to impress you. Sometimes Edwina you're quite naïve. A university degree sometimes protects stupid people; can you do the Rubik cube?'

'I've never even saw one I am only thirty! I bet you still have a working Betamax video recorder in your spare room. Do you want to hear, about my two weeks in St. Petersburg and my two days in Moscow?'

'You never told me you went to Moscow, what was the reason for the detour?'

'The helpful former ambassador, who now works in the oil and gas sector, gave me a name, he would text him my name, so he knew where to meet me, and the reason I was coming. It went very well. Some pieces of the jigsaw will fit now. And my Politics & History degree was most helpful.'

' Oh, dear…four years at university, and I can collate the same knowledge in an hour on Wikipedia…but do carry on.'

'Erm... can you learn to speak fluent Russian in an hour?'

He laughed she had bit, and he took paternal pleasure in seeing her defend her higher education. 'That would take slightly longer. I think it was perspicacious of our glorious leader to send you over to Russia on your own, it was less conspicuous. And the former ambassador seems to have been helpful.'

'It wasn't our superior officer who suggested I travel alone, I insisted. Anyway, did you manage to glean any more useful information about our suspect?'

He was clearly surprised at this revelation, that she overruled their pernickety boss

'He is a man of routine; he is flying to New York today, when he is in transit the guys will be in his flat setting up the surveillance equipment, that will make our job so much easier.'

'Who is he meeting in New York?'

'No one knows, but we have shared intelligence with the FBI; they will have eyes on him as soon as he lands at JFK. They will send over any relevant information that would benefit our nebulous case, Could be a wild goose chase, but time and information will be decisive.'

'I was thinking the same, could all be perfectly innocent, and if the information about his new clients is true, he could be more useful to us rather than the Americans. They always treat us as rednecks. I wish this was a British only operation. My concern is if our information holds up, they will extradite him, and their request is normally granted without too much discussion with us. International politics always wins over domestic matters.'

'Anti-American sentiment? I'm surprised at that, you'd be best to keep that to yourself, if this was common knowledge, it could lead to a glass ceiling.'

'You've changed your tune, nothing to do with that female American tourist you met?'

'Ha, ha and, no, and it's over, and I don't want to talk about that okay?'

'Okay. Has your Elbow songs been deleted from your Spotify account then?'

'You've lost me Edwina?'

'Well you getting the elbow… yet again.'

'Not funny .And it was a mutual uncoupling. Did you solicit additional information from the contact in Moscow?'

'You spoiled my entrance, yes I did, but I want to keep this 'off the books', or I don't reveal the information okay?'

'I'm fine with that, sometimes I've flown solo.'

'Well, this name came up, he's a person of interest not Jonathon Gove, but David Fisher.' He looked at her with indifference. 'Who is he and why was his name mentioned?'

'This is an anti-climax, but that was it, just his name and I was advised to put him under surveillance.'

'I'm concerned, if we put him under surveillance, we are not observing Jonathon Gove, we could be getting set up by the FBI or Department of

Justice, they grab Gove in New York and we are watching David Fisher. And who is this David Fisher anyway?' She didn't think of that scenario, and the former ambassador was a consultant with an American company which would have linkage to the American intelligence services.

'I scanned the internet; he's a Financial Advisor and Wealth Manager with a pristine record. Lives in Mayfair where he has an office. However, he lives in the same apartment block as, guess who?'

'Gove, Jonathon Gove?'

'They could be connected. If they are well…'

'…If they are, things could either become easier or more complicated. I'll run a computer check on him .Remember this is an off the books job. We don't want a trail leading back to you.'

'That's not a concern just now, later it may become a concern, but that's in the future. He's not been over to Moscow or St. Petersburg, in fact he's not been to Russia according to my source, but he ended by saying 'yet' which was enigmatic.'

'Now that is interesting, the logical implication being, but that will change? Hold on a minute, I need another drink; you've hardly touched yours.' At this she lifted her glass and the cider emptied down her throat. 'Another cider please and try to be quicker this time.' He melted into the throng of the animated patrons milling around the bar, she felt she was onto something; David Fisher was a left-field addition. 'Excuse me is anyone sitting there?'

***

Jonathon's enthusiasm for the trip to New York had dipped slightly; the limousine was proudly parked outside the red bricked apartment block. People walking their pampered pooches didn't give it a second glance. His eyes were not now transfixed on it; he was looking for a car that was parked nearby containing the two well-built unexpected visitors. The limousine driver stood at the car door which he held open, he was observing Jonathon with a puzzled look, why was he gazing to and fro and beyond the limousine. He skipped down the eight stairs and walked quickly to the limousine uttered a nervous quick hello and entered the back seat. The driver closed the door. In the front seat he entered the trip details into the on-board computer. Jonathon's curiosity overcame any latent fear. He took out his pen, and started circling some sections of the paragraph. Worry was leaving his furrowed brow, reading these economic projections for currencies, energy prices and emerging markets were optimistic but no economist could state they were inaccurate; he recognised some of the coloured graphs and the data. Nothing was untoward in these figures and projections over a five year period. His own data on emerging markets looked hamstrung; he would have to embolden the language to be more dynamic. The plan formulated in his head after each passing mile. He would *incorporate* his medium term plan with the bespoke addendum instructions that the two impatient *investors* thrust into his hands which he would showcase to his client in New York, and if he was being perfectly candid, his recommended companies seemed passive..

On prima facie evidence these impatient chaps that didn't knock quietly had enhanced his bespoke investment portfolio but why? He couldn't cognise this, should he try to? He took an executive decision. He would accept their recommendations in good faith. No coffee for him in the BA Executive Lounge, he would have a copious measure of Blue Goose; sometimes you have to break a mundane routine. Feeling ebullient he checked the weather in New York, cold but dry. He wouldn't be doing any sightseeing. This new client would be charmed; nothing would be left to chance, the restaurants were booked for the following two days they were directly across the street from each other; the Russian Samovar and the Pravda Vodka Room suitable for any age group and were on 52nd street. A wise choice?

***

The evening with Pavel had gone well. He was a £100 lighter than anticipated because of the generous tips he had given the waiter. However, if Pavel agreed with his investment choices, he would earn in excess of £20 million with fees and commission from Pavel's impatient £400 million. This negated the niggling £100 tips that hung about his chaotic mind. He gave himself a wry smile and made his way to the bar for a double Blue Goose, Beluga Noble was not beyond his wallet, but beyond his working class upbringing mindset. At the bar, he was unconsciously smiling; the barmaid took this as a flattering gesture. She had had her long hair cut, shaped and coloured. She walked over to him ignoring other customers' requests. 'Yes, can I help you sir?'

He was surprised at being served so quickly. 'Oh, great, can I have a double Blue Goose please, and you have one also.'
'That's very kind of you, are you celebrating something?'
'I am actually, but I can't say just now.' She turns her back and goes to the Blue Goose optic, she returns with the double. He hands over £20 took the drink smiles and walks back to the table. Celebrating? £20 million! He should be doing cartwheels, but he had a good anchor, namely his low-key personality. He never was one for being ostentatious. The flight was early the next morning; however, that was not a problem, the adrenalin was pumping through him, he was hoping the alcohol he had consumed would slow his effervescent mind down and allow his regular sleep pattern, a

paucity of 3 hours. If he was still tired in the morning he would catch up on his sleep on board. A couple of hours would be adequate.

It was near closing time, he would have another Blue Goose, a single. The barmaid came over as she saw him move from the table to the bar. He had that look of someone who had had a great day, but she wouldn't press him. 'Same again, sir?'

'Nah, just a single measure this time, please.'

'You're Scottish, from Aberdeen?' When he was getting drunk his concealed accent had made an unexpected appearance, it wasn't a broad Dundee accent but it had departed from his honed everyday Scottish accent. She gave him his drink. 'Nearly right, Dundee, can you hold onto the drink until I return from the gents please? He handed over £10. In the gents he replayed all the events of the day in his head; he had handled Pavel today very well, every question was answered with confidence. He washed his hands and caught an unforced glimpse of himself in the mirror; he was pleasantly surprised how happy, not smug he looked. The silver flecks in his hair were highlighted as well. He didn't look his age or maybe his vision was being influenced by the Blue Goose. Probably.

He returned to the sparse bar. 'Go to your table, I'll bring it over, and here is your change, from the last time as well.'

'Just keep it, and I'll have my drink at the bar, the view is better.' She welcomed the flirtatious comment.

'Maybe if you were wearing your glasses, the view would not be appealing?'

'If I was visually impaired, the view would still be beautiful.' He took his drink looked at it, and then downed it. 'Well time to go, I didn't catch your name?'

'Lena and yours?

'David, well Lena I bid you a good goodnight.' He then left the bar. He had made a positive impression on her.

***

Simon Corndale was looking out the window of his new apartment overlooking the Thames from the Victoria Embankment. This was his first day in the apartment; it had cost a cool £5 million. He was approaching fifty; business had been good; working for one of the top four accountancy firms for twenty years had been an educational and sobering experience. five years ago he had an opportunity he could not turn down, if he did, he would be in jail.

This multi-million apartment was his gilded cage, he could not venture abroad, if he did, he would not come back, even to be laid to rest, his body would have been disposed of instantly. He could not help thinking how things could have been so different, if only he had listened. He had been in therapy to train his mind not to over think things, but this did not work. A tumultuous decision had cost him his freedom and could eventually consume his sanity. He gazed at the workman changing a bulb on the thoroughfare; he would exchange his life and apartment with him now, if he could. There was not a tariff you can place on having peace of mind.

The electrician completed his mundane task on the Embankment, time to move to the next lamppost to replace another bulb. When he was retuning his step-ladder to his van, he looked up at the green clad affluent building, he noticed a man looking at him, holding a cup, I bet it was him who reported the lamp on the thoroughfare was not working, and he was making sure it was being replaced. Lucky bastard he thought, his apartment was worth millions, I bet he wouldn't fancy doing this for a living. If only he knew.

He couldn't mention the personal problem he had encountered with a client to his four frequent dining companions. They would all have much sympathy, but they would drop him from their dining roster simultaneously and immediately. Telephone calls, emails and text messages would be ignored or not be returned. It was he that had drawn up these draconian sanctions, if anyone transgressed their unwritten bespoke ethical business. His only sense of freedom was to go out running in daylight hours. But even this was fraught with danger; sometimes his acute paranoia overwhelmed him. Anyone in dark glasses was assumed to be a potential assassin. However, his frequent use of cocaine didn't subdue his paranoia. He had researched locating to countries in Europe, but on balance if he was going to come to physical harm, he would rather it came in London, because he was a patriot even though most of his purloined gains were 'resting overseas' in an offshore account. Irony always came second to his patriotism. But that was in the past, he had been issued with an unexpected get out of jail card. He had been instructed to return his misappropriated £6 million which he had, and then had sacrificed one of his dining companions whom he said had formulated the scam. When his companion failed to turn up for dinner; the bargain had been concluded and his life had been spared.

CHAPTER TWO

He felt better than expected; he was on his 3rd expresso in the Concorde Room (Lounge) at Terminal 5 at Heathrow. The over indulgence of the Blue Goose and Beluga Nobel had not affected his optimistic mood, or his concentration, three days away from London would benefit his mental health, work was piling up, he could have turned it down, but there was a chance that other clients would ease him out. They were all connected in business, and some socialised frequently.

   It was a stroke of genius moving to London, choosing the most advantageous and affluent location to live and then acquiring an office was imperative, and crucially it was down to him and not any celestial being. The lounge was well patronised for the morning flight, it was encouraging to see more business women, but some were so intense on their mobiles and tablets. Who was he to judge? He had spent many hours working through the night to complete a proposal for potential clients. He had learned to manage disappointment, and celebrate success. He was a challenging student. He picked up various newspapers, and flicked through them. His mind was not fully focused, Lena had entered his thoughts, and he had behaved, as he always did. She had sent him on his inebriated odyssey home with joy as his covert companion. He would have to make time to frequent The Iron Duke more often. She was younger than him, but God loves a Trier; however deluded they are. It would be to his advantage to leave this inchoate development until he returned. It would not benefit him pulling out the proposals again, he knew every comma on the pages, and there would be no need to pitch any additions. Pavel's representative had requested sight of the investment opportunities that he prepared for him and he wanted his advice; David took this as an affirmative plebiscite in his judgement. Pavel had seen a worried look appear on his face when he had mentioned the overseas business trip to meet another business advisor; he eliminated any concerns, however miniscule. The advisor spoke perfect English which was welcome; because some of his other Russian clients' advisors did not converse fluently in English, which could lead to expensive misunderstandings.

   The following year he would fly to China and attend a business fair in Shenzhen, money was flowing out of China and was seeking investment opportunities in London. Affluent homes to live in and expensive new developments were particularly attractive to the Chinese investors. Michael Ogilvie had invited him to accompany him; he was seen as the more mature and business savvy of the dining companions. If only his former teachers at Kirkton High School had heard this. An audible chuckle emanated from his smiling mouth. He looked at the departure screens, the gate was open, he had plenty time, but he would visit the gents, and then make his way to fast track boarding.

***

The curtains were tightly drawn together in her Fulham flat. It was two am and she looked at the scant information about David Fisher again. He was a successful businessman, modest background, worked hard. Nothing to suggest he had a hidden malevolent side. Could it be a coincidence that he lived in the same apartment block as Jonathon Gove? You can't choose your neighbours; to her cost she understood that sentiment. However, that battle could wait. But why did the endorsed contact in Moscow offer up his name, and say enigmatically, he was a person of interest. He wouldn't elaborate; she wasn't pushing at an open door. She could only examine officially lodged tax returns from individuals and companies if she had reasonable suspicions. Over the last ten years, overseas tax havens were being placed under the microscope, more so presently.

John Armstrong came personally to her flat with the news she dreaded. There would be no off the books surveillance of David Fisher. She played the devastating news down, by changing the subject, then coming back with the opinion; maybe the Moscow source was just being obtuse, maybe to take the spotlight away from Jonathon Gove? She suggested Gove was the fissure of light, and that could lead to credible information. And with that he said goodbye to Edwina, without the expected raised voice.

Edwina had his Facebook profile on her laptop. He is dull isn't he? He could do with a night out. One photograph was on his profile. He had participated in some conversations but never gave anything away. Most of his friends were in Dundee, he had very few in London. He seemed to become animated when he commented on old photographs of his home city. He became quite witty when he was taking a stroll down memory lane. Some builders had commentated on their contract in London; David had been the perfect host. He replied to the compliments not with words but the thumbs-up meme. If only his friends back in Scotland were aware of his accumulation of riches. Not too many incentives for entering his flat and secreting surveillance equipment. Then she had a disturbing thought, what if Armstrong *hadn't* asked about the off the books surveillance of

David Fisher? Or more importantly; how did he sell it? An off the books surveillance was not a jaw dropping request, nothing would be placed in writing, and if it went wrong, you were on your own. She yawned loudly, she looked at his profile photograph again; she thought surely you're concealing something? She closed the laptop down, and retired to bed.

***

Armstrong had parked his car around the corner from Edwina's flat. That had gone well; she took the news better than expected. He had seen her have a vocal disagreement with a condescending supercilious female colleague. She received the full gamut of expletives that a Millwall supporter would be proud of. He had been spared this evisceration. However, her trips to St. Petersburg and Moscow could lead to difficulties that could endanger her and his health. David Fisher had never been mentioned by anyone, but he was secondary; more important to him who was this mysterious contact in Moscow?

London was experiencing a tidal wave of Russians seeking political asylum; the government were granting most of them this request. There were no doubts they were extolling MI6 operatives and then passing embellished damaging vignettes about Putin; and that the MI6 operatives would not try to disapprove these *facts*. In addition the oligarchs were injecting unlimited capital into the flat-lining property market. However, some of the more established political dissidents were getting over confident in their new salubrious surroundings and were mirroring their unrefined behaviour that was prevalent in Moscow. The Russian Ambassador had an impromptu meeting with his British counterpart in Moscow and advised him, 'that the high-profile political dissidents' behaviour in London and the Home Counties were not going unnoticed, if the British government did not act to discourage this behaviour it would not end well for the laughingly labelled political dissidents or the British government.' This information was relayed to London and was duly noted. In reality it was ignored.

Armstrong's hand had been significantly reinforced by the rapid recruitment of Edwina Collins, a forensic accountant and polyglot. She was rapidly recruited to his small tight knit team. Unfortunately for an established member of the team on her first day, he made it clear that her rapid rise came because of her ethnicity not because of her innate intelligence. He was gone as the last word tumbled out of his savage mouth. No tears were shed. His pleading to be sent on a diversity training course to modify his behaviour rather than be summarily dismissed; was met with open mouthed rejection. His dismissal was reluctantly ratified by

John Armstrong. The perpetrator was leaked the minutes with Armstrong's punitive recommendation. He swore revenge on Armstrong, these words were not uttered in anger; they were measured. Armstrong was aware he had acquaintances from opposing sides of the Law. They had looked the other way to avoid their criminality, in return for information. The kaleidoscope had been shaken. Where would the pieces fall?

***

Simon woke at five am, fully refreshed, he had not felt like this for a number of weeks, the heavy clouds of dread and pessimism had gone. He reluctantly looked at the exercise bike with disdain; that could wait. Before he had retired for the evening he received an encrypted email with a link to an account in Cyprus, he had been expecting the email, the £6 million was retuned via the link. A confirmation email was received, and he felt no regret of returning the money. Nor any regret of potentially implicating his friend. He consoled himself by self-convincing that his friend would have done the same if *his* life was threatened. However, deep down in his conscience he knew this was incorrect. Nothing would infect his elevated demeanour today. He had been on anti-depressants for over three months, they had not helped. Stress related was the GPs diagnosis, due to long hours, poor diet, and recreational use of cocaine. If only that was the true cause, he would have welcomed that.

Being stopped and invited to an unsolicited odyssey in the car park of the gym in Kensington concentrated his mind. The game was up; he was manoeuvred into their car and driven to a house in its own magnificent grounds in Surrey. He could not admit the convoluted fraud, if he did, he would not leave this house, unless to be buried. He had the script in his head, he would deliver it with conviction; he had to show indignation, and go over the preposterous reasons why he would do such a thing?

He was not invited to sit down, but marched through to the large kitchen, in which the ceiling, walls and floor were adorned with clear polythene sheeting. He had to remain unconcerned about his immediate health. The large table was covered with the paper trail of financial transactions, to his surprise the 'smoking gun' transfer of funds was not there. Or maybe he is withholding it until the end of the interrogation? Time would tell or implicate him; he had to deliver a performance that would grace any of the theatres in the West End.

'Simon I'll give you five minutes to study these documents and emails, they are all in chronological order; do you require a coffee?'

'No Ivan, I'm fine, what is this all about?' His eyes were leaping from document to document.

'Are you sure? It could be your final cup,' He was grinning, he had the evidence and it was damming.

He decided to throw in some chutzpah; he had nothing to lose and only his life to gain. 'As you're in middle of remodelling the kitchen, I'll answer any questions.' He pulled the chair wrinkling the sheet on the floor. Ivan was not best pleased.

'Oh, I have no doubt about you answering questions, and as for the kitchen that is of no concern to you.' The more Simon studied the transactions, and confirmation emails the more he felt emboldened. 'OK, Ivan what do you want to know?'

'There is a gap in the accounts, money is missing, where is it?'

Simon's confidence collapsed, he had underestimated him. 'Ivan what date is it today?'

'It is the 21st, why?'

'The £6 million will be transferred into the main account on the 25th, the money is in an account in Cyprus, it is a new account, you told me to seek fresh accounts for the money before it ends up in the main account. And you may recall, I advised you not to have all your eggs in one basket. My friend uses this bank in Cyprus as a staging post for other clients. If you want me to cease using this bank or similar methods, I'll stop, but I think it is unwise. Executives at the bank have contacts in the EU, they had been forewarned to advise clients to close accounts, because the EU were going to confiscate or impose a draconian tax on all their funds; and it was all legal, that was in 2013.' He could now pull the incriminating email out of the hat, he had explained before he was confronted. Ivan looked at the bespectacled accountant. In response he agreed. Simon felt safer, but not completely vindicated.

'Why didn't you advise us of this new development, and what would have you done if it was not a genuine account, and how would you replace the £6 million?'

'But it is a genuine account, are you not aware it was Russian investors who injected much needed capital into the bank, and these investors now have EU passports? The Cypriot government were outraged at the confiscation of the funds in every bank account; the EU was forcing the Russians and their wealth to leave Cyprus, if the Russians leave, the economy collapses. To mitigate this; the Cyprus government offered Russians and other wealthy investors from other countries, invest in Cyprus and we will issue you with an EU passport. According to my friend 2000 passports were issued, of which 1000 went to Russians. I would replace any funds that could not be returned; £6 million would not cause me too much concern.'

'Did you transfer the money or was it your friend?'

'I and I alone transfer or invest. It is not professional otherwise.'

Ivan spoke in Russian, the men started pulling down and removing the polythene sheets. Simon had convinced him he had done everything in good faith. But it was close. He could not pull another stroke similar to this ever again. This had been a dry run with the money from Ivan's investors, and it was no doubt our bespectacled friend who had flagged this misunderstanding up. He had facilitated this route with other investors but not at this monetary level, he had imaginatively added an excessive charge, and then submitted an invoice matching the excessive charge to the account. Everything matched when accounts were submitted to the investors. However, these additional charges ranged from £5k to £40k. His prolific cocaine ingesting enhanced unwarranted confidence to this 'misunderstanding.' There would be no more 'misunderstandings.'

Ivan and the accountant spoke softly in Russian, the conversation ended with Ivan looking at Simon. 'Simon, you will receive an email link tonight follow it and send the money to the account. Now you will be returned to your car.'

***

It was good to be back in New York, he (Jonathan Gove) would have preferred The Plaza (Trump owned), but due to political prejudice, that was a forlorn hope. The Carlyle was being renovated on some floors, some of the reviews were uncomplimentary about the noise of the building work, but he had called the hotel in advance and enquired if his suite could be located as far as possible from the renovation? It was. The chauffeur from the hotel was waiting with his name on a white card he made eye contact with him. The forty minute journey was spent reading newspapers. Donald Trump was making the news again, apropos his early morning tweets. He turned the page quickly to the Broadway theatres. They were now in Manhattan (Upper East Side) the Carlyle came into view he pulled out a $20 note and tapped the chauffeur on the shoulder and gave him the money. He let the chauffeur alight and open his door. On the pavement he glanced up and down, the noise from traffic hadn't declined. He waltzed through check-in and was escorted to the elevator and then to his room. He slipped the bellhop $20. The one bedroom suite was of the Olde Worlde style. He filled the kettle, kicked off his shoes and walked over to the window to gaze over the Manhattan skyline. The kettle clicked and he made himself a coffee, then went to the living area and sat on the comfortable sofa. The quietness of the room unnerved him, he activated the remote control on the elegant coffee table, from the radio melodic 80s music filled the silent void; he felt better. He returned to the large window to gather his thoughts for the dinner in the evening. After a shower he would go to the Metropolitan Museum of Art which was only a ten minute walk away, if he was still energetic he would venture over to the Guggenheim Museum which was also close by.

***

Rain was battering incessantly against his office window, the door flew open; he turned around in surprise, in breezed Edwina. 'Still moping over that American woman?'
'Actually, no, I was just thinking about your original plan, to have an off the books surveillance operation on David Fisher, after some thought, I think we should go with it.'
'Has new information come in about him?'
'No, but I think he is worth watching, why would your contact in Moscow mention him, if he wasn't important? It just doesn't add up.' She was circumspect of this unexpected but worrying rapid change of mind.
'To be honest, I don't want us to split our resources, and, upstairs won't sanction this, maybe leave it till we have built up intelligence on Jonathon Gove?'
'Okay, perhaps you are right but keep this to yourself okay?'
'Sure.'
'What are you here for anyway?'
'Here is my meticulously compiled report from St, Petersburg. These are the names and alleged money laundering lawyers, estate agents, and financial advisors. Jonathon Gove is not on the list, nor is David Fisher. To be honest it looks as if it boils down to this: political opponents of Putin, namely the Russian Mafia are the good guys, their lawyers and financial advisors fly to Russia at least six times a year, without any problems. And money is systematically being extracted from Russian banks and transferred to Cyprus then onto London. They have money to burn or to invest. It is obvious to me, that some of them have intelligence links with the FSB otherwise no money would be allowed to leave Russia.'
'If Gove is not on the watch list, that means we will have to do the digging. The team is being overwhelmed with the amount of wealthy émigrés arriving in London, it will be difficult to prove that their money is dirty, if it is allowed to leave Russia all we will have is a legitimate electronic paper trail. What we depend on is information from a rival or someone honest from the City to leak information. Have a seat or do you have something else to do?'
'Nothing that can't wait, what time do the team go into Gove's flat?'
'That won't be happening I have been told not to go ahead until I have credible proof. There has been a change in policy, someone overstepped the mark on another operation, that's all I was told. However, if Gove is

advising wealthy Russians with no credible business history, that should not cause too much difficulty. That's where the Putin government can assist us; they want some of these individuals returned with their money.'
'Great in theory perhaps, but in reality how many of these businessmen or oligarchs have been returned because of this policy?
'I know, bit of a joke really. I don't completely trust the FBI either, that's why I was standing at the window, I want you to go to New York and keep Gove under surveillance, the flight leaves at 14.30.'
She was knocked sideways, normally Armstrong had a chronological timescale in advance .and he was not prone to impetuous decisions. Something must have cropped up recently. 'Will you be coming as well?'
'No, it would be best if you went on your own, less conspicuous. Going over there you might be able to save us a lot of time, rather than waiting for him to return then put eyes and ears on him. You'll just need a small bag. The FBI is not aware of this operation, nor is anyone else including our boss.'
'Fine, I'll go, and it won't take me long to pack a case, it'll only be for a few days.'
He moves to his desk and opens a drawer, and pulls out a small envelope. 'Here's some information about your business trip and new identity. The passport and dollars are also in the envelope *Gillian*. You will be staying in Gove's hotel which is the Carlyle and you return on the same flight as Gove but alas in economy.'
  She gives the passport a quick glance immediately memorising the D.O.B. 'Right I better get going. I'll send you any info as I process it.' Then she leaves his office. He returns to the window to view the rain drenched grey landscape, he was smiling for a couple of reasons, he trusted Edwina and he had manoeuvred her out of the way until Gove returns. Gove was not the principal target of his curiosity.

***

  David had checked in at the Gramercy Park hotel. He had showered and was ready to go out to grab a bite to eat and enjoy the vibrancy of New York, not anywhere in particular, but just to absorb the noise and bustle of the city; he had been to New York ten times previously to complete deals. His reputation was ascending with Russian clients, but his avaricious eyes were being averted to the less conspicuous young Chinese investors in London. They were business and technological advanced compared to the Russian clients. The nagging doubt that popped into his head years ago was if there were political problems with the West his Russian clients' assets and bank accounts would be frozen. Investing in Cyprus would avoid this draconian measure; he would invest £2 million in property in Limassol and in return the Cyprus government would issue the client with an EU passport entitling them to travel to 147 countries unencumbered. Of course it was a low tax country, and it was only three hours and thirty minutes from Moscow, similar to London to Limassol. He had fifteen Russian clients who took this advantageous path. New York had a similar light regulatory touch as London. Russians were tolerated but not loved. The New York real estate developers took the opposite view they were most welcome because of their riches and they were purchasing high-end properties.

On the sidewalk outside the hotel he took a left on Lexington Avenue the alcohol was out of his system, his appetite had returned, eggs Benedict would suffice until dinner with the client in the evening. He had asked the concierge about Rocky Sullivan's (an Irish Pub off Lexington Ave), he had enjoyed a raucous evening with clients there, but was told it had closed down, he thought in 2005. Wow! How time flies. Surely the concierge was wrong? He ventured onwards; he caught a glance of himself in the shop window, maybe the concierge was correct. He crossed the busy street to the delicatessen; he took a table and read the table top menu, he chose eggs Benedict, toast and coffee, he loved the New York coffee. The owner came over and asked him if he would like a coffee while he was studying the menu. He took the black coffee then gave him his order. He then came back with the Daily News, and told him he would only be five minutes, if he wanted more coffee just shout. Great service! He had planned to look on his phone for emails, but didn't want the owner to think he was rude by not accepting the unsolicited newspaper. He placed it on the table. The front page headline sent a shiver down his spine. He read the story; a Russian exile had committed suicide by leaping from a balcony from a high floor apartment that he and his wife were viewing. His wife was in the kitchen with the real estate agent signing the contract. The Russian had not been named; however, he was believed to be an investor in several New York properties, unconfirmed reports said he owned a £2 million property in London, and split his time between these cities.

His eggs Benedict and toast were brought to his table; his appetite had been blunted. He hoped his lack of sleep on the plane was fuelling his excitable imagination. Surely this unfortunate individual was not his proposed dinner companion for tonight?

***

No limousine from JFK to the Carlyle hotel for Edwina, she had taken an iconic yellow cab. Before entering she made clear she was paying the flat fare, she was not a tourist. The taxi driver offered no resistance. At the hotel the concierge approached the taxi, she handed over $70 (including $10 tip) he opened the door; she smiled stepped out and relocated her sunglasses from her head and positioned them strategically half way down her nose before stepping out.

'Welcome to the Carlyle hotel.' She smiled and waltzed past him, no tip. She checked in, and advised the bellhop she could manage to walk to the elevator and carry her compact overnight bag to her room on her own. No tip. She was enjoying playing the high-powered, impatient and haughty businesswoman.

She had only being in MLIU for just over two years; her confidence had never waned from her first day. Her course on money laundering was heavily influenced by the FBI; from their prognosis to the guest tutors. However, there was a conscious bias against Russia and Putin. She kept these views to herself. The FBI tutors were unanimous in their opinions that the 'Red Mafia' was more sophisticated, intelligent and brutal than the Italian, Sicilian or Columbian mafias. He skilfully veered from his prepared text to anecdotal former successful sting operations. He made it clear, however, there were many failures as well, or when they had been played, and had lost millions of dollars, you will not read about these failures anywhere. Brighton Beach in Brooklyn, New York, was the genesis of elaborate frauds and drug deals (cocaine). Putin had given hundreds of the Russian Mafia a literally get out of jail free card. Many were released from jails, and many were rounded up and given the option of a clean record and a passport to leave for the USA or Israel. Or being locked away for life, and they would be allowed to leave with their money, but which would be subjected to a swingeing government tax. Whether this tax would go into government coffers or Putin's alleged pension scheme was a moot point. The tutor was unambiguous; it went to Putin's accounts in offshore tax havens. He was running a *kleptocracy* not a democracy. The tutor gave Putin faint praise, however reluctantly. Under the vodka soaked leadership of Boris Yeltsin Russia was stripped bare by young oligarchs, they had been recruited as financial advisors, after Yeltsin was advised to begin a programme of privatisations of the countries loss making assets Yeltsin just signed the decree when his hand was not shaking.

The oligarchs systematically evaded tax; however all that changed when Putin came to power. The oligarchs would be paying taxes, and there would be no turning up at the Kremlin for vodka and zakuski (Russian equivalent to tapas) to suggest changes to government policy. Some oligarchs were invited to leave after selling their cash generating companies (former government industries) some foolishly decided to decline Putin's offer, and take him on politically. An oligarch on television said Putin's colleague in charge of a state oil company had overpaid for land. He made it very clear he was suggesting that his colleague had received a considerable kickback from the seller of the land, and the transparent inference so had Putin. It was a very unwise statement to make privately; complete madness to say this to Putin and on television. After this televised meeting with the oligarchs there would only be one winner. Putin confiscated their companies in lieu of tax that should have been paid in the Yeltsin years. There was little resistance. Those who did ended up in jail.

Then the FBI tutor returned to the main subject money laundering. '$49 billion was lost to the Russian economy in 2012 because of money laundering, some economists insist it was double that, but we settled on $49 billion, in one year. In 2014 $150 billion left Russia .Today no one for certain can say what the figure is, except it exceeds the 2014 figure. Now where does this money go? Simple; to cities where wealth doesn't get an inquisitive second glance. The money passes through the financial hubs of London, New York and Paris where millions of financial transactions are made every day. .In Spain for example many marinas were developed and sold.' The tutor then asked was there any questions. Edwina raised her hand.

'Yes, go ahead,' he said.

'When you said that the Russians were intelligent did you mean cunning or academically?'

'A brilliant question! And hopefully this will explain it vividly. When we did a sting and made arrests in Miami, we were all congratulating each other, when one of the team said what was the point of some of the Russians having fake PHDs? Then it was discovered their PHDs were genuine, they were economists, chemists and metallurgists. They were not what we expected, and they didn't have tattoos on their backs. So Edwina, they are Smart cookies as well as cold blooded killers and never, ever underestimate them.' She wouldn't.

***

He looked at the text, Perfect. The dystopian rain soaked London skyline was interrupted by the clouds changing from oppressive grey to white. The weather played havoc with his shifting moods. He instantly felt better; he could not make an appointment with his GP about his ever changing feelings about the pointless act of living to rinsing every second out of life. Behind his cheerful facade dwelt an individual who had difficulty coping with relaxing. However, today would be filled with a series of short adrenalin rushes.

The beat up electrical services van outside the property was occupied by a portly gentleman in his fifties consuming an unhealthy and lavishly filled roll who was reading The Sun. He observed the car pulling into the pavement, and the instant flash of headlights. He placed the partly eaten roll back into the plastic container, and returned the newspaper to the top of the dashboard. He retrieved the toolbox from the passenger seat, and made his way to the entrance. The occupant of the car watched with satisfaction as he entered the building effortlessly. Armstrong's elevated mood enhanced greatly.

***

Pavel was in Nigel's office, and it was very clear to anyone passing the office that the conversation was light-hearted, judging by the sounds of laughter emanating into the corridor. This was the exception to the rule. But when it happened, it meant money would be flowing into an account Nigel managed for a client that was an infrequent visitor to the UK, and the money was safely in the designated escrow account. Nigel's commission ran into millions. High risk equals high reward. The IPO (initial public offering) of the renewable energy company had been cancelled. Nigel's less cerebral colleague had leaked the confidential information that there would be a minimum 20 % rise in the share price when it was traded in London. He had told the confidant that the shares were undervalued. The hedge fund manager had invited Nigel to dinner; unfortunately Nigel was overseeing the prospectus for the imminent IPO.

'After tonight, you won't need to examine the minutiae, I have a counter and more attractive offer, however if you do not attend tonight, you are doing your client and yourself a disservice. That's all I can say at the moment, so I will see you at 8pm at Bonhams?'

Nigel was smiling. 'OK, but I'm sceptical; that is my professional opinion, but I'm obliged to examine every *credible* offer before the prospectus is compiled and sent out to my clients for their approval. No alcohol will be served, you understand, so there are no misunderstandings Claude; you understand?'

'Ha. Ha! But I am sure, you will order champagne, I have all the paperwork that matters, the normal padding out of the offer document will follow, these City lawyers have to justify their exorbitant fees, but you are the exception Nigel, you always earn your fees.' Claude ended the conversation. Nigel loved French cuisine; Bonhams in Bond Street was the perfect choice. His pitch would be laconic, but the numbers were larger than Nigel would be expecting, he was supremely confident that Nigel would be blown away. And when he heard his agreed fee in advance, that would erase any doubt. His fee would be paid into any off shore account that he required. Everything would go smoothly. It had to.

***

David was in the sitting area of the hotel lobby guests were entering and leaving at an alarming rate. He had been instructed to wait in the lobby sitting area, and a member of staff would take him to the table where his guest would be waiting. The working fireplace was the focal point, various chairs and sofas in striking orange upholstery were strategically positioned throughout the area. His excitable thoughts about the Russian leaping from the balcony had been placed in a calming area of his mind, of course, he could understand why he had instantly came to this unfounded scenario. But after dissecting this proposition, the odds of this being his client and dining companion were rapidly diminishing. To help time pass he looked at his paperwork for investment and wealth management and could not fault his compiled lists of fledgling Financial Technology companies in the UK,USA, and India. If the client concurred, he personally would invest *before* his client's money had been transferred to take a majority stake. When this had been completed, the share price would rise sharply. He was shaken out of these wealth creating thoughts, when the hotel member of staff approached him, asked his name, and then was told his dining companion was awaiting his presence.

Lobster would be his main course; young Russians were partial to lobster older Russians to steaks. The short walk from the lobby area to the restaurant emboldened his confidence, in the early days he never counted his commission before it was in his account. However, he would deviate with certainty on this deal. His confident smile waned as he was being led to his table, his client/dining companion was Jonathon Gove. Once he got over the shock he sat down in silence, it was obvious that Jonathon was not expecting David. David tipped his escort $20.

'This is not good Jonathan, not good at all. '

Jonathon was eyeing David's slim document folder. David took out the investment recommendations and pushed them over to Jonathon. Jonathon repeated the procedure with his documents.

'Are you acting on Pavel's behalf?'

'May I remind you of client confidentiality David?'

'Never mind that, why are we here in New York, when we could have concluded business in London? I am perplexed, as well as concerned.'

Jonathon was relieved David had articulated what he was surmising. 'Okay David, I am acting on behalf of Pavel, we are here to conclude business with each other on behalf of our client, it may be an unusual arrangement, but it still is a business meeting.'

'It now seems perfectly clear; we are acting on our mutual client's benefit. However, I am concerned. Why?'

'I know you are an excellent financial strategist, if you weren't you wouldn't be here. I have been acting for Pavel for a number of years, and you are investing for him for the first time. It will be on my say so, whether I recommend your investment plan. If I recommend your plan, you will be commuting to New York on a regular basis. Sometimes you may have to stay in New York for up to two weeks, but that is a very rare occurrence, staying here in a suite is hardly slumming it is it?'

'Wait a minute Jonathon this is moving far too quickly for me.'

'I have been surprised as well, I was told that you were or could be the new member of Pavel's investment strategists…You had been recommended, however, it is on my judgement whether you will join the team. Order some drinks, Blue Goose, while I peruse your investment recommendations and medium term plan.' David was being overwhelmed by this information and the stoical secrecy that he had kept his client to himself, when he would normally hint that he was representing a billionaire client. The diners at their Tuesday catch up at The Ivy would never divulge who their clients were, but some mundane investment plans were exchanged, but nothing of this scale. Jonathon raised an eyebrow while perusing the second A4 paper. David observed him, and he would be impressed; his inside man on this occasion was a woman in Silicon Valley. He sipped his Blue Goose while he was observing the other diners, he thought welcome to the 1% club. The majority of affluent clientele were in their thirties, a smattering of octogenarians was ensconced in the corner tables they were animated. I wonder how they all made their fortunes.

'I have underestimated you David, you really are a dark horse, and you obviously have faith in *fintech* (Financial Technology) and I see by your notes that you have been prescient about solar power, you ask the pertinent question, why are the Saudis placing their oil reserves in a Sovereign Wealth Fund with Goldman Sachs to place on the market? You do not believe that the Saudis need to raise money to finance public spending, due to spendthrift younger members of their Royal Families? You surmise that oil will be phased out throughout the industrial world. Solar energy and its source is infinite, and can be converted to clean energy and again you surmise there are high-technology batteries that are in existence or will soon come onto the market. Bit of a punt don't you think?'

'Not at all, I would happily invest a few million myself.'

'Well to let you enjoy your meal, I will on behalf of my client accept your recommendations. Welcome to the team. Normal electronic bank transfers procedures will take place when you fly back to London. Are you ready to order?'

'I am very pleased with that news Jonathon, regarding the *team* how many are in it and are any of our dining companions in it?'

'That's commercially sensitive, and a word of caution, this meeting is secret none of the others are aware and must remain unaware.'

'Okay, I fully understand that, I have another question, and that's it I promise.' Jonathon smiled and nodded. 'When did this New York vacancy become vacant?'

'Today, there was an unfortunate incident, one of our team fell or jumped from a balcony; it's in the newspapers. Unfortunate business.'

***

This was where Pavel would earn his money; he politely waited on the chauffeur to open his door. His suitor was waiting, going by his expression, good news could not wait. This suited Pavel, and he would not tease any information from this esteemed fellow. 'Great to see you Pavel, welcome to the House Of Lords.' Pavel shook his hand.

'Thank you for inviting me to lunch at such short notice.' They walked rapidly towards the restaurant where the impoverished and not so impecunious Lords and Ladies could dine in the salubrious surroundings with subsidies from the taxpayer. The £300 daily allowance does not stretch as far as it used to. A roast lunch cost an eye-watering £9.50, how do they manage thought Pavel. His host was a former rabid socialist that had eloquently morphed from an abolitionist of the House of Lords to a defender of the House of Lords. He had been identified, nurtured and introduced to Pavel; he was another useful, but expensive idiot. Flattery and filthy lucre concentrated his manipulative mind. The table was in the corner, out of earshot of fellow Peers.

'I know how busy you are Pavel so I have taken the liberty of ordering.' Pavel was pleased to hear this, the less important Peers who observed him with Lord 'Green fingers' the better. His official business was to thank Pavel for contributing to his environmental charity.

'That is most welcome, I have a very busy schedule; now how can I help you?'

'The Magnitsky act will not pass into Law, even if it is passed in the House of Commons, which I very much doubt, it would be an adverse reaction and would affect billions in trade with Russia. It's time to tell Trump to back off.'(In 2009, Russian tax accountant Sergei Magnitsky died in a Moscow prison after investigating a $230 million fraud involving Russian tax officials. Magnitsky was accused of committing the fraud himself and detained. While in prison, Magnitsky developed gall stones and calculous cholecystitis and was refused medical treatment for months. After almost a year of imprisonment, he was beaten to death while in custody. Bill

Browder a prominent American businessman and friend of Magnitsky publicised the case and lobbied American officials to pass legislation sanctioning Russian individuals involved in corruption. Browder brought the case to Senators Benjamin Cardin and John McCain who proceeded to propose legislation. In 2012 it became Law, and prohibited those who were involved in his death not to be allowed to travel to the USA or allow them to use the banking system.)

Lord 'Green fingers' was the beautiful flower that Pavel had propagated with very expensive nutrients. 'That is good news for Russia and UK trade. I will be donating to your charity, through a third-party which is not even tenuously connected to Russia or any Russian citizens.'

'The Climate Change environmental charity will be grateful for your generous and welcome donation, as the charity has grown so has the running costs, your donation or part of it will alleviate this.'

'You are the expert, you will use the money wisely, that I am sure. Your influence in the Chamber has not gone unnoticed; expect invitations from various energy companies to join them as an environmental advisor. Turn down the two most lucrative, and accept the two least remunerative; in the long term these will make you financially secure for life.'

'I will take your advice on board. I have formed a cross section of Members who are very interested in Climate Change; however, they have difficulty in following and reading the minutiae and request my expertise. The field trips to the USA, Caribbean and Europe to study Wind power, solar, and heat source systems are educational, so are the days when they see the sights, stay in five star hotels and dine in the best restaurants. There are no Climate Change agnostics, all are true believers.'

'You are a great judge of character and people. How have you settled into your new apartment in Kensington?'

'You are so kind, the apartment is lovely, and I can't thank you enough for contributing to the deposit, for the first time in my life I feel it is time to look after myself, all those years I looked after my constituents, then the press started writing unflattering stories about me. So when Labour wanted me to vacate my role as an MP, I demanded I be elevated to the Upper Chamber. They had no choice, if they didn't agree, I was staying put. And the higher echelons were fully aware that I knew where corrupt practices had taken place.' Pavel smiled, he was the source of negative information to the London and Scottish tabloids. Everyone was aware the maverick MP had alcohol and gambling issues. A confidant of Pavel's took the crestfallen and under financial pressure Member of Parliament under her wing. She subtly suggested he should be in the House of Lords, but while he was an MP this could never be so. He filled in the gaps. He played hardball. He was a welcome addition to the Climate Change esoteric group in the stuffy and privileged House of Lords.

Pavel always struck agreements in plain sight, meeting in mediocre restaurants attracted attention, everyone had an iPhone there was no hiding place; except in high-end restaurants and hotels. The MP was weaned off alcohol and gambling by his new female acquaintance that *happened* to bump into him ~~in St~~ Stephen's Tavern, a watering hole for MPs and their researchers. He was inebriated; he had been in the pub from noon, and boy he could drink. She was moving in the opposite direction, she moved towards him, and collided with him; both spilled their drinks and apologised profusely to each other. Even when he was inebriated he was polite and charming. He insisted it was his fault and he would replenish her glass, he invited her to sit at his table. This could be fate throwing him a beautiful lifebelt. Or it could be the alcohol taking his optimistic thoughts on a detour from reality. He didn't mind, he felt good, he was going to go with the flow. He returned to the table, she explained she had been on a blind date, but she had been stood up. They swapped life stories, and took comfort that they had similar relationship breakdowns. He pointed to the lager in the glass and explained alcohol was his only friend. As kismet would have it she was a psychotherapist specialising in alcohol dependency, very fortunate. He laughed uncontrollably. *Lorn*a enquired what he did for a living he modestly replied he worked in the civil service, through the haze of alcohol he judged she was not a student of current affairs, or she would have recognised him from the salacious stories in the national press; or maybe because his present ubiquitous unkempt appearance was appearing in the press frequently.

A campaign had begun to remove him as an MP, due to 'serious personal issues.' And so this fortunate meeting was the germane to Alexander Marr being unwittingly seduced and recruited to be one of Pavel's political expensive stooges. Alexander and Lorna started off as friends; however, he fell for her kindness big time. She convinced him to come to her exclusive gym, she would get his body and more so his mind back to being sharp, intuitive and prescient. He had forewarned the House of Commons about following the USA into disastrous regime change of dictators in the Middle-East. They laughed and mocked him then; they didn't now. He had to be removed from not only the Labour Party but the House of Commons forthwith. MI6, didn't need to initiate his downfall, he contributed generously to it himself. He was the man of the people, television and radio stations couldn't get enough of him; fellow comrades were envious of him, he was becoming a celebrity. Then the offers dried up, he sat alone in his flat in London with only boredom for company. Then alcohol made it an unlikely threesome, he was on the slide. Over a period of eighteen months he finally acknowledged he was dependent on alcohol; he needed a mistress; enter cocaine. He attended the House of Commons on rare occasions, MPs complained about his boorish behaviour in the Strangers Bar. He was becoming argumentative and challenged MPs from various parties to fight. He had sunk to his destructive nadir.

Fate intervened that day in St Stephen's Tavern. He pledged through a haze of alcohol induced pronouncements he was going to change his life utterly. Lorna was his guardian angel; he would not undermine or question her professional advice. He became fitter, he abstained from alcohol and more importantly he mended fences with political friends and foes. Life is too short, and so was his temper. Now it was subdued, he started to like himself again, and it felt good. However, the political establishment wanted him out. Lorna over lunch, asked him the question, do you want to leave politics completely if not trade your constituency for a Peerage. His eyes glowed. He excused himself from the table and made an impromptu phone call. He made the Chief Whip an offer he could not refuse, and he wanted an answer in five minutes, if the answer came back no, he would stay on as an MP as his popularity was soaring. Either way he was indifferent. It was the Chief Whip's choice. He returned to the table and placed his mobile beside his glass of water. It vibrated, he was to be elevated to the House of Lords, they agreed and a timetable was put in place. He gleefully explained this to Lorna. She smiled and congratulated him, and secretly congratulated herself. Pavel would be pleased.

***

Edwina peered over her imperious sunglasses, her heart beat raced; that's David Fisher dining with Jonathan Gove! Was Armstrong aware of this meeting? And if he was, was she sent here to confirm that they are connected? She took out her phone and took a selfie which captured in the background David Fisher and Jonathan Gove dining in New York. She examined her handiwork; very impressive Fisher and Gove were easily identifiable. She sipped her expresso coffee, it tasted delicious. Fisher and Gove were laughing like drains, and then she saw Gove stretch out his hand across the table; Fisher shook it, no vulgar high-fives for these traditional types. She typed these gestures into her notes on her phone. The night had only begun, and she had linked Gove and Fisher to some financial arrangement or agreement. However, this could be a completely innocent business arrangement. On the other hand it could be an insight into the convoluted world of sophisticated money laundering. Her professional opinion would favour the latter, rather than the former. She chased the chocolate cake around the plate with her fork. Her hidden eyes never left them; they were here for the long haul, judging by the food that was being delivered to their table. Copious amounts of vodka were being consumed; they didn't have a care in the world. When she sent Armstrong the photograph and notes, she would determine how her instinct would react to his reply. Fisher and Gove were dressed Smartly, would they be staying in the restaurant, then retire for nightcaps in the bar or venture forth into the New York tumult?

The restaurant was gaining clients, the noise level was raised. A younger clientele were now in the majority, polite society looked on disapprovingly at the various entourages that were being escorted to their tables. Gove and Fisher eyed some of the inebriated young women, she could only guess at the salacious comments that they were passing to each other. The various waiters ferried trays of drinks to two tables which were occupied by young women in their late twenties or early thirties, they looked like supermodels; stick thin. To her surprise the waiters returned with various foods; pasta, steaks and French fries. They all were wolfing them down, as soon as the food hit their plates; no one was waiting till the last plate had been served. Before the waiter had completed the servings, some of them were requesting second helpings. Loud but polite was her opinion of the phalanx of women. Now she was in a dilemma; sitting on her own could attract unwarranted attention, either from the two tables of raucous women, or from Gove or Fisher. Should she discreetly navigate herself from the restaurant to the lobby where she could observe the comings and goings from the hotel or retire to her room, write up her report and send the definitive proof that Jonathan Gove and David Fisher knew each other professionally and personally? These compelling questions were halted. A waiter came to her table and placed a bottle of her favourite wine accompanied by an elegant wine class. The waiter explained it was from an old acquaintance; he poured the wine and then walked away. Her hidden eyes darted to Gove and Fisher they were still admiring the young women at the two tables, they were not interested in her. She smiled and raised the wine to her red lips; her eyes could not locate her latent admirer. The expensive wine had not lost its allure. However, under her sunny disposition, she had been compromised, but by whom the Russians, FBI or the unlikely old acquaintance? She had to revert to damage limitation she would stay put and enjoy her admirer's unsolicited largesse. The intoxicating taste of the wine rapidly diminished as she saw Gove and Fisher leave the table. If she followed suit she was hot-wiring her attention to her opaque admirer. She poured herself a generous second glass, and rapidly came to the conclusion, she had unexpectedly come across David Fisher as Jonathon Grove's dining companion. A file was now opened on David Fisher. London, St. Petersburg, Moscow and now New York were all coincidently the top four money laundering cities in the world. Had some citizens of these 'laundrettes' had the benefit of David Fisher's advice? Jonathon Gove had been on frequent trade delegations to these 'laundrettes.' She had an alert on her phone. She observed with incredulity at the video, it clearly showed in High Definition a male in her flat, not an opportunistic burglar but someone calmly opening and closing drawers in a methodical fashion looking for something specific. He then moved to her Smart TV and activated it, she could clearly see he was in the settings section and he was connected by his phone not the TV remote, she figured out quickly he was from the Intelligence Service; she was now under observation in her own home. Was he from British, Russian or American intelligence? Then that awful feeling in her stomach; was Armstrong behind this in some capacity? Send her out to New York to get her out the way so the intelligence operative could activate her Smart TV to listen and observe her? Fear overcame her momentarily, which was replaced by instinctive loathing for Armstrong. The wine glass was now being emptied and replenished in similar fashion as she tried to gather her animated thoughts that were entering and leaving her professional thought process at an alarming velocity; she was experiencing an avalanche of cognitive dissonance .The hunter was now being hunted.

***

David and Jonathon were in a yellow cab on their way to the Russian Samovar restaurant & piano bar on fifty- second street a twenty minute journey. The copious amounts of vodka had barely affected them, they were laughing uncontrollably at being each other's client. The Russian Samovar was popular with Russian clientele; as well as discreet and indiscreet Wall Street traders. They never hinted or discussed during their heightened exuberant cab ride this was the most lucrative fee they had laughingly earned. Their adrenalin was a natural antidote to the potent Blue Goose. The pre-booked table would not see much if any food, except for snacks, the table was only a few metres from the iconic white piano. David had left nothing to chance. And to supplement this he would be accompanying the client to the dimly lit Pravda Vodka Room which was immediately across the street from the Russian Samovar.

Jonathon had been greatly impressed by David's meticulous criteria for schmoozing with clients future and present. However, he may wish to modify this opinion at a later date, his opinion was not set in stone. He could never have forecast the unexpected and unexplained death of his Russian colleague who had leapt to his death apparently smiling. His death deeply disturbed him; he did not wish to promote David to an untimely death. New York was very lucrative but more dangerous than London. However, the fees on offer superceded the constant danger. Through time, he would learn the reason that drove his colleague to leap enthusiastically to oblivion. But that was for another day; today they had each accomplished their objectives. This in itself had thrown up another in plain sight problem. Pavel, had orchestrated this meeting, was he meant to look for minuscule flaws in David's character or business acumen? If so there were none. Unlike himself, who had many but unnoticed flaws, and he could praise or condemn colleagues without a flutter of guilt across his unwielding conscience. The 'Flying Russian' would confirm this sentiment if he was not indisposed.

***

Edwina soon overcame her disappointment when she saw David Fisher and Jonathon Gove stand up place their jackets on and leave the restaurant, to her surprise they were no obvious signs of them being unsteady on their feet. The partly consumed second bottle of wine dissipated any feelings of despair or failure. Her phone had them bang to rights if any wrongdoing was suspected and proved or if they denied any professional contact. When they left she removed the oversized sunglasses and placed them on the table, she now felt she could relax. Her secret admirer was no longer in the shadows; he had called her and told her that he had sent over the bottle of wine. It was Armstrong. She was bitterly disappointed. A girl can only dream. He had confided in her that being served the expensive wine, would add cache to her alter-ego *Gillian* the successful businesswoman. She could have explained that this jape had curtailed her from monitoring Gove and Fisher, but she would hold that back. She told him to hold on for a moment, and then she sent the montage of images of Gove & Fisher dining together and shaking hands. He was shaken when the images came through, but he recovered to congratulate her on capturing them on her phone. It could be innocent or it may not was his conclusion. He abruptly ended the call, something had come up, 'order another bottle of wine, and keep in touch.' This she duly did. Her state of mind may have been altered by the alcohol but she was certain there was more to this innocent business meeting than Armstrong surmised. He didn't mention the obvious question why they went to New York to meet, when they lived in the same apartment block in London. It was patently obvious that there must be a third-party; hence the meeting in New York. But Armstrong never went near this. She had spooked him; he was not expecting Gove & Fisher to meet in New York. Either she was succumbing to paranoia or she was professional and diligent as per her training.

Armstrong sat at his desk pondering the brief conversation and the disturbing images on his phone. Gove and Fisher had concluded a deal, but for whom and the monetary value? Maybe there was no one else involved, it could be feasible and more sensible to fly to New York stay in separate hotels then meet up for dinner and conclude a money laundering deal, far from the prying eyes of police and MI6 in London. This was clever. The FBI had not spoken of any ongoing surveillance of any Russian or Person of Interest from London flying into New York for a clandestine meeting. Sending Edwina to New York on a fictitious surveillance operation, had unexpected consequences. But for whom?   He reached into the bottom drawer and retrieved a cigarette from the packet that had lain untouched for over a year the cigarette helped his mind slow down and reach a conclusion, however unpalatable. He searched for the lighter which was at the rear of the drawer, he hoped it would ignite. He gave it a good shake; he felt the tension infuse his body. But the lighter didn't let him down, he opened the window and sucked deeply on the cigarette, he felt so good, a flicker of a smile was battling to emerge, but it did. Then suddenly it was erased, maybe he had been premature to remove Edwina's racist antagonist? He could have used his overt antipathy and racism as a tool to subdue her, if the need arose? He would park that thought, he was gone and he wasn't coming back. The smile had not given up it returned triumphantly. The calming cigarette had formulated a kernel of a possible solution if it was required. He tossed the cigarette out the window.

***

Michael Ogilvie waited on the potential and lucrative client in his office. First of all the client was not Russian, or purportedly representing Russians which was welcome. Robert Samson, English and had lived in Jersey for the last fifteen years. A former fund manager who had accumulated £200 million, but his health had suffered; two heart attacks made him heed his Harley Street physician's advice, 'give up the City, stay in Jersey play golf and take up gardening, if you don't you won't survive another heart attack.' Divorced twice and two heart attacks before he was forty, the future didn't look good, he took his doctor's advice. He purchased another property in St. Helier, employed a team of builders, he would be the labourer as well as the project manager. The excess weight melted away with each passing week, he was gradually retaining his fitness from his early thirties. He was a keen mature student of the building trade; he struck up a respectful relationship with the tiler, soon he was not just fetching and cutting tiles he was laying or fixing them on the floors and walls. The tiler just asked innocuous questions about the City and how it worked. Robert was never evasive, rather than mention any illegalities he substituted 'sharp practices' and without prompting he added a visceral diatribe about Russian émigrés, how they could muster boom and bust in a very short space of time. He deduced Russian clients had contributed to his heart attacks, but he couldn't expand on specifics; the tiler viewed his face changing to a deathly white as he was telling this. He hoped he wasn't on the verge of another heart attack; they still had to tile another bathroom. Thus he changed the subject rapidly to future projects, the healthy hue returned to Robert's sporadic lined face. The tiler was relieved, another school lesson learnt; don't mention the City or Russians; Robert would still be on earth and could help him tile the other bathroom.

The telephone rang. 'Send him in please.' He came through the door with a confident smile and handshake. He had all relevant documents and his passport for him to copy and send to the relevant government departments. Michael had enquired discreetly about Robert Samson, 'a good egg, but had to retire as the City was killing him .And he doesn't like Russians oligarchs.'

'You're looking well Michael.' He sat down, Michael replied likewise. 'Appearances can be deceptive, now how can I help you?'
'Simple really, I have to take an arms-length position regarding investments, due to my health. I want to invest directly in property , and not in any funds that have any Russian investors, I firmly believe the United States government will impose economic sanctions worldwide, not just on the UK and the European Union also on companies that have Russian investors. This information comes from someone who has a contact in Washington D.C.' Michael could not suppress his laughter. 'Seriously? Maybe you've be on the internet too long studying conspiracy theories. I know what they say and propose, but if economic sanctions come in it'll be short-term. And if you feel strongly about this, why don't you short stocks with companies or funds that have major Russian investors, there are numerous funds that have major Russian investors that will be on the sanctions list?'
'Grandmothers that need to be taught to suck eggs?'
'I know, but in my professional capacity I think you're over reacting to newspaper gossip from Washington. But that is just my opinion. It is your money, and you are fully aware of the vagaries of the property market; big profits if everything stays calm in the City, but if economic data comes out suggesting a slowing down of growth that will cause concern for the property market in London'.
'That is my fucking point Michael!'
'I'm confused, what is the point?'
'When the sanctions kick in, there will be cash flight from the stock market, where will the cash go. It is very simple, into the relative safe haven of property. That's why I want to invest now, to get ahead of the curve, that is how I made my money in the City; anticipating trends not reacting to trends. I want to invest in London some short-term, when the

sanctions kick–in the money from the stock market will be looking for a safe-haven with a good return. This will cause property prices to rise, I'll liquidate my assets in London, and my other long-term assets not in London will be for the long-term.' Michael was not impressed. Maybe his medication has affected his cognitive facility?

'And if the sanctions are not implemented or they come in and are rescinded, the stock market will rise, outstripping any comparable return from property investment,'

'But you're ignoring the information from D.C, not at your peril but at mine, if that doesn't sound too rude?' Michael is having great difficulty understanding how this former City trader/fund manager made millions? It must have been insider trading. 'No that is not rude at all; and it is your money, you said other property outside London; where exactly?'

Robert felt much better, and he was at last on board. 'In Scotland… Dundee.'

Michael was now intrigued, he was looking at a spiv, that accumulated his wealth from insider trading and market manipulation. 'But why choose Dundee, Robert?'

'The Victoria & Albert museum, when it is open, there will be an unprecedented demand, six hotels are being built, and other established hotels are being refurbished and extended, obviously for the influx of visitors. I want to purchase flats nearby on the Waterfront area, and let them out on a nightly basis, through Airbnb, I have researched the area, and it is a growth area for tourism. Flats are being built as we speak, I want £2 million invested in them; here is the name and number of the developer; and here are the floor plans of the apartments, those marked are the apartments I require they all have the best views and I want them all altered to these specifications. (He hands over photographs) Obviously these flats are inexpensive compared to London, however, these are the discounted prices I am prepared to pay, I am sure you can use your skills to achieve an even better discount, if not don't worry. End the conversation with a follow up letter sent by email, which is in your inbox, apart from the prices of each apartment. I'll leave it to you to include the agreed price when you have agreed verbally. They have 24 hours to conclude the bargain. When the paperwork has been agreed with their solicitors half the money will be transferred into an escrow account; the remainder on completion of the properties and when a rigorous quality control inspection carried out by an established third- party has given the properties the all clear.'

With these precise details, he stood up, shook Michael's hand, and then departed from the office.

Michael was impressed by his clear strategy; there were no downsides to his well-researched plan, but why the indecent haste? Before any verbal or written contact with the developer, his first port of call would be David Fisher; after all he was brought up in Dundee and would have contacts in the city. Robert was sanguine that his investment would be bountiful. David would be a good sound board; was there any downside to this investment?

Robert stood outside on the pavement; he was waiting anxiously on *the* call. He looked at his expensive watch repeatedly, very anxious and fraught. The mobile vibrated against his thigh.

'It went like a dream, as you said it would. I should hear very soon, when, not if, the developer will accept my proposal. At 4pm today the police will be assisting HMRC when they seize computers, files and USBs from their office. HMRC received credible evidence that there has been a systematic and sustained VAT fraud over a prolonged period of time.' The call ended abruptly.

An unmarked battered grey van emerged alongside him, as he was placing the mobile reluctantly into his jacket pocket. The door slid open, he was grabbed and pulled into the van by two masked men, he had a hood pulled over his head, and was thrown into the rear beside various construction tools, bags of cement and sand. 'Don't say anything Robert.' He didn't recognise the voice; he was relieved it was delivered with an apologetic tone, and in perfect English. He heard him speak into his phone. 'Package picked up; zero damage, repeat zero damage.' There was an unnerving pause.

'Message understood.'

'Returning to base with package. Out.' Robert was bemused, how he longed to be back in Jersey up to his neck in discarded building material. This was not what he had agreed to; he had to face the fact he was going to meet someone from his past that he had wronged. He smiled under the hood, and thought it can be anyone from a list of over a hundred. He decided to fill the unsettling void of compelling silence by counting every second he was in the van until he reached his unknown destination. His phone vibrated in his jacket pocket. 'Aren't you going to answer your phone Robert, and take off the hood.' He removed the hood, rubbed his eyes and answered his phone. Armstrong was sitting opposite of him smiling.

***

Pavel was nursing his cognac; he glanced at the Thomas Schofield Grandfather clock, 11 pm. He had been alerted that the rat in New York had taken the easy way out. No one had any idea he was a very well paid informant until five days ago; but more troubling how long was he an informant? Everything had been in place; he was due to be relocated from New York to London. When he had been in London he would apparently hang himself due to business pressures. It would be leaked to the Press that he was 'an uninhibited cocaine user.' Now things had changed utterly but for the better? Time would reveal all. However, his replacement would be a man of unsullied character. He wouldn't be directly employed; he would be investing money at his intuitive discretion. He would be remunerated accordingly. David Fisher was the only one to fill this vacancy. David Fisher had been studied from near and afar. Nigel was Pavel's eyes and ears in London. David was circumspect when potential Russian clients were visitors to his Mayfair office. He used Nigel's experience and perceived wisdom to ascertain if the potential Russian was tainted in any way.

Pavel was a great admirer of David; he implored Nigel to arrange a meeting. Nigel made it very plain; David didn't covet an abundance of Russian clients, a polite smattering was adequate. If the mountain doesn't come to Pavel, he would encourage a financial earthquake to make the mountain seek financial assistance. Pavel spoke to one of his contacts in the City, he opined that a Merchant Bank was struggling, it had a client that was known to be involved in laundered money, might be best to investigate subtlety, without making any waves. Pavel was fully aware that his contact would embellish this information. Unfortunately for David Fisher this was the Merchant Bank that would be releasing the final tranche of finance for his commercial development. The Merchant Bank's difficulty was Pavel's opportunity. Pavel had imparted this forthcoming bad news to Nigel, when he was in his office on another matter. Nigel didn't react well. He was concerned for his fee as well as David's imminent financial difficulty. Pavel softly enquired if he could assist favoured clients or a client of Nigel. Nigel's melancholy dissipated. David's funding issue was the most pressing. In the back of Nigel's mind, Pavel's spontaneous gesture may require something reciprocal in nature in the near future. He wasn't willing to speculate at this difficult time. And his fee would be guaranteed. Nigel explained David's near completed commercial project quickly and clearly; Pavel jotted down the figures, and wrote down the terms of the loan. He handed the notebook to Nigel; the terms were more attractive in comparison to the Merchant Bank. He had to subdue his delight, he would have to go through a charade of being slightly disappointed; he glanced up from the notebook with his face covered in disappointment, Pavel without saying anything, smiled, Nigel changed tact, it was a deal that was very generous, he was sure David would accept.

Pavel showed little emotion, he wanted a two page contract drawn up before David arrived. He made it very clear; he wanted it signed as soon as Nigel explained the terms of the new funding. If David showed any reticence the deal would be pulled never to resurface. This could be difficult; David's custom and practice was to take the paperwork home and study it himself, and then return the next day with some caveats. Today this could not happen. Pavel was observing how he would get this deal over the line under tremendous pressure. Nigel lifted the phone and spoke to the Legal Contracts Manager he wanted the contract in his office in fifteen minutes, he calmly dictated the Terms & Conditions, Pavel sat stony faced eagerly listening to the one way conversation. Nigel was relieved there were no interventions from Pavel. His fee was being spent in his head as he placed down the phone with palpable relief. In Russia Pavel completed many short-term contracts in a similar expedient fashion, with one proviso; there would be one of Pavel's *administrative managers* holding a Makarov (pistol) against the reluctant lawyer's head to incentivise him. However, London was a more civilised city than Moscow; more corrupt but definitely more civilised. Nigel ordered coffee as the contract was being drawn up, he wanted to order champagne but he did not want to tempt the misfortune of an unwelcome intervention of fate. While he was shooting the breeze with Pavel he could imagine the despondent mood David would be suffering, and when he was in the office he would erupt with invective against *'these fucking corrupt banks.'* He would meet him at the elevator to disabuse him of the financial meltdown he was facing

***.

Armstrong was in a café near King's Cross station, he was on his third cup of coffee. Nightfall was descending. He looked at the photographs repeatedly that Edwina had sent from New York. There was no dispute now that they were connected by business; however, other invisible business arrangements could have been completed away from the gaze of others who wished them harm. He went to settings in his phone, Edwina's lounge came into full view, but more important her desk with her laptop screen could be magnified until it could be read. Now he understood why they were called *Smart TVs*. He didn't have one; wonder why? He was shaken from this comforting thought when he came in casually through the door without any outward sign of worry. He indicated he was going to the counter. Armstrong was livid; the amount of coffee he had drunk would play havoc with his intermittent sleep pattern. He was chatting up the attractive woman in her forties behind the counter; she was carrying too much timber for Armstrong's preference. He caught Armstrong's icy stare, and ended the conversation abruptly with the waitress. He had brightened up her bad day.

'And where the fuck, have you been? You should have been here an hour ago.'

He sat down and gave that thin lipped smile that Armstrong hated; he lifted the steaming cup of coffee near to his lips, paused then said, 'how what happened?'

Armstrong's face reddened. 'Don't fucking start…!' The waitress looked up suddenly at their table.

'Language please, there is a lady present, and a gorgeous one at that.' The waitress blushed and smiled, Armstrong got more annoyed. 'What fucking age are you?'

'Okay, I'm just winding you up, calm down.' He stared at Armstrong while sipping his coffee.

Armstrong took a series of deep relaxing breaths. 'So how did it go then?'

'As I said a walk in the park…your temples are going grey, I've never noticed that before…'

'Shut to fuck up, you're due for an assessment in five weeks and four days you're not laughing now are you?' The laughter melted away.

'Are you sure? I've not received a letter.'

'Well, I'm telling you, and guess who is compiling part of the assessment?' Now Armstrong was leaning back, much more relaxed and smiling, he held up his hand for the anticipated response. He smiled at the waitress observing them. 'Can I have another cup of your delicious coffee Miss?' The blush returned to her youthful and make-up free attractive face.

'Does your friend need a re-fill?'

'No, be best not, he gets incontinent after two cups, it happens when you get older, don't be fooled by that luscious head of hair, it's a re-tread… a cheap hair transplant, he goes to Bulgaria; every three months for maintenance, if you understand.' He gives her a slight wink; two older women in the corner are giggling, one uncontrollably. Armstrong leans over the table and urges him to do likewise.

 He slams down the coffee angrily, the clatter of the cup on the table echoes off the walls. Some coffee has spilt onto the table. The giggling stops abruptly, and a malevolent silence entombs the café.

'Now, do you want to continue this pantomime, or get down to real business? The choice is yours.'

'Certainly, I am sorry for taking the piss; I was just relaxed because everything went so well, as you had said it would. I knew you would be anxious.'

 The waitress came over smiling at Armstrong carrying his cup of coffee; she placed it on the table, and quickly glanced at his friend's 'hair' as she

quickly dried the table. Armstrong can't suppress his laughter. His companion, smiles as well. She moves away from the table. The air has been cleared. 'Well, I've not got all day.'
'Okay, okay, he talked but not at first. I encouraged him, if you understand…don't worry I didn't need to use any violence. You were a hundred per cent correct about the others, but completely wrong about David Fisher. He didn't know of him, he seemed genuine, in my opinion.'
'Oh, that's bad news! However, you did a fine job in the house; the surveillance comes through loud and very clear. In and out in fifteen minutes, it was a text book operation.'
'I'm glad to hear that. Officially it never happened, if she finds out. It's an off-the-book-operation.'
'Things can change; this could morph into an official sanctioned full-blown counter-terrorism operation. It could end up messy if that happens. Heads will roll, you understand that?'

***

The Blue Goose vodka had suddenly taken its exact revenge; he was unsteady on his feet as he emptied his bladder into the urinal. The smile of utter contentment would not regress, the absurdity of going to New York to conclude a business meeting with his neighbour, business associate and dining companion was not lost on him. Then the smile faded, the news about the Russian throwing himself over the balcony to his death came to the fore. He must have planned it; this was not a spontaneous moment of madness. The legal documents to the multi-million apartment had been signed. The widow of a few hours was now the legal owner. At last the torrent ceased. He zipped up and washed his hands. Jonathon was concerned at the length of time David had been away. His concern was unwarranted as he emerged from the rest-room. He stopped to speak to the attractive woman who was passing him, she had commented on his "beautiful accent." Jonathon emitted a wry smile at this comment from a few hours ago, as the drinks were consumed; David's accent reverted to a heavy Scottish accent, which at times was indiscernible, and when speaking to her now he would be calling her "hen" apparently a term of endearment when speaking to a woman. How strange.

Jonathon had already ordered another round. David left the woman who was laughing uncontrollably, and made his way back to his table. He was exuberant. And so he should be after earning millions of pounds in commission. He envied David's business and personal skills. However, he had formed the same opinion of the flying Russian. 'I needed that Jonathon, and I see you have ordered.' He sat down.
'I see you made a friend for life there.'

'I don't know about that Jonathon.' His face reddened.
'Oh, she has taken a fancy to you, I know these things… I have studied body language.'
'Don't, be daft, she likes my accent, she told me that earlier. You know what New Yorkers are like.'
'I'm just saying David that's all. You look so happy.'
'That's because I am, this was the deal of all deals. I am not saying the money doesn't matter, that would be untrue. But I felt really as though I accomplished something more than a business deal today, I can't explain it.'
 'That's good; that you've experienced a sense of achievement. I'm very pleased how professional you were today. The best deals are the ones that have a structure to them that a teenager can understand. Your documents were well-thought out and clear. As you will be taking up a new position in New York, I can see it as an advantage if you formed a friendship with your new friend. It can be lonely at times in New York.'
'Jonathon, do we have to talk about this just now?' He stood up and downed the vodka. 'C'mon, we are going across the street to the Pravda Vodka Room.' Jonathon looks perplexed; he shrugs his shoulders, and stands up.
'Okay, my Scottish friend, lead the way.'
'Are you not finishing your drink, in fact you've not touched it!'
'I'll leave it, lead the way, and your friend is looking at you.'
'C'mon Jonathon, if you're not drinking it, I'll drink it, waste not, want not.' Jonathon hands him the drink, it disappears down his throat in seconds. The woman is visibly impressed at this, she's pointing out David to her younger friend.
'That was braw! Time to go Jonathon.' Jonathon is smiling; David has yet again spoken with that peculiar accent. 'On you go David, the night is still young.' They move towards the exit, the woman hurriedly moves towards them with her reluctant partner in tow.
'Leaving already David?' She looks disappointed.
'We are going across the street to the Pravda, you and your friend are welcome to join us, this is Jonathon by the way.' Jonathon looks a little bit surprised at this invitation, but, business has been concluded, so what the hell. David has forgotten her name. He smiles. 'And who is your smiling friend. ?'
'This is Avery, Avery this is David and Jonathon.'
'That's all the introductions sorted out, are you both coming over the street with us?'
'I told you Avery he was a charmer, didn't I.' Avery smiled. 'We accept your kind invitation.'

David smiles; (he remembers her name; Gwen) and invites them to lead the way. Jonathan tips his imaginary hat at David. One thing can be guaranteed David would not talk shop, and he would listen very carefully what he said, an interesting few hours lay ahead.

***

Simon Corndale frequently woke up in a sudden panic covered in a cold odourless sweat in the early hours. How he managed to talk himself out of certain death he couldn't fathom on a cogent basis. He had at last managed to free himself from the pernicious attraction of cocaine. His mind was settling down, but some remnants of intense paranoia surfaced as the charcoal silent sheet of nightfall descended. He was still a self-imposed prisoner in the steel and green glass apartment building. However, he had *one* more lucrative deal in him; then he would be out of this business either free as a bird or prematurely deceased. His former client Robert Samson was exiled in Jersey, the stories behind this unexpected exile were wild and varied. The official reason was it was down to health reasons. Or he had been found out to have *inaccurate accounting practices* that disadvantaged his Russian client. He had been *encouraged* to deposit substantial compensation into an account in Cyprus that was favoured by Russians. If he demurred from this reasonable demand, he would not have time to reflect on this unwise course of action. He completed the transaction with the Russian client sitting beside him. He clicked send. £10 million pounds; took flight from his account instantly. The ping on the Russian client's iPhone sent an uncomfortable feeling to his bloated stomach. The Russian's mood elevated. He shook hands then left the office, twenty minutes later Robert suffered another cardiac arrest, as opposed to self-diagnosis of indigestion. When the cardiologist asked if he had suffered any stressful exertions that day his volcanic temper erupted; 'are you fucking kidding me?' It didn't help the cardiologist was from the Ukraine.

Simon was in, his instructions crystal clear. Follow the instructions in the email to the letter and the exact time. Do not reply to the email. This would be the double-cross of the most violent Mafia in the world; the Russian Mafia. Fear, excitement and the millions of pounds were the components that convinced him to be party to this audacious scheme. He had experienced a near death episode with the Russian Mafia earlier, it made his bowels over react, but the adrenalin rush was more potent than cocaine; but this financial transaction could prove lethal. He removed his headphones and stepped from the running machine. He was still buzzing; he looked at the exercise bicycle, and decided twenty minutes suffice. His thought process was stretching him mentally in a satisfying manner. His body and mind were in perfect harmony; a sense of peace enveloped him after his encounter at the farmhouse.

He was now a frequent visitor to the in-house gym of the apartment block. The participants who were there were predominately woman, most were in their thirties, four were in their fifties but were very well honed. There was hope for him as he looked at his paunch. They were all City types; driven and single-minded. In laconic conversations with him they were straight to the point,' just moved in?' and 'where in the City do you work?' His engaging smile elicited softer responses. He could understand the hardness in their voices; the City was full of sexist pigs; he used to be one of them. Smiles were not forced anymore; small talk became the new-normal. Life was looking more optimistic for him and the regular participants of the gym. In his experience most of the multi-millionaires who were his clients were the most miserable human beings he had the misfortune to meet. However, his worst nightmare had come true; he had replicated them; wealthy and miserable. But he had clicked his internal reset button. Some contentment, had elbowed out various dark and miserable thoughts. It would be a slow, maybe painful process, but he believed in the Promised Land.

He had been invited to a restaurant for an impromptu evening meal with six other residents and gym aficionados; however, the meal would coincide with the first email from Robert Samson. The text message said nine. That would be nine pm. Robert was obviously a man of few words and digits. He didn't want to attend the restaurant in a tense frame of mind, then suddenly depart or make an excuse. He would boldly suggest a rescheduling. If not he would definitely make the next dinner as he would arrange the date and pay for the meal to make up for his non-attendance. It was not in his nature to be so generous, but things had changed in his life for the better, albeit more dangerous. However, he could live with this juxtaposition. Fortune favours the brave (and the City).

His quickening feet punished the pedals on the bicycle; he was trying to predict the fraudulent scheme that Robert would come up with. He was unsophisticated, so an elaborate or complex plan was instantly ruled out. Then again, he may have underestimated Robert; he had been ensconced on Jersey for a while. Then he stopped peddling; Jersey is riven with Bankers of every nationality, perhaps Robert has assimilated with the banking community, and has picked up or been guided to good advice? He glanced at his watch five pm. The email will clarify matters.

***

Robert Samson was relaxed after the shock of being bundled from a London street into a filthy van. His first thought was, he had been betrayed by Jonathon Gove, and that his captors were Russians. When he heard Armstrong's voice, his heartbeat became less audible and frenetic. But he was still concerned why the kidnapping in broad daylight? Armstrong had instant information that he was back in London. Flying into Southampton was an exercise in futility. He was followed as soon as his name was on the flight manifest. He wasn't aware when he purchased his train ticket into London; his name was flagged up again. Armstrong had used the kidnapping to frighten him into being more security conscious. It certainly had. However, it raised a more potent question, why had he returned to London, when he knew this could comprise his personal safety? Samson's explanation was plausible; he was tidying up superfluous financial matters. Armstrong did not concur. He was lying through his recently cosmetically whitened teeth. And he had shed a considerable amount of weight. But he was still a fat bastard. By flying into Southampton, caused Armstrong some concern, and when the information came through that he had purchased a day return to London; something was awry.

Samson's injudicious visit to the financial advisor (Michael Ogilvie) elevated Armstrong's interest, who was he? If substantial sums were invested; then substantial took on a more sinister meaning. He asked him rudimentary questions; the answers returned were anodyne. He skilfully avoided the more pressing questions, while feigning concerns for his welfare. He would be driven to Southampton airport, and advised not to return to London; ever again. Samson took this very seriously. He would need a plausible proxy who would not panic under financial or personal safety issues. The insidious Simon Corndale came to the fore. He was his bespoke fraudster of choice. They were colleagues, but never friends. They had common traits; an insatiable appetite for making money, and retaining some of the accumulated wealth they made for their avaricious hedge funds.

***

Edwina woke but daren't open her eyes, her mouth had an awful taste; her head was suffering from residual pounding. 'Awake at last, do you want coffee?'
She bolted upright, looking quickly around her; she was in her own room. She was about to scream, 'who are you?' When it became very clear oh dear, he was the waiter who had brought over the second bottle of wine. The coterie of woman had dragged her from her lonely table over to theirs. It all came back in audio and in high definition reality. He stood there, about twenty-five she guessed, then she saw the attraction; he was very

similar in stature and looks to her ex-fiancé. She didn't even recall his name.

'No, thanks.' 'Ok, enjoy the rest of your stay.' Then he was gone. The quiet closure of the door; coincided with her leaping out the bed into the bathroom. She hesitantly looked at the mirror; she was pleasantly surprised that she looked relaxed and not too hungover. She turned round and looked for her handbag, she rummaged through it, everything was there and intact; she took out her purse, money and cards still intact. She took out her phone and went to music settings and jumped in the shower, she didn't attempt to recall the night of passion, if there were one. There would be no self-pity either, no one got hurt. One thing her night of alcohol proved, she still wasn't over her only love. 'Don't stop Believing' belted out from the phone. Irony or what? Not an ounce of guilt entered her head; the water was powerful and soothing. She was experiencing the first pangs of an appetite. She had to face reality, if the waiter were on duty in any of the restaurants; she would be polite but would not engage in any small talk or drift into conversation regarding spending the night together. It was his lucky night, but his luck had ended. Yes, she felt better with this strategy. And no alcohol shall pass her lips until she was back in London. The lather on her hair had a lovely scent to it; she rinsed her hair, and was simultaneously planning the day in her head. David Fisher and Jonathon Gove entered her consciousness at velocity. What were the reasons they were in New York, legal or otherwise? Then the big question she needed the answer to, her home was now under surveillance but by whom?

'New York Minute' by Don Henley emitted from her phone, she stepped out of the shower and began to dry herself, she glanced wryly at the phone as the words resonated with her thoughts, 'in a New York Minute everything can change.' She felt the first flush of embarrassment about the unexpected occupant of her bed. She stepped into the bedroom, the winter sun vitalised the room. Her eyes were drawn to the bottom of the door; an envelope had been squeezed under the door.

***

He sat on the bench in Central Park, near the Tavern on the Green, he was struggling with his daily run, due to his over indulgence of Blue Goose, he blamed David Fisher for this, with a wry smile. At least he crawled out of his bed in a manner that did not disturb Avery. He convinced himself after the run he would feel much better. He didn't. He took a long, greedy drink of water from the bottle, which was near empty now. Perhaps, after a shower and breakfast, the lingering hangover would lessen.

David was a very personable character, more tactile and effervescence than the quiet and studious dining companion, who listened more than he talked, and rarely interrupted to make or disagree with a point made by one of the other dining companions. He charmed the ladies without a doubt, and to his surprise, the alcohol didn't seem to affect him, even though he was quaffing the drinks at an alarming rate. This seemed to endear him more if that seemed possible to the ladies. David insisted Jonathon use this term. He lifted the bottle; two bullets entered the back of his head. The Central Park jogger completed the hit in five seconds. The unforgiving sins had caught up with Jonathon.

***

David catches the waiter's eye; again. He holds up his empty glass that was filled less than a minute ago. Gwen is amused at this; she is suffering likewise. The waiter comes over with a jug filled with orange juice. David smiles at him; he was getting embarrassed repeatedly holding up the rapidly emptied glass. He instructs the waiter to leave the jug; in contrast Gwen's glass has water, but has barely been touched. David's obvious discomfort from the night before has fortified her in a perverse way. She watched him as he filled up his glass again, and without ceremony guzzled the orange juice.
'Oh, how I needed that Gwen!' She is enjoying his discomfort, as it takes her mind off her splitting headache.
'So I see! I'm having great difficulty in lifting my glass of water, you obviously don't.'
'Needs come before dining etiquette Gwen, I'll feel a lot better when I have something in my stomach. Are you ready to order Gwen?'
'A croissant and a coffee will be fine.'
'Are you sure? You'll feel better with something more substantial.'
'Substantial?'
'Bacon, eggs, sausages and hash browns, best cure for a hangover, believe me.' He signals to the waiter, who comes over rapidly. 'Are you ready to order sir?'
'Yes, can I have; two slices of thick bacon, two eggs, two sausages and two hash browns. And for the lady, a croissant and a large mug of coffee please.' Gwen's spirit is raised once again, when he calls her a lady. The waiter smiles and departs.
'This is a lovely restaurant David. They serve lovely Italian meals throughout the day.'
'I have only sampled breakfast in here (Maialino) I always have breakfast in the hotel where I am staying. I will have dinner here this evening, but

only if you accompany me.' She stretches her hand over to his. 'Of course, I will. When do you leave?'

'That's great…I leave tomorrow evening. What are your plans for the rest of the day?

'Shopping with Avery…'

'…Oh.' He is disappointed.

'But I can change if you wish; I can take you to the sights?'

'Excellent! I want to spend the day with you, its cold but do you mind doing the Circle Line boat cruise, some lunch, and then the rest of the day shopping on 5th Avenue?'

'That sounds like my ideal day. You'll have to wear a heavy coat and scarf, it will be very cold on the river; the wind will cut through you.' The waiter comes over with their breakfasts.

  She has great difficulty watching him devour the contents of the enormous plate. She spreads jam on her croissant. The large mug of coffee is more alluring. It is very hot but comforting. Her mind wanders to Avery, guessing if she is in one of the lavish restaurants having breakfast. Or would they be in the gym? It was clear that David was the polar opposite of Jonathon, who was reserved. She would not be ill-mannered by calling Avery, and explaining the sudden change of plans for today, Avery would understand. She was relishing spending the day with David, he was interesting, but she was sure he had more to reveal about his life. She wished she had a less eventful life; but would keep her difficult past; firmly in the past. Her phone rang out; Avery's name was on the screen. 'Sorry David do you mind if I take this, it's Avery?'

***

  Things had not gone too well for Lord Alexander Marr. However, the tabloids were once again, running historic salacious stories about his time as a drink sodden MP, stories were repeatedly regurgitated. Why are they doing this? He couldn't understand this; he was now a *de facto* paid up member of the Establishment. They had printed the photograph of his flat, suggesting he was no longer a man of the people. He was wise to these exclusives, was the purpose to drive him back to the chaotic alcohol saturated dark days? And was it a coincidence that Lorna was back in Switzerland to raise finance for a franchise of gyms? Or maybe it was his erstwhile combatant paranoia creeping up on him on every occasion a story was splashed across a tabloid? He gazed at the drinks cabinet it was his inner strength to resist the various bottles. Lorna suggested the contents of the various bottles should be removed of alcohol and replaced with coloured water; how he argued against this, but he succumbed to Lorna's entreaties. Would he be tempted if the bottles were intact of their alcohol?

His shudder was the appropriate answer. Lorna was due back in two days' time, oh how he needed her. He pulled the curtain back slightly; the Press corps was encamped on the pavement opposite his apartment building. Why? The stories were old, there were no sequels. His curiosity got the better of him, he needed to be calm when a barrage of questions came at him, and he genuinely could not anticipate any unfortunate event when he had alcohol problems. His car was in the underground garage, there was a threadbare police presence to prevent the Press surrounding his white Range Rover when he exited the garage. He raised his eyes to heaven; forward into battle.

In the garage, he practised the insincere smile, it was convincing. The Range Rover edged forward the doors raised slowly; he could see the excitement and anticipation on the reporters' faces. He edged forward, the police were no match. As the car swung to the right, they all started to scream in an indecipherable manner. Calmness took over him, rather than forcing his car through in an incremental fashion; he spontaneously opened the door and stepped out, not in a rage but a friendly manner. He walked over to the muscular reporter with the fearsome reputation and whispered in his ear. He ordered the police to make the reporters clear the road; if they didn't he would call for more capable police officers. The reporter went into the underground garage. The rest were herded back onto the pavement. Lord Alexander Marr, closed the garage doors, entered his car and drove off. This was not his original plan. He had whispered into the tabloid reporter's ear, that he had an exclusive for him, but only him. He suggested if he wanted it, go into the garage, he would join him after some order was restored. No one would argue with the brash reporter, he was the king of the pack. Lord Alexander Marr had an epiphany after he and the police had brought order out of the noisy chaos, he had made up his mind to severely beat the reporter into submission, not with his extensive vocabulary but with his fists. There were no cameras in the garage. He was confident that the music from his radio would mask the savage blows he had intended to assail to the reporter's acne riven face. It would be his word against the vile tabloid reporter's. He was actually looking forward to this violent task. However, Lorna's training kicked in, breathe, think and relax. Leaving him in a darkened garage did more reputational damage than any physical beating. He would undoubtedly be subject to ridicule from his peers. Someone would be on the end of his anger. He was pleased at this line of defence against the tabloid reporter. He drove along the street, thinking how pleased Lorna would be after he had explained in a calm and precise manner how he had dealt with his anger at the Press, and how he did not return to the bottle. Lorna already knew; she was at the rear of the throng of the reporters. Dressed in hat, wig and glasses, she was in awe of him. He had been nurtured and now it was time to let him loose.

Pavel was correct once again; who would ever think that this near alcoholic Member of Parliament could be so valuable. She slipped away from the phalanx of sexist reprobates; her opinion of the Press would need a shovel to reach their true level. Pavel would surely be surprised how Lord Alexander Marr coped and used his initiative and *her* training to turn a negative situation into a positive conclusion. World events can change political thinking and smash political ideology, when politicians are under pressure they seek advice, and act on it quickly. If it turns out well; they bathe in the glory, if it turns out negative, they all scream in unison they were acting on advice: i.e. it was not their fault. They had a member of the House of Lords on their payroll, if he was needed in the future when a geo political crisis emerged, he and others would be of incalculable value; politically and monetary. She could now call off the Press pack; no more negative press exposure would appear again about *their ennobled friend & unwitting colleague.*

***

Jonathon Gove's demise in Central Park made the various indigenous and international news agencies go into speculative overdrive. Was this assassination connected to the Russian who leapt or was pushed to his death? It would only be a matter of hours until this news was broadcast on Sky and BBC news in the UK. In the Gramercy Park Hotel, David Fisher was experiencing great anxiety; as was his dining companion. The terse information was relayed by Avery's friend. She had been following the shooting of a jogger on the local news channel. She did not construe for a moment that it could be Jonathon. However, he had not returned from his run in Central Park. Now she was very concerned. She decided to call Gwen, in the faintest of hope that Jonathon had stopped by the Gramercy Park hotel to speak to David. The response did not lift the heavy blanket of foreboding. It was dawning on her, through the self-imposed delusion, that the victim was Jonathon. Her chaotic mind was jumping from different scenarios some had a trace of credence others were just plain ridiculous.

Her first thought was to exit the room immediately and take a cab to the Gramercy Park Hotel to seek reassurance from Gwen and David; they would charter the best course of damage limitation when the news agencies would surround her. And in the age of social media, it would be only a matter of minutes before some conspiracy theorist linked her with the assassination of Jonathon. How she wished she had declined the invitation to accompany the two Brits to the Pravda Vodka Room.

David stared into unforgiving space as Gwen explained the devastating content of the phone call from Avery. He never spoke or attempted to put up a dismissive argument to this bombshell news. She ended the conversation and explained that Avery had called the NYPD, and told them where she was staying, she would have no objection to being interviewed, and she hoped her identity would not be displayed on the Breaking News banner on the various news channels. David had not resiled from self-imposed silence as Gwen spoke of the news from Avery. Personal fear was at the pinnacle of his cognitive process. In his short period of time in New York, two persons had been killed. It was quite clear to him that Jonathon had been involved in illegal money transactions. The client had taken exception to this. He had to remain lucid; the information regarding Jonathon's demise would unfold throughout the day. The NYPD would be interviewing him, there was no point in trying to evade or revert to procrastination; he wouldn't request a lawyer. He came quickly to form a strategy, they would take a taxi to The Carlyle to comfort Avery, and give their statements to the NYPD when requested. He explained that Avery needed them, and the NYPD would be piecing together Jonathon's and Avery's movements the previous evening. It would be better for them to speak to the NYPD at The Carlyle, than the NYPD trying to locate them. Gwen acquiesced and was comforted by David's genuine concern for Avery. An eventful night couldn't come close to describe her evening. She would learn more from the forthcoming NYPD interviews and media speculation. All she and Avery were aware of was that Jonathon and David were in financial investments; and they were in New York to conclude a deal of some kind. When the deal was finalised they went out to relax and celebrate. Keep it simple was her Modus Operandi; and for good reason.
'I'll arrange a taxi to take us to The Carlyle, Avery's mind will be all over the place.'
'She will appreciate us going over; can you give me five minutes to go to our room to freshen up?'
'Sure, take your time. I'll make a few phone calls to London, to explain the situation. I'm glad I had breakfast now, if I hadn't I wouldn't be at my best answering questions.' Gwen had other things to do as well as freshen up.
'Okay, David I'll be quick as I can.' He smiled, and then she left the table.
When she was out of view he looked around the dining room, no one was paying any attention to him. He picked up his phone and expectantly waited on a reply. 'Hello David, all going well?'
'No, Nigel, the fucking opposite…'
'Calm down, what do you mean?'
'Jonathon…Jonathon Gove has been shot, murdered in Central Park, not long ago, it's morning here, we were told when we were having breakfast.'

'We?'

'Never mind that, he's dead, and to complicate matters, a Russian was killed or committed suicide yesterday.'

'You've got to calm down, it's obviously a distressing situation, but don't let your mind take off into other situations that may or not have happened. You're coming home soon?'

'Nigel it is very hard to calm down, I was out with Jonathon last night, we were in female company…'

'…call girls?'

'No, no, very nice women actually. Now where was I? We were out drinking, and hooked up, disregard that; no *met* these women, Jonathon went with Avery to his hotel and I went to my hotel with Gwen, at the end of the evening, well early morning. At breakfast Gwen took a call from Avery that Jonathon had been murdered in Central Park; he had gone out for a run, that's all I know.'

'You do realise the police will ask you all to account for your movements?'

'Yes, I worked that out for myself Nigel, we are going to get a cab over to Jonathon's hotel and speak to the NYPD.'

'That's very sensible David. As a matter of interest where was your last drink?'

'The Pravda Vodka Room. Why?'

'Well…all this anti-Russian sentiment in the U.S., a Brit gets assassinated in Central Park; his last known whereabouts was at a Russian hangout.'

'Again, Nigel that has resonated in my brain, that's why I want to speak to the NYPD to clarify matters. I want to fly home to London tomorrow.'

'It might not be as simple as that. Then again, it may go smoothly. As long as you make yourself available for interview in the future that should notch down any suspicion.'

'I won't know until I meet the NYPD, I'm less nervous than I was a few minutes ago.'

'It'll make the news over here, and it'll cause traction on social media. The Press will probably meet you when you land, my advice is, no comment as it's an ongoing criminal investigation and you are cooperating with the NYPD. A statement will be released in the near future. I'll arrange a car to whisk you away after you are through customs.'

'That's brilliant Nigel! I am more relaxed now. Do you think it is wise for me to decline any legal representation?'

'Yes; as long as you are a witness not a suspect,'

'What do you mean a suspect?'

'You're in a foreign country they do things differently over there. If the questioning gets invasive or you feel pressurised; request a lawyer, and if you do request a lawyer, don't utter another word until the lawyer arrives.'
'Surely it won't come to that Nigel?'
'You can't rule it out...better to be safe than sorry.'
'Okay Nigel, I'll mention this to Gwen, she maybe expecting a brief interview.'
'That's your call David; you know nothing about her…remember that.'
'I think I'll keep my own counsel, if I mention all of this she may get alarmed, she's coming into the restaurant I'll keep you informed Nigel... bye.'

Gwen showed no signs of undue worry. She had scrubbed up very well. 'Are you ready David?' Her calmness rubbed off on him.
'Ready as I will ever be. I hope Avery is being treated well.' They walked over to the concierge, David silently mouthed Taxi to him; he nodded in reply. 'I rang Avery, but it went straight to voicemail.'
'Nothing to worry about, she'll be speaking to the NYPD.'
'Yes, of course, I thought of that, but still have concerns.'
'Ditto, it's natural to have concerns, Jonathon has been murdered.'

Outside, the taxi is waiting on them; the concierge is holding the taxi door wide open. David allows Gwen to enter the taxi first. He slips $10 into the palm of the concierge's hand. 'The Carlyle Hotel please.' The journey is spent trying to anticipate the NYPD line of questioning. They were subconsciously trying to reassure one another. It was achieving the desired effect. David was conducting a more stringent interview process silently in his head. The conclusion of this unilateral exercise did not return the same outcome. He couldn't erase the negative consequences.

Gwen had skilfully segued his return to London tomorrow into the conversation. Yes he was anticipating a scrum of media awaiting his arrival, but he could endure that, as that meant he was going home. Approaching The Carlyle the sidewalk was a sight to make them drive on. Various media outlets were mingling at the entrance. It wasn't for them as they would soon realise; George Clooney was due to arrive, the assassination in Central Park took silver medal, George Clooney was gold. Relieved they had made their way into the hotel without the expected volley of rapid questions, infused a sense of calmness into them. David asked to speak to one of the managers. When he arrived David explained in a perfunctory manner the shooting of Jonathon and the relationship of Jonathon's overnight companion and Gwen; they had all spent the evening together, before returning to their respective hotels. They were here to assist the NYPD. The manager explained that the NYPD were in The Carlyle but were incognito, David was so relieved. Two detectives were in the room, he would advise them that David and Gwen were on their way up. They emerged from the elevator, a detective was sitting on a chair outside the room, he stood up held up his hand to them, they stopped their journey to the room. He rapped he door and entered, they looked at each other in silence. Anxiety was bubbling under the surface. The detective popped his head out of the door and nodded them in. To their surprise Avery was smiling and totally relaxed. Their joint fear of her tears sodden face and uncontrollably weeping were misplaced. Their interview was brief, what was his reason for being in New York, and places where they went, did Jonathon seem agitated; basic routine stuff really. David was relieved and worried at the same time; he thought when he mentioned his client who was a Russian, the interview would be ratcheted up, but it didn't the interview continued in a polite and relaxed manner; very worrying. However, he would be on the plane home tomorrow.

   No doubt they had a copy of his passport details from check-in. They would have compiled a background check on him, before he had entered the room. Gwen on the other hand would be different, she was a U.S. citizen. When the formal interview was due to begin, they were asked if they wanted an attorney, in unison they said no. David was tempted to add to his statement that Jonathon lived in the same apartment block; however, this would be clear when the details of passport, employment status and address were collated. They never asked. He decided to impart this information halfway through the interview. No eyebrows were raised or facial features were changed. They were aware.

   They were reticent when they asked the detectives what was the motive behind Jonathon's demise?
Their demeanour became defensive and sullen. "Too early to say," Then the interview was over and they could go. Relief permeated the room. Avery made no attempt to leave. The detective who brought them into the room escorted them out in silence. David was pleased there was no "we'll be in touch." Gwen took the polar opposite view. Something is not right; she was unnerved by the soft soap interview. But she wouldn't share this with David, his relief was palpable. As the door was closed laughter from Avery was heard, they almost stopped, but Gwen nudged him forward in silence. They entered the elevator and the attendant enquired which floor? They smiled and David said lobby.

   Their synthetic smiles dissipated when the elevator reached their destination, in that short period of time, obvious and less obvious questions queued up in their respective heads. David desired to go for a coffee rather than a drink. He had planned to take Gwen to the Bemelmans Bar in The Carlyle for cocktails and listen to the piano music in the background, Jonathon and Avery would be invited to join them, secretly he hoped they would decline. However, due to the "unfortunate incident" he had to slow down his pace of exit in case it drew attention to him. Any coffee shop would do. The ultimate aim was to exit The Carlyle in a nondescript manner. And never return. This promise to himself was set in stone. They took a right turn after leaving the hotel; David couldn't get the detective's phrase out of his head, "unfortunate incident." Not homicide, murder or a mugging going wrong. Maybe this was Avery's nervous reaction to the man she spent the night with, not returning. a warped defence mechanism? Who knows, but something was not giving off a reassuring fragrance. Gwen pulled on the sleeve of his coat. 'Where are we going? And slow down!'

He came to a rigid stance, if only his mind could do the same. 'Oh, I'm sorry…we are going for a coffee and have a chat about the detectives; I'm perplexed with them and paradoxically relieved, if I'm not being too nebulous?'

'Keep walking, that's exactly what I'm thinking. Something is rotten in New York City David, and I'm frightened and concerned. What happened to Avery? She wasn't acting like I thought she would.'

'That threw me instantly, she reminded me of someone who had lost a dog, and the police have turned up with the dog. But, we or you will find out what reassuring words made her very rational in an irrational situation.'

'*Inter alia.*'

'What does *Inter alia* mean Gwen?'

'Amongst other things, didn't you study Latin at High School?' He erupted into effervescent laughter.

***

Robert Samson sat on the unplumbed toilet bowl; a sense of satisfaction could not be diluted regarding his short trip to London. The smoke rings from his cigar, and the pungent aroma hung in the air. The discarded floor tile cuttings were stacked neatly ready to be removed at the end of the satisfying but physically exhausting day. Patience was his ally. His plan was for the police to be aware of his presence in London and his covert appointment with a relative unknown stockbroker. This would raise suspicion of a criminal enterprise .In reality he was leading them a merry dance. He looked at the stub of the expensive diminishing cigar. This cigar's cost exceeded the tiler's daily rate; it would be injudicious if he mentioned this or if he was asked. Resentment would undoubtedly ferment, and he would not be asked onto another building project. The tiler was back he heard the rear door open. However, there were no sounds of any footsteps. He didn't want to move from the toilet bowl to give his position away, or call out the tiler's name. The silence was unnerving, his fragile heart was rapidly pumping, sweat was pouring from his temples; his chest started to tighten. He took a series of deep breaths, he didn't feel any better, but continued with this futile exercise. A noise emanated from downstairs, then immediately stopped. The suspense and supposition were literally killing him. His mouth was creating saliva at an alarming rate. He had to make up his mind; does he fight or stay still?

Had Armstrong turned the tables on him instead of vice-versa? He could have been followed ever since he stepped off the short-haul flight. Self-satisfaction was an imperfect description of his well-being. The drip, drip element of revenge made his insipid heart beat healthily. No moving on for him. Cold expensive revenge sated him. Armstrong was a recipient of his largesse for years, but his avaricious appetite showed no sign of abating. His biggest misjudgement was explaining in absolutely clarity that the tap was being turned off. Then he went further than was wise; he explained his fall back plan if Armstrong passed information to various financial regulators.

Now in hindsight he should have refrained from this course of action. Armstrong continued to remind him of his statuary stipend, Samson ignored it. Stupidity on stilts. His office was raided by the Serious Fraud Office. The City of London made him a pariah; however he had his silver bullet to prove Armstrong was corrupt; various transactions of a multitude of financial payments. He took them to the top lawyer in London, to cut a deal if he was charged. The lawyer was sympathetic to his plight, prison was the probable outcome. The lawyer asked him to bring all paperwork and records of financial transactions conducted by phone. Robert Samson left his office with a sense of a deal will be cut, no open prison would be waiting for him. He wanted to send the dossier by courier, the lawyer persuaded him this could be compromised, the papers could be copied, before arriving at his office; or they may not arrive at all. After a sleepless night, he delivered the dossier personally; he was dressed as a courier operative; the lawyer smiled inside, and took the dossier. 'That's everything', then he walked casually out of the plush reception. Two weeks passed, no contact from the lawyer, the happiness that he had inured, was now non-existent, and the sleepless nights were the order of the darkness. Bad, bad karma was on his tail; he went against the lawyer's explicit instruction; "do not contact me under any circumstances in person, email, text message or phone."

The spontaneous visit to the office was halted at the front desk of the plush building. He was told to wait while the security guard called. The lawyer was unavailable; and requested him to desist returning to the building. He was escorted from the premises, and was advised if he returned the police would be called. His tortured mind was constantly in a state of uncontrollable flux. When he returned home in a dispirited manner, the police were waiting on him. His house was to be searched and computer equipment would be seized for examination. Life was becoming a less favourable option. He was seriously considering removing himself from society, before he was removed by an unknown source.

Through these dark periods, alcohol was consumed frequently throughout the day and into the early hours. No one was calling or visiting him. He had descended from a *bon vivant* to *persona non grata*. Salacious stories were being sent through the ether to land in the mail boxes of respected financial journalists, and it was entirely coincidental that they had robust differences of opinion. They all took different days to traduce his various investment funds; which lost value after each story gained traction. Normally he would rub his covetous hands in glee, anticipating a grovelling retraction and substantial damages. The cowed journalist would be ordered by their editors to read from a pre-prepared script to him. He would have the call relayed on speaker thus all the staff in the open plan office could hear the grovelling sycophantic apology. However, that was then, this was now. His lawyer advised he was no longer his client and could not act for him now or in the future. How he cursed Nigel, erstwhile friend and lawyer of fifteen years.

***

Simon Corndale landed at Jersey airport, in the parish of Saint Peter which was only four miles from St Hellier, and only two miles to the Longueville Manor Hotel. He was booked in for one night only. He was travelling on an alias passport. The hired car was signed for then he made his way to the building where he was working, he was desperate to tell Robert Samson, the good news. He had worked through the evenings on this deal; he slept like a baby during the day, and only needed four hours of sleep. The share manipulation scheme would net them both millions. Only one person would be held to account and it would not be him or Robert Samson; when the shares plummeted. In all intents and purposes Simon owned the shares and supplied the money for the purchase of the shares, Robert was not connected legally in any way, even though he supplied the money and he was the architect of the scheme. The ferocious focus of ire would not come near them. Robert had explained to him; how he had accidently found the alchemy of a healthy and stress free lifestyle to keep fit. Simon was not entirely convinced; but if it had the beneficial psychological and physical affects, who was he, a mere mortal multi-millionaire to dissent? Privately, he thought working long hours on building projects was an expensive and expedient route to an early grave.

The reason Simon worked nocturnally he thought it would only be a matter of time before Robert's next cardiac arrest would be his last. And he wanted to have the prepared paperwork sooner than later, so Simon could examine his notes and give the green light to the share manipulation scheme; of course on paper it was legitimate; if the scheme was deemed fraudulent it would fall back on Simon Corndale; who in turn would pass the ultimate responsibility to someone else. Simon would explain this *omitted* text from the notes verbally and in person, when the shares would be purchased and sold. He wanted the scheme to be up and earning within days. The funds were in Simon's account.

He decided to go to the property that Robert was working on, it would be a pleasant surprise, and he wanted to thank him for agreeing to release funds earlier than planned, which in turn and unknown to Robert he would instruct the third party to purchase the shares. The broker would not be concerned; a modest commission would be earned; this would come from Simon's fee. This was a small price even though to a lay person the sum would be substantial. And if Robert had a fatal cardiac arrest, that would be unfortunate but not for Simon. Jersey had never appealed to him when he was anticipating relocating from London, mainly because it was only a short distance by air from London. However, times change and so does intransigent opinions. His thoughts were exploring various options; permanent residency or split his time in London and Jersey. He would not discuss these lucid musings with Robert just yet, but sometime in the future, perhaps? The location was not too far away according to the satnav; he smiled and thought I could have walked here, he was instructed to take the left farm track on a steep incline, the farm steading came into view, it was lunchtime, no builders' vans were in view; they are probably in the pub. He mused Robert wouldn't be in the pub, mixing with the plebs was not his style. He opened the car door, no banging or cutting of wood assaulted his ears; he was pleased about that. He observed the steading was more imposing and substantial than he envisaged, he was less confident of Robert's physical endurance on this site over a long period of time. two skips lay to the right of the building, one was overfilled, the other half-full, and that'll be Robert imposing cost benefit analysis in reality to clarify his theory, and the builders smiling while thinking what a boring bastard this guy is.

Simon decided to wander around the property first, Robert maybe sitting on a pallet reading the Financial Times. He walked around the property; various pieces of scrap wood were burning in the rusty metal oil drum. That's positive thought Jonathon. He didn't want to spoil the surprise by calling out his name; he wanted to see his reaction when he walked in. He grabbed a green safety helmet from the unoccupied cab of the silent bulldozer, he stood for a few seconds; the only noise that he could hear was from the occasional sparks from the burning wood. He opened the door, stuck his head in, no noise, but he knew Robert is present in the vast building, he could smell his awful cigar. He stepped into the large hall with wood strapped on the walls ready for the plasterboard. He continued onto the other rooms on the ground floor, only joiners' trestles and plasterboard stacked neatly were present. He was surprised how much electrical wire that ran in various directions from the walls and ceilings. He must be upstairs, and not somewhere else, he crept up the creaky stairs, the pungent smell of the cigar increased his expectation, the bathroom door was opened by about six inches, his sense of smell indicated he was in there, Should he crash in, no, he might cause another cardiac arrest; he decided to rap his knuckles gently against the new oak door. No response, he repeated the procedure. No reply. He opened the door and saw Robert. He was hanging from the exposed roof joist.

***

In her hotel room she had no sense of guilt or shame about her night of passion which she could not recall in any slightest detail. No more surprises would come her way as she blow dried her hair. She could see the television in the mirror, but no sound due to the sound of the hairdryer. Her eye fleetingly caught the breaking news banner at the bottom of the screen, a shooting in Central Park, but the next sentence chilled her, a police source said "it had all the hallmarks of a professional hit."
She unconsciously switched off the hairdryer and turned round to stare at the TV. The banner headline went on to explain unconfirmed reports the victim was a British citizen. She dashed from the chair and grabbed her clothes which were laid out neatly on the king size bed. Her eyes were fixed on the TV; in her heart of hearts she was convinced it was David Fisher or Jonathon Gove. She quickly brushed her hair, grabbed her bag then left the room for some breakfast. Trust her and her closed mind to ruminate about no other surprise. If it was David or Jonathon the cops would be all over the hotel, her trained eyes answered her own question. When she spoke to the lift attendant she could see he was less talkative than before. He had a grim expression. It would be a pointless exercise in trying to extract any information about the shooting in Central Park. She stepped out of the elevator, various police officers were milling about. Her fearful thought was confirmed.
  En-route to the restaurant she suddenly changed her mind and carried onto the lobby, she would have a seat and grab a newspaper and eavesdrop on the chatter. Other guests had the same inclination, tiny minds think alike. Some of the young models she had spent the evening with drinking,

were being chatted up by various police officers. She removed her sunglasses from her bag, and placed them on to hide her observant eyes. As she made her way to the high-backed chair, she grabbed a newspaper from the impressive pile. She was halted by a model; she quickly learned that the victim was Jonathon by the comprehensive description. The model was quite visibly upset because she remembered Jonathon and the other dining companion. They were all impressed by their manners and politeness; they hadn't hit on any of them, though they were expecting them to come over to their tables. The brief conversation ended, Edwina pretended her mobile was vibrating, thanked her and moved towards the restaurant. It was unconfirmed, but not for too long. She called Armstrong, with the unconfirmed news, he wasn't expecting this news. He repeatedly said "are you sure?" Then he asked a left field question, where was David Fisher, was he still in New York? She was just about to say she would find out when he came into view. She relayed this information back to Armstrong. He sounded surprised, which she thought odd, but didn't dwell on it. He told her good work, he would contact the NYPD to confirm if the victim is Jonathon Gove, and the theory behind his assassination. It was very clear in Armstrong's mind he was not an innocent tourist killed in a random act of mindless violence.

    She sat at the table, the waiter took her order, it is going to be a long day, so she had to store up on carbohydrates; she ordered a full English breakfast. David Fisher would be called in for questioning; Armstrong would be able to obtain the transcript of his interview with the NYPD. It would be sensible and productive to monitor his movements in London when he returned. Knowing Armstrong he would have an operative installing surveillance bugs in his home and a roaming bug (software) installed in his phone. Orwell's 1984 had been superceded, and the public had slept walked into agreeing to various pieces of legislation in Parliament to thwart and disrupt numerous terrorist plots or planned atrocities. Thank you Anthony Charles Lynton Blair, a very common name in the social housing schemes of Britain she mused. She sipped the chilled water, she needed that, and she would never forget this trip to New York, eventful was an apposite description. A suspect who was under her surveillance was assassinated, she spent a night with a doppelganger of her ex-fiancé and George Clooney is staying here, yes The Carlyle memories would comfort her in her Autumn years   She refilled her glass and took the glass in both hands then lifted it up to her dry mouth, a coterie of the women at a table in the far corner raised the decibel level drawing disapproving scowls, a waiter walked across the floor to speak to them, the group returned to mute. Approving looks were sent into the direction of the waiter, a faint smile was returned without him breaking stride. Very civilised; unlike her noisy neighbour in London.

***

CHAPTER THREE

The view from The Shard hotel never bored Lorna. Pavel's Corporate Let apartment was rarely used. She was privileged to be here. Lord Marr would be here very soon. He had lobbied intensively former colleagues from Labour, Conservatives and his close friends in the Green Party. The draconian reduction in subsidies for renewable energy had been overturned in the House of Lords; Climate Change was on everyone's lips. The Conservative government were out of step with world opinion.

At home the Climate Change deniers were boosted when the intellectual colossus Donald J Trump was elected as President of the United States of America. Unfortunately, this was not *fake news*. Climate Change did not exist according to this President. It was rumoured he wore slip-on style shoes as tying his laces was challenging. However, he said this was *fake news*.

The dirty money evolving into clean money in London was coming under scrutiny. Buying expensive properties in London, then flipping them after a few months to another criminal oligarch was beginning to look very clumsy and amateurish. It was in Pavel's interest and the British government's to inhibit this practice. Pavel through his network of contacts was able to identify to the Economic Crime Unit which banks were being used as conduits to facilitate the blood soiled funds. This earned him gravitas with the Economic Crime Unit senior personnel, and removed any light that may be aimed at him, Pavel's myriad of shell companies and hedge funds were able to entice well-respected environmentalists to sit as non-executives on each company's board. They were keen on green energy and coincidently green backs. The dirty money expropriated from criminal oligarchs was invested in Wind Farms in Cornwall and Scotland. This renewable energy was sold to the National Grid, the profits were invested in more Wind Farms; some of the profit settled back in Russia, where the money was initially purloined by criminal oligarchs. Pavel and Putin felt a sense of a wrong had been corrected with this strategy.

However, the jigsaw was not complete. Lord Alexander Marr was the movable piece, he was unfailingly polite, intellectual and possessed a reservoir of kindness; three assets that few people possess no matter where they are in life. His mantra when he was a young MP, when speaking to his researchers from privileged and cosseted backgrounds when they met real people with real problems at his constituency meeting "you don't have to attend university to earn a degree in kindness."   Scotland would be his next port of call; the Scottish government were achieving impressive results in renewable energy and were keen to expand Wind Farms. Small isolated communities in the far north of Scotland and on the small islands would be receptive to new community halls and inexpensive electricity to heat their homes. An agreed sum of money would be deposited in a trust for the community concerned. Pavel's company would cover the construction costs of the Wind Turbines and new roads etc. Lord Alexander Marr's odyssey would take him to Universities throughout Scotland; he would discuss his plans over dinner with academics, suggesting that Scotland can do even more to promote renewable energy, if he can secure experts in renewable energy they will not be discouraged to think outside the environmental box. He would wish to meet them and discuss with the Scottish government, his plans to make small communities self-sufficient within five years. Then he observed his inbox filling up with academics and respected environmentalists sharing his vision. They would be brought down to London to stay in The Shard separately to discuss their plan. Believers do not have to be bribed.

  Lorna would sift through their professional C.Vs and their personal lives on Facebook, Twitter and Instagram. The cream would rise to the top. Pavel's contacts had influenced the E.U. to look again at the air quality in densely populated cities in Europe. The diesel cars that the British government had encouraged the public to purchase instead of petrol cars; were now seen as the egregious pollutants. Electric cars were the future. Pavel's companies were benefitting from the green revolution; electricity would be needed in unquantified amounts. Pavel's companies could help satisfy some of the demand. Then there was the question who would manufacture the millions of batteries for the cars? Pavel had the answer. His companies would build factories in post- industrial cities throughout the United Kingdom; 1000s of much needed jobs would be created, the UK government and Scottish government would compete to entice the factories to be built in high unemployment cities. Financial assistance would be offered and greatly accepted. Environmental disposal of millions of end-of- life batteries had not been raised. Pavel's top environmental experts would think through this conundrum; land fill was out. They needed a credible and profitable plan that would be met with universal approval. Lord Alexander Marr and his band of environmental experts would ensure this result was achieved.

While the solution was years away, Pavel had the zenith of renewable energy scientists working on a renewable battery. Time was not on their side; pressure would be applied, but no threats of physical harm. Money walked hand in hand with scientific prestige. Securing funding from the UK government would not cause him any sleepless nights; Lord Alexander Marr and his influential acolytes could charm or railroad any non-enthusiast to their cause. Trump had convinced America that cheap gas and abundance of coal would keep the economy from faltering, future generations would pick up the tab for the legacy of the inestimable catastrophic environmental damage.

***

The phones were ringing out continuously in the Economic Crime Unit's office. Emails were showing no sign of abating. Enquiries from the USA were overwhelming Armstrong's close knit team. Jonathon Gove's assassination could be connected to the Russian who committed suicide in New York; if there were a tenuous Russian connection, then they were connected. Armstrong quickly assessed that the State Department had undisclosed information about Jonathon Gove. David Fisher was not on their radar, but he was now. Things could become difficult if they discovered that Jonathon Gove had more than one string to his bow. Factors would become clearer when two agents from the Department of Justice landed at Heathrow tomorrow. They would be on the red eye flight 8 pm local time; and worryingly they did not request anyone to meet them. He would be there; the email was scant on information, no names, or request to be picked up and taking to their hotel. They were going direct to the US Embassy. It would not benefit him if he informed Edwina of this latest development in a difficult fluid situation.

Armstrong had seen this movie before; it would end in tears and recriminations. The US would be appropriating the investigation into Jonathon Gove's demise; the Economic Crime Unit would collate all information and forward it onto the agents. British governments were supine to any US requests. Armstrong would play along, he would not inhibit or obstruct them, he didn't have too much faith of them digging up any treasure trove of any connection Jonathon Gove had to espionage. It would please him immensely if the Russia phenomena of interfering or influencing the election of Donald Trump or Brexit proved fruitless. If they were that Smart, they could save the US taxpayer money by staying in New York and look at the myriad of Russians who were shitting on their own doorstep. However, when they eventually requested a meeting, he would have Edwina by his side. Both of them would be able to subtly elicit undisclosed information about Jonathon Gove.

Edwina would refrain from informing the two agents that she had been in New York when Jonathon was assassinated, and had photographs of them having dinner together. They would play the two agents, the Americans would not be able to keep information to themselves; they would behave similar to wide-eye Rednecks gawping at their superior knowledge. Yes, that was definitely the way to go. When they were all relaxed in each other's company, he would continue to play the subservient underling, he would suggest that they interview David Fisher, just in case the NYPD missed something, and if as he expected they turned down this suggestion, then his gut feeling would be confirmed; they had something on him, and they were not going to divulge this information to him or Edwina.

Edwina was switched on; she would concur and have her own tailored input. He would welcome that; she would not be surprised when she learned this would be an 'off the books' operation. She would divulge her intuition assessment of the *real* reason of the meeting in New York.

He had his 'spotters' at all London airports, they were all employed in various departments at the airports, from cleaners, administration, and the best of all cabin crew. They were all remunerated handsomely; they were trustworthy and unaware of other 'spotters.' He was the sole beneficiary initially of their information. His senior management never quibbled over the credibility of his information. He had too much success over the years. Cash was the seductive infinite currency; he would meet them personally in various locales in London; never in their respective airports. This was the tried and trusted method, and if Edwina was aware of this her well-shaped eyebrows would leave their mark on his ceiling. The unexpected death of Jonathon Gove had raised the suspicion level of a Russian state sponsored assassination. This would be the default conclusion if the CIA or FBI could not arrest someone for Jonathon Gove's death. He would not impart this information to Edwina; she may or not have a conscious bias against a particular foreign government. However, she would have to be impartial and forensic in her investigation as if her own life depended on her findings; because it did.

***

The shock and manner of Jonathon's murder, was just kicking into his cognitive process, he was relieved he was returning to London tomorrow. Gwen stretched across the table and placed her hand on his. He jumped back in his seat. 'Are you okay, David?'
'Yes, I'm sorry; I was away in a world of my own Gwen.'
'Things will become more manic as the day proceeds. The news will be hitting the media in England. What are your plans, when you arrive home?'

'I know, I've not even thought about it, too be perfectly honest. I'll take a few days off and try to get my head to make some sense of this. Jonathon was murdered for a reason, and I can see the Russian Mafia were the proponents of this. I have always stayed clear of Russians in London, and my intuition has been proven to be correct. To let you understand, not all Russians are in the mafia or criminals, but London seems to attract the worst of them, I know that for sure.'

'My advice is to throw yourself into an intense fitness regime at a gym. It will be beneficial to your mental health. Don't even think about running in London. Things are still dangerous. New York has Russian Mafia or oligarchs as well, the government talk tough, but give most of them a pass, on condition there are no deaths on the streets.'

'That's a good idea, about the gym, that appeals to me. I am involved whether I like it or not. I concluded a financial deal with Jonathon, probably his last one, and I'm glad to say there were no criminal elements attached in any part of the contract. Everything was above board and any scrutiny will reveal this to be the case; I'm relieved to say.'

'Of course it was all legitimate; if there were any suspicions you would be in Rikers Island (prison). But don't get too complacent, your personal history and financial history will have been examined or under examination as we speak. NYPD are rarely polite. Someone has told them to treat you with decorum most of the NYPD detectives are anathema to this.' David's sense of well-being plummeted on hearing this.

'And how do you know all this Gwen?'

'I'd rather not say, but you do believe me?' She smiled at him.

'I believe you implicitly, but why won't you tell me why you know all this, were you an officer in the NYPD?' She smiled, he was very vulnerable.

'Oh, David, I didn't know your opinion of me was that modest, you know how to hurt a woman's feelings.'

'Now we are getting into difficult territory…were or are you in intelligence or the FBI?'

'I think you have had too much caffeine today?' She had him exactly where she wanted him. He was not prepared to throw in the towel.

'You've not confirmed or denied my assertion or assertions Gwen. Who are you really?'

'It's too soon David, far too soon. You'll soon forget me.'

'Whoa! Forget about you, I don't know you.'

'Do you really want to know me? I suffered a mental breakdown in my formative years, but I am fine now.' He didn't want to hear this.

'No one is immune to mental health problems. That's life I'm afraid. You don't have to tell me. I won't feel offended.'

'Are you not curious?'

'No, not curious at all; just intrigued. Unfortunately I fly home tomorrow, where will that leave us?'

She leaned over. 'I can return home with you tomorrow? This was a seismic shock to him. She wanted an answer now.

'Do you fully understand what are you saying?'

'I just need an answer David, yes or no.'

'To be honest, I am not too sure Gwen.'

'Okay, that means no, does your heart ever win over your head?'

'It doesn't mean no, I don't like making decisions instantly, that's all; you must understand this?'

'I am financially solvent, if that is your concern, if it doesn't work out, I can leave and return to New York'

'Gwen, you don't know me, it didn't enter my head about finance, I'm more concerned how you would fill your day; boredom is not an asset.'

'I would just continue to do as I do here in New York. I would arrange a transfer; it's a simple process David, why do you place obstacles in my way. Just say no, and be done with it.'

'Transfer? What do you do?'

'In London, everything would crystallise. I can change your life, are you willing to throw that choice away?'

David studied her, undefined mental illness, unspecified income, and career path unknown. It was very easy to say no. However, with her history of mental illness, he didn't want to send her into an abyss of despair. He would have to reluctantly say no. He conjured up that little boy smile and reaches for her hand.

'Gwen, events have overtaken us, you returning with me to London would exacerbate and complicate our lives. Why don't you wait another four weeks then decide if you want to come to London?'

'I thought better of you David, it's time for me to leave, I'm sure everything will work out in your life…eventually. It was very nice to know you.' She stood up, smiled, and grabbed her coat and bag, then left at speed.

He was left devastated, he wasn't expecting that, but it achieved the desired result. He watched her pull the door open of the bustling café, the noise from the street rushed in, the glass door closed slowly and silently. The hubbub from the noisy New Yorkers reached a crescendo. He had to leave.

He left a $10 bill under his coffee cup. The waitress caught his arm gently as he gently squeezed past her voluptuous figure and whispered 'go get her.' He looked at her, he wasn't escaping the noise; he wanted Gwen to return to London with him. His head was reminding him; he would regret this.

***

Sipping his vodka, he watched the ticker tape at the bottom of his recently installed 60 inch television; Jonathon Gove's life was unravelling before millions of viewers, it was very easy to conclude that the media were being fed information from the NYPD. The reporter speaking live had ascertained without too much evidence that "Jonathon Cove was a financier from London; he was in New York to conclude a *series* of deals that ran into millions of dollars. Various sources have confirmed Russian money was involved; it is too early to say whether it was laundered money or legitimate money. It is premature to conclude if Jonathon Cove's murder was connected to a particular deal."

'Good grief' thought Pavel; the reporter even got his name wrong, he said "Jonathon *Cove."* And laughably after implying the reason he was assassinated was because a Russian money laundering scheme had gone wrong, then he said with a serious expression; "it is premature to conclude if Jonathon *Cove's* murder was connected to a particular (*Russian laundered money*) deal."

'Fucking unbelievable! He shouted out to no one in particular. He felt slightly embarrassed at his invective towards the ill-prepared reporter. However, Jonathon Gove's death had superceded the Russian who leapt into the New York air from the apartment. That was a welcome unintended consequence. He could actually write the script for the next twenty-four hours for the media, Laundered money, British Financier, Russian Funds, murder in Central Park, then the large yellow cherry on top; Donald J. Trump. Trump would be dragged into this story if there were a tenuous link.

It would only be a matter of time. Thank God, that Jonathon Gove was not staying in Trump Tower; that would have started the media frenzy, and someone would have asked Trump at a Whitehouse briefing without any doubt. 'President did you know the British financier who was assassinated in Central Park, and was staying in Trump Tower, and was alleged to be laundering *Russian* money, do you have any comment?' He would have paid good money to hear this question, and Trump's eruption at the impudence of the reporter, no doubt marking his or her place in history.

Pavel was always mystified at the media's fascination with Putin, he was an autocrat, and he was a billionaire. No proof had ever been presented to the public. Paradoxically, the United States citizens had elected a failed business man who had been declared bankrupt more than once as President.

He consumed the last drops of the vodka, and switched off the television; too much comedic content in a serious subject. His cyber fingerprints were all over the two unconnected deaths in New York. He hadn't thrown the Russian over the balcony, but his argument had convinced him to jump, and leave his wife and family's finances relatively intact. If he declined this once and only generous offer, his family would be penniless and returned to Moscow, where Putin had a personal interest in the family. The option was triggered with mutual satisfaction. He injected himself with a cocktail of hallucinogenic drugs (mescaline, psilocybin and LSD) in the bathroom of the apartment that legally would be his wife's as soon as he signed the legal papers. Then he leapt into a better place. His wife and the real estate realtor stated in their respective statements, that he smiled and kissed his wife after signing the legal papers. They assumed he was going to view the New York skyline. Close but no cigar.

***

Simon stared in disbelief at the lifeless body of Robert Samson it was swaying slightly; he was circumspect whether to feel if the body was emanating a modicum of heat. If he touched the neck, and it was warm, that would mean he committed suicide very recently. However, did that matter? He had to call the police; there were no doubt about this course of action   Then the reality of the death of Robert crept into his brain, he was his client; a dead client. Not good for business, and certainly not conducive to securing a home on Jersey. After a moment of pros and cons, he decided to call the police, but before this, he would call Armstrong.. He looked at Robert's body; a life lived with no regret. Thank God his fee for his services was paid in advance. The shock had made him think clearly, he took out his phone and called Armstrong. Please don't go to voicemail. His fear was not borne out. Armstrong picked up on the third ring.
'Yes, how can I help Simon?'
'Robert Samson has hung himself, I'm in Jersey, I was going to meet him at his development…'
'…wait a minute! He's dead! Where are you?'
'I'm in the bathroom; he's still hanging from the roof joist.'
'Have you called the police?'
'No…I thought…'
'…good, don't call them, get the fuck out of there, have you touched anything?'
'No, but I think I should call them, and to answer the question, no, I haven't touched anything, why?'
'Simon, things are taking a turn for the worst, Jonathon Gove has been murdered in Central Park; he was shot. Check to see if Robert's phone is on him or nearby; and if it is, take it, and get back to London.'
'Jonathan's dead, in New York? And why do you need Robert's phone?'

'No time to explain. Look now for the phone.'
Simon could see the outline of his phone in his work trousers, he extracted it
'I've got his phone, what next?'
'Get the fuck out of there, switch off the phone and get a flight home.'
'I am booked into a hotel, if I leave now that'll be suspicious, I'll complete my stay and then return as normal. I've got other business to attend to so that'll make my stay legitimate. The workmen must be on their lunch, it'll be best if I leave now.'
'Okay, if the police contact you later, just tell them that you stuck your head in the house and shouted out, there were no reply. No one was on site, and then you left. Keep it simple.'
'Well, that's practically the truth, apart from finding him. I'm not a police officer, but it looks like a tragic case of suicide '
'Simon, forget what happened, just get out of there, now!'
'I'm leaving now; I'll contact you when I get back to London.'
'Simon, move it...'

Simon ended the call, looked at Robert for the last time, and then departed from the bathroom; he returned immediately, he thought he heard something being disturbed in the rear of the property, the bathroom window was ajar. The barely inaudible sound was increasing; vehicles were heard but not seen coming into the grounds of the steading. It would be the workmen returning, no matter what Armstrong advised; he would contact the police after he explained to the coterie of workmen, of his horrific discovery of his client. Armstrong would surely understand it would be ludicrous to flee the scene of a suicide with workmen giving the police a full description of him and his car. On the plus side, he had Robert's phone which must have a treasure trove of financial information. Armstrong would be pleased that he would soon be in receipt of the phone. Jonathan Gove's death must have some implication or connection to Robert Samson untimely demise. Now was the appropriate time to inform and if necessary placate the workmen of the macabre scene in the bathroom. He would insist that no one should enter the house until the police arrived. He walked purposely down the recently installed wooden staircase; the yard was full of vehicles parked at awkward angles. They were police vehicles.

***

Edwina was thinking about her tumultuous short-time in New York once again, she kept on replaying all the incidents that occurred in her mind; however, her overnight companion's stay was erased with ease and little regret. She would love to return to The Carlyle, but not alone. Being single did not bring happiness, and was not as peaceful as she had thought it would be. Her break-up with her long standing fiancé was brutal and bitter. Her subconscious must have retained her former fiancé and the generous amounts of alcohol brought his memory to the surface. However, she couldn't alter the past; her future was still in front of her. She hoped there were episodes that brought laughter, however, tears were guaranteed. She was perusing the New York Times, but her eyes were drawn to her phone once again. She had promised herself that she would not reach out for it, for at least an hour. Barely ten minutes had passed when she came under its demonic power. She poured herself another coffee, and then grabbed the phone, nothing new, no messages from Armstrong, which was a good thing. Jonathon Gove's death was invading her thought process; the NYPD's investigation was not meticulous or robust. This was not complacency, this was constructed from above. Armstrong would hold a similar view; more information would be released to her when she was back in the office. The surveillance software installed in her Smart TV, didn't cause too much anxiety, she would just accidently break the screen while she was vacuuming, a simple accident. She would purchase a replacement herself. However, the elephant in the room had to be addressed, why was she under surveillance, and from whom?

    The images on her phone of Jonathan Gove and David Fisher who were neighbours in the same apartment block, meeting and socialising in New York perplexed her. There must be various cogent reasons. The first was very simple to establish; money. They were successful investors for other peoples' money, and no doubt invested their own substantial funds. However, one of them was dead; assassinated. Were they in New York for a *bona fide* business deal or were they lured to New York for the simple reason to remove one or both of them? Was David Fisher party to this conspiracy? Or was he just the bait to get Jonathan Gove to New York? The NYPD's report would be in Armstrong's hands. If the report alluded to money laundering; the Department of Justice would be the sole prosecutor; the United Kingdom would be the facilitator for extradition warrant(s) if they were required, and the warrant(s) would be expedited to the Department of Justice's satisfaction.

    David Fisher would now be a P.O.I. (*Person of Interest*) if he was not without sin, it would be uncovered. He would be offered an immunity deal from the D.O. J, only time would reveal if this was to be the case. Her natural instinct would reject this assessment, but facts always superceded instinct. Then the epiphany struck her; rather than change her Smart TV, she would put her house on the market removing herself from the unsocial neighbour, and thus expunging her from the surveillance operation. The Smart TV would be '*accidently*' dropped while she or her friends were removing it from her house to the hired removal van.

A waiter came over to her table to remove her coffee cup, she asked for another pot of coffee and some biscuits. She looked around the lobby, only a few of the distinctive yellow chairs were vacant. It occurred to her that this was the fourth time she had sat in this chair, and her melancholic mood had lifted. If she ever returned to The Carlyle; this would be *her* chair. It was perverse that she was in a heightened mood of optimism after the assassination of Jonathon Gove, however, this was a rare occurrence in her adult life, and wherever it came from she welcomed that. Happiness was an infrequent visitor. Then the silent despondent view of her life changed, it was obvious but she had ignored the rationale behind her often lonely and single existence. She had broken up with her fiancé simply because she was in the intelligence sector of government, her flying to different parts of the world would have caused his jealous trait to surface; it was either him or her career. There were no weeks of conflicting emotions. Her career would be life-enhancing and productive. Marrying him, would be tantamount to waking up each day and retiring to bed with the same recurring monotonous thought; imagine where my life would be if I *had* joined the Economic Crime Unit, instead of a well-paid but unhappy accountant? The tingling shiver ran up her spine. She had made the right decision.

Her unexpected sense of calmness and affinity with the chair was fleeting, when she was replenishing her coffee cup with a smile on her face, she saw David Fisher with an unknown woman take seats in the lobby, he had cases; they must be waiting on someone or were awaiting transport. She lifted her phone from the table as if she had received a message, and began to study it. She captured their images, and then immediately forwarded them to Armstrong with trepidation. The eventful stay in New York had not reached a quiet conclusion. The woman had a large suitcase on a trolley; He was booked on the evening flight, why was he waiting in the lobby? She had a decision to make; does she check-out now and follow them? Or does she stay put and catch her scheduled flight? She was staying put; she had collated photographs and made lengthy notes. It could be a very logical reason why he had checked-out earlier than she had anticipated; the woman could be a relative or associate of Jonathon Gove. She was relaxed that she had made the correct decision. They wouldn't be going anywhere soon, the waiter brought over a coffee pot and four cups. She captured this on her phone, but was reticent to forward the images to Armstrong for an unspecified reason, she wouldn't exercise any angst. Her anticipation that two unexpected visitors were expected and the two vacant chairs at their table would be filled. Nothing could or would surprise her anymore.

Jonathon Gove's murder in Central Park was still a feature in the New York Times, but the column inches were diminishing. However, in the Daily News, there were four pages containing plausible to fanciful but entertaining theories. In her professional thesis, the tabloid Daily News had caught the zeitgeist of the New York excitable public. The New York Times had published known facts, truthful but dull. The New York talk radio shows went full throttle, she could only listen for a short while as the conspiracy theories were too outlandish. She had glanced up occasionally from her newspaper; there were not much chattering between them, he repeatedly glanced in the direction of the check-in area. She was being irked at this, she leant over and grabbed his hand tightly and kissed him on the cheek to reassure him. Edwina glanced in the same direction which was busy with guests arriving and leaving, cases being taken to the front of the hotel and cases being brought in from arriving taxis and limousines. Suddenly David stood up, he was not smiling; the woman could have been glued to her seat as she made no attempt to greet or acknowledge the two imminent guests. It was a couple in their early 40s they were smartly dressed and seemed to be in a hurry; Edwina anticipated this would be a short visit. David invited them to sit down and poured them coffee, the woman was smiling but not talking, David's companion smiled and pecked her twice on the cheeks. The male was carrying a folder and placed it on the table and pushed it slowly and menacingly towards David, who took it but never examined the content, but placed it in his small case. His face lost ten years instantly, while his companion (Gwen) instantly sprouted wrinkles. This interaction was captured on Edwina's phone; again she declined to send it to Armstrong. It was very clear they would not be requesting another coffee; the male was becoming animated talking to David who also had become very agitated, the male was slurping his coffee in a hurry; he had to go was the message emanating from his body language. David was relieved he had the folder but his companion didn't share his joy. She made no attempt to initiate any conversation with her guests; in fact, she was projecting overt hostility which seemed to be received without any rancour. The woman just sat and sipped her coffee slowly and smiled sporadically which clearly annoyed David's companion. If ever Edwina took an irrational dislike to anyone it was her. That synthetic smile, natural beauty and sculptured tinted hair raised suppressed jealousy. When she arrived back in London she would be arranging a facial and have her hair restyled with various tints, similar to the self-assured smiling coffee drinker.

  David's laughter was drawing envious looks from some staid guests reading newspapers or drinking coffee in reverent silence; smiles broke out on a myriad of visages, Edwina's stony face succumbed to his infectious laughter. Various guests looked at each other with silent approval. If only they knew, they'd be running for cover. Her attention swings back to their table, the male has finished his coffee rises, and speaks to David's companion and then hugs David. The woman is not tactile and then she smiles politely, rises and waits on her colleague concluding his convoluted farewell. She furtively looks around, uncomfortable that David's laughter has been the focal point of a large percentage of seated guests. Her companion is less concerned, David is reluctant to let him leave too soon; he can't thank him enough. There is a healthy bond of mutual respect between them, his voice was quiet but now has become more distinctive; there was no trace of a Russian or east European accent. Edwina is ambivalent to this, if he was Russian that would have been less complicated, but the voice was of a gregarious and confident native New Yorker. He turned to leave, and buttoned up his ill-fitting suit jacket. On his bulging waistband a NYPD badge was visible.

***

Armstrong was enjoying his third cup of coffee; he didn't need any photographs to identify the two Americans that would be emerging soon from the arrivals. Dirk McCabe the senior attaché at the American Embassy was there personally to greet them, and definitely without a smile. He was the most virulent racist and duplicitous individual he had ever come across. McCabe and Edwina had an infinite bond between them, they hated each other, and he wasn't keen on Armstrong either. Eighteen months previous, Armstrong and Edwina had arranged a meeting with McCabe, laughingly it was meant to establish cooperation between the United Kingdom and the U.S. intelligence agencies. Edwina's skin pigmentation caused McCabe to utter subtle racial slurs, not directly at Edwina, but everyone in the room understood his sentiments. Only the Americans in the room laughed. Not an inspiring start. However, Edwina was not slow off the mark either. McCabe finished his anodyne speech which ironically was meant to place everyone at ease, it became apparent that when he said any questions, he didn't want or expect any. She raised her hand; he raised his eyebrows, and snapped 'Yes'!

Edwina sat in a relaxed position as if she was watching television. 'How long were you in the KKK?'

Boom! McCabe went into a rant, 'I am not a racist, if you're so sensitive maybe this was not the place for you?' Edwina just dismantled every argument he insipidly put up. McCabe called for an adjournment so the 'misunderstanding' could be cleared up. Edwina walked out of his office, back into the meeting room. She had made her point in an articulate and polite manner. She halted any riposte from him immediately. Enemies for life from that day.

Armstrong correctly identified the two individuals that arrived; he placed the coffee cup down, and followed them out into the VIP car park. His car was also parked there; he had completed many assignments similar to this. The only surprise was Dirk McCabe was there. He was excited and perturbed because of this; something significant was coming down the pike. What hotel would they be staying at? The Travelodge chain could be confidently ruled out. He waited a short-time, and then followed them out of the car park. They were not being transported in any of the pooled cars from the Embassy. He captured the registration number on his phone; it would not come up on any recognition cameras, only a government code. But he would run it through the computer anyway. The journey was completed without any impediment; they were dropped off at the front door of The Ritz, impeccable taste and perfect for the Green Park underground station. This raised confidence, he had a confidant in The Ritz, and he will be able to establish the duration of their stay. Dirk McCabe didn't hang about, he was heading back to the Embassy, there were no point in continuing tailing him, he would return to his flat; have a few joints, and then nervously attempt again a recipe from the dust covered cookery book.

Edwina would soon be returning she would have notes and photographs. Would she have additional information on the demise of Jonathon Gove? If she had, she would not be keen to share it initially with anyone. She preferred a complete picture with nothing obstructing her view. The surveillance software in her Smart TV may divulge undisclosed information which she withheld from him; he had come to the conclusion that she had harvested information from various fraud cases she had previously and successfully completed. She may be advising suspects under her surveillance that she could erase or modify information that various government agencies had stored on their computers. She was definitely one to watch. And he thought all of this without a sliver of irony. However, he convinced himself that *this* work benefited the security of the United Kingdom, and of course his pecuniary healthy off-shore bank account. He had rapidly lost faith in his department; the Oxbridge crowd were being elevated to positions that they didn't even know existed. They adhered to the hands-off and pass the buck way of thinking. They would not make a unilateral decision, which had cost lives because of their ineptitude. They were not held to account for their catastrophic mistakes. When he spoke informally to his superior, he was told that this was of no concern to him, but if he really felt that way put it in writing. He handed the letter to him as soon as the final word contemptuously erupted from his lips within earshot of his junior colleagues. He anticipated the arrogant response. If this utterance was directed at him in a bar, he would have laid him out. He would not be dismissed, but his career would be becalmed. His card was marked. And he was marking Edwina's; and it wasn't in pencil.

***

   They stared at the bench in silence; the trees in Central Park were swaying in the gentle breeze, David had placed flowers at the side of the bench. Normality had returned to Central Park, runners and people walking briskly talking into their phones, some were laughing some were not. No one gave the bench a first look never mind a second look; the New Yorkers attitude was what is the point crying over spilt blood? Gwen held his hand tighter she could see the pain and the embedded shock etched on his face. He insisted they go to the place of execution before they return to London. She argued against it, there would be no obvious benefit to his mental health. However, he was insistent, to the point of subtle malevolent anger. This may bring an unexpected dividend. He was vulnerable and his guard may be weakened. There was a chill in the wind as it blew her long hair into her face; they had not moved from the spot for five unnerving minutes, she had to break the silence, and prise the latent information from him of paying off the NYPD detectives, it was very clear to her that the detective was a past master in releasing or suppressing damaging information. When she asked why he was succumbing to blackmail; he disagreed with her assessment, it was a financial transaction that would allow him to continue to secure his wealthy clients the best return on their investments. Any rumour of inappropriate financial transactions would affect his business and cash flow overnight. He insisted there were none. But, information could be leaked that if Jonathon Gove was involved in any investment that was considered unlawful or corrupt, the inference could be easily translated that he was also involved.

   Gwen understood the sentiment behind it, and it was the simple and expeditious solution, but it may come back to haunt him; instead of the NYPD detective soliciting money from him, he would say it was David bribing *him*, and he had been threatened, he didn't want to end up dead like David's colleague Jonathon Gove. However, this was neither the time nor place to raise her concern. In London she would use all her experience to assemble all the information into a narrative that would confirm her suspicion. Jonathon Gove's death was formulated in London and conveyed in New York in a flawless manner. The media were unaware that they were confirming the narrative as was agreed in London, the leaks to the media and theories on Twitter were all being directed from London. And to her utter dismay the people behind it were total professionals; David Fisher was not seen as part of any conspiracy; he was portrayed as a victim, just like his friend Jonathon Gove. No photographs of David were inserted along with the narrative of Jonathon's death. Very strange.

He pulled her hand, they were moving. 'I feel a lot better now, and if you don't mind I'd rather not talk about Jonathan…ever.'
'You look better, and I understand, the only thing we have to do is collect our cases from the hotel and take a taxi to JFK.'
'We will have a bite to eat, in the lounge at JFK, I want to get out of New York, I would never have thought I would say these words. By the way how is Avery coping?'
'She's getting better, she's a tough cookie, she has had set backs in her life but not as traumatic as this; some deeply disturbing, but that's for another day. I'm looking forward to living in London, and of course living with you. She seemed very resilient; I didn't need to comfort her too much,'
'Have you told her that you are moving to London with me?' Gwen burst out laughing.
'Definitely not! She's fine in small doses; that's all I can say. Her personality can overwhelm you.'

David smiled, the worry dropped from his face. 'I get that, when I was a schoolboy I had a friend like that, great for a few hours, but not to be stranded with on a desert island.'
Their spontaneous laughter, made their steps quicken.
'I'm hungry now David, can we go to a little deli, not The Carlyle, for something, just a burger and coffee nothing fancy?'
'I'm glad you said that, I really am, it's been years since I had a burger, I'm going to have fries with my cheese burger, yes a cheese burger!'

She was bemused at how excited he was about a cheese burger and fries, but if it made him happy and relaxed, he might disclose something of importance. Numerous joggers had passed them since they left the bench, she was listening to David, but she noticed that he didn't flinch or pause when joggers approached them from the front or behind, he never turned round; her eyes were watching each and every jogger that passed them. He didn't even look at them. If he stopped or had a sudden panic attack, it was understandable because his friend had been assassinated. She felt uneasy.

***

Simon was shocked to see four police cars in the yard. Maybe the workmen had discovered the body of Robert hanging from the roof joist, and had panicked and went to the police station? It didn't matter the police were here, now he could explain. He emerged from the front door, some police officers were looking at his car and taking notes, others were taking photographs on their phones of the car from different angles. Two detectives were walking towards the front door; they didn't seem surprised as he walked from the house, before he could say anything about Robert Samson, they asked if he was Simon Corndale. He confirmed his name and why he was here. They lead him to their car and placed him in the back seat. The sound of the doors locking made him feel queasy, a police officer stood at either side of the car. This was looking ominous. He sat in the back seat trying to make some sense of this. The minutes passed by quickly, an ambulance came into the yard, obviously to take the body away. However, the crew just stayed put. Another large van came into the yard Forensics was emblazoned on the side of it. Four personnel carrying small metal cases went into the house. Twenty minutes later the ambulance personnel descended from the ambulance carrying a stretcher and pushing a trolley. The terrain of the yard would make it very difficult to push the trolley with someone of Robert's weight. The forensic team were standing by his car; the detective came over and opened the door for him to go to his own car. They told him they can take him to the police station and be interviewed under a police caution and have a lawyer present. His instinct said he should go to the police station and have a lawyer present, but his curiosity overruled his instinct, he wanted to know what the fuck was going on. He walked over asking various questions but they wouldn't respond, when they stopped at his car, they asked him, if this was his car, a fucking stupid question he thought in the circumstances. He confirmed it was his and he had hired it. They asked if anyone else had been in the car when he collected it, or had been in it when he drove to meet Robert Samson, he confirmed he had been alone. They asked him if there were anything in the car that could incriminate him or contributed to the death of Robert Samson. He laughed, 'of course not!' They asked him to remove items that belonged to him from the car, then they would do a preliminary search of the car with his permission or they could take it to the police station and it would be searched with a lawyer present. He removed his suitcase and then gave them permission for the forensics to search the car, it wasn't as if they would find a gun; he had nothing to hide and nothing to fear.

  Other vehicles were coming into the yard but were stopped some distance from the house, the workmen in three vans got out, wondering what was going on, the ambulance personnel emerged with Robert's body, they placed the stretcher on the trolley, they were not having as much difficulty as he envisaged. In the circumstances, he thought they were very respectful and dignified. On the other hand the workmen were amazed at what was unfolding before their eyes. A yard full of police vehicles, numerous police officers, a body being removed, a stranger standing beside a strange car, surrounded by strange people in blue boiler suits, videoing the inside and outside of the car. Even though they all had witnessed this surreal scene; they had no objection in leaving immediately; because they had consumed alcohol. Simon on the other hand, was regretting not accepting to be interviewed by the police in sterile surroundings and with a lawyer by his side. However, this would all be over soon, and if they wanted him to go to the police station, he would have his personal lawyer fly over from London. The interview would be brief, and he would return to London in the presence of his expensive lawyer. Suddenly as he thought this through a sense of calm and everything will work out imbued him. The sense of confidence was misplaced; he wasn't in the City anymore, shouting insults at people and boasting how much money he had made on currency exchange and derivatives. And the sole reason the abused staff tolerated him, was because when he made money, they made money. He subconsciously knew this all along, but he loved *Lording* it over them, especially the women. Removing himself from the trading floor and becoming freelance was the best decision he ever made. The Russians ensconced in London were odious individuals, but the criminal odour was masked by the compelling fragrance of millions of pounds, whether it was earned by sweat of brows, or at the end of guns, it never rippled his neutral conscience. Robert Samson was an obnoxious character, but he knew how to make money, and he knew that he (Simon) was better and more avaricious; that would cause the chalk face on his dead body to still blush. The shock of Robert hanging from the roof joist was diminishing, money had brought them together, but money killed one of them and it wasn't him. The detective was called over to the other side of the car by one of the forensic team; in the glove compartment was a hypodermic needle.

***

In Terminal 7 at JFK, David and Gwen are relaxing in the Business Lounge. Both are oblivious to the array of pampered clients. Everything is within calling distance. They both abstain from the impressive complimentary alcohol selection on offer. Any concern that David harboured regarding the brutal slaying of Jonathon was analysed and placed in a hermetically sealed recess at the rear of his mind, it would only be released when the police came to interview him in London.

His concern was Gwen, how would he cope having her living with him? Space was not a problem; he had been institutionalised in living and working alone. He enjoyed the unorthodox working hours and self-imposed isolation. He thought more than he spoke, and this gave a skewed impression of him being sometimes distant and aloof. There were no handprints on his broad back where he had patted himself after completing another successful financial transaction, domestically or with international clients. He only travelled overseas if it was absolutely necessary, and if he did it would be on Business Class and five star hotels with a minimum stay.

When they arrived in London he would take the week off, he would try to get inside Gwen's head, learn her foibles, if any existed, would she come clean and tell him, or try to suppress them? That was typical of David getting ahead of the present moment, instead of enjoying it. Nothing could prevent him from thinking ahead of any situation, although to the outside world and clients, this may seem a trait worth paying a therapist to discard, he was of the opinion it had more merit than concern. Perhaps it was because of his austere childhood? It was only a fleeting concern, and it made him driven to achieve the finer things in life; to live in a nice neighbourhood, self-educate himself, and to leave all the naysayers in his wake. He had one really eccentric trait, kettles, or more exactly how long a kettle would take to boil. The longer it took; the more energy it used. Idiosyncratic? Definitely. He didn't need a behavioural therapist to find the root cause, and relieve him of thousands of pounds to reveal the answer. He would place a substantial wager that Gwen couldn't come close to this idiosyncrasy. He was totally wrong; he wouldn't uncover it, or come close, even though it was in plain sight.

Gwen was a woman who planned every step of her life, she had not stumbled anytime, and she wasn't planning a misstep. She was only a few hours of reaching the epicentre of her tortuous odyssey, only the arbiter of time would decide if she was righteous or deluded. Both of these conditions have downsides. Sometimes fatal.

She couldn't muster any concern about moving to London, her satellite television would keep her up to date with the maverick President of the United States. Her online subscription to the New York Times would continue. She had places to go and people to meet, some who were unsavoury and actively criminal, or engaging outside the rule of law with confident impunity. She would visit locations which were unappealing at unearthly hours, and meet with characters of questionable morality. However, means would justify the satisfying end. It had been a painstaking, disappointing and costly endeavour, the end could be in sight or could she be looking through an optimistic and unrealistic prism? Her anger had evolved into positive energy that could be released when the occasion merited. Her body and brain were in positive places and she was in control, she was feeding off David's vista of the future.

Edwina, observed them sitting in silence, as cool as she could imagine and without guilt, she was well aware you can train your body to lie, she had implemented this practice with aplomb, whether it was a job interview or when she was in the field of subtly interviewing suspects regarding financial matters.

She intended to gather as much intelligence about them in addition to the information on file. David's file was now being updated; the information in the file would've been gathered in a perfunctory manner. The information would be coming in at haste, his file would be gaining credence; Jonathon Gove's murder had changed things utterly, not just for David Fisher, but now for his unexpected female companion returning to London.

Edwina had upgraded her seat to observe David Fisher and his companion, Armstrong never raised any objection, he was intrigued about the female companion, she was instructed to take photographs of them in the lounge at JFK from different angles; they would run facial recognition software over the photographs, a professional approach that would result in zero additional information. The flight manifest would immediately reveal who she was. Nothing of concern would bubble up to the surface, however later, information would alter matters irrevocably. Resignations would be demanded, some would be voluntarily, and others not so. Perceived injustices and obscenities would be screamed across rooms that should have been aired in the confines of the office; salaries and pension entitlements should be negotiated in an eloquent manner. But these were not normal times.

***

In the Shard, Lorna is relaxing awaiting the arrival of Pavel, she had information that he should hear not over the phone or by text message. Lord Alexander was concerned that someone had entered his flat, nothing was taken, but his fear was that someone from British Intelligence had secreted surveillance hardware in his flat. He was very vague about this assertion; but was convinced. Lorna wanted to run this past Pavel; she wanted the flat swept and any surveillance hardware removed.

When Lord Alexander Marr was an MP he was a critic of the Security Services; YouTube had a montage of his eloquent speeches in which he named certain individuals under Parliamentary Privilege; he was a part of a group of MPs that raised inconvenient truths about the Security Service placing political activists under surveillance, he had a mole in the Security Services. Whether he was being manipulated was or is open to conjecture. There were times when he was clearly under the influence of alcohol and was unkempt, but he miraculously managed to remain steady on his feet and be articulate when he was delivering his searing speech, even though he was being heckled from the government benches and from some of his own colleagues

He could have been a professional stand-up comedian; he had performed at the Edinburgh Festival for three years running. He was abruptly advised not to return for a fourth year. He had upset left-wing comedians, by saying "how come all these Left-Wing comedians were educated at Oxford and Cambridge, and operated tax saving off-shore accounts?"

It hit him badly, his self-esteem took a hit, however his popularity with voters ascended to rock star status, his many charitable endeavours remained secret; he had also helped parliamentary colleagues across the political divide who were suffering from the mental pressures of Westminster. The enormous amount of leisure time was the touch paper to lead to personal oblivion; the occasional drink became an everyday occurrence, and that stretched into the early hours in the Strangers bar in parliament. If only he had listened to his own advice; however, he had climbed out that alcohol pit of despair, only to enter into an open prison of loneliness. He may have said au revoir to alcohol but he welcomed cannabis with open mouth, then cocaine, which couldn't be sniffed at anymore. In bed he lay for hours in his mental cage; his recurring thought was the end would come sooner than he had anticipated; should he be cremated or buried, and would anyone attend his funeral?

Time was his enemy as well as his saviour, sitting every morning, and afternoon that blurred into evening in the various pubs in and around Westminster was his daily haunt, he needed all the gossip. He was still friendly with MPs of various political parties. Then Lorna 'bumped' into his life, and life became less frenetic, and his mind settled into a calming pattern.

Pavel entered the apartment, he was relaxed and smiling. Lorna had the coffee pot in her hand. He took off his overcoat and sat at the table at the cathedral window overlooking the London skyline.

'What's so important?'

She poured him his coffee then refilled her cup, and sat beside him at the table.

'It's Alexander, he said his flat has been broken into, no damage, or anything taken, he suspects it's the Security Service…'

'…he's totally correct, M.I.5 gained access to his flat and installed surveillance equipment in various rooms.'

'I don't understand, has he told you this?'

'No, no, I found out myself from a source, but there is nothing to worry about… lovely view from here.'

'I don't understand…he wants the surveillance equipment removed, that's why he contacted me Pavel.'

'It's been removed; I had it removed the day it was installed. He's got his old sharpness back, that's good. This experience will keep him lucid at all times, and he'll need it in the future; it was my team that left a calling card, so to speak.'

'Will I inform him that his imagination has gone into overdrive?'

'No, no, just meet him for coffee, then return to his flat then go through a search with him, tell him to purchase anti-surveillance equipment then you can go through the charade with him, listening for beeps when the equipment is operative.'

'Why is the Security Service targeting him?'

'He's been meeting someone who is a cause for concern, not just to the British State, but to us as well. When the Security Services' bugs were removed, we put in our own sophisticated bugs, it's the best available, the inferior anti-surveillance hardware will not pick it up. It's Chinese, and it is installed in the new billion pounds plus American Embassy. Complete irony, don't you think?'

The smile of complete satisfaction couldn't be hidden, nor did he attempt to conceal his undulated joy. Lorna was impatient for him to reveal who this person Lord Alexander Marr was meeting in clandestine surroundings. Past experience would chastise her not to ask outright. He enjoyed revealing devastating information in an incremental fashion.

''When were you aware that Alexander, was deviating from the original instructions?'

'There was a photograph of him and others from the Climate Change cross-party committee at a dinner. However, at the rear of the group was a new addition to the committee, he had been parachuted in, because of a long-term illness of a member of the committee, before he became an M.P., he was an N.C.O. in the British Army, he was in M.I.6, he was involved in unsavoury incidents during the 'Troubles,' he is a charming, and an intelligent individual. He is primarily on the Climate Change committee to gather information on our mutual friend Lord Marr. He was behind the go-ahead to enter and install the surveillance bugs. Unfortunately for our mutual friend he has been seduced by his charm, they're spending a lot of time in each other's company. And, I'm very surprised, Lord Marr, has not noticed this.'

Lorna was surprised at these revelations; Lord Marr had not been out of character or displaying any sign of anxiety. Was Pavel reprimanding her in an understated manner? He wasn't an individual for berating someone by shouting or demeaning them.

'So by leaving something out of place in his flat, you've put him on his guard, that this was unusual, and could it be coincidental that this has happened since he was befriended?, and knowing Alexander, he would be well aware of his position in M.I.6 when he was an N.C.O in the British Army?'

He rose from the table and gestured her to join him, he was walking towards the window with the panoramic view, coffee cup still in hand.

'You have listened, and processed this information, and you have reached the correct conclusion a lot sooner than I had anticipated. Lord Marr could be being playing a wrong game; he might think he is getting closer to the Establishment; thus cementing himself further to the Establishment, a vain, egotistical and reckless strategy. Now that you're up to speed with this latest development, I'm sure you can alter or adapt his behaviour to bring him back on course. And, of course to elicit as much information as possible from him, don't steer him towards the connection between his new friend and the break-in at his apartment. Don't ask if he has been spending time with any of the Climate Change committee, if his stress level comes to be replicated in his manners, gently probe is everything okay?'

Lorna had already formulated her next move as he sipped his coffee and stared far into the London sky line; he had more information but he would not share it with her today, she had ascertained that very quickly, today had brought many surprises, some disturbing that could compromise Lord Marr.

This ex-M.I.6 officer would have run her through intelligence agencies and computers; however, she had a pristine background, with no links to any foreign power. Her business was not a front as such, it was thriving, and her bespoke therapy sessions were fully booked and had a burgeoning waiting list from professional backgrounds. Most of the clients were in the City, burning the candle at both ends and in the middle, they were addicted to cocaine. Lorna would not say addicted as that would mean they were the same as the working class oiks. No, language was essential to mollify them, they were not addicted; they were 'dependent.'

There were not too many people on this planet that had three careers and loved all of them equally. She had lived the hedonistic lifestyle in her twenties, outwardly she had it all, career in the City, living in Canary Wharf, in a luxurious apartment which was a stroll to a job that remunerated her well. Wine bars after work most nights, and then when she and her friends were feeling the strain, and tiredness was engulfing them at midnight, they resorted to cocaine. She wasn't forced to ingest it she was an eager participant. Cocaine took over life and her mind, paranoia was growing, in the ritual morning shower, tears and an epiphany shook her mind and body in unison. She was going to get clean, and she took the day off and booked herself into rehab, her expensive insurance picked up the invoice.

Three months later she was clean, she decided to study and became a Psychotherapist specialising in drug dependency, she had a customer base on her doorstep; many of her ex-colleagues came to her. Familiarity did not bring contempt. By nature she was a kind and considerate individual, she broke the news over dinner delivered in a non-judgemental and gentle manner that she was breaking-up with him, he wouldn't give up cocaine or late nights, they had come to a fork in the road which was signposted he took the road marked 'Status Quo', she took the other road covered in leaves that had not been travelled marked 'Uncertainty,' and that has made all the difference.

She moved out of the apartment after receiving a favourable settlement in releasing her part ownership of the apartment. Her bank balance was displaying a healthy hue, securing a mortgage for another apartment from the bank that she was formally employed, didn't cause her any concern. In reality she could purchase an apartment along the banks of the Thames, but her punishing running regime had taken her to unfashionable locations in London, seeing skips and a myriad of tradesmen alerted her internal business antenna, and her superficial interest coalesced into a formal business plan. It was liberating, being her own boss and owning companies that purchased, renovated and sold houses. Accumulation of vast sums of money did not enhance her life or lifestyle in any visible manner. Her mental health was slowly being impaired, but she knew where the root cause lay and it lay at her golden feet. Her company were purchasing flats and houses in what were deemed to be working class areas, it was capitalist ethnic cleansing, she was an ardent capitalist, but a social conscience was born. And it would not attend nursery school; it would be enrolled into university immediately.

She sold her companies and bought a gym in an unloved and unused warehouse, her solicitor ascertained that permission would not or unlikely be granted to convert or demolish the warehouse into social or residential houses or flats. It was in an industrial area, this was monumental mood enhancing news.

She overseen the conversion of the voluminous internal area herself, local tradesmen were offered various contracts, some were too expensive, she advised them of that, some rapidly came to the conclusion she wasn't green as the grass outside the warehouse, and modified their tenders. Lorna had now a radical social conscience but she wasn't prone to bleeding heart syndrome. Halfway through the renovation she was chatting to the foreman over a coffee, politics were raised, to her horror they were all Conservatives, she listened intently, they were all bright, and politically astute, this really was a period of political uncertainty. If only they were aware that she was formally of the Right, and she used to conduct her life with supercilious fervour over 'ordinary workers.' She had made a decision the socially, egalitarian Labour and Liberal parties were just subsidiaries of the Conservative Party. Things had to change. And she was flummoxed how she could be part of social change.

The gym was completed and the membership applications were oversubscribed. One of her former female colleagues from the bank and an enthusiastic participant of after-work activities (cocaine) arranged an appointment to see her when she was personally accepting completed application forms for membership. Lorna was surprised and delighted to see her, she took her into the office, she got straight to the point; she wanted the position as manager of the gym. On first sight this was a ridiculous meeting, she was overweight and looked frazzled with life. Lorna first thought was a polite no, but she had made the correct decision to join the gym, to get fit, even though it would be a long process. However, she was trustworthy, a close confidant and possessed an engaging personality. She told her she would be ideal, the position was offered to her, the salary was dwarfed by the banks' remunerating package. Lorna didn't enquire why she had become dissatisfied with the City; she could only take an educated guess. She would confide in her at the appropriate time.

When the gym was opened it was a financial success, within two months numerous national renowned gyms made Lorna an eye-watering straight cash offer, she declined. She was not in period of divestment; she was going to expand and London was ripe for development. Her former colleague and now gym manager would be the general manager for all the gyms in London, her salary would be doubled. Lorna would now be able to concentrate and increase her client base for her psychotherapist practice. In her office she had been studying the client appointment list. Anxiety and sleeplessness were the problems that needed addressed; an hour's assessment was pencilled in, the client would unburden his or herself; therapy is also about self-healing from the inside. In a fleeting moment of introspection Lorna, self-analysed herself, a very rare event, she needed to go over her unhappy life, professionally and personally, she wrote down the cathartic moment that set her on the road to happiness in her personal and her professional lives. A life unexamined is not a life lived.

She worked back from that life changing moment, a mundane partner who was unambitious and she was infected by this sapping contagion. The mammal in the room was her dependency on cocaine.

That period in her life altered everything; a cold, clear view of her world was not a signpost to contentment. The notepad was placed back in the drawer of her desk; the gentle buzzer alerted her that the client was on his way up. She walked to her office door and opened it, there stood Pavel.

***

'Well, what do you think of the flat?' Her face was illuminated; she was *home*.

'I misjudged you David, I thought it would be nice and functional, it's very impressive, I noticed you are an avid collector of hotel toiletries, do you take them home to remind you of happy memories in various famous hotels?'

Sitting in his chair, he smiled. 'No I take them home because I paid for them, and they are of excellent quality. You are correct that the sight of them evokes memories. The murder of Jonathon will not be brought on by sight of shampoo.' She had to lift the colourless gloom from the conversation.

'I understand that…do you have a cleaner?

'No, I don't have a cleaner; do you think I need a cleaner?'

'So you clean the apartment by yourself?' She was genuinely shocked at this simple revelation.

'Of course, it's not the Whitehouse.' Sunday is cleaning day, thirty minutes and it's all done; these micro-fibre cloths are brilliant.'

'Good to see your feminine side at work '

He laughed. 'No, no feminine side, just working class ethics I always tidied my room when I was at school. That's my cleaning routine sorted… do you think you'll feel at home here then?'

She had underestimated him. 'I'll take things slowly, but I feel very comfortable with you and your apartment. It is very nice, and traditional, apart from the bathroom and kitchen, you certainly like your gadgets in the kitchen?' He rose from the chair, took her hand and guided her to the bathroom.

'You forgot to mention the bathroom, what you call gadget, I call technical innovation.'

They both stood in the bathroom, 'David why are we standing in the bathroom in darkness?'

'Move your hand quickly along the bottom of the vanity mirror?'

Did he really think she would be impressed that LED lights on the periphery of the mirror would illuminate the bathroom?

'Go on then!'

She swiped her hand quickly along the bottom of the mirror. The LED lights came on instantly.

'David, I don't want to disappoint you, but I've had various LED mirrors over the last six years.'

'That maybe the case, but does it have this?'

'Have what?'

'Close your eyes Gwen, tightly.'

She was laughing. 'OK, they are closed.' Immediately soft music filled the cavernous bathroom, the acoustics were perfect, the music incrementally grew louder. Her favourite love song of all time was now booming out from the LED Bluetooth vanity mirror. A trickle of tears ran down her cheeks. Memories that she had thought were dead and buried, rose from the mass grave of her past. She kept her eyes closed, the warm feeling that had been lost and which she thought would never return, tingled its welcome return. She searched for his hand, squeezing it gently, the song reached its chorus, the intermittent tears returned, David was alarmed at this, but he couldn't break the silence.

  Gwen felt light-headed, but paradoxically elated. She had never had any doubts about her returning to London with David, this was now a choice that endorsed her innate feelings in New York. The song was in its last throes, the bittersweet memories came at her from different directions; they coincided with tumultuous periods of her life. She had to exorcise them; they were guaranteed to revisit her when personal happiness came into her life; the negative and disturbing images won the race to be embedded in her mind. Therapy failed to remove them, the technique of 'parking' them worked for a few months, but as her life became less frenetic, the handbrake came off her 'parked' memories; they all resurfaced in the early hours of the morning. Sleep would be impossible after dissecting them. Gravity was drawing her and David together. "Honey it's been a long time coming and I can't stop now." The words of Gravity by Embrace were so relevant now. But how did David know Gravity was her favourite song?

***

La Route du Fort in St. Helier, (Police Headquarters) looked similar to many council office blocks built in a hurry throughout the U.K. But to Simon Corndale the building was foreboding, when he departed the building after the rudimentary interview; he wouldn't recall this place with any nostalgic affection. On the positive side, he wasn't handcuffed, and his poise and dignity remained intact. The two detectives' demeanour hadn't betrayed any conscious bias against him. They weren't chatty; they asked informally what was the reason for his relationship with Robert Samson? Normally, with nothing to fear, he would have given a comprehensive description of his relationship and why he was over to meet him, however, since the hypodermic needle was found in the glove compartment of the hired car, he told the detectives that he wouldn't be answering any questions until his lawyer was contacted and giving comprehensive details of why he was being detained and interviewed. The detective offered him his phone and told him to contact his lawyer. Simon's phone was in a sealed evidence bag, and it may or not be returned for an indefinite period of time.

He was processed quickly and placed in a holding cell until his lawyer arrived in approximately four hours. He had politely declined a State lawyer; too many historical cases in the justice system had ended in bitterness and jail time being served. His time in the holding cell would give him ample time to try to understand why he was here. Simon wasn't stupid; it was unlikely his visit and the death of Robert Samson was just an unfortunate alignment of the stars. However, the needle in the car, the hired car, he reminded himself, it had probably been left by a drug dependent individual but it still caused him some concern. Robert's death would be declared as a suicide, for what reason or reasons, still to be determined. He sat upright against the wall, his City trader ruthless persona came to the fore. He can benefit in monetary terms if he was economical in his financial disclosure to the police when he was being interviewed. And if the detectives confronted him with any undisclosed information he would play it in a nondescript manner. Robert's money was *his* now. As far as he was aware Robert didn't have any dependents, but death and money seems to bring out the worst in people. Robert's life was littered with failed romances, but no children were conceived.

This would be just another vexatious episode in a fractious meeting with a client. His life was not in immediate danger; however, if this was a Russian client he wouldn't be planning a five year financial exit with confidence. He felt his blood run cold, if this was a Russian client, he would not have left Jersey on his scheduled flight; he would just have vanished. It was not conducive to his mental health to place himself in any potential or life threatening situation, he had been there, and the experience was educational. Death was rarely polite or swift; hours of torture after information and bank account access codes were extracted along with teeth, and funds were transferred, only then death became instant. Fortunately, he had a gift for telling lies which seemed plausible; he had no conscience when it came to implicating others with dire consequences, he would not name them directly but reveal emails that suggested money was being skimmed and deposited in accounts that were not authorised. The unfortunate recipient of these undisclosed funds could offer no rational explanation why unscheduled deposits of millions of pounds were in this account that they did not know existed. Simon had the bulk of the missing funds in his secret account. No spotlight or suspicion fell on him.

Simon was charming as he was devious, with Robert undoubtedly feeling financial pressure from someone, decided to leave the stage early. However, his death would cause a whirlwind of rumours and conspiracy theories. When he was back in London, he would keep under the radar; others would raise concerns, when it was officially declared Robert had succumbed to depression, after suffering a series of health issues and hung himself. In the City former adversaries would dismiss this explanation out of hand. Money made him, and money was his executioner. He would say that to various traders, they would coin it as their own concocted phrase. He was quite proud of this strategy.

  He ruminated on the de facto reason why Robert took his own life, he agreed with his initial assessment that money was behind it. Why else would Robert give him access to an account in his name? (Simon's name) Where did the money come from? It was patently not legitimate, was this simply money laundering? Was Robert taking a hefty commission, and subcontracting him (Simon)? That was possible; at this point in time he had his commission and the funds in his account, all perfectly legitimate. There was no benefit disclosing this, it would only add to the legal bureaucratic morass that would take years to untangle. Without seeming cold and predatory, this unfortunate business might bring him some pecuniary largesse. His head was no longer spinning, he quickly got over the shock of his client hanging from the joist; he seemed at peace. Knowing Robert, his affairs would be incomprehensible, he was notorious for letting paperwork slide, and he was a novice when it came to computers; or this could have been a charade to give the impression that he was not good at retaining, updating records and recording financial transactions. Simon knew this charade was for consumption for gullible City traders. This holding cell had given him time to stretch his mind to second guess what the detectives would be thinking. If he can match their thinking his lawyer would be able to surpass his thoughts. He slid down the wall; he lay on the flimsy mattress, and looked at his watch, the adrenalin rush had made him sleepy, a nap of an hour would refresh him, he could only speculate when news of Robert's suicide reached the trading floor of the City, work would be cut short for the day, Robert's demise would be greeted with elevated cries of joy. When the euphoria dissipated; the serious examination and speculation of his finances would be the only subject discussed in the City and by financial journalists. This would be supplemented with damaging information passed to preferred journalists by Simon that was not in the public domain, or that the few traders in the know could ever imagine.

  Hands behind his head, he had not felt this good or wealthy in a very long time, he had to try and outthink his lawyer, the less he knew about Robert's funds in his account would be advantageous to his finances and his well-being. His accounts would stand up to any financial scrutiny from any forensic accountant. Nigel would insist that he had access to his bank accounts, and any financial transaction that raised a red flag would be explained in a detailed manner. Taxes had all been accounted for; he was a model citizen, compared to former and current City traders.

Nigel had been a criminal prosecutor then changed to a defence barrister, he didn't have a penchant for righting any perceived wrongs; it just paid better. Then he changed again, he was part of an experienced defence team from the most prestigious chambers practice in London, normally when they called the response would be simply yes; even before the case had been fully explained. The trial was expected to last sixteen weeks, the Serious Fraud Office were confident of being vindicated, the trial would cost the public purse an estimated £15 million. The blue chip practice had agreed in advance a fee of £10 million, if they were successful in the four defendants being acquitted; a £4 million bonus would be added to the negotiated fee.

Nigel had spoken to various lawyers in other practices; they didn't hold out much chance of any of them being acquitted. Their unanimous opinion was a legal technicality would be the most favourable route to achieve a mistrial or have the case dismissed. And why was he being recruited? Where were the usual lawyers that were normally drafted in? Was he the expensive mistake, if as expected the defence team were not able to overcome the overwhelming evidence against their clients?

Nigel's reputation was valued more than any fee; it was of no concern if it ran into seven figures. He was disappointed when a confidant disclosed to him that three high-flying lawyers had turned down numerous approaches from the blue chip practice; they acquiesced that they were not going to be *the* expensive scapegoat. With this information which he chose not to disclose to the blue chip chambers, he agreed to meet the leading barrister who specialised in financial crime at The Dorchester (his choice). It didn't go well, he was very condescending to Nigel; he wouldn't disclose any pertinent information that could be the silver bullet to damage the SFO's case. Before the drinks were served Nigel bade him farewell, they contacted him four times, and eventually resiled from disclosing the meat and bones of their defence. Nigel insisted that someone from the chambers other than the belligerent barrister should walk him through evidence that could be challenged successfully.

Nigel was now an enemy for life; even though they would act in a professional manner when they had to be part of the team. Nigel was a breath of fresh air, to the young professional lawyers; he wanted all of them to have an input without any repercussions which could cause them to fear for their positions with the blue chip practice. Nigel was fascinated by the financial shenanigans that the four clients were able to practice in plain sight. He was schooled by a twenty-five year old female lawyer she was on top of her profession; she encouraged Nigel to study and achieve a degree in financial crime/defence. And that was the course he chose returning to university and additionally being tutored by this young lawyer.

The four defendants were acquitted on a legal technicality; the SFO had concentrated on overwhelming evidence, and had a superficial view of legal procedure. Nigel's reputation and earnings soared, and his office in Canary Wharf was a monument to his tenacious work ethic.

When the call came from Jersey, his heart sank, Robert and Simon were formidable former clients of his. He never thought that he would be asked for his assistance in a criminal matter. Simon must have a financial connection to Robert, and knowing Robert, if he was going to commit suicide by hanging himself, he would borrow the rope. He arrived in Jersey, the information he had was scant, Simon would expect that when he was in the interview room, he would be asked polite questions and be answered with an unequivocal "no comment" This would not happen today.

***

Edwina sat alone in Armstrong's office, she was in a bullish mood; her trip to New York had exceeded all expectations. Armstrong had been in a meeting with the department's big hitters; they controlled everything amongst themselves. Jonathon Gove's death caught everyone unaware, apart from Armstrong. Apparently he had sent Edwina over to New York because he had long suspected that Jonathon Gove and David Fisher were involved in financial matters that were unlawful. Jonathon Gove's murder bore his suspicion out. When Armstrong explained to Edwina this was going to be his story, she was horrified. Armstrong explained by embellishing the reason for her trip, he could secure much needed additional funds for surveillance trips like this and for funding informants in and around London's airports.

When she had returned to London Armstrong told her to take a few days off so she can get over any jet lag and adjust to the UK time zone; this would be the perfect opportunity to visit various estate agents and view properties, she was careful to arrange property newspapers scattered around her home. Whether Armstrong was behind the surveillance embedded in her Smart TV was now a moot point, the noisy neighbour who had an alternative lifestyle would be the specious reason for her moving home. She would study Armstrong's face and body language when she informed him that she was looking for another house/flat. If he tried to hide obvious signs of disappointment; he was party to the surveillance operation. If his body language changed when she told him of the mishap of damaging her Smart TV, that would confirm he was behind it

The meeting must have gone well, she could hear him cracking jokes with some of her colleagues, he came into the office with a face that suggested this particular cat had secured an ample amount of cream. 'How are you…and before I forget, you did a magnificent job over in New York, these are not just my words they're from the Eton boys, every one of them, they have agreed to additional funding as well.'

'I've not seen you this happy since you hooked up with that American tourist.'

He sat down at his desk. 'Very amusing Edwina, but that was in the past… it must've been a bit of a shock to you that Jonathon Gove was bumped off in Central Park?'

'You could say that, when David Fisher met him in New York, I thought that would be the only surprise, but how wrong was I? Has there been any development on the reason why he was assassinated?'

'Officially it is like nothing happened, but my initial assessments are money laundering, or he had ripped someone off, do you have any theories?'

'I am thinking along the same lines as you that would be logical, but who and why? He was a British citizen; I thought you would have a copy of the NYPD's report?'

'I do, just a preliminary report mind you, they are looking into his stay in New York and who he had met. David Fisher's statement doesn't hide anything. He mentioned he lived in the same block as Jonathan. They worked for various clients, just a twist of fate that they had to meet in New York. However, this was David Fisher's only business in New York, unlike Jonathon Gove, who had a long list of clients; David was just one of them scheduled. Jonathon Gove was a person of interest to the authorities in New York.'

'Who told you that, or is it in the preliminary report?'

He removed his elbows from his desk, a sure sign he was ready to go on the defensive.

'It's not in the preliminary report and it won't be in the final report either, but don't press me on my source Edwina, okay?'

'Okay, I understand that…who is your source then?'

He stood up from his chair and kicked it backwards. 'Don't ask Edwina, things are changing, that's all I can say, but don't ask again… I mean it!'

'Okay, I understand, there is no need to shout, is there anything else you need to tell me?'

'I'll tell you once I have more info. I noticed you have advised HR you'll be moving house soon, something about a neighbour, do you want to tell me anything more?'

'He's just a pain, anti-social, music and the slamming of doors, I've spoken to him but he said I'm racist?'

'But you're British of Asian background, not white, I don't understand?'

'Welcome to my world.'

'Is there any particular area that you prefer?'
'No not particularly, but definitely near a gym preferably within walking distance of my new home.'
He smiled. 'Yes, I can understand that'
'Ha, ha, you can talk! You wouldn't get on Ryanair with that stomach you would have to place it in your hold luggage.'
'Your hips are expanding Edwina, you are doing yourself a favour; you've got to take stock when you're getting on you have to watch what you eat, and I'm talking from experience.'
'Fuck me! You've obviously ignored your own advice! And I'm getting on? I've not hit forty yet, I bet you can't remember your forties?'
'Just passing on lifestyle hips, I mean tips Edwina, and I didn't need to cause any offence.'
'I'm not offended; the only offence you cause is to your mirror in the morning.'
'Can, we please get back to the serious subject of Jonathon Gove please?'
'Of course, he was a keen jogger you know, have you thought of taking up jogging to shift your bloated stomach?' She was still annoyed at him.
'Forget my rugged figure for the moment, I'll try to find out more about Jonathon Gove's clients, I don't expect too much information from the American spooks, but they may surprise us, but I doubt it?'
'If they have intelligence on him, are they obliged to share it?'
'They should, but they won't reveal all if it implicates them in any way.'
'What do you mean implicates them, are you suggesting the CIA could have been involved in Jonathan Gove's murder?'
'I am not ruling anything out, we are in a surreal world of intelligence, and cooperation descends into adversarial turf wars. And the Eton boys bend over without any encouragement, but it's in their nature to do that anyway.'
'So what you are implying is coffee, cookies and small talk will be more beneficial than complaining about them withholding intelligence to upstairs?'
'Definitely. It's always been done this way, if they are obstructive, they could be involved either directly or having a proxy carry out their dirty work.'
'Even though David Fisher has passed the sniff test by the American's I think we should put him under surveillance, but not inform our American colleagues about this, what do you think?'
'We are of the same opinion, it wouldn't do any harm, but don't go overboard, this is a superficial surveillance operation, when he leaves home, who does he meet, and when he comes home.'

'Be best to do this while I'm gathering information on Jonathan Gove's clients. If we're fortunate some financial transaction might open the door to something more substantive.'

'I doubt if there is anything that is illegal in his records. He was a trader in the City for years, he would know all the methods to cover any dodgy trades; and he would have known people up the food chain, if there were any enquiries from outside organizations, the Serious Fraud Office or the City of London Police. History has shown, very few traders are charged or convicted.'

'Well we can only hope that the Department of Justice, CIA or a trader with a grudge or conscience gives us a lead.'

'Gives *you* a lead; this is your baby Edwina, and it's off the books. If you need additional resources come to me, no paperwork required, nothing to connect you to David Fisher, our mantra is if we solicit information about David Fisher it came from investigating Jonathan Gove.'

'I know I shouldn't ask, but any information that you have or comes available about David Fisher you'll pass onto me immediately?'

'Of course, and if something goes wrong on your surveillance of David Fisher, and you'll have to have a copper bottomed story why you were at a particular location?'

'I'm well aware of that, my proposal is to start immediately, I want his house under surveillance, externally and internally, there is a lamppost across the street from his block, a camera can be fitted up very quickly, and internally, it shouldn't cause too many challenges.'

He studied her momentarily; this was music to his perfectly attuned ears. 'I'll have this done externally in the next few days; once it's done I'll give you the code for accessing the camera and recorded footage. Internally might prove a little bit more difficult than I hoped, but we will see when I establish when he is not in the house, I'll arrange it.'

'And I would like to be present when the operatives are actively installing the surveillance in his apartment.'

He laughed. 'That ain't going to happen. So forget about that. Why the sudden interest in installing surveillance equipment?'

'Just curious, that's all; don't you remember it was you who told me to stay curious?'

'Yes, and I knew you were going to quote me, but this is an off the books operation, if things go wrong and you're rumbled, it's you on your own. If you are not there, you can't identify any operative entering the apartment. This is not America, there is no probable cause here, and thank the Lord for that.'

She was well aware he wouldn't agree, but she enjoyed pushing him to the limit. 'As it's off the books, I thought…'

'...no, and I won't budge on it.'
'Fair enough, I was just thinking out loud, but I can see from your point of view why it's not doable.'
'You may thank me in the future for declining your request.' She felt uneasy at this, but wouldn't ask for him to clarify this terse short statement.
'Maybe, I'm just getting caught up in the moment. When will you be meeting our American colleagues?'
'As soon as they request a meeting, that is why I'm perturbed, everything has died. When it hit the news that Jonathon Gove had been murdered while sitting on a bench in Central Park, communication was exchanged back and forth over the Atlantic as you would expect. But the NYPDs investigation has halted any further information requests. Again, most unusual, something's not right here, Edwina.'

It was unusual for Armstrong to raise concerns so early into an investigation. However, she shared his concern, but would not voice this. She couldn't envisage any goodwill by doing this.
'At least we all know where we stand with the Americans, they really are full of themselves, but if we had their funding, maybe we would have a swagger like them; our self-importance has always been at minimum, sometimes that's good other times not so good.' He perked up at this. It was not like Edwina to be too pessimistic.
'Feed their egos, tell them how we appreciate their help, and they can't help it, they'll let something drop, as I said they can't help it. And don't feel inferior Edwina, they'll pick up on it and clam up.'
She was just ready to explain why she didn't feel inferior, when he held up his hand he had received a text. He instantly looked at it, and smiled.
'Good news then, your American tourist back on the scene?'
'It's much better than that Edwina, but its personal, and I can't indulge you with any information' His text revealed two smiley faces.

***

The irritating rap on the cell door was not designed for him to gently awake from his peaceful slumber. The clanking keys turning in the lock concentrated his mind. Nigel walked in, he was not looking too pleased, perhaps he had plans for the day, and his unexpected flight to Jersey had curtailed them. He held up his finger to his lips, and sat beside him.
'Sorry for dragging you out here Nigel, but it is unavoidable. Who would've thought Robert would hang himself?'
'Is that a rhetorical question? 'He wasn't smiling.
' No, it's a genuine question...is everything okay Nigel?'

'We will soon see, but I think they have something to connect you with his death, but we will soon find out. Why were you over in Jersey, was it solely to meet Robert Sampson?'

'Wait a minute, Nigel, are you not getting ahead of yourself, a connection, what do you actually mean?'

'Forget that, for the minute, you were over here because you had arranged a business meeting with him, is that correct?' He encouraged Simon to confirm this.

'Yes, that is correct, I've known, or knew Robert Samson for years, he worked in the City…

'…okay. Do you have any concern for your personal safety at this moment in time?' He was looking into his eyes; he wanted him to say yes. Now he was concerned the in and out scenario after a brief interview was looking optimistic.

'Yes, but I'd rather not talk about it, just now.'

'I understand that Simon, have you felt less safe since relinquishing your services from a Russian client?' Simon was feeling queasy, Nigel must be aware of his spontaneous appointment and being encouraged to enter the car in the car park of his gym, to meet a concerned Russian client. But he managed to soothe their concerns, it was a misunderstanding. He required the same answer.

'Yes.'

Nigel stood up; he encouraged Simon to do likewise. 'That's all you have to say, we will be out of here in an hour tops, I came over on a private jet, and you'll be on it with me. There were no lines of anxiety on Nigel's face, he was not assuming this; he was stating this as a fact.

'Okay.' Nigel rapped on the cell door, after a few seconds the door opened; he indicated to Simon to follow him, they were walking to the interview room. After sitting down he stated his name, address and occupation. Nigel formally introduced himself to the two detectives. Simon explained why he was over in Jersey and the purpose of his meeting with Robert Samson. Then the polite questioning became devoid of any neutrality. Nigel was taken aback at this sudden change.

'Simon, it would be best if you explained everything today… Robert Samson, did you encourage him to hang himself, because he had not kept his side of the bargain in a financial matter?'

'Detective Wilson, it would be better for all if you removed the accusatory tone from your questions.'

He ignored Nigel. 'Why was the needle in your car?'

Simon looked at Nigel; he nodded for him to answer. 'It's not my needle.'

'Then how did it get in your car?'

'You and your colleague are the detectives, I'm just a simple ex-City trader who has made millions, and this fucking interview has ended!' He stood up. Nigel requested a moment with his client. Detective Wilson looked at his colleague smiled and asked him to terminate the interview at the lawyer's request. 'Take your time,' he said to Nigel. Nigel took Simon into the corridor.
'What are you doing, you're looking like you have something to hide!'
'I'm not taking any more of this, let's go in there and get this over. They can't charge me, can they?'
'Do what I say, and drop the belligerence, no they can't charge you unless they have evidence, and they've not disclosed that They're on a fishing expedition, look they want this to be suicide, they don't want a murder on Jersey. Your outburst has not helped, when we go in here, I'll apologise on your behalf, you're upset because he was a colleague, client and friend. Now, behave okay?'
'Okay, but the way he delivered the questions...what about the needle?'
'No problem with that that's his job, forget the needle, it's not yours. You didn't handle it?'
'No, I didn't know it was there, it was in the glove compartment. Someone's must've used it, then forgot to get rid of it.'
'It's not yours, end of. Now smile and behave, if I touch your arm end your answer immediately."

They entered and sat down; Nigel apologised and embellished how upset he was. The detectives acknowledged and accepted his apology. Rudimentary questions were asked and answered in a relaxed manner. 'To clarify, the needle in the car is it yours and did you handle it?'
'It's not mine, and I didn't handle it, I wasn't aware it was in the car...'
Nigel lightly touched his arm.
'Have you had or did you have any disagreement with Robert Samson in the past or more recently?'
'No.'
'Did you come over to Jersey to kill him or assist him in taking his own life?'
'No.'
'Are you aware of anyone who wanted harm to come to him?'
'No.' Nigel tapped him on the arm, and asked for the recording equipment to be paused while he consults his client. Simon was perplexed. Nigel and Simon returned to the corridor.
'Simon, this is where you say, that a few months ago Robert confided in you that Russians had threatened to kidnap him and kill him, about a deal that went sour, you don't know the details, you also feel your life is in

danger because of your association either through friendship or business with Robert Samson.'
'Whoa! I'm getting confused here, what's going on here, I'm getting dragged into something that's getting dangerous.'
'Simon do you trust me?'
'Up to a point... yes.'
Nigel wasn't expecting this less than fulsome endorsement. 'I'm disappointed in your answer…but you have to trust me, and follow my instructions, you have to trust me Simon.'
'You'll have to explain more, I'm not going to say all of that, no way.'
'Well, if that's your informed decision, you'll have to seek other legal representation, I can't risk my reputation.'
'What?'
'You heard me Simon; you either accept my legal advice in its entirety or you have to engage another lawyer who may or may not offer you alternative legal advice.'
'What kind of choice is that?'
'Your choice?'
'I'm not happy, I'll tell you that.'
'We either go in there together or you go in alone, I don't have time for this Simon.'
'We go in together, but I'm not happy.'
'You said that previously. When we go in sit down and say nothing until I explain to the detectives the background to what you are about to say. You got that?'
 Simon nodded and walked back to the interview room, his mind couldn't remove the warning signs that this was going to end badly. His life depended on Nigel's legal advice. He was not fully confident that his hurried agreement was a wise decision. He sat down and Nigel explained to the weary detectives; but perked up when Nigel mentioned Russian organized crime. Nigel sat down, Simon was perplexed when Nigel stood up and explained, why can't he just sit down and explain?
 Simon looked at the detectives they were eager to hear his worrying tale or web of lies. Simon was ambivalent himself. However, Nigel was the lawyer, normally his advice was sound. Simon explained how Robert was concerned by the Russian mafia using him to launder money, when he discovered this he told the Russians he was terminating their business relationship forthwith. All monies had been returned minus his fee. Nigel was not concerned he had gone off script; he certainly had the detectives' undiluted attention. Then tears started to settle on his cheeks, he made no attempt to wipe them away, some fell onto the desk, Nigel handed him his

handkerchief; he was impressed. Then in a hushed tone, he explained how he felt his life was in imminent danger.

The detectives were overwhelmed at the detail Simon had shared with them, they called for a halt of proceedings, when the recording equipment was halted it was clear to Nigel that this was above their pay grade. They had to seek advice from their superiors. Before they left, Nigel explained his client did not feel safe on Jersey, he wished to return to London, he then explained a private jet had been chartered, simply because no risk could be taken by using scheduled airlines. He then explained Simon had come over to Jersey on a whim, if he had known this he would have strongly advised against this course of action. His client could be interviewed in London at any time as long as it was identified as a safe location. They wished to return to London immediately, can they emphasise this to their senior officers? They left without any comment. Nigel was optimistic they would be leaving very soon. Simon's concern for his own life after discovering Robert's lifeless body hanging in the bathroom had now been shared with the detectives, however, nothing could guarantee that they would be allowed to leave without a more comprehensive explanation. The door closed, and they were left to contemplate what had just been revealed.

'It must have been difficult when you discovered Robert's body, but it may sound callous, but you have to be concerned for your own safety now. It would only be a matter of time before there is a leak from here, to a newspaper in Jersey or in London.'

'I can't see the police getting to the truth of Robert's death. His financial records will be scrutinized, but they can only examine what is in his records, not what he had left out.'

Nigel was not intending to discuss Robert's financial matters, but he agreed with Simon's sentiment, his tax returns would be exemplary; however, his other business which would have not been declared or would be operated by a third-party would be very difficult to expose. Nigel had assisted clients in establishing accounts that were not in clients' names, therefore could not come under any scrutiny. Simon was fully compliant in tax avoidance schemes. However, would he venture into criminal activity when he was a very wealthy individual? Highly unlikely.

***

CHAPTER FOUR

The view from the Sidlaw hills towards the rejuvenated city of Dundee was impressive and beneficial to the cross-party parliamentary committee on Renewable Energy. Lord Alexander Marr had studied at Dundee University he enjoyed the night life, but the city at that time was in the process of being deindustrialised, heavy industry and light engineering manufacturing factories were closed and plant and equipment transferred to former Soviet satellite countries in the European Union; and bizarrely the European Union allocated millions of pounds to assist the transfer, Dundee was not on its knees; it was prostate. But that was then. Now it had reinvented itself, the V & A at the Waterfront was the last throw of the economic dice for the Scottish Government, council and its weary citizens. But today could or should change the mood of the city into unprecedented optimism. The independent coterie of engineers, academics and environmentalists were a unified group, the Sidlaw hills would be the largest renewable energy (wind turbines) site in Scotland. Lord Alexander had taken the party to the newly constructed aircraft hangar type sheds where the wind turbines would be designed and constructed, 1400 well-paid jobs would be created, and other wind turbines for other sites in the UK and in the E.U. would be constructed and shipped from the adjacent docks. Dundee would be the hub of renewable energy. Fossil fuels would be discouraged in the energy markets; however, some extreme environmentalists were totally against the Sidlaw hills as the site of the wind turbines. However, there was an incentive that would overcome their genuine outrage; a bespoke factory to produce batteries for electric vehicles would be built in Dundee, in which the batteries would be charged from the wind turbines from the Sidlaw hills; notwithstanding the 800 permanent jobs that the factory would employ. The electricity would also be purchased to power Ninewells hospital in the city saving millions of pounds in crippling energy costs to the NHS. But the sweetest of all cherries on top of the environmental cake; the renewable energy would require no subsidy from the Scottish government, the wind turbines would be exporting electricity to the National Grid, earning the private company (Pavel's) millions of pounds in which the company would pay much needed corporation tax. The Scottish government had agreed to financially contribute to the construction costs of the green battery factory. It was rumoured to be £10 million. That was exaggerated; it was £9 million. However, the cost benefit analysis would make this £9 million assisted grant seem parsimonious. Right on cue the strong wind that was forecast made the group hold onto various headgear; they studied their individual iPads with the detailed map of each individual wind turbine, the proposed new roads for the construction site were highlighted on their maps, costs were in the sidebars and the estimated carbon savings, electricity produced and returns from surplus electricity sold to the National Grid were impressive. Then the costs to Ninewells Hospital were reduced significantly that they were planning another specialised treatment centre with the estimated savings.

Lord Alexander Marr was delivering information in a calm and reasonable manner, any concerns were kept to a minimum, councillors, MSPs and MPs were part of this renewable energy revolution, political differences were quietly tossed into the strong wind, money was needed for day to day services, the cash generated would see them embrace prototype residential and commercial refuse vehicles, thus saving money on fossil fuels and reducing their carbon footprints. The wind was increasing in velocity; they had all agreed this was the perfect site, however, Lord Alexander Marr would not curtail his verbosity; there would be no dissenters. At last he ended the informative speech with personal platitudes, they were the political pioneers who had overcame political ideology to benefit this generation in creating sustainable jobs, and making the air and environment cleaner and healthier, and sustainable for future generations, who obviously weren't here today, but would thank all of them when they are all just a memory, but a lasting memory.

Some hardened politicians were having difficulty in restraining tears at this emotive speech. Coat collars were being upturned by the ferocious wind. Lord Alexander Marr had the forecast sent to him three days ago, the wind was due to drop in the next thirty minutes, it was time to thank all of them for being brave politicians, it was time to return to the Apex hotel for a warming lunch, The wind was due to increase by another twenty-eight per cent in the next thirty minutes he repeated, they would all return to the electric vehicles and have a long lunch. There were no dissenters or searching questions they were all on board, and they all felt good about themselves. Future generations would remember them with affection. The afternoon had been meticulously planned and wind speeds manipulated, today Lord Alexander Marr was in tune with individuals who on paper could have proved difficult to deal with, but his well-researched personal dossiers had not required any financial measures to assuage them.

***

Gwen was in the bathroom; David was at his desk studying the screen of his iMac intently he now regretted boasting to Gwen about his vanity mirror that had Bluetooth; the music was loud and definitely not to his taste. He was never a fan of Michael Jackson. But he kept this to himself.
She shouted; 'I hope this music isn't too loud, and is to your taste?'
'No, not at all, I've always been a fan of 'Thriller.'
For his sake he hoped his neighbours were too. The music stopped, she came through to the lounge, dressed in emerald green silk pyjamas, her wet hair was combed back, the sunlight on her face revealed wrinkles that he hadn't noticed before, he was indifferent to them, apart from shaving he never gazed admiringly at his reflection. She came over and placed her hands on his shoulder and joined him gazing at the screen.
'Anything interesting today?'
'I wish... world markets are still in a bull market, and that makes me a happy boy.' Her eyes quickly processed the information, she walked away: 'do you want a coffee?'
'Yes but I'll get it,' the screen went blank and was locked. This didn't go unnoticed. She had an hour to kill before she went to her main office; she was an investment banker that had been headhunted from JP Morgan who was aware of her being disillusioned with her terms and conditions with her incumbent Investment Merchant Bank. She received $400,000 as a 'golden hello' and a generous relocation allowance. She was the one who had gone off-grid to confront her boss. He had been sending her meticulous researched notes to traders and passing them off as his own, without her knowledge, and collecting a six figure bonus. It was time to seek new pastures; a lawyer's letter was sent to the C.E.O, fraud and sex discrimination suits would follow. A 'golden goodbye' settlement was negotiated by her lawyer, and past bonuses were also recouped. She instructed him to draft another impromptu document. She returned to her apartment in Tribeca (Lower Manhattan) woke her recently unemployed husband of three years from his alcohol induced slumber and gave him the stark news. He had five minutes to sign these papers, the apartment would be hers; in exchange he would receive $700,000 in his account in ten minutes, and he would agree to a 'no fault divorce.' If he didn't adhere to her generous offer, she would contact the Security and Exchange Commission and hand over a flash drive (which she held between fore finger and thumb) that contained his trades and emails from another source

(insider trading). To assist him in reaching a wise decision, she said she would call the NYPD to report being assaulted by her drunken husband; if he didn't remove himself immediately from the apartment. He enquired who the men were outside; when no answer was returned he surmised to himself it would be her American-Italian relatives. The dull debilitating effect of alcohol soon left him in a clear state of mind. The previous severe beating left him with cracked ribs, and advised the next time he would be leaving the apartment by the window. He scrawled his signature on the document, took his wallet and car keys from the marble table and left with no audible sound. Her two cousins changed the locks on the large heavy door. Their advice to him was carried into the apartment. He didn't reply only the sound of his footsteps hurrying down the stone stairs could be heard. Another abusive husband bites the dust; the third–time lucky cliché was confined to the dustbin. Never, ever again would she walk down the aisle apart from the supermarket.

   She walked towards the large former garment factory window. How many impoverished women had gazed out of this window over a century ago with the same thought, "there's gotta be better times ahead?" She was not impoverished, but her soul was yearning for a meagre amount of happiness to visit her once in a while. New York City was the city that never slept, but how many torn people in the city couldn't sleep peacefully without a joint or sleeping tablets? Her childhood in Brooklyn was disfigured by poverty, but the house was filled with laughter. How she would exchange her worldly goods for a smidgeon of those hungry happy days. The years were flying past, but she knew out there in this crazy world there was someone who would love her and make her happy. But where?

   Her mobile rang and shook her out of the melancholic mood. It was her friend Avery, effervescent and the world's greatest optimist. She wanted to go out tonight; she had great news, but wouldn't disclose it to her if she didn't agree to hit the bars and clubs in Manhattan. She didn't need any encouragement, she had news for her as well, the conversation stretched and she felt better, for the moment anyway. She was on paid leave. Fate would smile on her tonight.

***

   Footsteps could be heard travelling at speed in their direction, Nigel smiled at Simon, 'here they come, now don't panic if they are playing hard-ball, just stay quiet and let me do the talking; shouting will get you nowhere except back to the cells, do you understand?'
 Simon was taken aback at this schoolboy scolding, he felt like informing him, that he is being well paid but decided that was unwise. The door opened the two detectives stood at the rear of the two younger men; they

were carrying thin folders. Nigel's heart sank; he hoped they had bulging folders; normally this was to instil fear into the suspect that they had an abundance of information about the suspect.

In the folders could be a warrant signed by a judge that they could detain the suspect for a considerable length of time. Simon took the polar opposite view, less information about him, the more chance of him being released. They introduced themselves, Nigel was perturbed that they were young and in important positions. They all sat down. The detective asked Simon, to listen to the recording carefully; after it ended, did he want to add, remove or change part of his statement or answers? They had listened intently Nigel made copious notes; this was just theatre they were of no consequence. Simon looked at Nigel for guidance, he looked away, and told his captive audience that he was content with the original statement and answers to the questions put to his client.

'This has been an experience that my client has had great difficulty in coming to terms with. He has extensive knowledge of international finance; he has travelled to inhospitable countries outside the European Union, he's an avowed capitalist the more risk the more reward, all legal I may add. However, he has come to genteel Jersey to meet his client, former colleague and close friend. The first sighting of Simon is his lifeless body hanging from the roof. He was not aware of any financial problems at the time, but he was aware that a business deal had gone awry with a Russian client, because of my client's close association with his former friend; he feels his life is under threat, and wishes to leave Jersey as soon as you have completed your interview with him, which I assume you have. I have given you his contact details; however, if you wish him to assist you in the future, contact my office and we will arrange a suitable place and time to meet at your behest.' The two detectives subtly acknowledged the nod from their two senior colleagues. They rose in unison and left the room.

'Here are the details of the appointment for next week, this is your copy, we have ours; we have been instructed to get you back to London within the next hour. We are not happy with this at all, but when Russians were mentioned, and a suspicious death occurs, I have to pass this onto London. I don't know what is actually going on here, but the information I have is your client is being less than truthful, and he has been tracked here since he left London. But I believe your client, regarding fearing for his life. A private jet flew in from Cyprus yesterday and is due to fly back tomorrow morning. The flight manifest indicates that four Russian businessmen are passengers; they are over here to combine business and pleasure; was their "business" to confront Robert Samson and have the "pleasure" of watching him being hanged?'

Nigel had to gather his thoughts; Simon's epic monologue was actually true! And it was accompanied by real tears. It had just been confirmed before his incredulous eyes and ears. Simon was looking very pale; his eyes were producing visible moisture that had not been missed by anyone. They wanted them off Jersey pronto; it would be a futile gesture to ask about these Russian businessmen, and if they would be detained and interviewed?

'Any questions?'

Simon was still clearly in shock, and was attempting to ask something judging by his body thrusting forward. 'No, none at all, and thank you for your understanding, we will get moving now. C'mon Simon, we've got to go now!' Simon obediently rose and left the room with Nigel.

The two senior officers high-fived each other; 'Now that was impressive, a private jet from Cyprus flying in; short and sweet, they fell for it hook, line and sinker.'

'That would be the least of their worries, *if* Russian hit men were flying into Jersey to kill Robert Samson and Simon Corndale. In reality their fate has been sealed in London. Samson's death is out of the Jersey police's hands, and it has fallen into our (MI5) lap. Simon Corndale will be on high alert, but when I speak to his lawyer next week, and advise him that his client has been eliminated from our enquiries, but no correspondence confirming this will be exchanged due to a live suspected international crime investigation.'

***

The large chapel was cold and uninviting in the east end of London; the priest did his best to overcome his disappointment at the lack of mourners; only David and Gwen were present. The priest read out a short biblical passage, he segued from the biblical text; he placed a sheet of paper in the large bible and closed it. He informed David and Gwen that Jonathan was a regular worshipper at his chapel; he always stood at the rear of the chapel, and a woman was always by his side, from his view from the altar he would guess she was in her forties. They made a conscious decision to stay apart from other worshippers, and they routinely left a few minutes before the mass ended, which he thought was unusual. He had never requested confession from the elderly priest. Jonathan's funeral instructions were clear; he would be cremated and no mourners should be in attendance only the priest. David thanked the priest and the funeral directors then left, only when he was at the end of the long aisle did he look back at the coffin.

Gwen was uncomfortable, she had never witnessed anything similar to this although she had been to a few private funerals, she shivered but it wasn't from the lack of heating in the church. This was odd.

Leaving the chapel in silence, David activated his phone, a slew of messages required his immediate attention, they all carried the same subject; Robert Samson had killed himself. He hadn't shed any tears for Jonathon, and his gut instinct would be to send a smiley face emoji in reply to the thirty messages.
'Good news on this sad day David?' He couldn't help smiling.
'It is very good news, it has made my day, I can't see the day getting any better.'
They were out of the church grounds standing at the tall rusted railings. The messages were coming in thick and fast. It was obvious that they all shared the unrestrained euphoric joy at Robert Samson's unexpected but welcome death, and by his own hand made it taste sweeter. The pubs would be filled all day, tales of duplicitous contracts drawn up by Nigel were legendry; they were legal but punitive. When numerous threats of litigation were relayed to Nigel, his stock answer was "your lawyer studied the contract, take it up with him/her."
Gwen was intrigued by the constant pinging of another message had arrived, it started to irritate her.
'Are you going to tell me the good news then?' He barely looked up at her, as he read the messages; she grabbed the phone from him, and read the vitriolic messages. She deactivated and returned the phone and looked at him and shook her head. 'Nice friends you have David, no one turns up at Jonathan's funeral apart from you and I, then a colleague kills himself and its champagne all round, what kind of company do you keep?'
'Let me explain, Robert Samson was not a nice man!'
'Really? I would have never have guessed!' There are some sick messages there.'
'I'm not going to defend these messages, but Robert drove at least two people to commit suicide, because of his pursuit of riches which he didn't need. He would take people into his confidence and promise them fantastic returns, sometimes he did other times he didn't, that's all I can say, I didn't wish him any harm…but.'
'That's a cop-out David you were smiling reading those sick messages. And I don't want to know what he allegedly did.'
He stopped her from taking another hurried step. 'There is nothing alleged, it was legal but not moral, that's all I can say… due to confidentiality.'
'I'm not interested, whether he was a bastard, that's the nature of New York, Wall Street and other financial cities in Europe, everyone has private thoughts, and may discuss the deceased with a few friends in a bar or over dinner, but not hatred like these individuals, but obviously London is not the city I had imagined it was.' He decided to keep his phone deactivated.

'Are you not going to switch your phone back on then, you can just mute it, that constant ping drives me nuts, I wish I hadn't read any of them.' He activated the phone and muted it; it would be difficult for him to deflect from today. He would stay silent until she spoke, which didn't take long.
'If Jonathan had no family or relatives, and he certainly had no friends, what will happen to the proceeds from the apartment when it is sold, and his other assets, who will receive the money?'
'I don't know, I really don't know.'
'He made a will, which included his funeral arrangements, and he must have named a person or persons to receive his money and assets.'

They reached his car she was going through all the legal requirements that Jonathan had probably formulised but didn't expect to be initiated so soon. In the car her curiosity got the better of her.
'Unmute your phone, surely there can't be anymore messages coming in?'
'I don't think that's a good idea, I'll leave it for another hour, I don't want you getting upset.'
'Just do it David, I promise I won't get upset.'

He did as instructed it was akin to being in a submarine with loud radar picking up a myriad of objects. She burst out laughing. 'There is something delicious of being hated so much is there? I have never met or ever heard of him, but at this moment, I have a sick admiration for him, isn't that weird?'

He sought to 'educate' her on the moral rectitude of Robert Samson, a self-confessed misogynist, but there would be no point, she would soon hear enough tales when she was in bars with her new colleagues, he would not assist in changing her opinion of City traders. London was just a citadel of greed and corruption; coming from New York, she had already unwisely formed a glamorous opinion of the City, on Monday when she took up her position; reality would leave its teeth marks on her well upholstered posterior. He was back in her good books; any contentious future opinion would be sanitised if it meant avoiding domestic conflict.
'Jonathan was a meticulous individual who kept his personal and business life private. Someone will be a very rich individual, who is that person? I don't know. Maybe some of Robert's former colleagues may have overdone the celebration of his death, but the City is like that. Hero or villain is in the eyes of the beholders, envious or misguided individuals.'
'That was very profound David, now can we return to the apartment or do you wish to go for breakfast?'
'I'm happy with either.'
'Breakfast it is then, I'll let you choose the café or pub.'
His eyes took on an unexpected sheen, 'let's go to The Iron Duke, a pub near the apartment, I'll park the car at the apartment then we can walk to

the pub. It's only about a ten minute walk.' He wondered if Lena was on duty, he smiled when he thought about her.

'You're smiling; I hope it's not you thinking about those sick messages again?'

'No, not at all, I was just thinking about breakfast, I'm hungry, that's all. I won't look at the messages I'll delete them instantly.'

'Yes, that would be a good idea, and I won't mention them again either.'

***

    He was not normally a person who felt his life was not in danger, he was contentedly boring in the way he conducted his life, but today after he heard the news of Robert Samson's death, he was shaken. Why would someone come to his office with investment proposals that were studiously researched as he had expected, then kill himself? He instinctively went into his computer to access Robert's account; it was deleted, no trace of it anywhere, nothing in backup, even though he saved it automatically. He rummaged through his desk drawer, silently congratulating himself for the USB that he saved all his high-value transactions. Panic set in, he couldn't find it; he stood back from the desk a sickening feeling was evolving in his stomach. He moved towards the desk closed the drawer and opened it again, he started to take out numerous unused highlighting pens, and scrap pieces of paper that he had shaped into neat squares; in case they came in handy, then it was there, elation ran through his mind. He connected it to his computer; confidence had returned, he studied the information on the screen, Robert Samson's account was not there, he checked the deleted accounts folder, nothing there. He wasn't a computer genius but came to the stark conclusion that his computer had been cloned or hacked; ditto the USB, if his office had been burgled the USB would be gone, but it wasn't. He sat slumped in his worn leather chair and propelled himself backwards from his desk, not removing his disbelieving eyes from the screen. The rumour that Robert had killed himself looked fanciful now. He placed his elbows on his desk and intertwined his fingers, and placed his head in his hands. His head slowly began to rise to study the screen. Paradoxically, this could be a good thing; if there were no digital or paper trace of his account with him; that was good news. Today would be spent diligently examining his computer and phone, including his own bank account on his phone. He took out the phone and accessed his account, nothing from Robert Samson, even though money had been paid through a third-party; that was not present either. The clouds of despair were gone. His money was not there in his statement but it was there in *his* balance. Someone had gone to a lot of trouble to eradicate Robert Samson from his life. He was not complaining, no business colleague or friend were aware he had been a client of his. Robert had accumulated a plethora of enemies; if his death was not suicide, there would be a long list of suspects.

Then the epiphany exploded in his head, he would contact the respected City firm that had been persistent in offering a healthy premium for his business. Time was marching on as his face reminded him every morning and evening. His wife yearned to make their holiday home in the Dordogne valley their permanent home, their two children were well rounded adults and had homes of their own; there were nothing to stop them. He took off his glasses, and spun them between his fingers; his mind was made up. It would happen but on his terms, he would have to sell the house in Surbiton, if he didn't it would always remind him of his life in England. He called the estate agent and explained he wanted someone to value the house today, and on the market within days of this call. His wife would be on the phone later in the day seeking an explanation. He would take great pleasure in informing her that they would be relocating to Dordogne. He had been planning it for over a year; apparently. Then he spoke to his contact that had been spectacularly unsuccessful in trying to woo him, to sell his business. Many meals and expensive dining experiences had all been in vain. His consort had great difficulty in coming to terms that Michael was retiring to France; his quantum that he required would not cause any difficulty in meeting. The prime location of his office was more important than his business, but it would be hurtful if he mentioned this. Michael agreed to meet him for a celebratory dinner that evening, the paperwork that lay in the folder moribund would be all signed and sealed that afternoon. There was no going back. He would inform his wealthy clients that he was retiring to France because of health issues, and that was the sole reason for selling his business, he would recommend them to the new company who had an excellent track record in emerging markets. They would be free to seek out advice about the new business, or go somewhere else. In reality, Michael was not concerned; he had made them millions over the years.

He opened the left hand bottom drawer and pulled out the bottle of malt whisky, and the two glasses, he placed them side by side on his desk, took the phone off the hook and poured two generous measures. He lifted the glasses, clinked them, then he thanked Robert for his business but did not mourn his death, he was sure the granite hearted Robert Samson would agree. If he was still alive he would not have any inkling about moving to the Dordogne or selling his business to his persistent suitor. This office had many memories all positive. Treat people well and they will reciprocate good feeling and generate trust. The hat stand in the corner would be coming with him to the Dordogne; many wealthy individuals had hung their wet overcoats on the four curved pegs. The smoked stained ceiling above his desk reminded him how heavy a smoker he was twenty years ago. Some clients thought it was a water stain from a previous water leak. He would play the reluctant seller at the dinner with a smidgeon of regret. Tears may surface; he would prepare for that moment. When the money was in his account then and only then would he would inform his dining companions at The Ivy that he was retiring to France. No one would ask the price that his business had achieved; as they would already know. Who would have ever conjured up his immediate future plan all came about because of Robert Samson's death? Life is indeed strange.

***

Simon was on his way in a taxi to meet Nigel in his office; he had been called at nine pm the previous evening, he said he couldn't talk over the phone, but he needed to see him in his office at ten am. He had good news. Simon's cajoling for further information was met with Nigel ending the brief phone call. Robert Samson's death was being reported on social media and the press as a businessman who had money problems, nothing was fleshed out. This was the touch paper for the ludicrous conspiracy theories to ferment. It was the Russians (obviously) or Chinese, maybe Americans or an irate husband on Jersey, all good reading for a slow afternoon. To his relief there were no reports of him discovering his body, it was discovered by shocked workmen after they had returned from lunch. He had checked all newspapers, domestic and international; it was only reported in the London and Jersey editions of national newspapers, and it was not prominent. Simon was an expert in transferring funds that would be of interest to curious governments and tax authorities from various bank accounts in the UK to banks dotted all over the world. Panama, the British Virgin Islands and Cyprus were the start of the detailed head spinning odyssey. Robert had broadened his knowledge base of concealing money; Simon was in awe of how careful he had been, and Robert had made it very clear, that he was the only one who was party to this. Simon was sceptical of this, Robert picked up on his scepticism, and took him into his office; he was going to transfer £10 million. And he watched with disbelieving eyes how the money was deposited in an account in Panama and where a green icon would illuminate, then in a nano second would change to red, this was the money being withdrawn then a green light would be illuminated in Cyprus, this process lasted thirty seconds, and had been in four hundred bank accounts throughout the world. The £10 million was 'resting' in Thailand. Robert observed Simon; he was overwhelmed at what he had witnessed in real-time. He took him into his kitchen, sat him down and poured him coffee. He stood at the newly installed granite worktop, and explained the bespoke software that manipulated the wanderlust bank accounts was developed by a Chinese student studying in London, he had called him in the City, he wouldn't explain where he got his number; but he told him to listen, and gave him an address to meet him, Robert laughed and declined. The caller told him to move out of copper in the next five minutes, because he would make the price plummet; when it did he would change his mind. Robert knew how to manipulate markets, he had done so after a tip or was party to 'adjusting' news that would raise or dilute share prices or the derivatives futures market; (for example agreeing to a price for a ton of copper, if you have information that a ton of copper is set to plummet by $1000 and is due to rise at a specific time by$600,if you had information that this was going to happen, you would stay out until the $1000 plummet, then buy.) Copper will be worth more than gold, when electric cars come on stream for the masses.

Robert was disturbed how the Chinese student knew he had thousands of contracts in copper, thus he sold all of them while copper was rising by the minute. Then he watched the value tumble over the next five minutes, it was the longest five minutes in his life, as the price declined various eyes turned to him from irate traders that had bought his copper contracts. From that day he was a titan of the futures market. He met the Chinese student who spoke impeccable English. His house was in Mayfair, he explained over tea that Simon had made *in excess* of £10 million in a day. He asked for £10 million as a commission. Robert laughed, not mocking him, but through fear, he didn't think he would leave his house alive. And he didn't have to ask how he was aware he had made this money; he showed him on his laptop on the table. Then Robert watched £10 million being removed from his account. He was in no position to argue, if he did, he was dead, but he was £30 million up in a day. But what did he want from him? The Chinese student explained in less than a minute. He would set up an account in a shell company in Panama, Robert would be the legal owner, money would be transferred into this account, then he would press transfer on the account and it would begin its journey. If it was that simple why did he need me? Robert thought out loud. You don't need to know was the curt answer. For every transaction completed he got paid £500,000. Simon was enthralled by this; he asked him where did the money come from? Russia was the answer. The Oligarchs stolen money was in numerous London bank accounts; he was removing the stolen money and returning it to the Russian government. He couldn't turn this down. He knew all the risks with dirty money, but he was 'earning' a commission of £500, 000 for clicking a button. The Chinese student had shown good faith by advising him of the lucrative information about the copper price, and because he acted on this information he had made £30 million net. Simon interrupted him in mid flow as he explained a litany of trades he had done with the information he received from the Chinese student, and of course he removed his commission personally. But why did he need Simon? He was doing everything that was required of him, and in addition, he was receiving lucrative inside information that was making him millions.

The Chinese student was 'indisposed'. What did he mean by that, he was indisposed? Robert casually explained he had hung himself at home. He was smiling as he explained, that was the reason he had moved to Jersey; he still had the software on his computer so he could still transfer money from his accounts to accounts abroad. If he needed money which he didn't, he just had to do a couple of clicks and the money would be in Jersey or London. No one had approached him about the laundered money; because they didn't know who he was or where he was located.

Simon was just acting as a broker for investing Robert's money; now he could understand why he was earning an envious commission; however, he was using trusted methods in transferring money to tax friendly countries. Robert had hung himself as had the Chinese student, this made him circumspect. Robert monotonously opined suicide was for losers, and if he were ever to consider suicide it would be by a bullet in the brain. Nigel would be deprived of this information, no matter what news awaited him; it would not be anything to link him to Robert's death. This was the narrative that the police in Jersey had released to Nigel; he would sound and be visibly relieved when Nigel told him in the office. He would only suggest that Robert's death must have been brought on by depression or money worries.

***

She just stepped into the shower, her outstretched open hand welcoming the hot pulsating water from her new power shower, she would be taking the shower when she moved, her old shower had a pitiful and ineffective water pressure; it would be returned to its former niche. Her mobile rang in the lounge, she decided to ignore the loud ringing; it would probably be Armstrong, the surveillance camera was signed off and would be installed in the street light across from Jonathon Gove and David Fisher's apartment block in the next few days. The hot water joyously battered her face, the mobile stopped ringing; then started again, it was Armstrong; she wouldn't be leaving this oasis of warmth, peace and tranquillity. Life was becoming less frantic; her viewing of properties had been narrowed down to three. Her revenge on her unsocial neighbour with a nocturnal lifestyle would be sweet; she would be having a party from two pm till late, she had learned he hated the Rolling Stones and Michael Buble, they would be the artists frequently played at the leaving party in which he would not be invited. He also hated Indian food as well. She would order in curries on the day of the party, so that when he was awakened by Michael Buble and looked out of his window, he would see the curries being delivered; his day would only get worse. The mobile rang again, her resistance remained robust. He would be in a terrible mood because she had not answered her phone; good.

   She wondered if her next house would truly become a home, this had never felt like home, the racist neighbour hadn't brought any serenity to this affluent neighbourhood. However, the sale of her house would bring in a vast profit when it was placed on the market it would be gone in a week. The fully fitted modern kitchen replete with LED lighting was her favourite room; she had not changed anything in her tenure there. Armstrong advised her to gut the whole place including the kitchen; his advice went unheeded, a wise choice. She would be advising him that she was taking a few days off to speak to builders about potential renovations at properties she had viewed; if he asked where they were she would mention affluent areas that she would not be moving to, just to annoy him in which she was an expert. She had to remove herself reluctantly from her Zen moment the mobile was ringing again.

   She terminated the soothing pulsating spray, and grabbed her bathrobe, she took the warm towel from the towel rail, and wrapped her hair loosely in it, her feet slipped effortlessly into her pink slippers. In the lounge she took the ringing mobile from the table.
'Hello?'
'Where the fuck are you? And what's so important that you didn't answer your phone?'
'I was in the shower.'
'Then why the fuck didn't you come out of the shower to answer it?' He was getting angrier.
'Because I have company, that's why.'
'You have company…in the shower?'
'Yes, and it would be rude to leave them…'
'…them?'
'Yes, what's your problem?' She was enjoying this.
'How many are there?'
'More than one less than ten.'
'Are you feeling okay?'
'I'm feeling pleasantly sore, but thanks for your concern.'
'I am concerned, are you suffering from any mental health issue that you want to talk about?'
'No, I've just got an alternative lifestyle, that's all; remember when I asked you to have a word with my racist and unsociable neighbour, and you said "let him live his alternative lifestyle" so your concern for me is wasted. Now what is so important? And get to the point my guests are waiting.'

'The camera will be live in two days' time I'll text the passcode so you can gather any information, and another thing Jonathan Gove's apartment is up for sale, very quick if you understand me, what do you think?'
'I agree, it was very prescient of me suggesting to keep the building under surveillance, anyway got to go, the ladies are becoming impatient, 'bye.'

  Armstrong took the phone away from his disbelieving ear, and stared at the phone for a few seconds. This job throws up numerous surprises every day. He felt vindicated in sending his operative in to install software in her Smart TV. His gut instinct kicked in again. Edwina was intelligent but he had major concerns about her; she could cause him problems in his professional and personal life. He would make sure that the cause of any potential future problem that impacted on him would be eliminated.

***

  On the London Eye, David and Gwen are admiring the view from the stationary pod. Gwen's thoughts are oscillating with her tormented past and the untold future. David was very hard to read, quiet and thoughtful. He came to life in the Iron Duke pub, he obviously enjoyed going there, but she was indifferent. She had tried to raise her numerous concerns about the file that the NYPD detective handed over in the hotel to him. David had shown her the file after the detectives had left. Jonathan Gove's business dealings in New York raised eyebrows when it was discovered he had dealings with Russians. David Fisher was not connected in any way to suspected Russian money laundering; Jonathan Gove was at the epicentre of convoluted deals. That was the NYPD detective's well-thought out and approved written assessment.

  However, things could have been more different and significantly dangerous in the previous informal interview the detective spelled it out to him; regarding Jonathan Gove's and his movements the previous evening and the subsequent violent death of Jonathon; his signed and sealed business agreement he had struck with Jonathan would immediately become invalid and a long and protracted investigation into David's business dealings over the last five years would begin and leaked to the media; to establish if there were any connection to Jonathan's money laundering. The NYPD detective didn't have to explain any more. The NYPD would email the file over to the City of London Police (Economic Crime Unit), he would be advised to contact his lawyer and meet them for an informal meeting; it would be anything but informal. His licence would be suspended indefinitely until all his financial transactions over the last five years were deemed lawful; if he didn't "voluntarily" turn up at their office. He was in a lose-lose situation. Word would leak out into the City, that he is a suspect in the murder of Jonathan and was laundering money for him. Clients would withdraw funds and banks or financial clearing houses would be reluctant to agree to any further loans.

The detective ordered coffee; his female colleague did not utter a single word she just sat beside the detective and stared at David which was unnerving. The waiter brought the coffee pot and cups to the table, after he had left; she poured David a coffee, and returned to her seat. The death of Jonathan Gove was still resonating and causing him extreme anxiety. He naively and politely explained that he was on business, and he was not aware if Jonathan was involved in money laundering. The female detective halted him from adding anything else. "Russian money laundering." Her colleague shrugged his massive shoulders and smiled at him, and encouraged him to drink his coffee. She bent down and removed her designer bag from under the table, the detective was still talking; David's mind was split at what he was hearing and seeing. Her bag sat in front of her, unopened. He then handed David a file, this was his initial findings; he encouraged David to peruse the single page document which was filled with bullet-points.

It didn't make good reading. He had met Jonathan Gove to transfer funds to Jonathan's trading account to purchase stocks, that would be sold immediately, and the purchaser was a bank in Las Vegas. The funds would then be transferred to London. The client of David's was Russian, who *could* be a conduit for the Russian Mafia. The detective's assessment was to arrest David on suspicion of arranging Jonathan's death, and money laundering. David's hand was caught in mid-air, the coffee cup was below his chin, he placed the coffee cup back onto the saucer on the table. He looked at them, they were smiling. He protested his innocence. Their smiles evolved more. The detective retrieved the page and placed it back into the folder, he then slid the other file which contained sheaves of pages. He was insisting that David replenished his coffee. Fear, took over his body as he was encouraged to read the pages. With ultimate reluctance, he read the pages; in utter contrast they stated the truth, he was in New York to conclude a bona fide business deal with a colleague from London; they were frequent dining companions along with other City traders / analysts at The Ivy restaurant in London. He (the detective) had liaised with the City of London police; namely the Economic Crime unit, he was not a P.O.I (*person of interest) although Jonathan Gove was*) conducting legitimate business with David Fisher this was a cover for his real business; money laundering for the Russian Mafia.

Jonathan Gove would replicate David Fisher's recommendations to purchase stock for his legitimate client and buy double or sometimes treble these stocks for the Russian Mafia. David Fisher was an innocent pawn in a carefully constructed strategy. His client is an innocent Russian exile who had British Citizenship and lived a lawful existence in London. His tax files were registered on time and he paid all his taxes that were due. He is a model citizen. Oh, how David enjoyed reading this fair, accurate and honest assessment. Then in all innocence he asked why there are two files that contradicted each another? He was genuinely perplexed. The Ice Maiden let her caged self-imposed reticence some freedom. Her smile and sonorous voice explained the situation, her smile grew thinner she removed an iPhone from her bag, and placed it on the file he had laid on the table next to the empty coffee cup. She then explained they would forward the file that he had just read to the D.O.J. (Department of Justice) and allow him to leave. However, if this was his preferred choice, $2 million would immediately be transferred to this account, her colleague, reminded David that this was not up for any negotiation, they were aware he had various accounts all exceeding this amount. Or if he didn't comply they would call in the two police officers outside the door to take him downtown, where he would be held overnight, and appear in court tomorrow morning in connection with Jonathan Gove's death and money laundering for the Russian mafia. He would be remanded in jail, and they would ask the judge not to release him on bail as he was a flight risk. He had never felt extreme fear in all his life as this was not a maybe or could happen to him; it would.

He didn't offer any resistance, $2 million was a very small price to pay from his commission, and the pound was rising against the dollar, he took out his phone and transferred the money. The ping from her phone indicated the transaction was complete. She lifted the phone, examined the screen looked at him and nodded. The detective was very casual as he explained the next step; they would meet for coffee and he would explain that everything is in order, and he would give him the copy of the file that would be sent to the D.O.J. and the Economic Crime Unit, exonerating him from the death of Jonathan Gove. She then rose from the table and encouraged him to walk to the door. They stood at the door, she rapped her knuckles on the door, it was opened by the police officer, and in his view and his colleague's he watched her smile, shake his hand and thank him profusely for his cooperation. He just stood there with a fixed slight smile as she shook his hand. The lonely walk to the elevator became less painful; the elevator attendant smiled and asked which floor. He answered the lobby. Gwen had told him not to worry, she was in and out when she gave her statement, it seemed he had been interviewed for hours; he hadn't.

She was waiting in the lobby; she commented how he looked very shaken; but understood he had been through a traumatic experience. She hadn't pressed him on the questions he had been asked, he just said he was glad it was all over. He wanted a drink, but changed his mind wisely and agreed with Gwen they should have a seat and have coffee. There were a few tables vacant. He was desperate to be home in London, he thought to himself this would probably be his last time in New York, even if it meant forfeiting future lucrative business. Then the thought, had these rogue detectives anything to do with Jonathan's death? Had they in fact murdered him? And also they were aware of his dining companions in London, and that they dined in The Ivy. How did they know that? Because Jonathan was under surveillance and they were all noted as potential moving parts in a money laundering conspiracy? He laughed at Michael Ogilvie being part of any conspiracy, a genuine and honest man who had maintained the old City mantra "my word is my bond." He wouldn't be asked in The Ivy how his trip to New York had gone. It was all in the newspapers. Or it may not be mentioned at all. Some of them may have known of Jonathan's undisclosed and unlawful behaviour, but no one would confess to this. Gwen was talking, but he wasn't listening, his thoughts were drowning out her small talk. She then pulled on his arm; the two detectives were en-route to their table. He hoped they weren't coming back for more money, he quickly chased that thought away; Gwen was in his company surely they wouldn't do this? He smiled and stood up and invited them to join them for coffee. Gwen didn't try to hide her antipathy towards her, for a NYPD detective the clothing allowance must be very generous; not so for her male colleague, who she surmised wasn't a member of a gym. They seemed to make David the centre of attention, he just smiled in return. Then his face lit up like the Christmas tree at the Rockefeller Centre. He handed his file to David; she couldn't understand what joy this could possibly bring him. It was obvious they were in a hurry; they smiled and left. As soon as they had left, Gwen asked why the file was so important. He just said it was for insurance purposes, Edwina had observed this curious meeting wryly.

***

In Norfolk the unending poly-tunnels were ready to unburden their treasure once again. Jonathan Gove may be gone but his legacy was still bearing fruit, if only he had been honest, he wouldn't have been released from his mortal coil so swiftly. He walked up the path with bountiful cannabis plants on each side touching the leaves, like a mother protecting a small child. These cannabis plants were destined for the lucrative overseas market, fifty countries had legitimised medicinal cannabis; these plants were being exported to Canada, the latest, but not the last country to legalise medicinal cannabis. Lord Alexander Marr had been the focal point in opening the door in the United Kingdom, for the government to consider legalising medicinal cannabis, after five years Jonathon had calculated that cannabis would be completely legal, whether consumers were using cannabis in joints or in vapes. Keep your eye on governments around the world was his byword.

In the United States, Governors in impoverished and underfunded states were minded to legalise and tax cannabis, opiates that were prescription drugs had caused an epidemic in drug deaths, cannabis was safer and raised revenue. Jonathan Gove had predicted cannabis would be the next dot.com phenomenon, banks and hedge funds would be investing millions into subscribed suppliers of medicinal cannabis, Jonathon had seen the future very clearly, cannabis being sold in vaping shops and high street chemists. His strategy would be to have cannabis shops in every town and city throughout the UK and in Ireland on a franchise basis; all would be operated and licensed by local government overseen by government inspectors. Jonathan had said that for this financial investment to succeed, respected politicians would be needed to lobby the NHS. Pavel knew the perfect fellow.

However, they had to play the long game before any intense lobbying began. A shell company was formed, and various legal cannabis farm owners were wooed in London, the new investors were ethical, they had studies that proved that cannabis in various forms, but especially oils, could alleviate pain from debilitating ailments. They wanted to invest in latest technology to assist rapid growth of the cannabis plants. The owners would have shares allocated to them and a golden "hello payment" would be paid. They would be on the board simply because they had the experience and expertise to expand their business. What was not said was that these owners had held a government licence to cultivate cannabis under strict conditions. Without a licence, it did not matter how much money was waiting ready to invest; they needed the incumbent licence holder on board. The last thing the new shell companies wanted was a wild-west auction for new government licences. Lord Alexander Marr would lobby to restrict any new licences that would become available when cannabis became legal. Big Pharma shared the same thought.

Pavel had studied the synopsis from Jonathan intently. Over £400 million had been invested in European cannabis firms in the last year, Jonathan had predicted with much certainty that MEPs and European Commissioners had been lobbied and incentivised. Cannabis would be legal in the European Union; investors from Europe would be allowed to invest and own companies that cultivated cannabis and exported to countries around the world that had legalised cannabis. This revelation was seared into Pavel's consciousness. Lord Alexander Marr in his days as a Labour MP was resolutely against the "capitalist EU that would drive down wages for British workers," he would be encouraged to campaign for the UK to leave the European Union. If this objective was achieved it would be the UK government and not the European Union who would award the finite licences to cultivate and export cannabis. Lord Alexander Marr would insist that the successful companies that were awarded a licence would donate cannabis in various forms to the NHS. This was Pavel's idea, but he would insist that Lorna would suggest this to Lord Alexander Marr.

A myriad of ideas were racing through his head as he bent down to sniff the aroma, the figures were impressive, £5 billion was the estimated figure of the black market value of cannabis in one year. Pavel dismissed this figure as not even half the true value. Ninety-five tons of legal cannabis / marijuana were produced in 2016, more than any other country in the world or in the European Union which was a moot point that did not cause any concern; 125% rise in shares in a pharmaceutical company that Jonathan had invested on Pavel's behalf over the last 3 years. Jonathan insisted cannabis was the future for massive returns in investment. Who would have thought placing illegal laundered money into cannabis would become *lega*l, *profitable and governments would extricate taxes from this?* Jonathan Gove didn't think it was absurd, where there was money there was corruption. Unfortunately he should have kept these thoughts to himself.

In the former Soviet Union states that are now part of the European Union, MEPs would be at his beck and call, the European Commissioners for all their verbosity about welcoming these countries in the largest trading block in the world, had many concerns regarding these fledgling democracies and with good measure. The European Commissioners were adamant that no cannabis farms would be granted a licence to cultivate and export cannabis products. Corruption was second nature to these countries and it would take a minimum of at least a generation before this was eradicated. Pavel thought otherwise. If the UK voted to remain in the European Union, the companies that owned and managed the cannabis farms would retain their licences, and the European Union would not deviate from advice from the European Commissioners who would follow Jonathan Gove's (Pavel's) instructions. All bases had been covered.

Again the projected figures were mind boggling; £110 billion was the estimated market figure for legal marijuana / cannabis by 2025, Jonathan Gove's research paper scoffed at this underestimated market figure. Quadruple the £110 billion was his calculated figure, and he was being conservative.

The heat in the poly-tunnel had made him feel uncomfortable. His thoughts came back on track, as a rule he delegated responsibility, Lorna was his eyes and ears on the ground. She watched him carefully as he walked back to his starting point, the solar panels that provided the energy for the poly-tunnels were first generation, however, they would be removed and replaced without interruption to the energy supply. The adjoining massive field had two thousand of out dated solar panels, the owner had been inflating his expenditure and embellishing the benefit of the latest government approved solar panels, however he had claimed that he had renewed them. This claim was patently untrue.

At the meeting in London it was pointed out to the owner that he had claimed that the solar panels were renewed less than a year ago. But after a thorough inspection of the poly-tunnels and also the solar panels in the next field they would have to be replaced, and the government informed; he would be charged with fraud and his licence would be revoked. The owner sat and listened how he would extricate himself from this premeditated criminal enterprise. The company would replace the solar panels at no cost to the owner, he would make an appointment with his lawyer, he wanted to increase his cannabis farm considerably; an additional six poly-tunnels could be erected in the field alongside the new solar panels. After the plans were accepted he would receive a bonus, as a director of the new company. Paperwork would be backdated to coincide with the cost of the removal and installation of the new solar panels. The relief he felt was palpable. He wanted to sign the paperwork to transfer ownership immediately; this was anticipated, Jonathan removed the relevant paperwork from his briefcase, and he duly signed.

Pavel had had invested a significant sum of money as well as faith in Jonathan, maybe it was a mistake to have him based in New York for weeks at a time? However, in the end his actions brought forward the unfortunate incident in Central Park, he was smart, but he didn't come close to the sharks on Wall Street who had met similar repercussions Some guilt was attached to him (Pavel), but action had to be taken which was fast and clean. He had given the go ahead. The surprise meeting with David Fisher and his investment strategy would have made him feel relaxed and less security conscious as Pavel had anticipated. Jonathan had great experience and confidence in removing himself from life-threatening situations, in London perhaps, but not in New York. Jonathan would undoubtedly be missed, he had forecast business opportunities every day; but he was also a thief of other people's ideas or thoughts. He was true to no one but himself. His death would not have come as a surprise, but not on that fateful morning in Central Park .The purchase of the myriad of cannabis farms was left field, but now they were an economic miracle in investment terms. They were his legacy.

He felt Lorna's penetrating stare, she had acquitted herself very well. She had brought to her partner Lord Alexander Marr, the plight of various children and adults who had to buy cannabis to ease chronic pain from street corner drug dealers; thus making victims of ill health participate in criminal acts. Desperate people were flying to Amsterdam and smuggling cannabis as the cost from dealers in their towns, cities or villages were prohibitive, that is not right? He nodded throughout her spontaneous persuasive argument, she didn't advocate for the legal use of cannabis, but for citizens to have *medicinal cannabis* from the NHS, instead of having to buy or worse flying to purchase cannabis from a civilised western country. The seed was planted and his ego was stroked. It was time to campaign on behalf of law abiding citizens to have *medicinal cannabis* available for certain agreed medical conditions. She suggested that he could be the catalyst for change, if he made a speech in the House of Lords regarding this matter, and some other peer stood up and agreed with him, the press would be all over him requesting interviews, he was the darling of the environmental movement, he had room for others to bestow gratitude on him. The government were in turmoil over Brexit they would welcome anything to debate to avoid their ludicrous plans for Brexit.

***

Simon had paid the taxi driver, and unusually for him tipped him, not out of necessity, but he had stayed silent throughout the journey. He stood outside on the pavement beside the concrete monstrosities that were home to synthetic palm trees. This was psychological; any client coming to meet Nigel from the Middle-East or the west coast of America, would notice the two palm trees and think of home, they would feel more relaxed as they made their way through the vast lobby to the elevator, they hadn't commentated on the palm trees because they weren't consciously aware of them, but endorphins had been released, any anxiety would be diluted, and good will would come out later as they signed or discussed contracts. From the moment clients stepped out onto the pavement, Nigel was influencing their thought processes and moods. Personally greeting them as they stepped out from the elevator emphasised the feel good factor, and they had not entered his office yet. In the office, tea or coffee would not be offered, water for middle-eastern clients with no alcohol on display. However, the air would be infused with the scent of various flowers that were a reminder of home. However, Russian clients were less refined; a myriad of premium vodka bottles were strategically in the line of the client(s) vision; and the temperature in the office barely above freezing, even though Nigel was in a white shirt, with no jacket. Simon waited on the elevator door opening, and Nigel standing there with a fixed grin, he practised his worried expression. The doors opened, Nigel was not there, he didn't need to feign a worried expression; he was concerned. He stepped out and made his way to his office, Nigel had always insisted there were no need to knock, if someone needed to talk to him, come in without the polite knock, unless he had a client in. He took a deep breath and walked in, Nigel was not alone, the two young senior officers from Jersey were sitting talking to Nigel, who was reading the document as they gleefully explained what they meant; he was playing for time until Simon arrived. Nigel just gave Simon a furtive look, and returned to reading the information on the sheet of paper, he was told to sit down at the far end of the office. They stood up and said they would be in contact later. Nigel did not stand up, he nodded then they left, not before smiling sarcastically at Simon. As soon as they were out the door, Nigel indicated for him to take a seat at his desk. There were no fragrant aromas pumping out from the air conditioner, Nigel could only smell fear. Simon sat down, and Nigel passed him on the way to the cabinet that was closed but contained the premium vodka, he took two glasses out and half-filled them. He returned to the desk, and handed Simon the vodka, who declined, but Nigel wouldn't take no for an answer. He took the glass reluctantly; Nigel encouraged him to sip the vodka; he consumed his vodka in a short series of gulps, and returned to the cabinet for a refill. He watched as he sipped the vodka, more relaxed and in silence he handed him the information packed document

  He read it with premeditated consternation. It identified a number of curious financial transactions, all legal, but would bring scrutiny to the names on the list. Simon's was not there, he was relieved, but disappointed at the same time. How can Michael Ogilvie and David Fisher been on this "watch list" but not him? Very strange. Their dinners at The Ivy were alleged to be a conspiracy to launder money for the Russian Mafia and cohorts of Putin. Jonathon Gove's murder was the catalyst for intense scrutiny of his dining companions. Now Robert Samson's death or suicide; was shining a light from New York on them. This was a copy of the document held by the D.O.J. The NYPD had completed their investigation; the FBI would have great concerns. They would be prepared to extradite them and place them in custody until a Grand Jury was formed. Now he could understand why Nigel forced him to accept the early morning vodka, he eyed the glass jealously and downed its contents. He held the glass high in the air; Nigel subserviently returned with it full, he was completely relaxed. His name was not on the list, he had to ask, there had to be a cogent reason. Robert Samson's death was reported as a suicide, he had no blame attached to him; all the questions in Jersey were delivered in a perfunctory manner. Scrutiny of his financial dealings with Robert did not raise any concerns. He lost the worried look, and placed down the document on the desk; all were allegations, no empirical evidence to even suggest any wrong doing, either financial or personal harm. He finished the vodka, and was ready to ask Nigel, why was he here and why was he not on the list?

'Nigel, very interesting reading, but it's not clear why my name is not on the list, and…'

'…The hypodermic needle.'

'I don't understand, that needle was in the hired car, it had nothing to do with me.'

'It has your DNA on it.'

'It can't for a number of reasons, I didn't touch the needle and I didn't give a DNA sample.'

'You did, they took it off your coffee cup, it matches the DNA on the needle, which was used to inject Robert Samson, and render him unconscious, and then he was hung from the roof joist.'

'Not according to the press reports?'

'Yes, but at the end of the press reports, it said "enquiries are ongoing."'

'But, but, what does that mean?'

'Those two jokers were in here, for what reason I just don't know. Time will reveal all, that I'm sure. The paper you have just read is a favour to you," it's a watch what you do and be careful who you meet warning." The favour will be recalled sometime. Don't mention the contents of the document to your dining companions.'

'Is that not the least of my concerns? I mean, me being behind Robert's death?'

'I'm lost with that allegation, they showed me the DNA matches, but they could be fabricated, they want something from you, do you want to tell me anything?'

'You're joking?'

'I'm very serious, why haven't they arrested you, if they have this evidence? And why did they allege you had participated in his death? Someone else must have assisted you in setting up the ligature to hang him, and lift up his body; he was a very heavy man.'

'Did they mention a motive?'

'Of course, money or a transaction that had not been fulfilled, and they seemed very confident…they are withholding something Simon, are you sure you can't recall something that you did?'

'Seriously Nigel? I'd be here all day, sharp practice, and insider trading, we all did it, come on!'

'I know all that, but no dodgy deals with dodgy Russians?'

'Again Nigel, all Russians are dodgy as far as I'm concerned, but as long as the money has been scrutinised by government agencies, I'll invest and take my fee, you must have Russian clients?'

'I can't confirm or deny that, but we are talking about you, they have something on you, normally you'd be arrested, so why have they told me this about your DNA, then do you a favour by keeping your name off the dining list?'

'I really don't know, but I'm concerned about this DNA, and a link to Robert's death? Do you really think they are at it?'

'Absolutely! Robert could have been involved in some unethical or criminal enterprise, such as money laundering, he might have crossed someone, who was wise to his fee structure, and didn't take kindly to it?'

'You certainly have a way with words Nigel, in plain English he ripped a dodgy Russian off, and he didn't fancy lodging a complaint with the Financial Conduct Authority, and sent a couple of thugs to kill him, but they wouldn't get back their money?'

'How do you know? They may have persuaded him to transfer money before killing him?'

'Persuade? Really, don't you mean hold a gun at his head, he would know they were serious.'

'It's all conjecture, but what you and I have discussed are perfectly plausible scenarios, and don't think we are the only ones to have a brainstorm of what might have happened.'

'You mean the police, from Jersey?'

'Yes, but in saying that they look very youthful and confident, maybe that's the way they recruit in Jersey, go for highly-educated graduates.'

'They seemed full of themselves, I give you that…'

'…They unnerve me, they definitely know something, and they can spring it on you or me, that I won't waiver from, now for the last time, are you holding back anything that would make them frame you for a murder?'

   The moment he dreaded had finally arrived, whether it was the generous measures of vodka, or Nigel's chumminess. It was the perfect time to come clean. Nigel had watched a confident man being reduced to someone who couldn't live with a past deed. In silence he refilled his glass; he hoped he wouldn't have to return to the drinks cabinet. He refrained from topping up his glass even though he craved it. Nigel would wish he hadn't asked him.

***

   Gwen observed her drawn face in the LED mirror; she quickly turned the lights off. Time was leaving its mark on her youthful features, and it wouldn't return to collect the visible etch marks. Her sleep pattern was in turmoil; at first she put it down to the UK time zone. She couldn't surpass the real reason any longer. She had to make a decision; the outcome would inevitably be a return to New York

She had settled in London quite comfortably, her position was less stressful than in New York, but the recurring thought would return to her throughout the day but more often in the small hours of the morning as she struggled to sleep. The reason for her anxiety was David paying off the two detectives in New York for an embellished version of his business transactions with the now departed Jonathon Gove. In her opinion he was now a hostage to disaster. He had disagreed, and had no choice.

The detectives were very clear; specific damaging obstacles would be put in place to have him detained with maximum media coverage, which would blemish his business reputation and destroy his personal life. He couldn't take that risk, he quickly assessed he was not the first person to be subjected to this shake-down, and he doubted he would be the last. It had crossed his mind that Jonathan Gove had went through the same financial gymnastics with the corrupt detectives, and knowing Jonathon, he would be relaxed about their petty pay-off. He would simply shrug his shoulders and treat this as a business expense, and then make up the money from his clients. Jonathan had once remarked "in this business if you lose your temper you can lose your life." This quote hit him right between the eyes; then he remembered him saying while they were in the Vodka Room in New York "better to take a hit in the wallet than a hit in the head" this earthquake quote stunned him when Jonathan was assassinated in Central Park. The $2 million fee was his get out of jail free card; it was a business expense, nothing more, nothing less. He was learning fast from Jonathan's grave.

However, Gwen took a less pragmatic view. She had written down in her practical illegible writing in her notebook various thoughts what could be the outcome of David's pay off to the detectives. Would they return to the trough for more? Were they extorting money from Jonathan? And did they kill him because he didn't play ball with them anymore? With Jonathon gone, the trough was empty, was David the next one to shake-down, a resounding yes to that. David was holding something back; she had to confront him with her concerns and his fears. He was more ebullient now that he was back in London, he was back to his chatty and charming self, he had nothing planned for tonight, but she had.

The Iron Duke was his favourite pub, he seemed more at ease in its surroundings; she would carefully and softly voice her concern about the venal detectives in New York. Gently probing had they been in touch? And interspersed with how his business was performing and how happy she was to be with him. A confident smile that had went AWOL had made a welcome return, she activated the LED mirror with newly found confidence, she touched the Spotify app on her phone, the music loudly descended from the mirror into her eager ears. No negative thoughts would be taking a room in her head today.

***

Simon left Nigel's office higher than when he was a prolific user of cocaine. He had unburdened himself to Nigel, and to his surprise he didn't emit any emotion, he just noted certain points of his story down. He was not concerned that he was doing this. Robert Samson's death would benefit him financially; there were no smoking guns or vapour trails connecting him to Robert. Nigel had encouraged him not to leave out any detail however insignificant. When he had comprehensively explained his modus operandi to him, Nigel had commented "ingenious." Nigel would agree everything was in Simon's name; there were no legal challenges however it would be helpful if the soon to be retired Michael Ogilvie handed over the client list to the new owners of his business and building. Simon couldn't see the significance of this, but Nigel could. He was on very good terms with the Senior Client Investor Manager he would advise it would be helpful if he could send it over so he could scrutinise Robert Samson's file. There would be no resistance or any questions why he needed to scrutinise the file.

He just wanted to be certain that Simon had not omitted any damaging information. Nigel was acting for his client (Simon) he just wanted to clarify that there would not be any undue delay to capital being returned. Simon was thrilled at this unexpected good news. Nigel would ensure that there were no links to Simon being the conduit for Robert Samson's undeclared investments. Honesty was the best policy on this occasion; it would be placed back in solitary confinement after today. Honesty may be the best policy, but it certainly was not the most lucrative. The two pimply youthful detectives from Jersey, had met their match in Nigel, he was devious and duplicitous, but knew where his bread was buttered, and he had an abundance of that particular dairy product.

Nigel had ingested all the information he had imparted to him, his spontaneous confession was anything but, it was premeditated. Robert Samson's estate would be frozen and all bank accounts and financial transaction scrutinised. Robert's main bank account did not hold a substantial amount, the bank account which held millions was controlled by Nigel, who was fully aware that Simon was conducting various investments on behalf of Robert Samson. Nigel had ran rings round Simon, much to Simon's annoyance and admiration. When Simon had finished his tale of investing on behalf of Robert, Nigel poured them both a generous measure of premium vodka. He kicked off his hush puppies loafers and placed his feet on his desk. Simon had never seen him so relaxed; it had unnerved him, he assumed Nigel would have been concerned that Robert's third-party investor would cause him a degree of anxiety, he had misjudged Nigel. So had Robert Samson.

The vodka had started to affect him as he listened with disbelief as Nigel systematically educated him on money laundering, and why people get fearless and careless, which leads to a lengthy prison sentence or an early grave. He congratulated Simon for avoiding both. However, a percentage of Robert's funds which was in Simon's name would be removed and placed into an account in Cyprus, he went onto explain in a dutiful manner, that *he* had nominated him (Simon) to be the proxy investor. Now was the best time to execute this transaction. Simon understandably became flustered as this information had just been thrust upon him. He never asked what the percentage was; he didn't have the details on him to activate his account to transfer the unknown percentage. Nigel removed his feet from the table opened his laptop, and in a matter of moments turned the laptop screen to Simon, to his horror all the details were there. Nigel had logged in for him as well; he was very kind in that way. The amount transferred was £1.8 million. Simon did this without any protest. He chose not to ask why he had access to his account, and the percentage was 15%. He had been played; but the music didn't cause him any displeasure. Today had been an education indeed. There were many questions to ask, but he decided it could imperil his stay on this earth. Simon was in total admiration of Nigel.

Nigel placed his hush puppies back onto his feet. He said he wouldn't detain him any longer as he must have work to do. Simon stood up and was unsteady on his feet, whether it was from the alcohol or the revelations from Nigel would be difficult to distinguish.

The fresh air heightened the effect of the alcohol as he stood on the wide pavement outside the imposing office block; he looked at the synthetic palm trees as their leaves swaying from left to right in the light breeze. He had to stop staring at them as they were inducing him to feel nauseous. His mind was clear, but his breakfast wanted to leave his stomach. He averted his eyes, his stomach became becalmed, he took deep breaths and he began to walk nowhere in particular, when he felt better he would use the Uber app on his phone to return home. Walking would help him make sense of this unexpected knowledge that Nigel had kept hidden. Then he stopped suddenly; had Nigel anything to do with Robert's death, after all he had just benefitted from £1.8 million. And the two detectives from Jersey were in his office, prior to him arriving. The heightened pleasure was replaced with fear. He began to walk again, but taking lengthy strides, he had to go to a bar, sit down and collect his thoughts. His mouth was dry and his mind was racing; how he wished he hadn't thought that Nigel could be involved in Robert's death, but he couldn't shake this thought away. Then the old calculating avaricious side of Simon removed any concern of Nigel being involved in Robert's death. Too be frankly honest, he was not too concerned of Robert's death, he didn't like him, and he had *also* materially benefited from his death by the not insignificant sum of £15 million and change. Surely Nigel would be coming back for another percentage of this money? He would not allow his mind to question where Robert had acquired this money. He was sure that Nigel would be in touch very soon regarding the money in his account. He had paid the piper, but he was not picking the tune.

***

Edwina had made an appointment to view Jonathon Gove's apartment, what she hoped to achieve was unclear; however, her instinct compelled her to arrange an appointment and view the apartment. It would not be in her interest to advise Armstrong of this off the books venture. Her dress sense would be conservative but chic topped off with omnipresent sunglasses and blond wig; and a Russian accent to be used sparingly. She would arrive by taxi, but depart on foot. If she could locate anything to unveil his contacts or paperwork relating to his clients that would be conducive to a few hours spent well, saving weeks' of mining and sifting innocuous information. The taxi pulled up outside the impressive and imposing apartment block. The blond young woman was smoking on the steps to the entrance of the apartment block. She disposed of the recently lit cigarette into her coffee cup, and projected an engaging smile as she elegantly stepped out of the taxi; she was being instantly assessed about her wealth. The smart designer Hermes Gris Tourterelle bag screamed affluence even though it was a convincing copy, purchased on Oxford Street from a street trader in 2010. The Harrods bags accentuated the perceived wealth. Edwina had done her homework. She was handed a bespoke brochure described in grandiose terms, would it disappoint or attract buyers? The door of the apartment was firmly closed, a ploy of the estate agent. When the door was opened in a slow and inviting manner, it didn't disappoint, the brochure understated the ambience of the apartment, if she had the money or capable of raising the exorbitant asking price she would have bought it without viewing the other rooms. Impulsive but ludicrous thoughts came into her head; maybe she could afford this apartment? Then she looked at her £20 handbag; maybe not. She was walking on air as she moved from room to room capturing the beauty and elegance of every room on her phone. No incriminating papers or post notes were displayed on the antique writing desk or the kitchen reminder board, but a phone number was written obviously in a hurry; interesting.

She declined to ask any questions, she just smiled a lot. She was invited to view the flat on her own and at a leisurely pace; the estate agent must be keen to infect her lungs with cigarette smoke. She returned from the kitchen with a tiny ashtray, and then vacated the apartment. Edwina was circumspect if there were hidden cameras throughout the apartment, she would carry herself and behave like the lady that was within her, but yet to make an appearance, she smiled at that ethereal thought. The second more critical assessment of the various rooms, didn't uncover any concerns; it was still a beautiful apartment; she could still dream. Her eyes had been attracted to the small coffee machine in the kitchen; she couldn't recall the name at the top of the coffee machine. Jonathan Gove had taste in furniture; modern and antique that had to be grudgingly admired.

An unprofessional spontaneous thought crashed into her calm mind; she would help herself to a coffee from the expensive machine; and she would buy one no matter the cost. The coffee pods were stacked according to each brand; she was embarrassed she didn't recognise any of them. She captured them on her phone. She took the small Italian coffee cup with saucer into the lounge and sat down into the leather sofa. The ornate cornicing made her feel jealous and envious. She would never, ever be able to afford an apartment like this; reality sometimes suppresses optimistic thoughts. The coffee was so smooth, she kicked off her designer shoes and folded her legs under her, this must be her epiphany she had to do better in life; the years were racing past her, she had to find her niche in life but where and how? London is a lonely place when you are single and work anti-social hours. She coveted the vista from the large comfortable sofa, the large windows looked onto nothing in particular, but it was a better view than from all her previous homes. She walked over in her stocking soles to the window; even the under floor heating seduced her. Nothing was going on in the quiet street, then a council lighting department drew up parallel to the apartment block; the "eyes and ears" squad were ready to install the camera aimed onto the block, it was time for her to leave. She slipped on her shoes, washed the cup and placed it beside the object of her desire; the coffee machine. She couldn't help once again fantasising about living in the apartment, her jealous eyes raised an envious smile; what had she learned today? Very little about Jonathan Gove, his lifestyle was planned; there were no signs of him being spontaneous; he was a calculating individual in work and in his limited leisure time; she had learned more about her inner self and her unbridled ambition. She had to improve her financial situation forthwith. That was a promise that she had to uphold. She stopped as she was leaving the state of art kitchen. The reminder board was different; it was slightly askew; she straightened it, stood back and admired her handiwork. Then the self-satisfying grin fell away; the mobile phone number had been wiped clean from the board.

***

The Iron Duke pub was quiet, Michael Ogilvie preferred it that way, he was nursing his Chateau Cardinal Ville Maurine this was an expensive wine, but if all his plans came to fruition, he would be exporting his own wine to Europe including the lucrative London market. His calm and laid back personality had paid dividends in friendships and business contacts over the years; now near his imminent retirement, his second career would prove more lucrative. He had sought out the best man in the region for advice to improve the neglected vineyard with the ultimate aim to produce a wine not for the mass market but the niche for top class restaurants in Europe and for individual collectors for the investment market. The scientific advice was sent by email, to improve the vineyard he would need to spend a minimum of £400,000 if he wanted to produce a top quality wine. Next year would be the maiden launch of his first crop; the results were impressive word had leaked out that the vineyard would produce the finest grapes within a hundred mile radius; Michael had studied hard and put his business acumen to good use.

David Fisher was the youngest of his dining companions, he was thoughtful, kind and intelligent, he listened more than he spoke. He was meeting David to tell him of his future plans, and as he wasn't one to stand up and tell his dining companions that he had sold his business, and was moving permanently to France, David would break the news, and he would give David the money to pay for the farewell meals and drinks. He had anticipated this day for a number of years. He felt much happier now that day had arrived. An hour chatting to David, and then the evening meal with the purchaser of his business and building, and that would be his diary cleared for the day. He looked around the pub, and he could see why it appealed to David, friendly staff, convivial atmosphere and close to his home and office. And if he was honest he eschewed the unflattering comments outwith earshot range of David, this was down to jealousy and David's lucrative investment strategy, David didn't follow the herd; he led the herd. However, soon he would be in his paradise, his wife was delighted and so was he, he hoped she shared his undaunted enthusiasm for his vineyard; he inadvertently failed to notify her of this new business venture he had purchased a few years earlier.. He would let her blue eyes decide in France.

He would limit his alcohol intake this evening as he had his routine medical the following morning, his type B diabetes was in retreat, cakes, sugar, and salt were banished from his home, he had shed three stones from daily walks and using the gym equipment in his home more frequently. He brought the wine glass up to his nose, the aroma excited him, he sipped it, then placed the glass down, and glanced at his watch. David was late, which was unusual for him, he felt uneasy for some unknown reason, he tried to banish the feeling of impending doom by raising the glass to his nose, the aroma was less appealing, he placed the glass down and glanced at his watch again, he's only ten minutes late, he tried in vain to gauge some perspective, then he glanced at the door David came in with his trademark smile, then he walked over to the table and apologised to Michael about his late arrival and went to the bar to retrieve the bottle of beer waiting for him by the barmaid. After a brief chat he returned to Michael's table. Michael noticed beads of sweat on his temples; he had casually loosened his tie and was breathing in an irregular pattern. Michael took the decision not to enquire if he had been running, he would let David explain.

David took the bottle and the content disappeared down his throat very quickly, he turned round and the female was at the table with another beer, she didn't say anything and placed the full bottle on the table and removed the empty one. When she walked away, David's casual smile disappeared and his face was etched with concern.

'Are you alright David?'

'No, not really, I assumed you are going through the same shock as me, and that was the reason for this impromptu meeting in The Iron Duke, but going by your demeanour, you have good news of some kind?'

'I haven't a clue what you're talking about, I am here to tell you that I am moving to France permanently and setting up a wine producing business. I wanted you to tell the rest of the guys, I didn't want any fuss, that's all. But you're in a state, and I also thought that something was wrong because you're such a stickler for keeping appointments. Now what is this "shock" that you have mentioned?'

'Just leave it, maybe I'm over reacting, it obviously doesn't concern you, forget it. Now tell me about this move to France and a wine producing business?' The worry lines were replaced with laughter, but Michael wouldn't push him to reveal what it was that caused him this serious concern, was it a business transaction or was it something to do with Jonathon Gove's death in New York? He took the decision not to ask. He had made the correct decision to relocate to France, seeing David like this reinforced his judgement to sell the business and move to France.

***

Gwen was in high spirits as she turned the key in the lock, music was playing louder than normal in the background, David was home, she couldn't contain herself any longer, David had been very moody, but her news would lift his gloom. She opened the lounge door, the two NYPD detectives were sitting together on the sofa, drinking coffee; David was not in sight. Gwen dropped her bag onto the wooden floor; she assessed the situation instantly, rather than say 'what are you doing in my apartment'?, she changed tact.

'I've been expecting you both for some time, what took you so long to come here?'

This put them under pressure to answer. They looked at each other; this was not going as planned. Gwen went to the kitchen and poured herself a coffee and returned to the lounge where she sat on the seat near the large window.

'We are concerned you have gone rogue…what's going on?'

'Now you listen to me, I kept my side of the bargain, I manoeuvred Jonathan away from David, killing him was not included in the plan. He was meant to be confronted in his hotel room. Not killed in Central Park, I didn't sign up for that. I'm out, and I'd advise both of you to leave, now.'

'You're out; there is no dispute about that. '

He stood up took his gun from the rear of his waistband and shot her in the forehead, he walked over and felt her neck for any sign of a pulse, he smiled, no pulse. He put on the latex gloves and rummaged through her bag for her phone. He removed the phone and placed the bag beside her seat.

The female detective rose and took the coffee cups and took them into the kitchen and closed the door. He looked around the lounge, his professional eyes were satisfied. His colleague joined him in the lounge, she also cast her eyes around the lounge; Gwen was still holding her coffee cup on her lap.

'The coffee cups have been washed and returned to the kitchen cabinet, our work is done here.' She removed her latex gloves. He nodded in agreement, they walked towards the door and listened; all was quiet, he opened the door, once out in the lobby he removed his gloves. It was time to make a call from Gwen's phone.

***

Edwina had reached the end of the road; she stopped outside the designer shop to have an envious glance at the latest fashion, and to have a chortle at the exorbitant price these fashionista chumps were paying for ludicrous shoes. She wasn't surprised at the price tags, then her internal ambitious imagination called back to her if she lived in the apartment block she would be a frequent shopper at this shop. She turned her head in the direction of a cacophony of police sirens; nothing unusual in London, but very rare in this affluent part of London, the sirens were heading in her direction, the wailing grew louder and louder, she estimated there were at least four police cars and an ambulance. Soon the speeding convoy came into view, she lowered her sunglasses to calculate if her eyes confirmed her tutored ears assessment that there were three police cars, one tactical firearms unit and an ambulance, the convoy whizzed past her, she was correct four police cars and an ambulance in the middle of the speeding convoy. She turned her attention to a particular pair of black shoes; £1500. The sirens stopped filling the air, she moved onto the middle of the wide pavement. The convoy had halted at the apartment block. She moved quickly away from the shops, people were coming out of eclectic shops to observe what was going on, a few excited women were conversing in Russian and joining a throng of pedestrians moving towards the apartment block, roughly four hundred metres away. This was not good, it would be a pointless exercise assuming what had occurred at the apartment block, but it was serious if the tactical firearms unit were present. Her pace quickened, she was swimming against an inquisitive tide of humanity moving towards the apartment block, at last she reached the junction, where were all the black cabs? She saw one approaching, she moved onto the road to hail it, it glided past, the driver smiled at her, she smiled and gave him the finger. Etiquette was suspended at this moment. A BBC news van screeched around the junction, she didn't need to guess where it was heading; she had to remove herself from this area. The amount of people who were walking and some running in the direction of the apartment block were increasing, however, she noted there were women who had various hairstyles and were wearing sunglasses similar to hers, and more importantly their hair matched hers; blonde. A private hire cab pulled up, she gave the address, the eastern European driver was not one for conversation, she was grateful.

***

Simon had stepped out of the shower; he dried himself and flirted with his reflection in the mirror. Being clean from drugs, and being an eager participant in the apartment block's gym had definitely paid visible and invisible dividends for his physical and mental health. Apart from recurring flashbacks of Robert Samson swinging silently from the roof joist and being held for suspicion of his death, it had been a good day.

Nigel had revealed part of his curricular activities that went beyond the humdrum of being a corporate expensive lawyer. Had he inadvertently or purposely drawn back the curtain? Was he being warned off from Nigel, by him releasing his commission from his bank account in real time? And the obvious question; Nigel knew Robert Samson's bank details? Had Robert Samson concocted a less than truthful account of the Chinese student contacting him and advising him how he can manipulate the price of commodities; namely copper? Nigel was a large moving cog in this, there would be no other logical explanation. It would not be in his interest to impart Nigel of the story about the Chinese student. He was alone in the world now; it was time to make friends.

***

David arrived at his apartment block a police cordon had been erected, a phalanx of media companies and rubberneckers were on both sides of the entrance. He went over to speak with the media police officer. He quickly and quietly explained who he was and that he lived in the apartment block. She quickly asked which apartment; she already knew. He was told to stay where he was, someone would be with him to explain "the incident." two detectives quickly took him away from the media scrum. They would not tell him what had happened; they in turn incessantly repeated where had he been? When he explained he had been in the Iron Duke pub having a drink with a friend, they took all the details. David could not hold back any longer. 'Do I need a lawyer, if I am going with you to Police Headquarters?' He knew he would. To his surprise they answered unequivocally. 'Yes.' Thank God he had a gold standard alibi.

***

Armstrong had taken a call from his informant at The Ritz hotel; the two Americans had just left and were heading to a police station; not sure which one. He called Edwina who was just settling down at her desk checking media outlets for news regarding the convoy of police vehicles that had sped past her.
'Suspicious Death.' was the banner headline on the media web page. Her blood ran cold. She couldn't glean too much; doesn't say male or female. She had ignored Armstrong's call, now she would return it. She would explain that she was just on her way to view Jonathon Cope's apartment.

Her story was water-tight. She came off the phone in a state of panic; the victim was David Fisher's partner an American citizen; he was concerned that the Americans would lodge a request with the High Court for the extradition of David Fisher. The two FBI officers were at the station insisting they ask David Fisher questions after they sit in when he is being questioned. Armstrong laughed 'his lawyer will never agree to this. I'll keep you informed... and cancel your viewing.'

She held her head in her hands briefly, then stood up and moved away from the desk, aware of the spyware in her Smart TV. Was Armstrong observing her now or was it another Intelligence agency?

This was her sliding door moment. Things had now changed utterly. The Smart TV had to be incapacitated soon. She had accidental damage on her Home insurance policy, she would have some food that left crumbs on the floor, then she would get the vacuum cleaner out and accidently hit the screen with the handle. Keep it simple. That was that problem fixed in her head; more pressing who was David Fisher's 'partner'? Armstrong would furnish her with the personal details probably within the hour. How he hated the Americans. Had Jonathon Gove's death in Central Park been political? Why that thought arrived in her head she was flummoxed, but exhilarated simultaneously. She decided to have a coffee then peruse the photos on her phone; the wiped number from the reminder board. The kettle came to the boil. She poured the water into the mug and flicked through the video and photos of the flat. She zoomed into the kitchen reminder board. The number was Armstrong's 'off the books' mobile. Troubling.

***

Simon had been summoned to Nigel's office, he wouldn't elaborate why he needed to talk to him urgently at ten am, Nigel had texted him at three-thirty am. After he read it he leapt from his bed, it was pointless trying to get back to sleep his mind would be in a vortex of dangerous thoughts. In times of trouble the default route was the kitchen, he promised himself he would not delve into too much what lay in store for him. While the kettle was switched on, he returned to the bedroom to retrieve the grey soft throw that would literally be his comfort blanket as he lay on the sofa, idly watching something on TV. His lounge had a bespoke fitted bookcase that ran the length of the wall directly behind the corner sofa. The shelves were filled with the classics and the great philosophers; all for show to give any infrequent visitors that he was well read. Harry Potter was his passion. He kept his signed First Editions in his safe. Stirring the coffee, he felt more relaxed, the positives were he and Nigel had benefitted handsomely from the universally hated Robert Samson's untimely demise. He smirked at this morbid thought. No guilty conscience; no regret. He moved into the lounge and rather than settling down and wrapping the throw around him and flick through the channels he was drawn towards the floor to ceiling window; why is it people always without fail stand at their window and stare out in times of trouble? The lights on the Embankment were all eerily lit; traffic was sparse, only the occasional couple passed by. And when they did, he wondered where they had been or where were they going at this unearthly hour?

The coffee and stillness of the early hours had slowed the expected turmoil of the phalanx of random thoughts, he was about to return the coffee mug to the kitchen, when his curiosity compelled him to pause this action, a black cab taxi halted abruptly outside the entrance to the apartments. A figure emerged from the taxi, it was Nigel casually dressed but carrying his briefcase.. Those serene philosophical musings he had been comforting himself with seemed premature and fanciful now. This was bad news; he hadn't come here to borrow some milk. He took the concierge's expected call and admitted Nigel, he returned to the kitchen and switched on the kettle. The gentle rap on the door could be heard in the kitchen, he smirked, ever the cautious Nigel. He would let him sweat for a minute; he took the two mugs from the wall cupboard. It had been sometime since he had a coffee with someone. Nigel was a black coffee person; he carried both mugs and placed then on the large coffee table; took a deep breath and went to the door to greet Nigel. No worry was on his face. This changed when he opened the door with his professional customary fixed smile when he was hoping to land an affluent but crooked client. The smile dissipated immediately when he opened the door, Nigel was prostrate on the lobby tiled floor, a hypodermic needle lodged deep into his neck He held back the urge to scream, this would be in vain anyway, there was only one other apartment on the floor and the overseas owner didn't live in it and had apparently only stayed in it for one night. He ran back into the apartment and instructed the concierge to call an ambulance and the police, the concierge didn't ask any probing questions, and in a casual manner replied, "certainly sir."

  Should he touch his neck to check for a pulse? No, better not do this, as his DNA would be on his neck and all the problems that would arise *and* another hypodermic needle, but this time in his lawyer's neck! This is going to be a very difficult period of time. Should he remove his pyjamas and place on casual clothes or a suit for the inevitable detention at a police station? At the least the concierge would have noted the time, name of visitor etc. a small comfort; but still a comfort to him amongst this madness. The intercom came to life, again the concierge in his monotone delivery advised him the police and a ambulance team were on their way up, was there anything else sir? He felt like saying can you get me a gun and come up and shoot me? Certainly sir and anything else sir?, would undoubtedly be his reply. At the far end of the lobby the elevator door opened, two paramedics, two uniformed officers and two detectives. The paramedics immediately went to Nigel and one felt for a pulse, he shook his head; it wasn't a surprise. The elevator door opened again, the forensics team emerged. Simon was invited back into his apartment. He was ordered to sit down gather his thoughts and take a few minutes to think what he was going to say. While this was going on the other detective noticed the two untouched mugs of coffee, Simon in the circumstances was in full control of his thoughts, he came to the decision not to bring up Jersey, unless they asked. They were calm and courteous, took routine details, how long had he lived here, did he know Nigel, and what was the purpose of his early morning visit? Simon explained everything, he showed him the text. Then they asked did he plunge the needle into his neck, and what was the content of the needle? Did he have any other needles in the apartment? Questions that anyone could see coming. One of the detectives went out and had a brief conversation with the senior Forensic Officer.

The other detective told Simon he would need a lawyer as he would be questioned at the station, Could he be kind enough to change into outdoor clothes and place his pyjamas into the bag that the forensic team would bring in? The forensic team moved into the apartment. Meticulous videoing of the apartment began in earnest. While changing into his casual clothes, Simon became calm. His strategy was not to divulge anything that could cast suspicion upon him. He had a list of competent criminal but expensive lawyers stored in his head. He knew which one to call and meet him at the station. He would do this before he left the apartment.

When the police had confirmed with the concierge the time of Nigel's arrival this would go some way to confirm his story. However, Nigel being killed at his door was something he had great difficulty coming to terms with. If it came out that there was a similar incident in Jersey, the dark clouds of depression would be upon him. Then he cast his mind back to Nigel saying he was not on "the list." If that was the case, why would the Jersey police inform the police in London? He had to stay positive, and keep the Jersey incident from his lawyer. Ignorance is bliss, and less expensive in this case.

He called the lawyer, he was not moved at being disturbed at this unearthly hour; he told him briefly and calmly what had happened. The lawyer knew where he would be taken; it was not too far from his home in Belgravia. He told him not to say anything in the car or at the station until he arrived. And the most comforting sentence, 'you won't be held long ...that I can assure you.' With this ringing in his ear, he started to ask why had Nigel turned up at his apartment, someone must have followed him all the way to his apartment, came in approximately the same time, got in the elevator with him, watched him leave the elevator and go to the apartment door, swiftly creep up on him, plunge the needle into his neck after he had rang the bell, returned to the elevator and made good his escape. Case solved and closed. The various cameras inside and outside the apartment block would confirm this plausible theory. It would be in his best interest to keep this theory from the police and his lawyer. Let the police do their incompetent best. When he informed two detectives, that he was ready to go to the station, he was told to remain for another five minutes as Nigel's body was still there being photographed and videoed from different angles.

The detective tried to engage in small talk, but Simon stuck to his lawyer's advice rigidly. 'Don't get involved in any conversation however innocuous even in their car... it will have recording equipment fitted.'

He politely but firmly told the detective on the advice of his lawyer he was not to engage in any conversation until his lawyer was present at the police station. The detective was not offended at this retort. They were advised it was safe to leave the apartment Nigel's body had been removed. Simon did not feel any sad loss that Nigel was dead; it seemed if anyone was involved in creative financial practices; death was an occupational hazard; especially in London. Nigel knew the risks. On this occasion he had lost. The City of London Police would be handed Nigel's file in due course. Nigel's financial records would not show any criminal or unethical transactions. He had friends in the City of London Police.

***

It had all started so well for Nigel that day. But the opposite was true for David. After learning Gwen had been shot dead in his apartment, he immediately thought this was undoubtedly connected to Jonathon Gove's brutal assassination in Central Park. Nigel met him at the police station, Nigel's face and demeanour did not infuse him with confidence, the detectives were thorough but sensitive to his immediate loss, and the life changing events in New York. Nigel was less assertive; he nodded more than he spoke. The detectives advised him to return to his apartment gather his computer, laptop etc, grab some clothes throw them in a suitcase and lock up the apartment. His life was under threat. He would be moved to a safe house. David rejected this offer immediately. Nigel intervened to tell the detectives he had various properties in London, which were in twenty-four hour concierge buildings. David nodded his head in agreement with this suggestion. The detectives went on to explain, they couldn't force him into a safe house, but they would strongly recommend this course of action. They agreed David would return to his abode the following day, and collect his personal belongings, and electronic devices. They did not mention that the computer and laptop would be analysed and stripped of the myriad of financial information that could help them to piece together the chain of events that led to the deaths of Jonathon and Gwen, *prima facia* evidence pointed to his trip to New York, his meeting with Jonathon for business, and his chance meeting with Gwen, Of course they did not mention that they would do all this without his permission, or rather the Economic Crime Unit would.

They left the police station in silence, both were held hostage to their own cataclysmic thoughts.

David decided to break the silence. 'Nigel, we are connected by Pavel, you're his lawyer and I'm his financial advisor. So was Jonathon. Do you think the Russian Mafia is behind this, I mean them killing Gwen as well, and if I was in my apartment, they would've killed me too?'

Nigel stopped and pulled on his arm. 'That's what I'm thinking too. Gwen was unlucky she was in your apartment on her own; they must've thought you would have been there too. Luckily for you, you were meeting someone at your local pub.. I can't help thinking about Pavel also. If it was the Russian Mafia, they are not being subtle, when news breaks in the media, and on social media, that these murdered individuals were acting for him in various financial roles, the public's imagination will run wild, and who can blame them?'

'I am going to speak to Pavel, and advise him, I can't work for him anymore, I'm sure he'll understand, don't you think?' Nigel let out a spontaneous series of laughter. He forced David to keep walking. 'I'm sure he'll understand? Have you forgotten he stepped in and covered your loan, when the Merchant Bank, withdrew their final tranche of the loan, due to suspected money laundering? 'Even if you have the money to repay him, and that would be an insult to him, he and others would ruin your business. Forget that plan David. The Russian Mafia is sending a message to other legal firms and financial advisors, working for Pavel *will* damage your health.' David stopped walking. 'Then what do we do?' 'Keep walking David, we carry on regardless, you've made out a will, I presume in Dundee?' 'Fuck sake! I can't cope with this!' 'We will just have to, what else can we do David? The police can only do so much, for your information, some officers will be passing on our whereabouts, and mobile phone numbers and email addresses. So be careful. Look if they want us eliminated they have the means to achieve this, think of Jonathon in New York and your friend in your London apartment. And the safe house would've been anything but safe. That's why I mentioned one of my apartments. I don't trust the police, it would be inconvenient if one or both of us were eliminated, but not a seismic event.' How prescient of Nigel, in less than twenty-four hours he would be dead a fatal inconvenience or coincidence?

***

Edwina sat at home, waiting on Armstrong calling her, it was two hours since she had left the "Mansion Block of Death" as the media had christened the red bricked mansion block because of the untimely deaths of Jonathon Gove in New York and an unnamed American, believed to be a woman various online media outlets had pronounced.

Leaks from police officers to the media were the new norm; she didn't spend too much time ruminating this modern day of news management. Her cerebral fortitude was focused on David Fisher. Was he meant to be the main target, or was his partner the target to advise him of his latest financial transaction in New York, the final straw? She would keep this theory to herself until Armstrong held a meeting with her, to share information that was not in the public domain. Her eyes were drawn inadvertently to her Smart TV. Things had become so opaque and complicated. She was watching others and others were watching her. She had to ramp up trying to secure another home. Her sleep pattern had become discombobulated; her bags under eyes were affecting her confidence, she was starting to feel sad and lonely. She would start going out for early morning runs, her face broke into a smile at this random but welcome thought, while she was out running she would scope out different areas where she would like to live. And perhaps meet someone? That would be good. Her phone rang and brought her back into the here and now. It was Armstrong, she answered it with trepidation. Things were moving fast, he needed her to return to the office ASAP, he'll speak to her when she had arrived. Always conscious that he could be observing her from her Smart TV, she acted normally by removing her coffee cup and moving to the kitchen and placing it in the sink. She grabbed her coat and handbag then left for the office. In the car, she had difficulty in locating LBC news, she had come to the obvious conclusion her car was bugged internally and externally by a tracker. No phone calls would be made from within the confines of her car. Her mind was trying to connect Armstrong's number on the white board, then being quickly removed. A thin smile emanated from her thought process; he was connected innocently or not was the question, that only time would answer. She would have to limit her questions to him regarding the sudden demise of Gwen; the footage from the camera on the lamppost across from the mansion block, would undoubtedly help in revealing the assassin or assassins. Again were they Russians, Intelligence, Mafia or the CIA? She would tread carefully when she was probing Armstrong for theories.

***

David had made up his mind. He was returning to Dundee; not to stay with his dad in Broughty Ferry, but in a flat he kept separate from his portfolio of properties that he had sold before moving to London. Nostalgia had won him over; the flat had been used sparingly over the years as an Airbnb for golf tournaments at Carnoustie and St. Andrews. Getting out of London was a priority; his story for Pavel was simple. He was returning to Dundee to visit his dad; he would be available to the police if they wanted to ask any more questions about Nigel or Gwen. Of course he didn't want to suggest to him he was fearful for his life. Getting back to Dundee would help him process all the events that happened in New York and London. He had confided to Michael in The Iron Duke that he was returning to Dundee, for his own personal safety, he wouldn't be able to tell his fellow diners at The Ivy that Michael was relocating to France. Michael was genuinely shocked to hear of David's spontaneous plan to return to Dundee. Was it for good? David shrugged his shoulders as he gulped down his beer straight from the bottle. Michael was saddened in one way, but David's departure firmed up his relocation to France was the correct decision. He did not wish to burden David with the curious meeting with Robert Samson who had purchased new apartments in Dundee, and he (Michael) acted for him in purchasing the apartments. Then all the financial details were wiped from his computer and his USB flash drive. However, his fee was in his bank statement. His blood ran cold at that moment. They were all linked however tenuously, and the chain was being broken link by link.

As was becoming more apparent, the 'links' were being removed quickly and violently. Michael saw the fear on David's face; he had made a wise decision to return to Dundee. The Ivy dinners had prematurely ended. Not by choice but by design. David had stood up after gulping the beer till it was gone. He wished Michael well, but ended with the words, 'it would be best if we didn't keep in touch.' Shocking last words but clear in their meaning. Then he was gone. He was a man with a mission to preserve life. His own. What could he have replied? He just said 'take care,' and nodded. David smiled turned around and walked through the door, with wise words that echoed through his head as he left Dundee all those years ago. "Never look back." Lena lifted the bottles from the table and wiped the table. 'I see David has gone, he seemed in a hurry, I'll probably see him later tonight.' Michael sipped his expensive wine, swirled it in the glass and placed it under his nose. 'I very much doubt it...'

***

David is in his apartment saying the last goodbye? I hope not. He can almost hear the broad Dundee accents and laughter from the scaffold, when the brickwork was being repointed. Yes the workers had certainly made a favourable impression on the residents of the proud mansion block. They worked hard, but played harder. Who would've had imagined an unremarkable young Dundee man makes good then heads down to London, and makes millions? Certainly not him. He knew of erstwhile friends who had fought their way out of Kirkton, to make a good life for themselves, he had *thought* his way out. The brain always wins over brawn. The melancholy started to lift; the sun faintly was streaming

through the blind; his trademark smile returned. He was genuinely optimistic about his future; and he would return to London once again. How would Dundee greet him, a return of a favoured son or as a blowhard with an abundance of stories to forcefully impart on unwelcome ears? His neighbours would welcome his return, even though murder and mayhem had followed him to and fro across the Atlantic, his name was never mentioned in the media. He was just a financial advisor who had completed a deal in New York with another financial advisor who was murdered in New York. And his partner who was murdered in his apartment? Nothing unusual in these incidents? Then the fear returned. Why no press turning up at his door? As far as the outside world was concerned, he didn't exist. When he was settled in his old flat in Broughty Ferry he would explain to the inquisitive neighbours that he was up to visit his dad, but needed his own space to continue his work. Keep it simple. How long would he be up in Broughty Ferry? Probably months, his apartment in London was being refurbished. Yes, that's his story. He would text his neighbour, explaining his imminent return.
One thing he could guarantee; he wouldn't encounter seeing and being interviewed by so many police officers in Dundee. Oh dear.

***

Edwina was cautious as she entered his office; Armstrong was sitting on the old school style radiator blowing smoke out of the window. 'Fuck sakes. Can't you knock?' He threw out the newly lit cigarette onto the roof. He was clearly embarrassed. She couldn't stifle her throaty laughter. 'Oh, get a grip, wont you.'
'Look, I'm sorry, I've been under pressure lately...'
'Oh, do you see me wearing a bikini.' He laughed at that. 'Yes, you've been under pressure as well. Well things aren't getting any easier. Just to let you know some of the teenage scribblers have reported me for smoking; I've had an official warning. Can you believe it? Apparently one in particular said my selfish smoking is having a detrimental impact on her health. I told the Eton boys, then she should stop visiting Greggs, they were not impressed by my advice. Anyway, onto more serious matters, the murder of David Fisher's partner....'
Edwina sat down, '...new partner, he only met her in New York when I was there.'
'Really? That throws a different light on the investigation, and she had moved in with him? Wow!'
He moved from the radiator, to rumble through his drawer for a cigarette, Edwina let him be, he was going to come out with information he hadn't intended to, or a bullshit theory. He excitedly sparked the lighter, and drew on the cigarette and returned to perch on the radiator. 'Now Edwina, how

about this then, perhaps she wasn't his partner, it was a cover so they could work together in London. Maybe she had with David Fisher's blessing arranged Jonathon Gove's murder in New York, then they get out of Dodge, apparently grieving and...'

Her face does not concur. 'What's in your cigarette? Are you fucking kidding me? I don't have confidence in your theory, but obviously upstairs will have the same view, thickos think alike, but I wouldn't mention it to the FBI? Or is it CIA?'

'The FBI...we are getting the cold shoulder from them regarding Jonathon Gove's murder, how do you think they'll react to Gwen's murder..?'

'Does she not have a surname?' He laughs. 'She has several. Now why is that do you think?'

'Now that is interesting.'

'Gwen is an American, so I expect them to use their sharp elbows to our ribs in this investigation.'

'But she was murdered on British soil. End of.'

'You think?' He starts blowing a series of smoke circles out into the air

'The British Government has to be resolute in this case. Thanks for your suggestion (FBI) but we will keep you informed, we'll call you, don't call us.'

'Great in theory, but the Eton boys won't put up even a feeble argument. They'll want a joint investigation. And they may want to extradite David Fisher to the U.S.'

'Why would they do that, he's not a suspect?' He removed himself from the radiator. 'You have a lot to learn. We are like the fifty-first State when it suits our U.S. friends, and you can thank that prick Blair for that.'

'Is David Fisher a suspect?'

'Officially no, but things can change. You obviously haven't heard... his lawyer was murdered'

'When did this happen?' He slowly slid the thin file towards her. 'Read it now, it can't leave this office.'

***

CHAPTER FIVE

David's old house emerges into view. The lights are on; great my neighbour has made it welcoming for me just as if I was an Airbnb client. Gillian Watson was a retired nurse; she welcomed and took care of all the bookings. David had to convince her she was doing him a massive favour; he was too busy in London to take care of the Airbnb bookings. He had given her a list of plumbers, electricians etc, in case anything went wrong. She loved her little job; she convinced David that she would do the cleaning and all the changeovers. She was being driven mad with boredom. David rewarded her well, he had her bank details; he would occasionally place a bonus alongside her regular payments. The taxi drew up outside the flat, he could see her plumping up the cushions; he smiled. He paid the driver and walked up the path; he gave her a wave, he always used the back door to exit and enter the house, the garden was looking good even in the twilight, it wouldn't be long before the solar lights on the fence sprang into life. He opened the back door; the air freshener permeated the air. He felt safe. He placed his suitcase on the granite tiled kitchen floor; she shouted tea was in the pot. He strode into the well lit lounge; the new television was larger than he thought. She came over to him, and hugged him. A myriad of small talk went back and forth between them. Then her face became stern. 'Something wrong Gillian?' She pointed upwards in silence. 'Is something wrong with the lights?' She burst out laughing. 'No no...It's the new people who have moved in. They have been awkward with the gardener, they refused to pay him, as there was no contract signed, the gardener is okay with that he doesn't cut his grass and leaves the drying green uncut when it's his turn.'
David is visibly angry, he has used Andy (the gardener) for years; he didn't want to lose him.

 'He dictates where cars are permitted to park on the street, and what time bins are allowed to be taking out.' Gillian's laughter had ebbed away, when she saw David's anger emerge. 'And there is something else David, he doesn't want your Airbnb guests to use *their* path, or Andy to move his plant pots to access your two front lawns. The Savile Row suit suddenly became tighter.

'What!' The dormant 'Kirkton' persona emerged. 'Oh really? I think it's time he introduced himself to me. Still like AC/DC's Thunderstruck Gillian?' He didn't wait for her reply. He took out his phone paired it with the speakers on either side of the fireplace. Then boom! The heavy metal music not only filled the lounge but echoed into the normally sedate street. Gillian had not told David that the new neighbour had tried to impose his rule bins are only allowed to be taking out on the morning of collection, and not the night before was 'unacceptable, this was Broughty Ferry not a housing scheme...' When Gillian heard this she smiled inwardly, wait till he meets David. However, all the neighbours complied with the new rules. The bin men were coming tomorrow, David would take the bin out tonight would it be remiss of her to deny David this information? I think not. God she nearly forgot to thank him, for the three night break in New York he paid for. Her husband's ill-health had returned and had to go part-time in his construction consultancy business. The Range Rover had to be downsized; some neighbours took great pleasure in hearing of this. She knew that was the reason for David's unexpected but welcome bonus payments. He had offered them two weeks holiday in his flat overlooking a golf course in Portugal. With the music booming, it was time to leave she would talk to David tomorrow, and thank him for the trip to New York. She could hear movement from upstairs. David must've heard the same; he removed his jacket and placed it on the brown leather sofa. She stood up and said they would speak tomorrow. That engaging smile returned; he escorted her to the door; the deafening music followed them along the oak floored hall. She reminded him that the bins were being collected tomorrow. He said he would take his out once he got out of his suit. This would be interesting. She would observe from her lounge window the imminent conversation when the neighbour came down to complain about the music, and the bin being transported along *his* path. He would form an opinion of David that he was a rebel to authority.

  David sat on the leather sofa, cup in hand and music assaulting his ears. He placed the cup on the wooden floor, stood up and rolled up his sleeves. He heard heavy footsteps rapidly descending the stairs from the upstairs flat. He picked up his phone from the coffee table and paused the music; he heard his neighbour's front door open then being slammed shut. He stood observing from the lounge bay window; the irate male passed at pace. The door bell rang out incessantly. David removed his watch, placed it carefully on the coffee table and made his way to the large front door, and opened it. 'Yes, can I help you?'

The neighbour stood there struggling to get the words out in a coherent manner. 'The music! The music!'
'Let me introduce myself, I'm David...'
'I don't give a fuck who you're, get the music off now!' David stood there a smug smile expanding by the second. 'What music is this? I'm not playing any music, is everything alright? I understand you have mental health problems, do you want me to call a doctor or an ambulance?' His face was now puce coloured. 'Are you trying to be funny? You've turned the music off, when you heard me coming down my stairs; just keep the music off, not down.' David moved from his vestibule onto the step, he was still a few inches shorter than the well-built neighbour. This didn't cause David any anxiety. He took the phone out and pressed play; then descended onto the bottom step. He was inches away from the incandescent neighbour. 'And now I've turned it back on.' The next track came on; it was James, with the immortal line. 'Were you born an asshole?' On cue, David piped up, 'Well were you?'
He had to make an instant judgement; should he use his physical advantage and try to intimidate him. He stepped back, 'I'll get the police...'
'And an ambulance would be advisable.' David stepped forward, forcing the neighbour to step back. 'And don't ever, come to this door again. And a wee bit of advice, take a shower, you're emanating a sickening odour. Now leave.' The neighbour had difficult matching his fixed gaze. He turned away, without another word. Gillian observed this guessing the content of the conversation. On first sight, it looked like fifteen love to David. He departed in an incremental manner from his door rather than in Tasmanian devil mode when he arrived. This was not the start of a beautiful relationship she thought as she cupped the coffee cup in both hands. She was glad David was back in the street. Silence would be fractured while he was here He had not mentioned how long he would be staying.

 David had jumped into the shower, and thought about the obnoxious neighbour, he had brought chaos to the street when there was sedentary order. This little local difficulty had taken his mind off the carnage in London, he enjoyed the pulsating shower; it was removing the tiredness and anxiety that infused his lethargic body. If the police came, he would play the harassed neighbour, if the police were unsympathetic, his pre-London persona would come to the fore. He would surprise his Dad in The Tayberry restaurant tomorrow evening; he never tired of telling him of the extensive menu and how it was so enjoyable seeing his friends, which were thinning out. Of course, he would desist from informing him of the body count that seemed to follow him from London to New York, or the two million dollar bribe to two corrupt New York detectives...he would crowbar into the conversation about his petrol lawnmower. It was his pride and joy, way beyond his brand new Mercedes. He stepped out of the shower cubicle, feeling good in body and mind, towel drying his hair, the grey hair was becoming more prominent, unlike his dad's hair which was black, and combed back. Of course he would subtly mention his hair going grey made him look older; then casually bring out his steel comb and converse while attending to his black hair with a smile on his lined face. Better to be grey than dead he thought. The echoing bell filled the hall, he placed on his jogging bottoms, and top, placed his feet into his slippers, and went to answer the door. He opened the door, two police officers one young and very tall, the other smaller and near retirement age.

'Yes, can I help you?'

The younger officer was derisory christened G.I. Joe. He apparently defeated the Taliban when he served in Afghanistan...single handedly, with a little help from his comrades. However, when he was an inexperienced police officer, he was headstrong and enthusiastic but devoid of common sense. He may have confronted the Taliban and indeed defeated them, but was handed his arse from feral youths who had been paid in advance of their benefit money and were strung out because they had blown their money on a cocktail of drugs, now they were lacking drugs and money to keep their body and soul in harmony. The Hilltown area of Dundee on a Saturday was not a place to spread peace and goodwill. Trying to tell hordes of strung out youths to be quiet and go home, asked for a violent response. G.I. Joe was the catalyst and target for their non-passive response. Had he learnt his lesson? David Fisher would be the ideal arbitrator.

'We've had a complaint from Mr. Gibbon, about excessive music being played. Can we come in?'

'Hold on a minute officer I have to get something.' He returns with his phone and starts recording them.' G.I. Joe is alarmed at this invasive response.

'Are you recording me sir?'

'Did you use to be a detective?'

'No.'

'I thought not,' David is mockingly smiling holding the phone in his outstretched hand.

'Are you trying to be funny?'

'No, just making a casual observation, now why are you here?' His tone was more serious now.

'We have had a complaint from Mr Gibbon...'

'Never heard of him...'

'Can we come in...?

'No, again for the record why are you here?'
'Your upstairs neighbour has made a complaint of excessive music...'
'...Do you hear any music?'
'No, but...'
'Then put the following in your little note books, when we attended there was no music whatsoever playing, have you got that?' G.I. Joe is far from pleased.
'You do realise we can by law confiscate the music equipment...'
'Right, I've heard enough, are you here on a criminal matter, yes or no?'
'We don't know your name; we'll take some details if you don't mind?'
'Actually I do mind, you've not answered my question, are you here on a criminal matter yes or no?'
'We are here to advise you in case things escalate...'
'I don't need your advice, now as you refuse to inform me if you are here on a criminal matter yes or no, I'll give you a piece of advice, you are here to enforce the law, not make the law, now you have wasted my time and at the public's expense, and as a matter of interest, all quiet in Douglas (council housing scheme) tonight gentlemen?' G.I. Joe was lost for words; his silence was the opportune moment to close the door. They hung about for about a few seconds then did an about turn to their car. David moved to the lounge bay windows and dropped the blinds in a slow and uniformed manner. G.I. Joe watched each blind drop slowly. He looked at his colleague 'he may have won this battle, but I'll win the war, I've served in Afghanistan with distinction, someone from Broughty Ferry won't get one over on me.'
'He might put your performance on YouTube. It wouldn't be the first time would it?'
'The public have too much freedom nowadays; it should be illegal to film a police officer when they are carrying out their duties, and definitely a mandatory prison sentence for uploading it to social media.'
'I think you're wrong there, Police Scotland upload content to social media every day.'
'But that's my point, we should be allowed, but the moronic public should not be.'
'I don't think you've thought this through. One thing I liked about your new friend was when he said "all quiet in Douglas?" now that was funny.'
'I didn't get that one?'
'He meant you come to his house about music, which isn't playing when we arrive, his point was how can he turn it down if no music is playing, and we the police have nothing better to do with our time, when there must be something or someone needing our assistance in Douglas.'
'And is there?'

'Not at the moment...' Over their radios comes a request for officers to assist urgently in Balunie Avenue (Douglas) tasers may be required.' G.I. Joe, removes his flat cap and replaces it with his baseball cap, his colleague looks at him with a mixture of pity and dismay. G.I. Joe responds to the radio request. 'On our way, over.' He looks at his colleague. 'Now we're talking,' A manic glee emerging.
'Remember, the Hilltown... don't be too much in a hurry to get to Balunie Avenue.'
'The Hilltown was a personal crisis; I was suffering from PTSD, from my time in Afghanistan...'

***

Pavel sat at the office desk with various broadsheet newspapers in a neat pile to his right. On the front page was an article about the latest apocalypse warning about 'climate change.' Fossil fuels including gas should be phased out sooner than advised. In the House of Lords various members of the Climate Change Advisory Group had been successful in securing debates over the next few months. Lord Marr had cultivated and chosen well. Some of the C.C.A.D. were giving speeches with messianic zealot delivery. It would only be a matter of weeks before the various climate protester groups would be activated, then released on to the busy thoroughfares of London. Maximum global media coverage would ensue. Phase One was completed. He glanced at the various headlines on the broadsheets, the narrative was homogenous; fossil fuels would be a thing of the past, the public was being softened up; the future was renewable energy.

It was time to arrange lunch with Lorna. At her gyms were a burgeoning young affluent climate conscious clientele. Various posters would be strategically placed around the gyms; inviting them to various protests around London. Suggestions how to maximise various civil disobedience activities that may be unlawful were encouraged, "Maximum disruption, minimum damage" was the apt idiom. Various climate change protest groups had emerged very quickly, the demographic of the protesters when they were interviewed on television seemed to be retired academics who had sold their villas in Tuscany, their properties in London, then moved to the Cotswolds, ditched their gas-guzzling Chelsea Tractors for e-bicycles and used wood stoves for heating, while having a healthy bank balance from their sale of properties. Or young middle-class erstwhile students, who portrayed themselves as defenders of the planet, but in reality were middle-class parasitic deadbeats, feeding off their parents' goodwill. To the population in the deindustrialised cities of the north of England, former mining communities of Wales, and drug ravaged communities of the cities of Scotland they were seen as affluent chancers. However, Edinburgh (Holyrood) would be the next city to fall under the spell of the C.C.A.D. The Scottish Government would be in a quandary, open new oil fields that would finance independence or call a moratorium on proposed new oil fields and close existing oil producing fields? He or she who wears the crown carries a heavy burden. However, the prophet in his place of birth would be the lubricant to invite the various self serving MSP's who fortunately were in prominent and influential positions to board the climate change gravy train in first class compartments of course.   Lord Alexander Marr had been a thorn in the Labour Party and the Establishment, he had been invited to address the Scottish Parliament, he was a passionate and persuasive orator. It would be a great and momentous opportunity for the Scottish Parliament to hear that the battery plant for Dundee would be expanded and the workforce doubled. If any city needed good news it was Dundee, which had been ravaged on the altar of Thatcherism. A false god as history has proved.

  This news would be kept from the Scottish Government; they were incapable of keeping their mouths shut. Too many of the Ministers and Westminster MPs, were using politics to further their media careers. And a by-product of this headline grabbing news from Lord Alexander Marr about the battery factory was; they would get planning permission for the factory extension. How could the local council uphold the objections from the environmental lobby?

  On his left side lay a single piece of A4 paper. On it was the pace of Armageddon increasing, unless the West (European Union) were the pioneers of eradicating fossil fuels in a more challenging and minimum timescale. Too many COP Conferences that agreed to combat climate change but when they were back at the ranch, the agreements would be thrown on the fire, and the old practices would continue. Brave decisions would be taken by brave political leaders. There was a cadre of narcissistic politicians who would convince themselves when Lord Alexander Marr was talking, imploring *them* to step forward and replace the incumbent soporific party leaders. *Old wounds would be reopened. Scores would be settled but that was for the future.* The unexpected but life-changing news about the Dundee battery factory mesmerised the star struck MSPs. He would be handed the speech by one of his aides just before he took to the podium at the Scottish Parliament. After the speech there would be the media frenzy. Exactly as Pavel had foreseen

***

.

Edwina and Armstrong are in his office, used coffee cups sit idly on the tray on his desk, stale remnants of second hand cigarette smoke still hangs in the air, even though the window is open about two hundred millimetres from the top. It's been a fraught, tense but fruitful night in connecting David Fisher's friends and colleagues' untimely deaths. There was no conscious bias against David Fisher being involved in their deaths, even vicariously...yet. His personal and business relationships on the face of it were free from acrimony. Armstrong had liaised with an established and reliable contact in the FBI. David Fisher's former partner Gwen Russo had a very interesting background in business finance and personal finance. She was very astute in assessing potential returns from new funds that invested in China. She was meticulous in researching the fund managers, who bought and sold shares in various fintech companies. However, she and other savvy Wall Street investors lost millions to a sophisticated scam. An established and trustworthy Walls Street conglomerate established a new Fund; they would purchase emerging fintech Chinese companies for inflated sums, they would multiply their investment by placing these companies in a shell company then incentivising influential market analysts to tip journalists that these shares were set to increase in value over a short period of time. These journalists wrote for investment columns in newspapers and investment blogs. First of all the protagonists behind the premeditated fraudulent scheme bought a defunct Las Vegas company then merged the Chinese companies into the American company. Then after a short period of time the company would be on the NASDAQ offering shares to the public. Wall Street brokers acting for the conglomerate would offer hedge fund managers shares at a discounted rate, the hedge funds would then offer the shares at a discounted price before the initial trading started. The public would be last in being offered these shares; (Initial Public Offerings). All went well for the first six months, the shares doubled in value, however, that's when the fraudulent part of the scheme emerged; Pump and Dump; they started selling their shares; soon the hedge fund managers followed suit, they had been advised to 'reduce their holding.' Thus they did banking hundreds of millions of dollars in profits. Other Hedge Funds were left to exit at their leisure, and they didn't lose money, as they weren't party to inside information...apparently. The public were advised by influential journalists to hold tight. The reason for this curious advice was to allow the Hedge Funds to exit the market at a favourable price. Less shares for sale the better the return on the Hedge Funds shares. Shares were traded in nano seconds; millions could be lost or made in seconds. Gwen's family had millions in this company; she felt guilty recommending the company and the directors. It was her job to research companies. The American directors had been conned by their

Chinese counterparts; they couldn't go to the FBI as the shares would be made worthless when their Fund was suspended while 'investigations were continuing'.

The Russian Mafia had 'invested' hundreds of millions into the Fund. Thus the 'suggestion' from the Russian Mafia to buy the Las Vegas company merge the Chinese Fintech companies into it, and elevate it onto the NASDAQ after the financial journalists had written various puff pieces in prestigious publications, now this company was ripe to join the NASDAQ and Hedge Funds would be clamouring to secure shares.

Edwina let out a series of expletives after reading the bullet points of the background of the double-cross from the Chinese businessmen investors on their American partners. She suspected that the Chinese investors must have been very slow and methodical in luring in the Americans by verified accounts and acquisitions, which in a very short period of time would exponentially increase in value. She was not too far off the mark in her theory. In fact, it was more rapid and simpler. Other Chinese companies wanted to buy the companies (that the Americans wanted to purchase or rather purloin) with the backing of the Chinese government. The Americans had to move quickly and exceed their counter offer by $50 million dollars. And they still came to the optimistic conclusion that they were stealing the company. However, Edwina would be excluded from this information on the order of Armstrong.

She looked at him then whistled. 'I didn't know you could whistle.'
'Long story... Where does David Fisher fit in here? I know everyone who comes into contact with him, ends up being murdered, but apart from that...'
'Are you fucking kidding me? Apart from that...?'
'No, I'm serious, if he had anything to do with their deaths he would be in jail, obviously there is no empirical evidence,''
'I think I've worked that out myself Edwina. But there has to be a link somewhere. He's returned to Dundee because he feels safer there rather than in London, good luck with that I say.'
'I would do the same, return to kith and kin. Dundee can't be that bad surely?'
'Well, I went and perused Facebook, lot of grim people on there, no optimism for the city from the random posts I read.'
'Hardly a scientific survey, don't you think?' Look at the stats for stabbings alone in London how many were there in Dundee, over the same period of time?'
'How do you expect me to know that?' He's laughing.
'You've just ripped Dundee apart, because you've read a few posts on the Dundee Facebook page. Wow!' He leans back in his chair and has a thin

smile. 'Getting very defensive about a shithole place (Dundee), and before you start, I'm quoting from a poster on Facebook.'
'As I've said it can't be any worse than London, and the Scots have a good reputation for being friendly.'
'Well you'll be able to judge for yourself... you're going there next week. Remember and take plenty warm clothing, and an umbrella... and a stab vest; no strike that, better make that two.'
'Why?'
'Some bastard will steal one of them,'
She looked at him with a mixture of laughter and tears. He didn't half lure her into the trip to Dundee. She admired him for that. He wasn't as thick as she had thought. Then she thought he just got lucky. She composed her thoughts. He dipped his hand into his 'magic drawer' and pulled out a manila folder. 'There you go hen,' he said loudly in a piss poor Scottish accent. She stretched across his desk and retrieved it looking at him.
'Hen?'
'I did my research...'
'Ten minutes on Facebook...?'
'As I was saying, after extensive research, "hen" means a woman.'
'That's curious? Does that mean the women in Dundee don't give a cluck?' He claps his hands. 'Very good Edwina, very good, and if your assessment is correct, you'll fit in perfectly.'
'Well we or rather I will soon see. London, New York and now Dundee, I'm getting to be a bit of a traveller. Does Dundee have an airport and can I fly from London?'
'That was a bit of pessimism there, are you sure you are not on the Dundee Facebook group?'
'Does it have an airport yes or no?'
'Now, now, *hen*, don't get ratty like that in Dundee or someone will bang your *puss*.'
'Puss?'
'Face, I've educated you today, not bad for ten minutes on Facebook?'
'And where will I be staying in Dundee then?'
'An Airbnb in Broughty Ferry which is or *not* in Dundee according to Facebook'
'I'm puzzled, it's a part of Dundee or its not?' He pulls out his phone to access the Dundee Facebook page, he's scrolling to find the comments about Broughty Ferry.
'Well, let's see, ah, here are a few choice comments. " Picturesque Broughty Ferry lovely little fishing village/town " "Broughty Ferry, an open prison for the wealthy" "Snobby bastards all up to their ears in debt" That's a fair assessment of the more sober comments. I'm sure you'll find

out for yourself. And the reason you will be staying in the open prison, sorry picturesque little fishing village, incidentally no fishing boats there, David Fisher lives there, so he'll be easy to keep eyes and ears on.'
'That's even better. It'll make my task easier.'
'Well, I'm not too sure about that, just be switched on 24/7. We've got a tracker on his car, nothing unusual has been thrown up, we are working on accessing his house but he seems to be a bit of a home bird, which means he's working during the day and sometimes through the night. He's been out for a run a few times, but we have to ensure he's out for at least twenty minutes. Ultra fibre is being installed in his road, Grove Road, perfect cover for us, as its curtain-twitcher territory'
'I see, so when I have eyes on him the operatives can enter his flat and put surveillance equipment in?'
'Exactly, he holds the key to at least some of the deaths, he's connected somehow,'
'I'm surprised he goes out for a run after the murder of his colleague in Central Park.'
'Unless he *knew* his colleague wasn't coming back, plenty time to feign, shock and grief, *after* the contract was signed, he'd still get his commission.'
'Can't see it myself that he's involved, more he was the bait for Jonathon Gove to be assassinated in New York, his friend, colleague and neighbour was the business contact he had to meet, must've been a pleasant surprise, then after business has been concluded they celebrate by going to restaurants and clubs.'
'And he *met* Gwen Russo by chance...what do you think?'
'I think you're moving too fast to a conclusion without any facts to back it up. You've got to slow down, it'll take time.'
'Edwina, we don't have time, it's got to be wrapped up with a bow very soon.'
'But that's when mistakes are made and the wrong people go to prison.'
The colour fades from his face, he shrugs his shoulders.

***

The two New York detectives are having lunch, under their casual subterfuge they are observing Michael Ogilvie who is chatting animatedly on his phone, the wine bottle nearly finished, he removes himself from the phone conversation momentarily, whilst he orders anther bottle of wine, the two detectives smile at this spontaneous bout of generosity to himself. Then he glances at his watch, he shows no concern. However, the two detectives take the opposite view; is he meeting someone? Or is he confirming the time he expects to be home?

Either way they would adapt or modify their timetable. The waitress brings over the wine, he tips her well, she is ebullient with his largesse; she pours him a generous glass, he encourages her to increase her measure. The detectives are relaxed at this; Michael has indeed being informing his wife that he will be home early evening, he just has to return to his office to satisfy himself that he has taken all relevant documents and collect his ancient stapler; his wife was not surprised, he was nostalgic and sentimental.

***

Simon's interview at the police station was laconic and unnervingly relaxed; more routine questioning rather than probing. After all he was innocent. The detectives were not aware of the syringe death in Jersey. He was conflicted whether to mention this to the expensive lawyer after the interview. His lawyer told him there would be a news blackout regarding Nigel's death due to "National Security". He came to an executive decision; don't mention it; no good will, would emerge of divulging this potentially damaging information. He wasn't a detective but he definitely knew that Nigel's murder was linked. How could they not be? He didn't believe in coincidences. If he had to make an educated assessment this was international crime or perhaps geopolitical. He quickly emptied his head from over thinking; his lawyer did all the talking he would just write the cheque. Ignorance was bliss. Would he be permitted to remove himself from the UK for a short period of time for his mental health and more importantly his personal safety? Or would they decline his request while the investigation was ongoing? Again he would decline from asking his lawyer for advice. For the first time he felt he would be safer abroad rather than staying put in London. In the taxi returning home, his lawyer said he had information not in writing; that the detectives would not need to interview him anytime in the future. Instead of being elated he felt engulfed by impending doom. Why was that? He was dropped off at his apartment building; he was greeted by the concierge, who didn't mention a thing about Nigel's murder. In the apartment he made himself a mug of coffee and took the well worn trip to the panoramic window. He felt the view of humanity moving in different directions and at different speeds on the Embankment made him appreciate the here and now instead of stressing what fate awaited him in the future. The hot coffee tasted more pleasurable than before, this brought a calming influence to the maelstrom of negative thoughts that were multiplying by the minute in his head. He would be spontaneous he would travel to Paris on the Eurostar, stay in an Airbnb instead of a hotel, this made him feel he was back in control of his life. Money was not an impediment to his freedom. When he heard

"National Security" now that terrified him, he was formulating a method how to survive outwith London. Paris would be the ideal city to escape from pointless speculation of what will or could happen next. Nigel's death at his door propelled his desire to move out of London, Simon's death in Jersey and the complex financial trading methods screamed out money but onerous terms and conditions were attached if a trade went awry. He was released from these thoughts when he observed a man and a woman that seemed to be staring back at him from the Embankment. Was this paranoia?

***

Edwina is settled in her upper floor apartment in the contemporary curved glass fronted building in Beach Crescent in Broughty Ferry; darkness is falling at a leisurely pace. The beautiful furnished and decorated apartment makes her feel envious, she makes a promise to furnish her new home in a similar mode. At the window is a telescope which will be frequently in use to study the plethora of emerging stars that populated the charcoal sky, she knew nothing about astronomy, but her intuition assured her it would be a joyful experience. The cold nights were incrementally and subtly displacing the last remnants of late summer. She could be content to snuggle up on the Italian white sofa and watch a movie on the wall hung television, however, it had been a long day, she was famished, she had pinpointed the myriad of pubs, restaurants, and cafes that were all within walking distance; she chose The Ship Inn, it had impressive reviews, however, she would have her meal in the bar instead of the upstairs restaurant. A sprinkling of rain gently ran down the curved window, now was the time to visit The Ship Inn. She placed her snug fitting hat on and long camel overcoat and exited the building, the wind was increasing by the minute, she struggled to open her small umbrella, the journey would only take a few minutes. A man studied her hurrying, he slowly left the white battered Ford Transit van, he made his way to her apartment building; he bypassed the security entrance with a blank card. He would be in and out of her apartment within four minutes.

Edwina entered the bar and was immediately greeted with a warm smile and was asked if she required a table? 'Yes please.' Settled in she ordered a generous glass of house wine. The bar was sparsely populated, she took out her phone sent a brief message to Armstrong, 'all well, apartment gorgeous, out for dinner, contact you tomorrow.' It was read immediately. He smiled at the live feed of her apartment; he couldn't disagree with her assessment. He flipped the phone closed. He smiled; all going well he mused; he flicked the cigarette out of the window, closed it, then whipped the jacket from the back of his chair, he was in a hurry.

The homemade soup had been consumed in an elegant manner, her Italian pasta; Vesuvio ai Ragu di Salsiccia was also well received and consumed gratefully. Suddenly she felt exhausted, her body was telling her it was time to rest, she had a challenging day tomorrow, scoping out David Fisher's abode on Grove Road, which she would study as a nondescript jogger, Her urge for another wine won her over, then after that a return to her spacious apartment. Her hired car was to be delivered tomorrow at ten am. Her run would commence at seven am, after her studious assessment of David Fisher's flat she would continue up to Strathern Road take a right then continue through the sedate streets to the Esplanade, the crisp fresh air would do her the world of good. She was in Broughty Ferry for five days, she was determined to make the most of her trip and enjoy the company credit card. The bar is starting to fill up she looked at the group of mixed aged boisterous males; immediately she formulated her innate assessment they were detectives, and they were all well oiled; time to make her excuses and leave by the side-exit door. As she was placing on her hat, she and the senior detective locked eyes; however, no words were spoken. She felt overpowered by a sense of fear; she ignored this temporally debilitating feeling, and hurriedly made her way to the exit. His face was imprinted into her subconscious. She remembered she had left her umbrella under the table; the weather had become more inclement; however, nothing in this world could tempt her to return to the bar and retrieve it.

***

Lord Alexander Marr lay in bed ruminating over his busy itinerary while Lorna was having a shower; he was exhausted in body, mind and soul. The tour of Europe's most prestigious universities, with his chosen few of cross-party UK politicians was a remarkable success.

The young impressionable students were treating him as a climate messiah; they passionately believed they had converted him to their cause. In Germany he was welcomed at the Reichstag Building (parliament) by enthusiastic politicians of every persuasion. The Green Party had taken control of the media, they were reporting Lord Alexander Marr as the bulwark who had single-handedly converted the *climate deniers* and difficult UK government to acknowledge and embrace renewable energy technology. Wind, solar and tidal wave were the future for producing energy for domestic and commercial use. Lord Marr as an experienced and wonderful orator and had the crowd cheering and clapping loudly, however, he knew when to return to the simple working class man. He had always been against Nuclear energy; he had multiple police arrests to prove it. This sent the ever increasing volume of the crowd into a frenzy however, he was compelled to thank the Green Party who were far sighted to acknowledge that the planet was hurtling towards extreme weather patterns, they had convinced the German public to vote for them year on year in increasing numbers, and the public's faith was restored in the political system, by ensuring no more Nuclear plants would be built and the existing Nuclear plants would soon be closed and *not* mothballed. This would be replicated in the UK sooner than the political class would realise. Fossil fuels would soon be extinct, and the planet would begin to heal.

However, in France, things were more problematic and realistic. President Macron was a mirror image of Lord Marr in public, and in conversations with the international media. In a *tete e tete* with Lord Marr far from the adoring crowd, he was advised France would only close or limit nuclear energy when the renewable energy sector was fully operable in practice rather than theory. All the while he was smiling as he explained France's immovable position; this was all *off the record*. He was taken aback at this consummate politician frank but unhelpful advice, and if he was not endeared by this pearl of wisdom, another vignette accompanied this. It was Macron's opinion, that Germany would not dare close their Nuclear reactors, private energy companies in Germany had spent billions of euros on partly financing the Nord Stream gas pipeline from Russia to Germany, and there were imminent plans to construct another Nord Stream 2 pipeline. Macron was a former civil servant, then a Rothschild Investment Banker before he entered politics. Lord Marr had read the laughable claims online the he was *encouraged* to enter politics at the behest of Rothschild's, to counter act the Green energy cult; a ridiculous idea never mind theory. Lord Marr couldn't formulate a cerebral response to Macron's advice, however, the political mood music was changing from soothing classical music where the elite would sip their expensive coffee on the tree lined boulevards in Paris to out of tune and ear piercing punk anthems, which intended to smash up the tables and chairs that festooned the fashionable parts of Paris. *Mouvement des gilets* (Yellow Vest Protests) were out in their thousands protesting against Macron's increasing diesel prices, Macron said it was to fund climate change renewable energy research; two hats Macron, was Lord Marr's polite moniker he told close friends he had gave him after their *off the record* laconic chat. Other European parliaments and leaders of political parties were less resistant to his vision of a less fossil fuelled energy market than Macron's vision of the renewable energy replacing fossil fuels and overtly scepticism about the rapid transmission to renewable energy. He told friends that the French Government have always been against *green energy/issues.* Who can forget the French Government's attack on the Greenpeace boat the Rainbow Warrior, which French Intelligence bombed in Auckland in 1985 killing a photographer? Trust the French Government? Highly unlikely. When Lord Marr was leaving the Ritz Hotel along with other delegates to have lunch in the Eiffel Tower, he was approached and stopped by a beautiful tall slender woman in her early forties who advised him not to have the steak at the Eiffel Tower, but to change it to veal at the last moment. She then walked away. This brief conversation stunned him into silence. How did she know they were heading to the Eiffel Tower, and steak was his choice? Other delegates witnessed this rapid conversation, and equally rapid departure. He was clearly upset, should they intervene or let him compress the conversation and talk about it at lunch? They unanimously and wisely chose the latter.

***

If David had a relapse he had the therapist's number to call anytime. Today was the day when *that* David Fisher sat in the expansive kitchen; he had had it decorated in the fashionable but depressing colour grey, his helpful neighbour had arranged a close relative to decorate the recently fitted kitchen, she knew two Polish tradesmen, who were half the price of national kitchen fitters, David gave them a £200 bonus as a thank you. He studied his laptop and sipped his tea slowly. Nothing recent about Gwen's demise in his apartment in London, while he welcomed no news is good news, he still felt perturbed. He had to adhere to not over thinking the matter. The noise from pneumatic drills drove the anxiety from his mind, he decided to declutter his mind with a run; he smiled at this impetuous thought, running through the various affluent side streets away from the main streets and roads. He heard the anti-social neighbour had pulled himself from his chair, and run down the stairs at some speed, no doubt the workmen were using their drills and other tools at an unacceptable decibel level, or maybe they were disturbing his beauty sleep; and boy, did he need it. This he had to see, he quickly changed into his running attire, he was halfway to the front door, when that sickly smile emerged, rather than exit via the front door; he would leave by the back door and walk with a confident smile down *his* path. The unsocial neighbour was having a screeching row with a few of the workmen. When he saw David walk down the disputed path, he left the nonplussed workmen who had been on the end of numerous sharp rebukes from him, hence they didn't remove their ear defenders and kept their eyes to the ground and their pneumatic drills pounding the pavements, however, when they saw him confront David they all stopped in unison. He was much taller than David, who was not intimidated by his hulking posture.

'Are you fucking stupid? What have I told you about using my path; do you want me to call the police again?'

David looked at him with utter contempt. 'While you're calling the police call the ambulance as well, because if you talk to me like that again, you'll be in the ambulance, do you get my drift, thicko?'
'Are you threatening me?'
'And you called me stupid; no I don't threaten individuals I deal with them in a thoughtful manner. And for your information, thicko, this is a "common" path, so I will be using it on a frequent and annoying basis, you'll see that on your title deeds, but because you have a mortgage you don't have the title deeds. So do yourself a favour and get to fuck out of my way, or I'll throw you into your unattended rose bush.'
He was left to contemplate his unwise action, and he had a dispassionate audience pondering his next move. He turned round to the workmen whom he had been castigating earlier.
'Did you hear him threaten me?' They in unison adjusted their ear defenders and resumed digging up the pavement. David gestured with a contemptuous hand gesture for him to move out the way. He moved past David at apace. All the workmen's eyes were on David, who was going through a charade of warming up exercises in full view of them. They halted their drills to give him a spontaneous round of applause as he emerged from the path onto the pavement, deliberately leaving the ornamental gate which he had paid to get painted wide open. He smiled at the workmen; then turned round to see the neighbour at his lounge window on the phone. An educated guess it would be the police because he had threatened him and then onto the fibre company complaining about the incorrigible workmen. Returning to more pleasant thoughts; should he take a left up towards Albany Road or a right towards the Dundee Road? He decided to take a right then cross the Dundee Road onto the bridge then Douglas Terrace when the inspirational view of the River Tay would keep him company. He would continue onto Beach Crescent then all the way up the Esplanade up to the Barnhill Rock Gardens, he would take a seat and gather his marauding thoughts and stare across the Tay at Tentsmuir Forest in Fife, it never failed to decompress any anxiety when he was younger and fitter. The years' had flown past, but the view was still frozen in time. The Esplanade was being reconstructed with flood defences and a cycle path, it was looking impressive. He was afraid that the pull of Broughty Ferry on his heartstrings would curtail his eventual return to London; however, Broughty Ferry wasn't Devil's Island was it? The forecast was rain, he better complete his run before the grey sky grew darker, if the police turned up at his door; then so be it. He had more virulent thoughts to contend with.

Edwina had observed him gliding past her apartment, she received the text that she hadn't expected, the police were at David Fisher's door; they would have to enter another day, not to worry. To say she was disappointed was untrue she was irritated. She was going to go out for a walk that took her past his flat in Grove Road, she had been briefed about the dispute with his neighbour; she didn't want it to escalate. However, she had experience with her neighbour so she understood the frustration David would be experiencing, and using her own rationale it would be a lengthy but hopefully not a violent dispute. Her eyes reached for the sky, not inspiring she concluded, rain was rolling up the Tay estuary, time to make a move.

***

Armstrong was shaken out of his confident and congratulatory mode when he saw her leave the lounge then return with heavy coat, hat and scarf. This could be counter-productive. She left the flat and exited by the rear entrance onto King Street, she crossed the road heading towards the under bridge, she would meander through the streets then eventually onto Grove Road, what she planned to do there was not clear, she was to study the area for some undefined reason, illogical but compelling. Armstrong lifted the phone and dialled, the conversation was short but never sweet, 'get in and out, she's on her way.' No debate or questions. 'It's done.' Armstrong replaced the handset with a palpable sense of relief. The window was opened, the "occasional" cigarette was in his mouth and lit, worry returned and the cigarette was red with long nervous draws on it. Edwina was meant to be part of the solution, but she could be adding to the problem, or it's him overthinking things once again.

She was sent up to Broughty Ferry to get her out of the way, so he can deal with the events in London. Her contact in St. Petersburg had had an untimely death; when his apartment was searched he had a file on her, which was unflattering if not criminal. He was long suspected of being a free lance font of information which was available at a price, there were a holdall full of American dollars under his bed, why it was not in a more secure location in his apartment defied belief. His apartment had been used as a meeting place for gambling and illicit affairs. There were no cameras secreted anywhere in the apartment, so this was a solo and self-serving operation and extremely lucrative. The file on Edwina had information about her dispute with her neighbour and her friend (waiter) who had shared her generous offer to stay overnight in New York. Where this information in the file came from was a mystery, however, would it be used to compromise her into revealing information about individuals who worked for the Economic Crime Unit or persons of interest to the Economic Crime Unit? Armstrong had secrets that were best left undisturbed .If it came to the ultimate sacrifice he would willingly unburden the sins of his onto the unwilling participant; Edwina. The information in the file would add ballast to allegations against her; he hoped it would not come to that, but if he was left with no alternative Edwina would be perfect. His mood was lightened as he rapidly thought through the end game. Edwina had demurred from informing him of the conversation she had with the unexpected ex-diplomat, but he knew now; devious or a guardian of confidential information? That was a moot point at the moment. How he loved sitting at this window, it calmed him down, many seemingly impossible problems were eradicated or minimised here. He thought forward to the future, it was his settled will Edwina would be the eraser to his misdemeanours if he had no alternative. He looked at his watch then closed the window. The familiar rap on the door, they were on time. 'Come in' he shouted, the two New York Detectives walked in, they took their seats without an invitation. They laid the briefcase on his desk, He manoeuvred past them to lock the door

***.

David Fisher had enjoyed ruminating about his impoverished childhood while he sat drinking in the view and enjoying the serenity of the Barnhill Rock Garden, the bench that he was sitting on was dedicated to a worthy soul, it was good how good people were remembered and their kindness lives on as long as the bench was in situ, How many hearts were broken or lifted on this simple bench? Worries spoken and eradicated? Now to complete his run and return to Grove Road, running down Dalhousie Road, then past the Post Office bar, he would increase the pace, then increase it again when he came to the steep gradient at Grove Road, the rain started to lightly hit his face, he naturally increased his speed, he viewed the gradient with apprehension, the rain became noticeable, there was no noise from the workmen installing the Ultra Fibre, he would be able to work in the lounge. His breathing became heavy and rapid, he arrived at the communal gate, he was struggling he bent down to increase his breathing, however, when he brought his head up, he noticed a camera on the side elevation of his property. All tiredness vanished. He marched up the disputed path and entered his property; his volcanic temper he had from his youthful days returned. The shower would calm him down, the music was being played at a vexatious level, this was designed to bring the neighbour to his door, then justice would be delivered in a rapid manner; no need for a jury to deliver deliberation.

To his extreme disappointment, his door was never darkened. Sitting in the lounge with the music at a subdued level, he opened his laptop; the rain was increasing and making audible sounds on his lounge windows; he was in a quandary to abandon the lounge and increase the music level in favour of the kitchen with an adequate supply of coffee. While silently hoping the recalcitrant neighbour came to his door about the music he would instruct him to remove the competitively priced camera. He made an executive decision; he would hunker down in the kitchen, closing the lounge door behind to confine the music's path onwards and upwards. The coffee was bubbling away merrily; the kitchen table covered in strewn papers with various financial graphs and information in the margins; some ominously in red type. Then he took his seat, sipped the coffee, then music to his ears; the doorbell rang not incessantly which disappointed him, He decided to wait a period of time, then make his way to the front door. He removed his slippers and replaced them with heavy hiking boots, his anger increasing as he threaded the leather laces through the eyelets, once this mundane task was completed; he made his way along the stretching hall to the front door with alacrity. He opened the vestibule door; there his eyes were met with disappointment; through the double paned opaque glass he saw the hulking silhouette of a police officer. Change of temperament and mood was required immediately; scowling face was substituted temporarily for a visage of unfettered joy. When he placed his hand on the handle to open the door, he remembered his phone was on the kitchen table. He rapidly retrieved it and returned to welcome his long lost amigo. Camera on; he opened the door so quickly that the officer jumped back. 'Yes, can I help you... again?' It was GI Joe. Not a challenge to his intellectual capacity. 'Is that a camera? Are you recording me?'

Fuck me! he's definitely not a fan of spy movies. Holding the camera in his outstretched hand he had to subdue his mirth. 'Officer did you used to be a detective by any chance?'

'No, why do you ask' If he scratched his voluminous head, his steps would be covered in sawdust. He was enjoying this. 'I've got an obvious phone in my hand and... forget it, why are you here, a plant pot been moved in a suspicious manner?'

'Are you trying to be funny?' GI Joe was rattled.

'Ironic.'

'What do you mean?'

'This is going to be a long conversation; shall I get my shaving gear or sandwiches?'

'I can arrest you, you do know that?'

'For...?'

  GI Joe was feeling this was going to be a difficult conversation; he'd rather negotiate with a Taliban warlord. 'Look, I'm trying to be reasonable, I'm here to contain things, and not let neighbour disputes escalate, and offer advice.' David noticed the plaster over his eyebrow. 'If you are here to help, come with me.' He stepped onto the small path that ran parallel to

his lounge window, he invited the officers to follow him; they did reluctantly. David points at the camera. 'What do you make of that then?'
'It is a camera.' David looks at him. 'Yes, I know that! Are you sure you weren't a detective?' Your friend upstairs has placed it on my property, and it's illegal.'
'I think you are wrong there.'
'In what respect?'
'It is not illegal to have a camera on private property.'
'I agree, but it's on my property?' Now what are you going to do about it?' GI Joe, steps back into the garden and study's the position of the camera, then returns to his mute colleague and stares at it again. David is getting impatient. 'Well?'
'How do you know it's your property?'
'Because I bought it! Look I'll break it down to you so a five year old would understand. My property is painted, your friend's is not, look all around you, the buildings are divided by obvious painting.
'But I'm not a property lawyer.'
'I kinda worked that out for myself. Now ask your friend upstairs to remove the camera and advise him he is breaking the law, to corroborate with what I have told you; you or him can check the Information Commissioner's website, it's there in black and white, and if you're struggling to understand it take a five year old with you.' The silent officer laughed. GI Joe shot him a disapproving look.
'Right remove the competitively priced camera from my property and give him your aforementioned advice, then remove yourselves from my property without further ado.'
GI Joe is bursting with anticipation to counter this argument. He pokes his finger to raise his cap. David laughs at this puzzling move. 'How do you know it's your neighbour's?'
'Well that's your job to find out, or maybe pass it onto Interpol, or find a five year old they'll manage to ascertain who owns it.'
'I'm here to advise you to turn down the music, not find out who owns the camera.'
'OK, OK, I'm not turning down the music, now what?'
'You really think you're a smart ass don't you?'
'Compared to present company...absolutely. Now I have this entire conversation on camera, if you don't ascertain who this camera belongs to, I'll remove it. Your move officer. And the camera is still rolling... are you on Facebook?' GI Joe takes the sensible option, and turns away and walks towards the police car. David watches them depart and gave them a cheery, sarcastic and enthusiastic wave. When they are out of sight, he films himself removing the camera and popping it through the neighbour's

letterbox. The workmen in the portable canteen were observing this comedic encounter. All this palaver happening in the sedate, affluent suburb of Broughty Ferry, which rumour has it is an overspill of Douglas, Hmm?

David returned to his sanctuary; he could use that cup of coffee now. The local difficulties he was experiencing took his mind off the serious events in London, and anything that achieved this however banal was a major positive. Everything had remained quiet; no information either positive or negative had made its way from London to Dundee. He was meeting his dad at The Fort tomorrow for evening dinner; he daren't mention his curious experience with the police; that would send him into a incessant rant. Less information, the better the dining experience. He activated the laptop; the financial graphs were displaying positive sentiments towards his recent multi-million investments. It had been sclerotic experience with GI Joe. He forecast he would return to enquire where the camera was, he would assume his neighbour had removed it; due to the advice from the police.

Edwina had observed this shambolic public relations disaster from her car positioned between other cars on Grove Road, near the workers' canteen, she couldn't hear the conversation, but heard the bursts of uproarious laughter from the men, who seemingly were enjoying impromptu street theatre. All that aside, she was relieved to see David remove the camera, and return it via the letterbox; very strange. The street was eerily quiet she had never encountered a street with such few passing cars or dog walkers. In London the only experience she could compare it to when there was an ongoing hostage situation. A property in a similar street in London would be unaffordable. Tomorrow the forecast was dry and sunny, the surveillance hardware would be installed before David had broken sweat on his run; she was super confident that the installation of the surveillance hardware would also be removed easily and within a five minute or less timeframe. The only slight concern was the dispute with the upstairs neighbour. If it came to it, the police would be discouraged to pursue any 'erroneous' complaint against David Fisher, The plans of mice and men.

***

David's ebullient mood had been managed professionally once when he was in his early thirties, cocaine use was rife; he had been encouraged to take it against his better judgement. He was the catalyst for many successful takeovers of potential profitable companies, his personal wealth and reputation seemed to have no limit; all the corporate American merchant banks wanted him badly. Golden hello incentives starting at £3 million seemed paltry; he would bide his time. Friends could not believe when he eventually broke the news he was going solo. He would fall or fly by his own decisions. And that was the day he finally gave up cocaine. He had sought professional help. Don't get too high when things go well, and don't get too down when things don't go well. In this case the mantra had to be adhered too.

He had taken a laconic but disturbing call from the City of London police. They had discovered the reason for the murder of Gwen and the people who were the architects and executioners; the Russian Mafia. Gwen had invested her family's substantial income which were invested in steady income trusts; she had persuaded the family members to liquidate the trusts and place the money in a new company that had recently listed on the New York Stock Exchange; she failed to disclose that she had been financially incentivised to persuade high-net worth individuals and hedge fund managers to liquidate their assets into cash and buy shares in the new company. Gwen had an enviable reputation for impressive returns; it was all there on the internet. She was nobody's fool. However she was the unwitting facilitator to a scam. The people behind the scam were employed by a California Bank; Gwen had dealt with them on a professional basis over a number of years. The bank earned millions of dollars in fees from hedge funds. The bank had invested in Chinese Small Companies who were insanely profitable; the bank had been approached to secure a listing on NASDAQ (Technology) from other various Chinese Small Companies. The strategy was once they were on the NASDAQ; the companies would go public. However, the Hedge Funds and certain individuals; including Gwen would be offered shares at a discounted price compared to the public. This was a classic "pump and dump" scheme. And it worked like a dream. Unfortunately for Gwen, and other hedge fund managers; they were not party to this information, all they were left with were multi-billion dollar losses; Gwen had lost millions. She had done her due diligence everything was in order. At the exclusive road show for the new capital venture featuring various profitable Chinese companies; there was a former president of the USA in attendance; an expensive worm to give credence and probity to the bank's exclusive lucrative plan. Millions were spent and creating this lavish scheme; the bank had purchased a defunct American company, merged the profitable Chinese companies (reverse merger) to all and sundry the Am*erican company was increasing profits every year.* The 'dirty money' was invested by unwittingly hedge funds; the Russian Mafia who would reap clean money long before the scam was discovered. A substantial amount of the newly cleaned money would end up in the London property market. The FBI didn't discover this; Gwen had, and that had sealed her fate. She knew that Jonathon Gove was behind this fraudulent scheme; David had been manipulated by Gwen, she had used her 'chance' meeting at the Russian Samovar club. Her Modus Operandi was to separate Jonathan from David. Gwen had vicariously murdered Jonathon; she had organised the 'hit' on Jonathon, and she had the perfect alibi; she had spent the night with David. None of this would appear in the Press, as it was under National Security. The Attorney General had successfully taken out an injunction against any media reporting or even commenting on Gwen's murder. This was the time to call his therapist without going into the case; a difficult situation on its own. In the kitchen his head was unsuccessfully trying to construct a cogent story to explain to his therapist. He would wing it. He placed the coffee back on the oak kitchen table, his heart pounding. He looked at the discoloured business card, and punched in the number on his phone on the table. It was answered immediately; 'Hi David, how are you?' 'Not too well to be honest Lorna.'

**

In the UK media all the headlines pointed to a concerned mother who was caught at Schiphol airport (Amsterdam) with cannabis for her pain-racked son, the cannabis eliminated the multiple seizures he suffered every day. She was a working mother who was spending over £1200 a month to purchase the cannabis. Now she was being treated as a de facto drug dealer. The NHS refused to prescribe or treat similar patients with the cannabis as it was not licensed. Lord Alexander Marr in the House of Lords gave an impassioned speech that captured the hearts and minds of the sparsely occupied benches. However, this was designed for public consumption. 'What kind of society are we living in, if governments both sides of the border are proposing legal consumption of heroin overseen and administered by NHS staff to addicts, but a child who is suffering, cannot be prescribed medicinal cannabis? This anomaly must be rectified in months rather than years. I do not hold credence to the professionals who say and have been quoted that there is no positive proof that this cannabis alleviates pain or seizures. With the utmost respect, I think this hard-working mother is the best arbiter of this situation. Why would she fly to Amsterdam and pick up the cannabis every month if it didn't work? The UK is the world's chief exporter of medicinal cannabis to countries throughout the world however; the public in the UK cannot purchase the indigenous medicinal cannabis? This is beyond cruel, and legislation must be rushed through the House of Commons as soon as time allows.'
Sitting in the public gallery was Pavel, he was so proud of his protégé Lord 'Green Fingers'

Had earned this moniker not as a pejorative term, but as a compliment, he could cultivate any political heavyweight to his cause even though they were devoid of any knowledge of the subject. Looking around the Chamber, he had made certain allies with his thought provoking speech. Obviously, when the UK acknowledges the contradiction in its present policy, medicinal cannabis will become a multi-billion industry in the UK alone. And the government would derive impressive tax revenues, to help fund the NHS, Lord Alexander Marr would have this written in the Bill, even though he was unaware of it yet. He glanced over to the Press Gallery he could foretell the headlines tomorrow. The British public were outraged; he would ensure *his* outraged but articulate members of the public would be on LBC and BBC 5 live call-in shows the next morning. They would add to the momentum. Other people who took cannabis to manage pain would be praising Lord Alexander about his moral outrage; however, he had come up with a solution to benefit society and the government would have envious tax revenue from an unexpected source. The Treasury would be lobbying to get this law passed in the least amount of time. As expected, a social commentator in the Daily Mail had echoed Lord Alexander Marr's critical points, "the governments in the UK were going to administer and finance heroin addicts, but working mothers had to fly to Amsterdam and purchase cannabis at *their* own expense, and in addition could be jailed for being drug dealers? And she was unaware that the UK was the primary source of medicinal cannabis that exported to the rest of the world. Has this once great country of ours taken leave of our senses? This cruel anomaly must be rectified as quickly as possible. How can it be safe to *export* medicinal cannabis to Europe and afar, but the citizens of the UK cannot get the same medicinal cannabis for them or loved ones? Absolute impaired logic and financial cruelty. Over to you Parliament." The airwaves were choked with horrifying and heartbreaking personal stories. Savvy MPs were quick to offer to appear on these gladiatorial radio and television programmes. They would be raising these points with the Health Secretary in Parliament and in a letter. Other MPs were fighting each other to raising the matter in a Private Members Bill. The fortunate member that had had their bill passed would never be forgotten by the affected public or more important history. Many hard-right MPs of the 'hang them and flog them' brigade had their granite hearts immediately replaced with a heart that showed empathy. There was no coincidence that the government had became stale and lethargic and immune to public concerns, and various opinion polls predicted that these well-fed entitled individuals would be spending more times with their families, and filling up their expensive cars and stomachs no longer at the public's expense.

Social media was in meltdown, with the common thread why was this allowed to happen?
Various 'influencers' observed the moral outrage, and added their voices as well and increase their clicks on social media and views on YouTube, nothing wrong with capitalising in financial terms and empathy with an outraged public and devoted followers. Everyone was a winner it seemed, apart from MPs who were being assailed from every direction and every political view. One savvy 'influencer' had started a fundraising page for the "Amsterdam Nurse" it raised £40k in six hours. All branches of the media and social media citizen journalists turned up at her house without invitation, but this was publicity that money couldn't buy. The influencer structured the informal interview and uploaded it to her YouTube channel it was viewed and shared worldwide by many millions; her bank balance surpassed the meagre sum that was raised by the fundraising page. The nascent of legalising cannabis had begun. One thing politicians cannot argue with was vociferous public outrage that threatened to quickly morph into civil disorder. Members of Parliament of every political stripe have a tendency to legally and some illegally pillage the public purse at every opportunity, those who enter parliament with the best of intentions and convince the public that they are different, soon succumb to the trappings of power and influence. The pharmaceutical industry in the United States of America spends billions of dollars lobbying members of congress. Why are the public surprised when this happens in old blighty? Pavel was a student of democracies and totalitarian governments they all fail on outside influences. Big Oil and Big Pharma. And it is no coincidence that when there is political unrest even in democratic elected governments to third-world tyrannical governments that are either removed by soft power or bombs and bullets; in the wreckage you'll always find a McDonalds wrapper. Pavel had recruited well, he had winced at the tactics over the decades of the so called world's most democratic country; the United States of America. However, since the advent of the internet, he was the catalyst to abolish interventions by tanks and infantry; soft power was more influential, and cost effective, no one with two single brain cells that would ultimately collide and create an idea in the most vacuous of craniums, would understand that Facebook was a private company, however in reality it was a government project. Edward Snowden now a resident in Moscow had let the cat out of the bag when he disclosed that the government were gathering information and spying on the American public. However, every word or photograph uploaded to Facebook is now in their gift to do what they will with this information, the public agreed to this as it is incorporated in Facebook's terms & conditions. Ingenious.

It was only a matter of time before medicinal and recreational use of cannabis was made legal. Pavel's timetable for this momentous day had been brought forward by years. His investment in the cultivation of medicinal cannabis had been underestimated; there would be a General Election in less than two years' time. His 'bots' would be flooding Social Media urging politicians to bring forward a date when cannabis would be legalised. And the tax revenues could not be ignored by any of the mainstream political parties. When cannabis was legalised in the UK, he would organise pressure groups in the European Union to follow the UK in legalising cannabis. He had an unlimited budget to finance these pressure groups, and pay their spoke persons an attractive salary; these persons had to be selected and must have an academic or medical background. He had a person in mind. His becalmed mind turned to his protégé Lord Alexander Marr, as well as an articulate orator, he had an engaging personality and a endearing social conscience; and he connected with young people instantly. The warm countries of southern Europe were ideal for growing cannabis; it would grow quickly and be ready to export economically within the EU, the savings in energy and transport cost were phenomenal. He or rather his companies would be buying arable land in poorer parts of Spain and France. When the day came that cannabis would be legal, he would clear the fields of their produce and prepare the land for the acres of cannabis plants. Obtaining the necessary licence would not prove difficult. There would be a finite number of licences, big Pharma would have the bulk of them; he would be awarded his, away from the glare and scrutiny of the media. However, that was in the distant future, he would concentrate his time and money in convincing the politicians in parliament to expedite legislation when the new parliament sat for the first time. It did not concern him which party
formed the new government; it would still be the same wheel but different hamster. Lord Alexander Marr would articulate in the House of Lords that MPs of all parties were showing great courage and respect to science and the public when cannabis was legal. He could be mischievous by adding 'as some of you are already aware of medicinal properties in combating anxiety and stress" but thought better about it, it would be about the 'Amsterdam Nurse' who had opened the door to out of touch politicians to the harsh reality of their neglected constituents.

***

In The Shard apartment Pavel is pouring out coffee for Lorna and himself; Lorna is transfixed by the London skyline, even though the dark brooding sky will soon release torrential rain. Both are pleased with the unfolding events in major cities throughout the world; these were not spontaneous climate demonstrations; the seeds were planted into the minds of the receptive, malleable, fertile students of a plethora of prestige universities throughout Europe. The days of bombs and bullets were archaic, discriminatory and lethal methods to subjugate populations. Soft power was the vogue persuasive narrative without the need for violence and spilt blood. Donate vast sums to supine idealist university lecturers, influential journalists, and media personalities. Journalists influenced the older population; the millenniums were addicted to social media and short videos; money was catapulted towards this modern phenomenon; whoever controls social media controls the narrative. Any individual who were unwise to post a counter narrative were swamped by personal insults and subtle threats. All financed by various environmental charities and NGOs (Non Government Organisations) controlled by Pavel's acolytes. However his potent and productive bulwark was Lord Marr who was expensive but worth the millions that financed him; notwithstanding the money he purloined from the various charities and lobby groups. Old habits die hard. He was setting in motion future difficulties. His jurisprudence would be called into question about certain unregistered withdrawals from an environmental charity that could or would lead him onto the road to destruction; alcohol.

Pavel felt he was intruding into Lorna's inner peace as he placed the coffee mug on the table below her gaze. 'Thank you Pavel. I love this view.' Pavel sat to the left of her. 'The reason I asked you here, was to personally thank you for your efforts in recruiting your members of your gyms to engage in the climate change movement; whether by placing the most vocal in touch with various environmental charities; and the three cerebral individuals have become paid employees after they resigned from prestigious banks or hedge funds; all at a financial cost to themselves. However; blue chip lawyers will be contacting their erstwhile employers regarding various discriminatory and illegal practises that forced them out. I am confident that when they receive the hand delivered letters and the name of the legal firm acting for their erstwhile female employees; they will settle in fourteen days.'

Lorna averted her eyes from the compelling skyline and fixed her gaze on Pavel. 'None of them have mentioned this to me.' Pavel raised the mug to his smiling lips; then returned it to the table.

'That's because you have to break the unexpected good news to them; someone from the legal department will be in touch to invite them separately for an informal appointment. We are talking about six figure sums with no fee for the service of the legal firm. They will sign an NDA. (Non Disclosure Agreement) the three women launching their claims will

not be able to discuss with anyone from the launch of the claim to the settlement. They will be advised of this at their individual meeting which will only take a maximum of fifteen minutes. I forgot to mention each sum will be tax free; the various offending companies will pay the due tax.'
'What an unexpected bonus for them; it will be difficult for them to remain silent about this, and obviously I will be oblivious to these recent events. The three of them are personally invested emotionally in each charity, and are content than in their previous careers... *that they were forced to leave.*'
'Exactly Lorna! They are more fulfilled human beings exiting the insidious pressure of the claustrophobic corporate culture that awaits every individual that sits at their computer day after day. And without doubt when these cases are settled the news will leak from the corporate circle in the bars; head will roll.'
'I've been there and it is only when you are outside of this poisonous culture that you can become whole again if you battle the demons It is a false happiness; booze and cocaine, lack of sleep; is a heavy price to pay for a large salary.' Pavel noticed her eyes become moist and return to the panoramic skyline; the incessant rain is periodically accompanied by the boom of thunder that makes her jolt forward. Lightening crackles the dark sky, the darkened room becomes eerily silent. Pavel removes himself from the chair to turn the various lamps on, and this gives Lorna the space to harness her thoughts and dispose of the pernicious ones. The gloomy vista engulfing London comforts Lorna.
She brings the coffee mug with both hands to her lips and sips it as though she doesn't want it to end.
The news of lawyers and non informed future litigants brought a wide smile; the women involved were well-educated but hated their careers, Lorna knew the angst they had suffered; they wouldn't be the last. Pavel returned to the table, Lorna's phone rang out breaking the silence. She looked at the name, and rejected the call to voicemail. It was David Fisher.

***

Michael has consumed the last bottle of wine; he looks around the walls with personal pride, he wasn't a frequent visitor to The Iron Duke but every social or business engagement left him more fulfilled than when he entered. David Fisher had left an endearing impression on him more than any other individual. It was his honesty when it came to discussing business; he was not a charlatan. On the surface anyway was his assessment. There would be no tears when he left London; the sum for his business was life changing to the mere mortal, to him, it was a welcome bonus. His wife thought he was joking when he advised her he would return to the office to retrieve the old stapler; this was the reason to return, however, he wanted to sit in silence for a few moments, go down the nostalgia route, then depart without any doubt that he was doing the right thing. London was changing rapidly Russian businessmen had altered the financial landscape to the detriment of the old boy network. This was applicable to Michael. Spivs were the majority in the City, there were numerous government compulsory financial checks to be carried out; however, these were opaque and traders, hedge fund managers and financial advisors came to the ubiquitous decision each decision was based on interpretation of the law. Michael was old school; if someone didn't pass the sniff test; they were politely declined; due to overwhelming current business.

  He stood up slightly unsteady on his feet, the two New York detectives observed this and were not perturbed; the hovering waitress (Lena) moved quickly to steady him and advised he had obviously enjoyed the wine. Her eyes locked with the female detective; the return gaze was met with approval. Michael left, after composing himself, and made his journey to his soon to be former place of employment.

The New York detectives gave him a few minutes head start then made their way to the exit. Lena cleared their table the napkin was dispensed into the black bag then she felt for the envelope which was secreted within the discarded New York Times newspaper which was in pristine condition and discarded them also into the black bag; she returned to the bar area where she picked up various newspapers and placed them into the black bag. She went into the rear office and retrieved the envelope. £5000 was in the envelope as promised; she had handed in her notice the week before; this was her last day. She had earned £5000 by eliciting background information from David Fisher in the guise of gentle flirting; nothing too clandestine. He was not boastful of any successful deals he had completed. The only innocuous information he had inadvertently divulged was his imminent and catastrophic trip to New York. This was invaluable to the detectives; but seemed a bland routine business trip at the time. However, to the detectives this was gold dust as they could elevate their murderous plot from theory into practice. She had unknowingly contributed to Jonathon Gove's violent death on a bench in Central Park, New York City. At the time she was advised the David Fisher's life was in danger from the Russian Mafia in London, she would be able to engage him in conversation about life in general. No matter what she thought would be trivial everyday chit chat could maybe avert danger from his person. Therefore she was helping protect David Fisher, and "National Security" she would be pecuniary compensated for this task. When she heard their distinctive New York accents this triggered immediately the business trip to New York. She texted the number they had given her, after David Fisher merrily made his way home. This was invaluable. When the news broke that Jonathon Gove had been murdered by the Russian Mafia, she was visited at the bar, and was told she had "saved" David's life as he was due to go out running with Jonathon Gove; the Russian Mafia had murdered Jonathon Gove by mistaken identity. Then she was advised to pick up the New York Times as there was something of interest that would benefit her. Lena felt a good feeling engulf her how she had saved David Fisher's life by advising of his imminent business trip to New York. However, her happiness was heightened by the money stuffed envelope within the New York Times newspaper, the first of three envelopes. The last envelope she removed from the black bag; she had no need to count it, looking at it was the mandatory sum of £5000; life changing for her to alter her unfulfilled benighted life. Unbeknown to the two New York detectives Lena was also friendly with a genteel polite gentleman; Pavel. Therefore he was numerous steps ahead of the detectives, Pavel had found out where David Fisher socialised, Lorna had had lunch at The Iron Duke; she had invited Lena to join the gym at a discounted rate, where was her apartment? Lorna had told her an apartment was becoming vacant in a month's time, when Lorna was told her rent; she immediately said she knew the landlord (Pavel) and she could negotiate on her behalf to make it more competitive than her present rent. She was ecstatic at this news.

***

David sat at the kitchen table staring out at the birds that had settled in the Rowan tree. When he had moved into Grove road the Rowan tree was a sapling; it had grown sturdy and confident over time; a bit like himself apart from his height. After consuming a light lunch; he was back to the laptop with renewed vigour; the stock market was in bear territory as it had been for the last few days, his laptop was in split-screen mode; shares and Bitcoin. Bitcoin was rapidly appreciating in value but he reigned in his compulsion to sell a portion of his holding and await further profits. However, when the facts changed on his laptop screen and there were a tsunami of sell offs he would follow suit.

The door bell chimed; he was expecting the visitors. He had to dispose of his thin smile before he answered the door, he glanced at the laptop, shares were still being sold off, the market was down two percent but Bitcoin was increasing in value. He opened the door the scourge of the Taliban had returned, he casually retrieved his phone from his rear pocket and started recording GI Joe and his new colleague.

'Yes, can I help you?' 'Are you recording me?' David shook his head sadly in reply. 'Why are you recording me?' 'To make sure there are no misunderstandings when I put my complaint in against you, now why are you here?' GI Joe was taken aback that a complaint against him was going to be lodged. However, that would be confronted when it had arrived; he was here on a more serious matter. 'Can you tell me whose plant pots beside the path belong to?' David aimed the phone at four plant pots of various sizes which contain various weeds and a crop of dandelions. 'The pots that are situated beside the *common path?*' GI Joe's demeanour visibly sank; this was not going to be a congenial meeting. 'Yes that's correct.' 'They belong to your *friend* upstairs, are you here to remove the weeds and replace them with flowers?' 'No, we are here because we have had a complaint that you've been repeatedly moving them, and you have admitted the pots don't belong to you, do you have a valid reason why you are moving them?' 'Officer, I admire your testicular fortitude, you have disturbed me at my home when I am working, and ask me why I have moved pots that are full of weeds, are you fucking kidding me?' 'Calm down.' 'No I won't calm down, the reason I moved the pots was to allow my ladder onto my property to remove the camera which was on *my* property; I can't believe you are here because of that. Do you want to interview the pots to see if they are alright?' 'Sir, you're being ridiculous.' 'Obviously there are no mirrors in your house, now leave my property or I will have to call the police to have you removed, and tested for drugs, and for your interest I saw in the Evening Telegraph last night there were four cars set ablaze in Douglas, which weren't taxed, were there any plant pots harmed from the intense heat?' The younger officer pulled GI Joe away, and had a conversation which was short but never sweet. 'Are you willing to take a fixed notice penalty, and that would be the end of the matter?' 'Have a guess...no scrub that, you find that concept too difficult, how about this... no way fucking.' 'Ok, I'll pass this onto the Procurator Fiscal's office; it is out of my hands.' 'Yeah, you do that, can't have plant pots being moved can we? While you are here have you advised your *friend*, that it is a criminal offence to erect a camera to observe or record on another person's property?' 'No I won't, we don't intervene in trivial neighbour disputes we have more important matters to attend to.' 'Of course like let's see, he starts to stroke his chin, I've got it, someone moving a plant pot.' GI Joe is rising to the bait. 'Are you trying to be funny?'

   David looks at him from behind his phone. 'Trying?' The younger colleague leads GI Joe away, who can't resist another bite at the bitter fruit. 'Anymore questions before we leave?' 'Funnily enough yes how is your granny?' GI Joe can hardly contain his contempt for David; revenge is on his minute mind. How did he know he is a Freemason? His colleague had to leave as he was suppressing his laughter. 'Anything else officer that I can help you with?'

GI Joe had been humiliated, he had advised his inexperienced colleague "watch and learn" this is how to deal with and educate low-brow members of the public. He high-tailed it back to the police car, and observed the curtain twitchers were out in full view at their windows, some pretending to clean windows, adjust blinds or curtains. He casually looked at them with utter contempt as he removed his hat and bent down to enter the police car.

His colleague was in uproarious laughter. 'I don't know why you found that so funny, where was my back up, I'm glad you weren't guarding my back in Afghanistan, I wouldn't be here today.'

'That wouldn't be a bad thing, watch and learn, he handed you your arse. How's is your granny? Now I wasn't expecting that, nor were you!' 'We will talk about this later, I fooled you as well as him, this was part of my special ops training, this is not the end my friend.' 'You'd be better to drop this matter, David Fisher is not daft, be best to quit while you are behind.'

***

Michael had never felt so relaxed and optimistic about his future in France. He had few friends; quality before quantity. He had invited them out to dinner where he had divulged his future plans; and expressed fears that London had become more dangerous for investment companies and individuals because of Russian investors; not all of them were thugs in suits; but there were too many for his personal liking without specifically mentioning certain individuals that had met untimely and in some cases horrific deaths that were deemed suicide. He had never lectured his friends on accepting certain clients that on the surface seemed totally legitimate, but his sole weathervane advice when it came to accepting these wealthy clients with millions to invest was, if your instinct is alarmed study the client's hands, if they look smooth and manicured; relax. If not decline immediately and pass them onto other financial advisors who have a superficial view of financial regulations. If you disregard my observations you will I guarantee not live to regret it. The three of them were far from surprised at this sage advice; he would not be in London for advice he would be far away in his vineyards. They had unanimously feigned surprised at his sudden retirement and sale of his business; but there had been whispers from within; namely the company that had purchased the building, secrets never stay secret in the City. Michael had just confirmed the rumour.

Now it was their time to feign surprise and feel excited for him, he was embarrassed with the lavish praise and advice he had gave them over the decades. When Michael explained in a downbeat manner about his plans for the processing of the grapes into a fine wine; that was when the one of his friends mentioned that he had a client which sourced fine wines for a major high end supermarket. Michael was visibly excited about this news; he would be furnished with the details sometime later in the week. He quickly compartmentalised this lucrative information and returned to advising them, do not under any circumstances be involved in any way in Bitcoin. And if anyone is, get out immediately; it is a scam or a Ponzi scheme in my opinion which is far from humble. He explained that hedge fund executives with selfish concerns for themselves and not their clients were being paid millions by Bitcoin future trading companies that were flourishing in the US and London. It had attracted shady characters to shiny coins. When the music stops all chairs would be occupied. And numerous traders would be standing some with one leg. They suddenly were less enthusiastic about the future, and one by one admitted they had Bitcoin accounts that had burgeoning millions in profits. They were naturally reluctant to fill in this well. However, Michael had given his advice without hectoring and they unanimously decided to sell their profitable portfolios on separate days the following week.

It had indeed been an interesting dinner; Michael was aware of their foray into Bitcoin for a matter of months; he had followed the inexorable rise with puzzled logic; it was not a tangible asset similar to property, stocks or bonds; it was based on faith in the future. They had all banked the profits of the sale of a high percentage of their Bitcoin portfolios and had placed the profits in a cash deposit account. Later they would use this cash to purchase government bonds which were safe and were steady in providing a handsome reward over ten years. Boring is good was Michael's mantra. He had also made it a requirement that if they needed advice he would be offended if they didn't call him; no matter how trivial. With these reassuring words they opened up the newly arrived wine on the table. Michael had exceeded his alcohol intake in The Iron Duke, it had been a rewarding day, but recovering his old stapler from his office when he placed it on the table brought forth with laughter and mystery. Michael was in full flow as he spoke earnestly about the stapler tantamount to a favoured retired colleague, was he extracting the urine from them? Not in the slightest; it had always been there in times of mostly good and very few bad times. He couldn't bear to think of the stapler being discarded into the skip when his office would be refurbished by the new owners; no, it was coming to France with him; a permanent reminder of his previous life and his momentous decision to depart for pastures new.

Michael encouraged the introvert and modest friend to pour the wine. He was filled with pride when he had heard this instruction; when it came to hover the bottle over Michael's glass and pour in the expensive wine; he ignored Michael's request to stop. Cheering from the others brought a cackle of laughter to their table. Michael shook his head and laughed; they all stood up and raised their glasses to Michael a loyal friend and a fine gentleman. Michael was surprised that he was not embarrassed by this spontaneous show of gratitude. He had been mentored by someone who was his age now, they were in their forties; finance had become more complicated and dangerous; however, to many in the City this was an occupational hazard. Nothing to worry about was the universal mantra. He had seen all this before; it was exciting but less dangerous. He didn't envy their lives, wealth or future.

His biggest concern was that Bitcoin would get the green light from the government through time. He had Bitcoin explained to him in baby steps; he was correct after the third time it was explained to him, the previous explanations were explained without any questions from him; however the third time he quoted from his copious notes. To condense his fears and they were not without foundation. The only people who can benefit from trading in Bitcoin were drug traffickers and wealthy people dodging tax. He explained a bank in the US offered no contest to the fine of in excess of $800 million. That suggests to me that the bank had made more than the fine through unconventional and illegal financial transactions probably for the Mexican cartels. And the litmus test Bitcoin was unregulated by governments. The person who gave the explanation regarding the block chain working could not satisfactorily counter Michael's concerns. Avoid at all costs. Periodically, he would come across articles of Bitcoin billionaires either going missing along with millions of dollars or committing suicide; definitely a downside to trading or owning Bitcoin.

His young mentor removed his casual jacket and confessed he had the same concerns; but he was enjoying the lucrative ride. He went further and explained that the plethora of Bitcoin Exchange platforms were ripe for legitimate scams. This focused Michael's intense concentration and requested more information in a child like explanation. His mentor told him that he underestimated his understanding of Bitcoin; they both smiled at his accurate summation. He explained that the world had utterly changed due to social media, newspapers to Millennials also known as Generation Y are not interested in newspapers unlike your information, he eyed Michael's copy of Private Eye the bible of satirical political corruption and negative behaviour of upstanding and talented politicians in purchasing expensive items and dining in expensive restaurants; all at public expense. The strategy was to get Hollywood stars, rock stars and former politicians to endorse their version of Bitcoin; the gullible public would take confidence these multimillionaires were purchasing; so why shouldn't we?

The public would be infected by FOMO (fear of missing out) and enthusiastically part with their savings or pension pots.

  This confirmed Michael's latent fears; former UK politicians who were lax with the public finances were being actively being recruited onto various futures Bitcoin exchange boards whose shares would be offered to the public. Why change a lucrative and successful venture that was the norm in the land of the brave and free. No concerns were raised that these Bitcoin exchanges were registered off shore in British Tax Havens. It was a risky investment where there are big winners there are big losers. When there was a sustained sell of Bitcoin or various other crypto; the market would crash; there was no doubt about that. However, the mentor's point was that is for some time in the future. Not a ringing endorsement. Michael's painstaking research had been confirmed by his tutor; who exuded zero concern. When he left he poured himself a politically incorrect whisky. His decision to get out of the financial market had been confirmed by the young knowledgeable tutor. The markets would turn in on themselves into a sustained period of self-harm, the public and of course politicians would be looking for scapegoats; he would not be one of them and nor would any of his protégées; if they listened to his advice. One can only but try. Staring into the glass, he hoped the venal politicians would not be able to proselytise their friends/comrades on various influential committees and former cabinet members to convince the Bank of England to adopt a regulated version of Bitcoin. Once they hear the click of digital currency on their phones; objections will be very few and far between. Michael was of another time; he had always welcomed and adapted to new technology; however this was too fast and without serious investigation how would the new digital currency affect the butcher, baker and candlestick maker? The rush for profits would be phenomenal anyone who had not entered the race would be left cursing their natural caution. Michael certainly would be in the minority that took the opposite view and he would be richer for it; he had confidence in the future but less in the political class who were being subjugated by former university students who were highly-paid advisors to politicians who were former students with poor marks; a recipe for economic vandalism that would last for years.

  However that was for others to unravel and correct, he would be in France and watch the financial carnage live on his Smart TV or probably his phone. When this financial Armageddon comes to pass; his protégées would be requiring advice how to exit the market without their hair being on fire. He would ensure that they would not require the Fire Brigade by advising them not to enter the Crypto market and if they had to exit the following morning after his farewell dinner.

***

    In Beach Crescent Edwina is on her laptop forwarding her report to Armstrong, she has observed that she is not the only person who has been observing David Fisher, and she is also being followed. She didn't forward the reason. Armstrong is concerned that she may sweep the apartment from top to bottom for hardware that conveys her movements in the apartment; if they are found she would depart and return to London which would require modification of his plan. And if she came to the shocking disclosure that it was MI6 who had entered and secreted the camera, he would allude to her it came from the Eton boys to protect her. However, that was the fall back excuse and there was no need to implement this...yet. Edwina ended the email by saying she would explain later; she wasn't too concerned.

    In the kitchen in Grove Road, David was holding a mug of coffee to his mouth; his eyes were transfixed watching the market rise steadily. He glanced at the large kitchen clock a present from Margaret a neighbour when he had moved in, it was approaching one o'clock, he placed the mug down slowly, he glanced at the clock again, he pulled his chair into the kitchen table, his alarm on his phone activated. Furiously, he started selling bonds worth millions, two minutes later he had completed his task. He stood up and observed the market in bonds decline in price, which in turn would hit the stock market; the split screen was turning red. He had played his part in bursting the bubble; Pavel in London was observing the same scene of carnage with utmost glee. He raised his cognac in thanks to David Fisher. In eight days time David would repeat the same procedure but in reverse. While the market would be in decline by thirty percent the shill financial reporters in the international financial press would be talking the market down, they had been paid well to distort the market to Pavel's advantage. Observing the excitable icons of Wall Street hold onto their diminishing assets fooled no one, a rumour was circulated that the Russians (who else?) had inculcated malware into algorithms that distorted the stock markets throughout the world. Close but no cigar. Governments had to react, and react quickly, the printing presses started to spew out money to purchase government bonds at first to steady the market and slow down the sale of government bonds.

    The schmoozing of the Titans of Wall Street had began, they were asked to come to the aid of the government; start putting money into government bonds and they would be rewarded in the future with tax credits and tax reductions. The government would even deposit the money in their accounts so the purchase of the bonds would start. Pavel was party to the date and the time when the purchase would begin. David Fisher would not be party to this privileged information. Pavel had told him through a third-party that he would have an additional mobile phone delivered to Grove Road, he gave him the four digit code to unlock it. The instructions were stark; switch on the phone on a certain date and time and wait on the text message with instructions. David was not concerned; he was fully aware phones and laptops of financial advisors to Russians were subject to backdoor infiltrations based on National Security a catch-all anti-terrorist law. The mobile phone was thoroughly examined before it made its way from London to Dundee. As David had observed the markets of bonds and shares declined steadily he was not too concerned; as far as he was concerned no law had been broken he was just executing his client's orders. He had run this past Nigel who explained he was acting inside the Law. David had no qualms that someone was manipulating the market to a schism of influential market manipulators; he was now one of them, and there was no doubt they were not aware of each others' identities. This gave him a veneer of comfort and security. His commission from the execution was £5 million, when and only when he purchased the government bonds. It would be a difficult time to set aside his *potential* commission from taking residence in his head. When he was out for his daily run, he would scope out potential detached stone built villas in the various leafy and tree lined avenues and streets of Broughty Ferry, the disturbed neighbour upstairs behaviour had swung his future to the fore; home is where the heart is and that was Broughty Ferry rather than London. Would he sell his London home? He was ambivalent, a nice problem to resolve. Then the unnerving questions returned, why was there no contact form the police in London regarding the deaths of Jonathon, Gwen and Nigel? Again he didn't want the police to get in touch but, there must be a reason or reasons.

   In London, Pavel was very far from exuding any concern, political influence led to financial benefit, if people had to be removed from society for a myriad of reasons, he would not lose a wink of sleep. If society benefited that these persons were not on earth any longer he could or would not show any concern real or otherwise. Lorna was of the same mind. Assets could be disposed of quickly and without remorse. So could money. Every tangible asset human or pecuniary had a disposable value.

   Michael had no regret about his over consumption of wine and his sage advice to his protégées regarding Bitcoin, ambling towards the tube station he could not refrain from smiling and feel fulfilled. The tube journey would only take roughly ten minutes to the main line train station where he would catch the train home. He reminded himself not to close his eyes on the tube train, thus missing his stop; this would never happen as he was concerned of the malcontents that were prevalent on evening trains. His wallet was in his front pocket as a precaution, due to his experience of having his buttoned back pocket relieved of his wallet a few years ago even though he had not consumed alcohol. Then his thoughts turned to his vineyard, it would keep him in physical shape and mentally sharp, he was also anticipating his wife's reaction to his impressive master of the French language which he had learnt from YouTube over the last nine months. The future was looking jaunty. The goodwill towards the world was suspended as the tube station was entered; the commuters were looking strained and various east European males were hovering in the foyer studying women descending to the platforms with designer handbags over their elegant shoulders, he felt his wallet for reassurance and immediately became more aware of his surroundings and being alert to potential dangers. He removed the Oyster card from his wallet then ambled through the barrier and returned the Oyster card to his wallet, he returned the piercing gaze of the gang member with interest, who immediately turned his head away. He felt vindicated, fire must be fought with fire; he was more relaxed as he made his way onto the platform stacked with humanity mostly with glum faces; he elicited a thin smile; he wouldn't miss these depressing scenes for much longer. He had felt the urge to nonchalantly glance over his shoulder; the gang member was in the midst of humanity and apparently waiting to board the train, he again felt for his wallet for reassurance, he had no doubt he was not his quarry, some of the female commuters were relaxed, others were lax in holding their handbags close to them, and were on their mobile phones and had left their bags open; an invitation to the skilled pickpockets. He had politely mentioned this a few years ago to a young woman about the perils of leaving her handbag not closed but was met with a torrent of abuse with his advice as she carried on her inane conversation, no doubt her experience with her 'stalker' on the platform would be the topic on her Facebook page with numerous others venting their spleens and telling of similar experiences. He averted his eyes without his customary despairing shake of the head at the open invitation for the pickpocket. He would keep his own counsel on this occasion. The phalanx of commuters edged forward to indicate the train was approaching, the pressure from the mass of humanity behind inched him forward, once again his right hand felt for his wallet. He heard the screeching train approach, he glanced over the heads of the commuters there was no sign of the pickpocket. He smiled.

***

David shut down his laptop with an abundance of euphoric triumph. When he was out in the rear garden the previous day he became aware of scaffold being erected in the affluent next street; where the houses were built for wealthy Jute Barons; his curiosity got the better of him and he had walked without thinking to find out what was going on. The scaffolder told him that the roof was being repaired and the client was going to cover the roof with a protective 'tent' over the roof so that the slaters would be able to continue to work even when the weather became inclement. It was a massive house; over £150,000 of internal updating was intended but costs would undoubtedly rise. Well it wouldn't be me thought David, fixed costs, any overrun in budget would be met by the contractor; and if the timeline was not adhered to there would be an agreed penalty all this when the contract was drawn up. There would be no maybes. As he was walking away, a well-dressed man in his forties approached him, and they struck up a casual conversation; he was on a fishing expedition, David extracted more than he espoused. The client was in charge of a hedge fund; David played the wide-eyed innocent imbecile. His learned friend took great delight in being the knowledgeable braggart; there was no stopping this guy. David lodged all the facts and figures in his head; and with the pleasure of meeting him in the future when he purchased the future substantial detached house; probably 4-6 bedrooms with drawing room and separate lounge. The £5 million he had earned in commission was in reality chump change; his irascible father's favourite phrase. Obviously he would not mention this figure to him. He left the braggart feigning wonderment at his knowledge of the building trade and his estimated overall profit. Why someone would do this; he couldn't understand. He struck out his hand and rubbed his knuckle. Oh dear; he wouldn't mention this to his dad; who had an intense antipathy to the fraternity; he never asked why. Would he go out for his run, or would he search online for his future abode? He didn't have to choose, he had a call from the police in London two officers were on their way to Dundee to meet with him to discuss certain matters that couldn't be discussed on the telephone. This didn't come as a complete surprise. He promised himself he wouldn't overthink what was the reason they would be coming up to 'discuss' not interview him, this rudimentary analysis was hardly critical thinking but it certainly kept his mind from overtly going haywire in thinking things would get worse. The reason would be the deaths of Jonathon Gove in New York, his partner Gwen in his apartment in London, and his lawyer Nigel whose death was described 'as violent but positive leads were being followed', apart from this he assumed it was a client who was unhappy with Nigel's service which would be about money. He made up his mind after the phone call that his time in London was done; Broughty Ferry was his home. No doubt he would have to shed some clients in London if it required him personally to return to London with face to face meetings; he valued his safety more; his accumulation of fees from investments for clients had made him super wealthy; he was sure he would spot a niche in the financial/pensions market in Dundee, he didn't need an office, all work could be conducted at home in his future detached abode in Broughty Ferry. He would not have any difficulty in selling Grove Road at a premium, it had served its purpose but there would be no tears or regret when it was sold. He had a cold heart when it came to business and affairs of the heart; what was for you won't go past you, as his mum often quoted.

***

Sipping coffee in the sunshine outside the small coffee shop, he placed it down upon the circular wooden table; he felt safe in Paris moving from Airbnb apartment to another in the affluent suburbs of Paris. He wore his mandatory sunglasses as an external safety mechanism, his hair was much longer and he had piled on the pounds; a deliberate choice. Reading London news every day on his laptop reinforced it was a wise decision to opt for Paris in the short-term at least; the body count in London and Surrey of former wealthy Russian clients were mounting and reading the police reports seemed to allude to suicide or unfortunate accidents, however, inquiries were still ongoing. Yeah...of course they are; is the jovial thought of Simon Corndale. Changing identities with accompanying bank accounts was a straightforward procedure; knowing certain individuals who were expensive but trustworthy were worth their weight in Bitcoin, however, favours not a favour were called in. Russian start-up online banks were the ideal choice. He was also supplied with a mobile phone that had EncroChat software installed which was encrypted. It was the preferred choice of drug and gun dealers. No real names would be used in phone calls or texts. He paid 1400 Euros a month for this premium service. His lawyer through a third-party had arranged this while he was in London, he was elated to be informed that the police would not be contacting him in the future in connection with Nigel's death outside his front door; but later he advised him to depart from London immediately, as he had learned that recent Russian émigrés had required his address from a source in the Economic Crime Unit in London; it would not be a social call. He didn't need to be convinced; he was advised a mobile phone would be delivered in a few hours' time to his address; start making plans. Which he did, a 'friend' had a domestic repair shop, which sold and repaired washing machines, dishwashers etc. He would use the critical phrase; and the passport and bank cards would be able to be picked in 48 hours. The cost he paid could buy the shop and give each of his returning customers a new appliance. In the 48 hour window; he had booked various Airbnb apartments in Paris, a city he knew and loved. There was no intention to wait and worry when his time on this earth would come to a sudden, bloody and violent end. He would plan his way to live a safe and fulfilled life in Paris. He was a polyglot, (he was fluent in French, Spanish, Italian and bullshit). The experience in Jersey of witnessing the swaying body of Robert Samson in the bathroom; convinced him that he had entered a massive financial fraud or laundered money from unethical Russian businessmen. It was fortunate that because of the unforeseen death of Robert Samson; he was the sole beneficiary of his financial largesse; them's the breaks I suppose. He peered over his sunglasses at the couple who had just sat down; by their attire they were neither Parisians nor tourists, he lifted his cup slowly but keeping the couple in his sight. The old Arabic owner came out smiling and threw the dish towel over his shoulder and smiled, they ordered in English, but in soft voices, the owner confirmed their order in fractured but understandable English. He picked up the Le Monde newspaper and stared at the couple who would assume he was reading the newspaper; they had made him feel uneasy, if they were after him, it would confirm they had their quarry if he suddenly left when his glass coffee pot was nearly full. He would put his student thespian skill into practice; breathe easy and relax, but no sudden movement from him would go unnoticed. They didn't lift up their heads from the menu to discreetly eyeball him, he looked beyond them, no cars were present, this was a bohemian part of Paris; Montmartre. The side street was very narrow; he observed the male, if it came to it and he had to remove himself from this peaceful setting, he had an escape route, his physique suggested he was a regular at a bakery rather than the gym. He turned over another page, while plotting his casual departure, he didn't know who they were but his instinct urged him to vacate the cafe. He lifted the glass coffee pot and poured another coffee. A young couple came into view and were not communicating they either had a recent row or they were concentrating on something that required their full concentration; hopefully not him.

    He ignored his natural instinct to move immediately; they took a table directly behind him. The caf☐ owner came out and spoke in French, they replied in French in unison, with a few laughs interspersed, they had an unfortunate experience with a taxi driver who had overcharged them, he was pleased to hear this, and relaxed, however, the latter part of the conversation caused him concern, the male presented the taxi driver with his police warrant card, and adjusted the fare. He returned his attention to the couple in front of him. One more sip of coffee and he would lift his newspaper, leave 10 euros, and then depart without raising any issue. He stood up, tucked the folded newspaper under his arm, and placed the euros under the coffee pot, he may have emitted indifference to any observer, but his heart was beating rapidly. He consciously regulated his breathing he wanted to depart without his usual conversation with the cafe owner. He moved away and tucked the chair under the table, then made his way up the steep incline to the busy thoroughfare. He was tempted to glance backwards but overcame this foolish notion, he increased his motion, his heart beat was settling into a pleasing steady rhythm, in concert his breathing replicated his heart.

He promised himself never to ignore his instinct again, it proved to be absolutely correct, the silent couple; the male was a police officer, if his instinct was human he would buy it a drink and offer thanks. The hubbub of the tourists trudging their way up the steep incline to Sacr☐-Coeur Basilica (Roman Catholic Church) brought a rare smile to his tanned visage, he would melt into the throng and make his way to the Church as he had frequently done even though he was an atheist, the contradiction irked him. The world's languages could be heard in the crowd, he casually turned round slowly his relief was instant, the two couples from the caf☐ were not in his vision, he decided to plough on, the sun started beating on his neck, this aided his well-being. His instinct rang his warning bell again; it was time to move earlier than expected to another pre-booked Airbnb apartment, and a more salient point; he would not return to the caf☐ where he was a regular customer, in fact he would return to speak to the owner sometime next month and advise he was going to Peru, to research for his book. That way if someone was snooping for information regarding his whereabouts; Peru would be the ideal country to throw them off his trail. Life was looking more optimistic; he was living in his favourite city, in glorious apartments and riches that were a fantasy a few years ago were scattered in various bank accounts. He would offer up a prayer for his beneficiary the deceased Saint of Jersey, Robert Samson and place €50 in the poor box on his behalf, just a pity he couldn't receive an invoice and make his donation a tax deductable expense; old habits die hard. He plodded his way onward to the Church amused at the random thoughts that made him smile. The numerous souvenir hawkers were selling rosary beads and various stylish small badges. He would purchase the rosary beads even though he didn't know how or the purpose of them. He stepped onto the pavement from the cobbled street to take a breath and have a reassuring view of the tourists following in his steps. All well, an elderly rosary bead seller was on the other side and tourists seemed to be avoiding her; he made his way towards her, her face suggested she did not succumb to Botox; he calculated she must be in her late 80s. The closer he got to her he realised why the tourists were bypassing her; her rosary beads were treble the cost of her compatriots; however, after catching her smile he couldn't in good conscience turn away from her. She held out her outstretched arms with rosary beads of all the colours of the rainbow;

including LGBT rosary beads; good to see her entrepreneurial spirit thriving; alas there seemed to be slow sellers; he chose the jade (emerald green) rosary beads, the woman pointed out they were €15 more expensive than the 'standard' rosary beads; she would have done well as a City trader. He loved her chutzpah and gave her a €5 tip and thanked her profusely in fluent French, only 100 metres from the Sacr☐-Coeur Basilica, his body may be tired but his mind since purchasing these expensive rosary beads was invigorated; maybe there is something in this religious malarkey after all? Again an infrequent smile came to the fore.

***

The rain showed no sign of abating, the rattle on the curved window did not distract from her collating the information on her laptop; to be honest, entering and secreting hi tech miniature cameras in David Fisher's flat seemed to be overkill, she had concluded he was just another financial advisor employed by wealthy clients to enhance their wealth even further. Nothing from his history raised any concern. The Economic Crime Unit had maybe over thought that David Fisher was more interesting than he really was. Who could blame him for exiting London when colleagues, friends and his lawyer were killed? Seems a perfectly sensible decision to return to Dundee, he had been married twice, both of his erstwhile spouses lived in Dundee far from Broughty Ferry; unfortunately for them, his wealth came after the relatively short marriages were dissolved; no children. Armstrong did not take kindly to this assessment; and when asked to put meat on the bones of this professional view; he could not. However, he advised her to keep her opinion till she left Broughty Ferry. She thought this was a warning that something or someone would alter her premature evaluation. She was not convinced.

The telephone conversation with Armstrong made her feel ill at ease, she studied David Fisher's history once again, to reassure her and look for hidden clues in his CV. She came to her original conclusion; he was diligent with his clients, no money laundering had been found on any of his accounts or accounts of clients; perhaps they had been recommended to seek out David Fisher? She was innately annoyed at Armstrong's inert criticism of her professional view reinforced by solid facts, it would not be the first time he had confused facts with his threadbare opinion. She rose from the computer desk to the kitchen to make herself a coffee. She filled the kettle and returned to the desk, however, the white van with someone in it was in the parking bay, this set an alarm off in her head, she heard the kettle click, she activated the camera on her phone, casually aimed at the window to capture the white van in the view finder, when she was working at the desk she would be able to glance at her phone which had a close up of the van, and the male, she ran the registration of the van through a colleague; it was a 'ghost' registration plate that she had hoped was perfectly legitimate. The rapid response was reassuring to her colleague but doom laden to her; it was an MI6 vehicle. Armstrong's assessment was correct in certain matters; however, he omitted to mention she was under surveillance and it would not be a leap to assume that her flat had been entered and fitted with cameras; as her flat in London had been. Had her phone likewise? She closed down her phone, and attached it to the charger on the floor, she had to remain calm and act normal; she would make her coffee bring it through to the large table and to her observers just surf the internet for household lamps, newspapers ,etc. If the rain eased she would go to Tesco to purchase a pay-as-you-go phone. She returned to the computer desk and lifted the laptop and returned to the table, she was careful not to glance at the still occupied van, she averted her eyes from the Smart TV; she sipped the coffee slowly and refrained from holding her head in her hands in despair. How she wish she had her joint to calm her down and harness her chaotic thoughts. Was Armstrong protecting her or preparing to bring her career or God forbid, her life to an end? What did he know about her? She came to an executive decision; if she couldn't have her joint she would have a few glasses of wine and something to eat, her choice would be the Royal Arch where she would assess where she was in relation to David Fisher, was he just an excuse to remove her from London while Armstrong would be initiating a full-disclosure on her computer records and phone records, including personal phone? She had retaliated first; she had compiled a file on him when she had discovered her Smart TV had surveillance software installed when she was in New York; then her blood ran cold; the man in the white van was the same man she watched install the software in her flat in London. For the first time her thought process convinced her that her life was in danger; nothing could make her think otherwise. The warm coffee mug comforted her; she searched her favourite fashion site for jeans, while her mind was dealing with frightening and disturbing thoughts that she successfully removed with measured logic. Aware she was probably being watched; she took the near empty coffee mug emptied the contents down the sink, washed and dried it per usual. She hoped it was only Armstrong behind this internal surveillance of her; if so; her call to her colleague regarding the van's registration plate would not come to the fore; unless all departments were instructed to pass on any requests from her. Even so, this request in reality was not unusual; she was being professional and diligent. She felt she would be vindicated in this sensible view when all the cards were revealed. She placed on her heavy coat and hat, and left the flat to venture into the sparsely populated streets that would lead her to The Royal Arch. Rather than leave by the communal entrance at the front of the apartment block she elected to exit at the rear of the building; despite her training she would be tempted to confirm the male in the van was the same male that had entered her home in London. She was in a foul mood similar to the weather, she had not returned to the Ship Inn to retrieve her forgotten umbrella after the silent but unsettling experience with the icy stare from the detective. On Brook Street she purported to anyone observing her she was stopping at the myriad of small shops, to study the goods on display but she was watching in the reflection of the windows to clarify if she was being followed, to her relief she wasn't, the short walk to The Royal Arch was mundane and uneventful as she had hoped. The Royal Arch was quite busy but she managed to secure a small table, she ordered a small steak and baked potato and a generous red wine.. While she was sipping the wine she gave herself time to evaluate where she was in relation to David Fisher, she quickly returned to herself being under surveillance electronically; she had to figure out and quickly why? More patrons and obviously regulars in there sixties all casually but smartly dressed came through the door in droves they were mostly in black and had been at a funeral, she was glad her timing was fortuitous; all the tables were now occupied, the unlucky few made their way to the bar, the steak meal was delivered to her table and she took the opportunity to order another wine. Suddenly and without any warning a fight broke out a woman whose partner had a beer poured over his head retaliated with vicious fists against his assailant, and her partner had joined in. She watched the mayhem unfold amongst the affluent clientele and was able to decipher the disagreement was between a dissatisfied client towards his financial advisor. The client's face had suffered badly with the rapid reign of blows that pummelled him; he stood strong but didn't attempt to defend himself; which she thought was strange. He was obviously a regular as the patrons seemed to turn on his victors and they were asked to leave immediately, he didn't offer any defence nor did his partner. Then her mischievous side turned to Armstrong's caustic comments regarding the Dundee Facebook page that had generous comments from former residents about the city and the 'picturesque fishing village' and from the residents in less salubrious abodes and neglected parts of the city 'The Ferry' was the target of their ire, whether justifiable or not she couldn't in all good conscience answer. However, for a vicious assault it was accepted in good grace. After the 'victim' was cleaned up he was driven home by a member of staff. In a matter of minutes polite society decorum returned to the bar. She imagined when the local newspaper was undoubtedly informed of the difference of opinion the irascible comments would be spewed on the Dundee Facebook page comments section. She could ascertain Armstrong informing her of the pro and con comments regarding The Ferry. 'My gran lives in the Ferry and her postie said it was an argument about their 'winter heating allowance' seemingly the guy that got battered and had a great tan and was boasting he was just back from Spain after three months, and was thanking the government for his drinking money. And a guy who was in a wheelchair took exception to his remarks.' Or it was a drug deal that went wrong, the guy who got filled in, was due the dealer £20k, and the dealer lost it when the guy offered him a couple of drinks and a meal and that would be the debt erased, then he lifted up his Ralph Lauren jumper slightly to reveal a handgun.' Then another post would say' it was a Pringle jersey, and the guy was mocking him, that's how it started.' She felt a lot better; the excitement in the bar, and the wine had been an elixir of merriment. Staff members were approaching all the tables, the young man was coming over to no doubt apologise about the commotion; in fact he informed her that her meal and drinks were on the house because of 'the unfortunate reaction of medication with alcohol to a customer...who raises a lot of money for charity' She smiled at this explanation and was offered another refill. The day had started in a disconsolate manner but laughter and good fortune had elbowed their way through. Looking all around the bar no one seemed to be overtly annoyed at the fracas, no eternal psychological damage was wreaked on these elderly patrons. She finished the wine and left the bar with good feeling it would be interesting to read the Dundee Facebook page tonight, the bile and hatred would be permeated throughout the comments.

    The sun had burst through the grey clouds and the short walk back to Beach Crescent would be taken at a leisurely pace, the afternoon had not been uneventful which she would deliver to Armstrong with glee, he would absolutely love to hear about the violence and mayhem in an upmarket bar in The Ferry. He loved to say 'The Ferry' in a menacing tone; she would enter the apartment block by the front entrance studying the much sought after parking bays. As she made her way past the Fisherman's Inn she would have an evening meal there if time was kind to her, the van was not there; this gave her some respite from anxiety, the wind took her breath away for a few seconds, she looked up at her apartment, conscious of it being under surveillance internally and externally. She took the lift, and stepped out; her feel good factor emptied, on the doormat was her umbrella from the Ship Inn.

***

    In Asda G.I. Joe is rummaging through the discounted sandwich section, beside him is a recently graduated female officer who is silently embarrassed at his burrowing hands. His phone has a dated ring tone, Rod Stewart's 'Do you think I'm sexy' is playing loudly and he has questionable disapproving looks from passing shoppers whose faces are smirking with a definite no to the question. The female officer asks him to answer it; he ignores her as he continues to seek the cheapest sandwich. He ignores her pleading, and she walks away with the song still belting out from his phone. His face is illuminating unfettered joy as he holds up a cheese and tomato (sundried in the Tuscany sun) he turns round to show his prize like a big game hunter to his newly qualified colleague, and is puzzled where has she gone?; he is soon over his disappointment and answers his phone. It was an off-duty colleague informing him that a long and lengthy list of complaints has been lodged against him. In it was the legal term *ultra vires* which the definition was he had acted beyond his powers, (civil complaint) in regarding a 'common path' the colleague went through the numerous complaints one by one, he knew it was David Fisher as soon as mentioned the 'common path'. The decaying limp sandwich looked less appealing. In the email carbon copied to his solicitor he advised the police that the dismissive generic reply 'that we have unable to contact you' should be avoided at all costs, as he would refer Police Scotland's 'no basis for a complaint' response to PIRC (Police Investigations & Review Commissioner) and he added in bold 'he was an experienced and successful litigant.' This would not be a complaint that ran out of patience; he was overtly advising this will go all the way to court if it is not taking seriously. How he now wished he had listened to his senior colleague when he had overstepped his legal duty regarding the complaint from his neighbour about him using the common path. David's Fishers' words came back more audible. 'You are employed to uphold the Law, not make the Law'. How was he going to get out of this Gordian legal knot?

  He tossed the unwanted sandwich back into the orphan pile; his voracious appetite had waned considerably. He made his way out of the store in a depressed state of mind; he had been successful in being granted a transfer from his crime ridden beat areas in the social housing schemes to the peaceful, idyllic and affluent area of Broughty Ferry, where he noted that the denizens filled their bird baths with Perrier water instead of tap water. He had only been in his new beat for less than a month and *this* David Fisher had caused him nothing but anxiety and could be the catalyst that would see his formative police career come to an ignominious end. He would be compelled to investigate his character and use the flaws in it to make him withdraw the complaint. He would never have thought that fighting the Taliban in Afghanistan would have been less stressful than his beat in Broughty Ferry.

  Walking in a dutiful manner his mind played over and over in High Definition the bulk of the conversation with David Fisher in which he

could erase or minimise in his response; however, he had recorded every syllable and movement on that fucking phone, and he seemed to enjoy every moment.   The swish of the doors opening hit his face with a rush of cold air which brought him back to the here and now, his colleague was in the car stuffing her face; not an unusual occurrence, his mind returned to his immediate problem; he would have to bring a solution of one kind or another; legal or otherwise. He was not shocked at this malevolent thought; it was part of life, and his fledgling career depended on a solution. Some of his senior colleagues had survived more pernicious complaints and these complaints that had been rejected were not an impediment to promotion. He would seek out their advice; this problem had to be eradicated; they had formed a pungent alliance with various criminals; perhaps David Fisher could be *persuaded* to reflect on his complaint and reconsider? A smile erupted through his disconsolate face, his pace quickened; his female colleague a season ticket holder at Greggs returned his unexpected smile; she had been told he was a fantasist regarding fighting the Taliban; and he had influence from family or friends that swayed the senior management in requesting a transfer to Broughty Ferry because of the behaviour of the young scamps in various social housing schemes in Dundee. This rapid transfer was accentuated because of his PTSD. Hmm.   His colleague informed him she had received a text that said that there had been numerous complaints lodged against him. He dismissed this with rapid candour. Tittle-Tattle. He looked at the message no mention of David Fisher or the source of the complaints; he was relaxed, nothing to worry about he told her. She returned his nervous lingering look. She wasn't buying it, she wouldn't probe it would
be discussed over the tight Whatsapp group that evening. He started the car and moved off, his mind would not accept what she had said, he was in a difficult situation, he had been the subject of numerous complaints to Police Scotland over the last few years; none had been investigated as the complainers had given up when Police Scotland had failed to respond in a timely manner. However, David Fisher's email had left everyone who had perused it in no doubt; that he was not prepared to be ignored and had the means to accelerate his complaint further if there were any sign of impediments.   He was fully aware that he was seen as a figure of fun amongst his colleagues; his self-importance because of laying his life on the line fighting the Taliban, even though some of the Taliban only had cycles for transport and wore sandals compared to the multi-billion equipment the US and UK armies had at their disposal, and were repeatedly thwarted by these simple goat herders. On reflection maybe he had slightly embellished his time in Afghanistan, but being ambushed by the Taliban on cycles was an experience he could not forget. And after

telling numerous tales about his army career his stock was less valuable after he and a colleague were ambushed at the erstwhile Alexander Street multis by yobs. He did not cover himself in glory that evening. And the yobs did not have cycles; they had metal poles and loud voices. After he returned to work from six months of sick leave, he was convinced that he was being forced out of the police, however, he managed to get his wish into a more safer area of Dundee; Broughty Ferry. Careful what you wish for?

***

Edwina lifted up the umbrella from the door mat, she was hoping there was a note to explain the return of her umbrella from the Ship Inn, but alas her hopes were dashed. She entered the flat, closed and locked the door firmly behind her. Her idyllic sojourn to Broughty Ferry had shorn all its perceived lustre. She was counting the hours down to her return to London. She entered the lounge and picked up her phone it was fully charged, there was a missed call from Armstrong. This was a relief; if there were missed numerous calls she would have been concerned. She returned the call, Armstrong explained that David Fisher was no longer a Person of Interest, she was being stood down; she would be on the morning flight to London from the local Dundee airport. She did not ask why? She was losing interest in David Fisher, even though she was going through the motions; the surveillance equipment had been removed from his property explained Armstrong. Then the latter end of the conversation hit her hard. A colleague of David Fisher was pushed into a speeding passing train at the underground station; a homeless vagrant has been arrested and is being held for questioning. This was the vagrant that the police were wishing to interview as his description matched a previous incident when he had pushed another waiting passenger from the platform. Things were fluid; he would update her when information became available. She was lost for words she reluctantly placed the phone on the table. She moved into the kitchen to switch on the kettle and process the information that Armstrong had delivered in a casual manner, acutely aware she was being monitored she kept a decorum of professional calmness. The kettle clicked and she made her coffee and returned to the lounge, she activated her laptop and searched for details about the tragic death of Michael Ogilvie, there was a story repeated through various news agencies. She stopped her cup reaching her mouth, apparently the station was undergoing a refurbishment; the CCTV cameras were 'inoperative' due to the refurbishment. Nothing about a homeless vagrant; however, a witness described a couple standing behind the passenger just before he fell or jumped into the incoming train. The article went on to describe an unconfirmed report 'that sources within the British Transport Police have revealed he had made an appointment with his doctor as he was feeling depressed.' She lifted the coffee to her lips her thoughts oscillating between Armstrong's casual conversation with her that did not correlate to the report on online reports. The bodies were piling up, and David Fisher was no longer a Person of Interest? Now her own assessment was called into question. Should she call Armstrong back and advise him of the alternative facts regarding his understanding of Michael Ogilvie's death or suicide? She continued to contemplate her next move, constantly conscious she was under surveillance; but from whom friend or foe? Then the return of her umbrella, was it a customer conscious member of staff who was diligent and found out her address, and just left it outside her door, and didn't leave a note, in case she thought she would be obliged to offer him or her a remuneration? Probably this was the case. Her low mood was slowly lifting, she was returning home to London, more enthusiastic than she had imagined; she thought she would be sad to leave Broughty Ferry with fond memories; the opposite was true. However her opinion of David Fisher was now nebulous, his life was being protected and he wasn't aware, or he was a major moving part in their deaths, while he had the perfect alibi, he was in Dundee, was he directing the removal of his colleagues, and is the reason financial? Then her spine tingled, was Armstrong involved somehow, and her recall to London made it easier to eliminate David Fisher? Was he a saint or sinner, and how could she discern? Either way she was being played. And her ears were not enjoying the music. The miserable rain returned no longer was the pitter patter on the windows comforting when she curled up on the sofa with her coffee held tightly in both hands and her mind was no longer free from any concern. She had to make a decision should she pursue David Fisher alone or raise her concerns about Armstrong? And while she was distilling the news about Michael Ogilvie was it suicide or murder? It would be simple enough to find out whether Michael Ogilvie had made an appointment or not. If he did, it was an open and shut case; suicide. There were no CCTV cameras operating to disapprove the foregone verdict. The doctor's surgery's computers were not difficult to access; the appointment would be on his record as would be his death.

However, if no such appointment was recorded then this was a more complex situation. Then a cataclysmic thought added to her mental burden, was her home being searched or surveillance equipment being installed while she was in Dundee? Her phone did not concur with her thought; all was well, the phone had not been activated, but she still felt uneasy. She looked at the unwieldy rain hitting the windows more vigorously, she sighed and took a deep breath; she had to get out and think things over where better than the Ship Inn for a warm bowl of soup, and casually thank the person for returning her umbrella.

***

   In the locker room GI Joe is changing from his uniform into his 'stylish' attire; his colleagues and many detractors commented 'where did you get those trousers, from the Primark branch in Kabul?'
Someone had left a turban beside his locker a few years ago; he said it was offensive and activated his PTSD which resulted in him being unfit for work for three months. His colleagues knew how to play the system; but they secretly admired a serial manipulator of the system. His supervisor has hung about till it is only GI Joe and him are in the locker room, he is holding an A4 sheet of paper, it is the complaint from David Fisher, he hands it to GI Joe to study and comment. He moves away from GI Joe and sits on a chair he hears laughter coming towards the locker room, the person who is emitting the laughter steps into the locker room and is told to fuck off by the senior officer, the order is obeyed immediately; however, the scene in the locker is described and sent to the Whatsapp group; silence is no longer golden in the modern age. GI Joe peruses the complaint and returns it to his supervisor and senior officer.
'No big deal, I was trying to arbitrate a peaceful solution with the warring neighbours...'
The supervisor stands up walking towards him shaking his head, he is apoplectic he raises his voice. 'There is a big deal, this is someone who has obviously a high profile solicitor; and accompanying video, what the fuck were you thinking? You should've twigged this guy is different, apologised for misunderstanding the situation, especially when he sticks a fucking phone in your face and what do you do? Wise up? No, you say are you recording me? I'm surprised David Fisher didn't drop the phone with laughter.'
 GI Joe is desperate to leave, but to his supervisor's annoyance doesn't exude any remorse. 'You may be concerned, but I'm not, I've faced more difficult and life-threatening situations...'
'Don't fucking mention the Taliban! That card has been overplayed; it didn't help you when the gang of emaciated junkies set about you on the Hilltown did it? Now if this complaint is upheld you are gone, and your Police Federation representative agrees with me, and too be perfectly honest he won't put up a credible defence; not even with your PTSD.' GI Joe is non-plussed as he pulls the yellow beanie tightly over his head and checks himself in the mirror, and is obviously impressed he gives himself a smile.
 'Anything else on your mind sir?'

'I'll reply in the usual manner, without rejecting it with sentences of management speak, but if he does go to PIRC, you're gone, so you would be better to change his mind, and persuade him to reconsider his complaint.' GI Joe is perturbed at this advice. 'And how do I go and persuade him to do that?'

'That's up to you.' He walks out the locker room. GI Joe had already thought that through and came to an unorthodox solution. Like in Afghanistan he was by himself, his life was not threatened but his career was coming to an end with no medals according to his supervisor. He would dispute the senior officer's bleak assessment.

***

Her eyes gazed admirably towards the Kingdom of Fife, what she would give to live here or in Fife. The brief pessimistic view of Broughty Ferry had lifted, Dundee airport is small, the passengers waiting alongside her were commuters heading to meet various business colleagues in London, going by the chatter amongst them. They had the best of both worlds, living in an idyllic location, commuting to London City Airport to initiate or conclude a business deal, then return on the last flight in the evening to Dundee. London seemed a hellhole compared to the idyllic fishing village or open prison for the wealthy depended on your opinion, she sided with the former. However, David Fisher was never far from her thoughts, she hadn't spoken to him but she had formed a positive opinion of him; he had been brought up in social housing in Kirkton, and had worked his way up to become a multimillionaire; however, his feet were still anchored to the terra firma. His former childhood area of Dundee; Kirkton had made the national news; an outbreak of anti-social behaviour, that some excited journalists had compared to the Gaza Strip was pure hyperbole; however, the uploading of numerous videos to social media of youths attacking riot police with various fireworks for hours on end; brought derision from most sides. Local politicians offered the usual excuses, poverty, the pandemic or even Brexit. Some of the climate change activists took exception to the youths at being called malcontents; they were victims of global warming, and they were not rioting, it was street theatre, hmmm? The previous night's riot or street theatre had been covered by London journalists who were comparing notes whiling away the time until they were called to board the small plane to London City Airport. Her portentous mind put her time in Broughty Ferry to the side, she would return to the events later, however she would be concentrating on the here and now. She was returning to London where the erstwhile colleagues or friends of David Fisher were piling up. The death of Michael Ogilvie had intrigued her, the contradiction of his death, was he pushed or did he jump? Armstrong would not be party to any of her interchangeable thoughts on his death.

Would he bring up that her flat in Beach Crescent (Broughty Ferry) had been wired for her protection? Or was she under surveillance as she was suspected of some malfeasance?

    The tannoy sparked into life, time to board, she lifted her petite suitcase, and made her way along with the other passengers, then she was fixated on the passenger near the end of the queue, it was David Fisher. Whether it was wise or not she immediately texted Armstrong to advise David Fisher was on her plane returning to London. What could possibly be the reason for him returning to London with the knowledge that his compatriots were diminishing in increasing numbers and not through natural causes? Then logic kicked in perhaps Michael Ogilvie's death compelled him to return to London? Definitely makes sense, however, if his death was murder, was this a trap to lure him back? Again she would refrain from explaining this to Armstrong she had a pang of regret sending the text forewarning him that he was returning to London. When the plane touched down at London City airport it was easier to reach the centre of London very quickly rather than arriving at the main hub Heathrow. Armstrong would have a couple of his team waiting on David Fisher and then follow him to his unknown destination, would he return to his apartment first? Undoubtedly Armstrong would instruct her to return to the office for a quick debrief, once that was concluded she would segue Michael Ogilvie's "accident" into the conversation she was skilled enough to allow Armstrong to express his opinion. She moved forward, checked in her suitcase and walked the short distance to the aircraft, once aboard she located her window seat and settled down, she wondered where David Fisher would be sitting. Her curiosity was sated as soon as that thought entered her mind. He was on the left side seated at the window side. He seemed to be in good spirits, he had the Private Eye magazine in his hand, obviously a man with a curious mind and a sardonic sense of humour. Her eyes strayed away temporarily from her quarry, looking through the window at the sloping expansive green space of Magdalene Green and the proud bandstand, and instantly became curious about it; should she return to Facebook Dundee and see the divisive comments about it? She would do this when she was ensconced in her house snuggled up on her sofa with a mug of coffee it was fascinating to read the caustic comments about an impressive Victorian bandstand that was well-maintained and painted in understated colours. She wondered if bands of different musical genres did play there. The remnants of passengers were thinning, a woman with striking long hair sat next to David Fisher, they were not unfamiliar to each other; that was evident, she felt uncomfortable, but didn't know why. The woman was Lorna and they subtly exchanged mobile phones.

***

The white battered van sat motionless in Beach Crescent, the driver was reading The Courier, judging by his expressionless face, nothing seemed to upset or interest him. The aircraft was gathering speed down the runway; the observer of the aircraft smiled as it took to the sky, he pulled out his mobile and sent the message. The van driver acknowledged the message; it was time to retrieve the surveillance equipment from the apartment. He folded the newspaper and stuck it into the top shelf panel. He casually observed the numerous dog walkers that passed in either direction passing his van, he was careful not to make cursory eye contact. Armstrong was being kept aware of the situation, but when Edwina texted to say that David Fisher was returning to London, that was concerning however he concurred with her that he was returning because of the death of Michael Ogilvie; he could not think of any other reason. He would make his way to London City Airport himself, rather than send others; he would not inform Edwina of this out of character impulsive strategy. He was in numerous minds whether to avail himself to Edwina when she landed, why he had no idea. The text came through; the flat had been relieved of the surveillance equipment. At least something had went smoothly, he reached into the drawer and retrieved a cigarette and lit it, the cool wind from the open window slowed his speeding thought process and removed the multiple body sapping doubts from his mind. He drew on the cigarette and smiled, he was well aware of the health hazards that smoking did to his lungs but he convinced himself that he was an occasional smoker, and it did bring him enormous pleasure, sad though that might be. The clock hands seemed to be stuck in time; he would use public transport for the journey to London City Airport, it was good for the soul to mix with the good plebeians of London. He tossed the cigarette onto the sloping roof below the window; he reached for his jacket then left his office.

Edwina had a perfect view of David Fisher and his female friend, the exchange of mobiles heightened her suspicions of David Fisher; was it that he had been advised that taking a burner phone to London would eliminate any tracking software on his bona fide phone? She couldn't argue with the obvious. But who was she? Was she a member of the intelligence community that had been advised that he was returning to London, hence the last minute boarding of the aircraft? Her doubts and questions of David Fisher were multiplying. When she returned to the office to debrief Armstrong she would eloquently extract as much information from him regarding Michael Ogilvie and his assessment what really had happened at the tube station, he wouldn't concede to browbeating, she would feed his ego and praise him for sending her up to spend some time in the 'open prison for the wealthy'. He would respond to that, there was no doubt.

Monitoring David Fisher's time in London did not cause her any concern he would be identified, and his apartment would be under observation internally and externally. But the recurring thought emerged again, if he wasn't in London regarding Michael Ogilvie's death, then what was the reason? Could the answer be the woman that was seated next to him chatting? She didn't capture her image on her phone incase her own phone was being micromanaged by Armstrong. She had a burner phone in her apartment secreted in the utility room.
It would be sensible to use that when she was in London. If Armstrong came clean and told her what was really happening that would be her best expectation, but it was fanciful. She settled down for the short flight to London City airport. Her notes on her phone were building up and were not leading her to form any conclusion good or bad. She was careful not to input any suspicions that she had of Armstrong when she added to her notes. However, this woman next to David Fisher must be identified if Armstrong advises her all was well with her, then why would they exchange phones and for what purpose? Her professional steeliness once more imbued her when the pilot informed the passengers how near they were to London and the expected time of arrival. She then had a change of heart rather than return to the office she would follow David Fisher and his female companion without informing Armstrong. This made her feel more in control of a compulsive mysterious situation, the different scenarios if not for Michael Ogilvie, could be a client or David Fishers' own financial business needing signed off. She just had to see what was on the beach after the tide was out. The pilot updated the weather in London was not unexpected, cloudy with outbreaks of rain. This triggered a disturbing thought that she had expunged; who had returned her umbrella and left it on the door mat? That would have to be revisited another time, at the moment her thoughts and forensic mind were on David Fisher and his female companion.

***

   Armstrong made his way to the Docklands Light Railway to take him to London City Airport cautious of being followed he took the tube train, alighted after a couple of stops and boarded the next train, all the while scanning the passengers who were waiting patiently on the platform. He was comforted that Edwina's trip up to Dundee was uneventful, however she was still at the forefront of his mind, her bank accounts and credit card statements were not of one who was living beyond her means. But the nagging doubt about her trip to St, Petersburg and meeting with an undisclosed male was a fluttering red flag, the corruption in Russia being mirrored or exceeded in London made him feel ill at ease. David Fisher's lawyer dead, ditto his friends and colleagues was bound to raise concern for David Fisher's well-being due to the nature of his work and clients. Was David Fisher next to meet an untimely death or accident, or was he the architect of their deaths? The two Americans who were seconded to work with Armstrong despite his objections cleared any ambiguity where their investigations were leading them. They were convinced David Fisher was pulling the strings that led to his friend being eliminated while drinking from a bottle of water on a bench in Central Park. However, they had the proof but were not prepared to share the proof with Armstrong. Armstrong's conscious bias against them was reinforced at hearing this. Armstrong smiled and told them 'that's the slight problem, he couldn't put him under surveillance as we had Laws in the United Kingdom which were not flexible unlike the Laws in the US which were flexible, solid or non-existent depending which party was in power'. This observation did not go down well with his American colleagues. They looked at each other and left with the parting words; 'we will be in touch', there was something menacing in the tone in which it was delivered. Armstrong smiled in defiance; he was not prepared to play ball with them; i.e. share information with them regarding David Fisher, and in return we will not give you anything. An offer he could easily refuse and made it clear without an utterance that he rejected, facial expressions and silence emit utter contempt than an avalanche of invective. However, he knew instinctively he would be under surveillance for what reason other than discomfort was a moot point. He would mention this in a casual manner after Edwina had debriefed him of her uneventful time in Broughty Ferry; should he mention the umbrella being returned to her apartment? Nah, be interesting to hear if it was of consequence, he smiled at the thought that would remain dormant for the time being. He made his way to the front of the now sharp elbowed commuters who suddenly became animated as the train could be heard thundering through the tunnel towards the platform. The thought of Michael Ogilvie edging towards the platform ready to throw himself into the path of the train saddened him. He was moving to France, and decided to end his life in a gruesome and horrific fashion; something didn't add up. He like others shared the similar view this was the reason for the return of David Fisher, as a friend offering his deep condolences and also he may have invested money for Michael Ogilvie? He couldn't shake himself free from the laconic encounter with the two American spooks, they said they were NYPD but they were above this due to their exuding intelligence, expensive clothes and their hotel of undoubted choice The Ritz. They mentioned all the deaths of David Fishers', friends, colleagues and some unknown Russian investors, but not his partner in *his* apartment. Now why this omission, was she a person of no consequence? Follow the money was his unspoken mantra. Her death was headlines for a day then it seemed she was no longer newsworthy. America was becoming too influential based on sharing information with a multitude of UK intelligence agencies and they were impatient to have colleagues (FBI) *advise* HMRC the most expedient method of locating and neutralising money launderers. Only the US would benefit from this, when the Eton boys brought this up and asked for thoughts, Armstrong suggested when they had cleaned up New York they could offer the UK their methods of how they achieved this, and apparently the EU had rejected this partnership as the Americans had tapped Angela Merkel's phone and other prominent EU commissioners. I think the EU were being a tad prejudicial don't you think? He was met by outright hostility and called impertinent. 'You are most kind', he removed his feet from the large table placed his trainers on (it was dress down Friday after all) gathered his papers shook his head and returned to his office away from the madness of the Eton boys. His colleagues had organised a sweepstake how long he would last in the meeting, wearing trainers with untied laces annoyed his superiors, but they had suggested that they had to move with the times; Armstrong dismissively raised his eyes to the ceiling while stifling his mirth. It was time to take his pension and run far away from this asylum, he would keep this brooding thought to himself. He pulled out his mobile and texted Edwina he would meet her at London City Airport.

The commuters were unruly and impatient as the train emerged from the tunnel, he was behind some unruly commuters as the train approached some moved to each side, however someone was at his back edging him forward; he 'fell' into the path of the speeding train.

***

Edwina was observing David Fisher and the woman as they made their way from the airport to the taxi rank. The woman kissed him on the cheek and departed as he entered the taxi. She moved away and entered a car that was obviously waiting for her, Edwina knew where David Fisher lived; she instructed the taxi driver to drop her off at the boutique not far from his abode. She checked her phone she had a message from Armstrong he would meet her at the airport, then they would go for lunch. He must have got side-tracked, she was not concerned. The taxi that contained David Fisher suddenly put its hazard lights on, and David Fisher emerged in a state of distress talking excitedly into his phone, as her taxi passed him she glanced backwards at him, as he paced the pavement ignoring pedestrians weaving past him, the car his female companion entered at the airport pulled in behind the stationary taxi, she got out took his mobile from him, removed the SIM card and ushered him in to the back seat, she handed the taxi driver his fare and did not wait for her change.

Edwina hoped that they would carry on their journey ending at his apartment. Then her phone pinged incessantly, the messages were universal, Armstrong was involved in an accident at the tube station. He was dead. She advised the taxi driver she had a change of plan, she told him where to drop her off.

For the first time she felt really afraid for her own safety. She would play dumb when the internal questions of his lifestyle; and the inevitable had he been compromised? Of course it was a loaded question, to elicit a response of some kind, where the body language experts would have a field day. Then the heavens opened up and the noise on the roof of the taxi from the pounding rain, heaped misery to her low mood. How she pined for the calmness and serenity of Beach Crescent in Broughty Ferry. She did not respond to the myriad of messages that were continuing to inform her of Armstrong's "accident" was it the same "accident" that befell Michael Ogilvie; then it hit her, was David Fisher informed of Armstrong's death the same time as her? And that was the reason for the sudden stop of his taxi, and him being irate on his phone? Then the unwelcome debilitating chill came over her, what was the connection between Armstrong and David Fisher? First of all she could not for certain determine that this was the reason for David Fisher to advise the taxi to pull over, and then his friend suddenly arrives and takes him into her car in a state of distress, however, she did remove the SIM card in a professional and obligatory manner. Her instinct would not waiver from this theory; she concurred. She formulated her questions that she would be asking; her stay in Dundee was 'off the books' if they asked where she had been she would say having a short-break. She would only offer the minimum of relevant information; going by Armstrong's withering and caustic comments how standards were slipping, her interview when it came around would not be forensic. Sad and cold hearted to say, some of the Eton boys would be ecstatic that Armstrong would not be darkening their door anymore. Their facade of shock and sadness would be lifted after they retired for the evening at their gentlemen's clubs. She had to concentrate on collating as much information as possible when her colleagues' states of minds were in an excitable and period of sadness, they may let slip something or another that they had heard Armstrong say. She was an expert in dissecting innocent conversations and distilling hidden truths. She was suddenly removed from these thoughts as the driver pulled up, she paid him pulled her suitcase from the floor and grabbed the small umbrella with ambivalent emotion. She walked the short journey trying to be calculating and forensic without creating an atmosphere of interrogation amongst the throng of questions that would be coming forth in her direction; it would be a torrent if the Eton boys were aware of the real reason of her 'short break', Soon all will be revealed, there would be a period of numerous questions then social media would ramp up conspiracy theories, there would be no doubt about that, however, on this occasion rather than loudly dismiss these crackpots as she had vocally called them in the past, she would be more measured this time. Her colleagues would be thinking out loud for the next few days then a period of normality would engulf the office; she would listen more than she talked; this would be a Herculean task. But she knew that every minute that passed was a minute wasted unless there was an inappropriate or throwaway observation that could move her in another direction completely. Her infrequent headache was emerging, information overload was taking root. She walked past the security guard, from his facial expression he was aware of the death of Armstrong, she made her way past him but was quietly informed to stay put; someone would come to meet her. She saw two imposing figures come down the escalator with their eyes fixed on her; the two NYPD officers. Her impenetrable confidence crumbled, fear and a pessimistic outcome replaced her structured defence mechanism.

***

David Fisher sat in his old chair that he had retained since he was a brooding teenager in his Kirkton bedroom all those decades ago. This was his touchstone; which he ruminated on when problems arose and would be dissected and a logical solution would emerge from his calm and measured mind; and it had reminded him where he had come from in the social economic landscape; now he was at the apex of wealth and material acquisitions. Surveying the walls and ceiling of his multi-million London apartment didn't surpass his abode in Grove Road Broughty Ferry. However, his capital had increased beyond his dreams since his brief sojourn to Broughty Ferry, Dundee. But his mental health was in a detrimental and damaging downward spiral; hence the call to his therapist Lorna. Deaths of friends and colleagues had taken its toll not only on his physical health but the burden and mysteries of their deaths created havoc when darkness befell Grove Road. Of course he knew there had to be a malevolent Russian influence behind their deaths, but the police did not seem to be too concerned; he had more interest from GI Joe about the plant pots being moved. And who cared about his partner murdered in this apartment; has the world become that indifferent? He rose from the chair and moved towards the window; for solace or inspiration? How he would trade all his millions for peace of mind. Michael Ogilvie's death seemed to invigorate the police into a more detailed investigation, now why was that?

They would be coming around to his apartment to interview him as a witness. As a witness and he didn't need a lawyer; that bit of advice he would ignore; he would have Lorna as a note taker. And it would be recorded by Lorna. The police were fine with this and before the telephone conversation ended; they repeated he had nothing to be worried about. He would call Lorna later in the evening
and prep her of the pitfalls of the police luring him into a false sense of security. Plant pots anyone? He laughed out loud at the absurdity of a phalanx of police officers continuingly returning to him about advice they had for him. And deaths of colleagues and friends were treated as trivial. Did the police advise him to leave London for the safety of Dundee, but fail to advise his friends and colleagues of credible threats to their lives, if this assertion was valid, they wouldn't admit it.

   He returned from the aimless gaze out the window with his mind becalmed, he went to the kitchen and switched on the kettle to make a coffee. His laptop was removed from the snug case and he opened it to seek the Evening Telegraph Facebook page to view what innocuous events had enraged the denizens of Dundee. The kettle's reassuring click pulled him away from the laptop, he returned to the table mug in hand, he was feeling less stressed, the headline was Pink Caravan sprayed with obscene images in Grove Road Broughty Ferry. He spluttered at this headline; the old neighbourhood is declining before our eyes commented a neighbour. While another said it was a sexual Banksy artist behind the mindless vandalism. Plant pots getting moved, and phallic symbols sprayed on the side of the caravan; civilisation was coming to an end was his facetious verdict. Good to see that Police Scotland was treating the matter in a serious matter though; "this was not only an attack on a person's property but on the rule of Law and the democratic process and no stone will be left unturned in pursuit of the culprit or culprits". And who was uttering this hyperbolic statement but GI Joe; fuck me! He needed to read this again even if it lifted the gloom for a short period of time. He read the article again; apparently this was a systematic attack on a single female parent. It was against the Law to set up a camera to catch the culprit. Hmm. How times change. He'll keep an eye on this developing story; shouldn't be too long before CNN pick up on this He closed the laptop as his mobile vibrated on the table; it was Lorna. She would be coming round tonight, she couldn't or wouldn't discuss it on the phone; then ended the conversation abruptly. The melancholy returned as he sipped his coffee; the call was on the burner phone, why the cautious tone?

   He would order an Indian takeaway for his evening meal; in the meantime he would have to either order his shopping online or venture out into imminent invisible danger? He felt like a subdued caged lion, the feeling of hope was fading; Lorna would stop him from falling into despair. He yearned for hope to end this unending fear of the future. His mind turned to Michael Ogilvie; he had everything to live for, he didn't leap into a speeding train, why would he? He was excited to start his new life in France and walk in his vineyard; his accumulation of money over the years made them become a reality. As for the others who had prematurely demised, they mixed with or advised Russians, their deaths could be connected, but not Michael Ogilvie. He wouldn't take any business from any Russian; now or in the future, trouble would emerge. Life was too short to risk their business and wealthy clients; there were enough wealthy clients without being tempted with dirty money. How correct he was, but who or what was the reason that led to his death?

***

His hair was long and he had grown a close cropped beard, this bohemian lifestyle which he previously despised as middle class vagrants too lazy to be in a regular career made him assert that this view was outdated and reactionary. But that was the bigoted view of Simon Corndale; who no longer existed as he had adopted other identities, circumstances can change a person's ingrained view. This was his opinion now. He was never beset by the heavy but silent burden of loneliness that he could not shake off when he had settled in to his comfortable apartment and lifestyle in London. Now in Paris he embraced the once fear of being alone for the rest of his life living under various identities. He was never to be confused with the mythical James Bond; but he was a natural in picking up nuances whether in a cafe bar or sitting in an out of town small restaurant. He paid much closer to his instinct now more than ever; this was because his life depended on it. When the winter was becoming noticeable he made a detailed plan to relocate to the Cote d' Azur (French Riviera) being a polyglot was another layer of protection in secreting his real identity. There were a plethora of currency apps that dealt in transactions in seconds, euros was his principle currency now, his phone had the apps to complete mundane transactions shopping, restaurants and SIM cards. His evenings were spent reading the various blogs about the deaths or accidents of various former Russian citizens who had envious wealth but factory habits, these blogs had unlimited information on these oligarchs and poked fun at their eating habits and academically challenged grey matter. He always thought these bloggers were fearless or sponsored by Putin. However, he could not dismiss their information as he had known some of these unfortunate people who had met untimely deaths, some quickly others gruesome. And most importantly no one had ever being arrested and the narrative came to a shuddering halt; no further investigations from the police or journalists. This troubled him but paradoxically since he was a man of different identities and abodes he was no longer dependent on sleeping tablets; did the life threatening reality of day to day danger act as an antidote to imminent death? He had no ubiquitous yearning for London; his multi-million pound apartment was registered to a shell company in the British Virgin Islands; he was the master of his own destiny; today the public's knowledge of their phones was really unimpressive. Facebook, texting and the ominous social media apps were their only functions and of course the seldom used talk facility. But to him, it was his world; finance made the world go around and it kept him alive. He had a bespoke VPN embedded in his phone, but he used the phone sparingly; his burner phone (EncroChat) was used in a more leisurely fashion when sourcing articles from the news and financial internet sites. He dreaded the thought of an insignificant future in France but these fears were embellished in his mind and didn't converge with reality; he was enjoying life and instead of dreading the incremental darkness that enveloped over Paris; he recognised the beauty and safety of it. With the warm night air silently comforting him as he sat in the ancient comfortable chair at the veranda with the large windows wide open observing the lights of Paris with the Eiffel tower overlooking the city and shooting shards of hypnotic light intermittently across the city; he wondered how many other citizens were thinking this, this minute and drinking a cheap but pleasant red wine? Then this comforting and heart warming thought was suddenly snatched from him and replaced with his concern for David Fisher. They were the only ones alive from the cadre of dining companions. He had escaped the ominous death in London that was pencilled in for him; he was rational and was able to dissect and come to a logical if not comforting decision; but David Fisher? Was he really the meek modest working class oik that had fought his way up the summit of the financial mountain; if so; he was ruthless in his heart and his polite manner was a facade? If this was the case, was it beyond reason that to continue on his odyssey of self-aggrandisement nothing or nobody would inhibit his grasping hands?

   The view lost its benevolence rapidly; he had to find out the answer; if David Fisher was involved in some capacity of his dining companions deaths for pecuniary benefit, *his* life was in imminent danger; he couldn't ignore this fact not opinion. But why would David Fisher continue on this murderous course? The wine glass he had held to his stomach in both hands he raised to his lips, like the panoramic view of the lights in Paris had lost its appeal. He placed the glass on the wooden floor; the unfeeling and selfish persona of the erstwhile city trader was unceremoniously replacing the calm, considerate and kind persona. He walked across the room to the pre-war large double wardrobe, and fumbled furiously along the top shelf; he pulled it free from the untidy bundle of clothes; a Glock semi-automatic pistol. He had used it before.

***

David Fisher's thoughts turned to Gwen and their fleeting but passionate romance, he had had it all, but since she was murdered in his apartment, too many memories would cast him into a sea of despair and depression; he knew through time he would sell it and return to Broughty Ferry. After having experienced the imbecilic GI Joe in Dundee, meeting the detectives in London would make him feel more comfortable. Imagine the tension if he was still living in Grove Road, it would have been reasonable to expect GI Joe to darken his door once again, and to subtly accuse him of setting fire to the pink caravan; yes, he was that dumb. His natural smile emerged and was accompanied by a shake of the head. His videophone sparked into life it was his therapist, (Lorna) he invited her up, and strolled to the kitchen to make her favourite coffee. She was blessed with the personality to make people not just clients feel at ease and lift the silent invisible heavy burden from their shoulders in the first few minutes of their meeting He had learned over the years not to overthink problems perceived or otherwise. She entered the apartment with a radiant smile. This put him at ease immediately; he had briefed her on the circumstances of the deaths of his erstwhile dining companions, and the informal request from the detectives. She had ordered a taxi to drop them at the police station, he concurred with this sensible arrangement. She sipped her coffee and surreptitiously studied his face and body; not too much too worry about. She had consciously applied more makeup than usual to highlight her almond eyes and high cheekbones to minimise and deflect any conscious animosity towards her and David Fisher. She would let the questions flow without any interruptions from her or David. If the interview strayed past 30 minutes she would politely intervene and remind the detectives this was an informal interview and if it did not conclude in the next 5 minutes she would bring the interview to a respectful halt, and arrange a further interview in the next few days with a barrister; hopefully this was the option she didn't need to choose.

However, and not for the first time, she had worries of her own that would surpass and eclipse David Fisher's, serious but not insurmountable difficulties; but maintaining her professional poise and eloquent analysis was her *de rigueur*. However, her problems which could end her career in a catastrophic manner would be revisited and met head on; but on her terms. They spoke to each other on very friendly terms and rehearsed the script she had on her phone. He would give the required laconic answers in a calm and measured tone, it would be no secret for him to learn that he was a P.O.I (person of interest) and the interview would be recorded and analysed to unearth any hidden answers that he had unconsciously retained, the only thing that he had to remember that it was an informal interview in name only. She had calculated that the Russian influence would be scratched upon but no deep incisions would be even attempted to release toxic information that they were not aware of. He was relaxed at hearing this even though he had surmised all of her bullet points himself over and over again; the police were not his friends. After she had closed down her page of bullet points on her phone she shut it down and she encouraged him to clear his mind, and tell her about his time in his old residence in Grove Road. The subtle reserved tone of their voices went up a few decibels when she heard about the antics of the police officer he had given the sobriquet GI Joe; they had 30 minutes to fill; she was in hysterics after he told her about their memorable exchanges she was laughing so loudly all because of a plant pot being moved, she had a stitch in her side. He then backed up his recollection of the vacuous and witty conversations by showing her the recordings from his phone so she could view GI Joe in full imbecilic mode; again uproarious laughter. He was on a roll now; he showed her the video that was on Facebook about the pink caravan. She pulled a face of confusion; he gave her the background of the obscene sexual art and the heavy police presence; door to door enquiries began in earnest much to the annoyance of the polite society that resided in Grove Road. Again Lorna had not anticipated this slapstick event; but as David pointed out in a mock dramatic ham actor fashion; things had turned serious. She watched on the screen of his laptop GI Joe's excitable retort to the press and for the benefit of social media his 'attack on the rule of Law and Democracy itself' speech. She naturally assumed this was a deep fake video and stopped laughing when she realised he was telling the truth. One word ventured from her mouth; Wow!

Her phone rang; it was the taxi; it was outside the mansion block. All mirth and laughter were deleted; serious faces and comforting words took over. They stood up picked up their phones and left the apartment. Unpleasant times lay ahead for one of them.

***

Pavel had a pre-arranged meeting with Lord Green fingers a political fellow traveller was keen to hear of medicinal cannabis being the product for future pain relief; he had seen the suffering of so many people that he could not ignore the evidence of the trials that had taken place in various EU states. And of course he also considered when medicinal cannabis was licensed the company that owned the licences to grow cannabis would after a short period of time be worth billions of euros.

Pavel was well aware of various Global Pharmaceutical companies who were buying up the majority share holdings in small niche companies; that would not happen in this case; he had secured the majority of these niche companies and his exit strategy would see him leave with a substantial profit in the hundreds of millions; all tax free as he had a myriad of shell companies in the British Virgin Islands. However, this would have to wait an unspecific number of years.

Green energy would be the focus of his infinite funds; Lord Alexander had convinced and converted the sceptical and technophobes that it would benefit the UK as well as the EU, and gradually the rest of the world. And of course it was amazing how political donations could drip from the House of Lords to the cesspit of financial impropriety; the House of Commons. The standards of Members of Parliament were mundane, uninspiring and charlatans of the lowest calibre. However, this made the sceptics more easily to convince that they were mistaken in their views. The General Election would be held in less than a year; MPs of all political hues were bought and paid for; no matter which political party was in power Pavel pulled their strings into the direction he wanted them to go through; and the puppet master was Lord Alexander.

An MP had spoke under Parliamentary Privilege that all but named Pavel as the money behind certain decisions that had escaped any serious debate in Parliament about Government legislation that had been rushed through late at night when the chamber was sparsely occupied; he had suggested this was part of an elaborate conspiracy to achieve certain decisions. Of course; he did not name Pavel, not because of his fear of legal action if he repeated his accusations outside of the gilded Palace of Westminster and went further and named the "malevolent Russian with British Citizenship" but his concern for his life. To the relief of many MPs, he refused to reveal the name of this person; he was goaded and verbally abused to name and shame this person not in Parliament but outside in the real world. Pavel did not bat an eyelid; there were many other businessmen from Ukraine and the Middle-East who were doing likewise but not as skilful and lawful. Pavel predicted to himself that this malcontent would be spending time with his family before the date of the General Election was announced. He would not stand again due to "personal difficulties". How right he would be. Wrestle with a chimney sweep and you end up dirty. Wrestle with Pavel and you'll end up dead; fact not opinion.

***

The taxi glided to a halt, David Fisher and Lorna were showing no sign of nerves; they entered the police station and an officer showed them to an interview room, they were offered hot or cold refreshments; they both politely declined. Fingerprints and DNA would be swabbed from the cups or glasses. In the room they sat at the desk; noting subconsciously the cameras on the walls. Nothing could shake their confidence. Lorna placed her phone on the desk; she was making a play to the observers; she had been in this movie before. No words were uttered; they sat in stony silence for 10 minutes, then the two detectives came in with faces frozen; the informal part was no longer on their agenda They briefly introduced themselves; Lorna advised them she was a friend and she had training in police interviews so nothing would surprise her, even blatant mistruths; and of course she would be recording the informal interview. And before the detectives sat down; she asked their definition of informal. They advised that recent events had made this informal interview had now changed to interview under caution; they could leave if they wish and return with a legal representative? David was unnerved by this volte-face of interview; Lorna displayed no sign of discomfort or surprise. She whispered in David's ear. And he began to smile inanely and nodded in agreement. The detectives were blindsided by her nonchalant agreement; they decided to leave the room so they could consult a senior officer on what grounds they kept to themselves. As they were leaving Lorna told them to take their time. She had instructed David to emit laughter and confidence; they would be out of the station in a matter of minutes. She had little confidence in the police's assurance of an informal interview; she knew this was a blatant lie and that the police would change tact and announce that the interview was no longer informal, and as David Fisher had no legal representation they assumed that the interview would continue as they wouldn't relish another visit to the station even with a lawyer. However, Lorna reversed the outcome; they would cancel and reschedule a formal interview. David was ambivalent he had nothing to hide he wanted the interview to commence and be over as quickly as possible. He kept this thought to himself but had admiration for Lorna's intuition. The detectives returned and asked David if he wished to continue the interview when he was under caution; he was ready to stand up and be ready to leave; but Lorna intervened and to the detectives' surprise, she agreed to continue. This was a complete shock to David but he tried to exude some misplaced confidence, but he was intrigued as well. The detectives were young, the same detectives who had interviewed Simon Corndale in Jersey. They started asking David Fisher about any links to Russian clients; he answered 'client confidentiality prevented him from disclosing names however; if you have a warrant and my lawyer is content I'll answer your questions as long as they are legal and relevant to the particular client.' Lorna was impressed; he had obviously taken legal advice and had expected this scenario to unveil itself. The detectives were showing no emotion, and then they came to the epicentre of the interview Michael Ogilvie. 'Why did

Michael Ogilvie in his will bequeath you substantial property interests in your home town of Dundee?' Lorna was shocked as David. 'I am unaware of this, and have not been officially or unofficially advised of this, you must forgive me officers the death of Michael has affected me, and I wasn't' aware of Michael having property in Dundee, now why would he have property in Dundee, and why would he leave it to me?'

He had sidestepped their next question, why are you the sole beneficiary of property in Dundee?

The detectives changed tact. 'Did you supply the funds to Michael Ogilvie and he purchased the flats on your behalf as part of avoiding taxes?' At least he was aware the property is flats not a flat. His confidence is returning and he feels less intimidated. 'Now why would I do that?' Lorna watches her protégé with a mother's pride. He is interviewing the detectives and is slowly extracting salient information from them, without asking. 'So you have no idea why Michael Ogilvie has left you property in Dundee, and for the record you did not supply funds for the purchase of the flats?'

'For the record, I have no idea why he left me the flats as I didn't know he had purchased flats in Dundee, and I can't see the reason why he would buy flats in Dundee and leave them to me in his will, it's bizarre.' They look at each other and smile; they have been expecting this wide-eye butter wouldn't melt in his mouth interview. They suspect they will know soon enough. They are expecting him to ask the location and value of the apartments but he declines to raise this; again very suspicious.

However, this bequest is small beer, they have more questions that they know the answers to, but they have to encourage him to reveal more than he intends to. 'The death of your partner is connected to the death of Michael Ogilvie; you must've worked that out?' This visibly throws David, sweat breaks out on his brow; his mouth is dry. 'Can I have a drink please?' 'No David, that is not a good idea, we can cancel the interview and rearrange it where your lawyer will be by your side.' He clears his head, and agrees with Lorna, scolding himself in getting suckered into requesting a drink at his own volition and the police swabbing and fingerprinting the glass; this was not GI Joe clones he was dealing with.

'No I've not worked out any connection with their deaths to each other, enlighten me please?' 'Gwen, your partner; was a client of Michael Ogilvie; and we have established he didn't take on any new clients; you must've recommended Gwen?' How he longed for a cold drink of water, the sweat had surfaced on his brow and had not gone unnoticed; they enjoyed seeing him visibly uncomfortable. He wanted to loosen his tie, he looked at Lorna for support, he knew they wanted him to abruptly terminate the interview. She gave him that look; stay calm and answer every question. 'No I didn't know Gwen was a client and I didn't recommend her to Michael, our relationship was a whirlwind one, I knew she was in finance in New York.' That was the words they wanted to hear; New fucking York! 'Yes, you formed a relationship with her in New York and continued the relationship in London where Gwen started a new position in finance; your friend, colleague and neighbour Jonathan Gove was assassinated in Central Park; were you involved in arranging his death?' Lorna was too confident; these detectives were not detectives they were intelligence; they didn't need to water board David to extract information from him, and she had encouraged him to play along. This was a lesson for her which was difficult to accept; however, she had to acknowledge their soft spoken skill in real time; and she had to find out how much they knew and more important who from. David was expecting the siren call from Lorna becoming indignant and terminating the interview, but it didn't arise. He couldn't second guess their next question or questions, the deaths of Gwen and Jonathon in New York and London, had hit him hard mentally at the time, but now he was being visibly consumed by despair and regret. The detectives were exuding confidence ; Lorna on the other hand was on the horns of a dilemma; should she curtail the interview and arrange another interview with a legal representative or plough through and establish what they knew and did this pertain to Pavel and of course her? She doubted her decision to continue the interview was in her and Pavel's interest; studying David was a cruel and pity less observation; however she was thinking of the future consequences; it was more sensible to watch David bear this burden without any sympathy from her. David was pleading with his moist eyes at Lorna to intervene; she displayed no acknowledgement of his mental anguish. The detectives on the other hand were making progress seeing David mentally crumble. They were following a script and it was bearing dividends.

'When you returned to Dundee were you in contact either electronically or physically with any foreign nationals?' Lorna had to stop her leg from shaking; this was not what she had anticipated.

'I don't understand....foreign nationals?'

'Russians to be specific.' David felt a sense of relief. 'No, I don't think there are too many Russians in Broughty Ferry nor Dundee, it's too cold.' He smiled at this comment. They were not infected by his lame humour. 'Now are you sure about that David, it is a very important question.' He shook his head. 'I can categorically deny I have been in any contact with any Russians or foreign nationals.'

The detectives stood up. 'Time to let you gather your thoughts and have a chat with your advisor. We will be back in 20 minutes with more questions.' The recording of the interview was halted and they left the room. 20 minutes without a word spoken between Lorna and him would seem an eternity; Lorna pulled out her notebook and pen, and wrote no talking with exclamation mark. He nodded in relief. She then wrote Russians with a question mark, and pushed the pad to him. He wrote a question mark. She wrote in response in capitals ARE YOU SURE? In response and clearly annoyed he wrote FUCKING OF COURSE!! Calm down. He was embarrassed. Sorry but definitely not been in contact with anyone. They have something on you. He grabbed the pad. I know, but what? She was pleased at his outburst even on a writing pad. When the detectives returned they would open the door wider with their questions; she had to use all of her knowledge to anticipate where this interview was heading. Then she had an epiphany; it has to be Nigel's documents about Pavel stepping in and authorising a new funding agreement to David to complete the commercial building; if this was the case they had nothing to worry about. She kept this comforting thought to herself, David was not unaware of her lips forming a smile, which made him feel less worried. She took the pad from him and returned it to her jacket pocket.

She studied her watch and whispered in his ear; the detectives would be returning in a few minutes time; they had to disclose their hand. They heard their uniform footsteps echo along the corridor. They had walked past their interview room; David's eyes were fixed on the door which he anticipated to open. The disappointment in his face he could not hide; Lorna was not surprised at this technique, she placed her hand on his arm to reassure him; it did the trick. The footsteps did an about turn; David was elevated mentally at this movement. He felt more comfortable when the door opened and the recording began again. Lorna was waiting on the first innocuous question followed by laconic but unnerving other questions, of course David was not. The detectives gave them a copy of the flats title deeds and the considerable late caveat to his will stating David Fisher is to inherit the properties in Dundee. Of course with the avalanche of deaths and David was the sole recipient of a substantial property portfolio she could accept why there would be raised eyebrows at this sudden change to Michael Ogilvie's will. Did he change it after the meeting in the Iron Duke pub with Michael Ogilvie? David continued to study the property portfolio with ambivalence. Grateful for the flats from Michael but also wish he had not been left them as it aroused suspicions. He knew exactly where the flats were; a short distance from the V&A museum; Michael had obviously thought of turning them into Airbnb flats which would generate a steady and lucrative income stream to supplement his income in France. However, he was mystified why Michael would do this as he was not short of money. He still felt uneasy about his inheritance; because he didn't need the money and was mystified why Michael bequeathed the properties to him; baffling.

Lorna had to find out whether the Russian national they were alluding to was Pavel, and if this was the case were they aware of Lord Alexander? There had been a series of former Russians now settled in London and in the Home Counties of being victims of bad luck that curtailed their asylum applications due to their unexpected deaths of natural causes and suicide. The Press were becoming hostile to these individuals and offered no sympathy or reasons behind their demise. This was due to Pavel's malevolent and pecuniary influence with political journalists of different political viewpoints.

However, Michael Ogilvie's death had shaken the political and criminal kaleidoscope; where the pieces would land was open to conjecture. These detectives were cerebral and were more than curious. Through her experience they were using Michael Ogilvie's death as an unofficial gateway investigation into political influence into the body politic. While they were subtly extracting information from David Fisher without threats of forthcoming or immediate investigations into perceived financial irregularities or corruption of political figures, they touched on these serious matters speaking in the past tense, either to warn or reassure David. They skirted around the matter, then implied something and waited on David's response. She rapidly came to the clear conclusion that there had been no inculpatory evidence against David, either in his statement or this interview. This formal interview had not been foreseen; Lorna's strategy was to relocate David Fisher to New York where he would be the overseer of Pavel's financial investments due to his insight and evaluation of present and future trends; Pavel had tracked all David's investments during bear and bull markets; if he had to blow his own trumpet about his successful trades in the stock market alone. St Paul's Cathedral would crumble.

It was her singular view removing David from London and Dundee and relocating him to New York would obviously benefit Pavel's expanding portfolio and the political and financial establishments in the United Kingdom. However, on this occasion her opinion may not converge with reality.

The detectives' strategy was to make him feel uncomfortable while he was in London, they interrupted each other as the volley of questions some of which were banal and innocuous, Lorna took solace from this, the interview was reaching its conclusion without too much being revealed. There would be no last minute revelation that would impede David's innocence that shone through the gloomy and sometimes intimidating process. Her endorphins kicked in and her optimistic intuitive nature came to the fore. She stood up and to their surprise she announced that the interview was being terminated and they would gladly return with a barrister if requested, but she opined that David had answered truthfully all relevant and irrelevant questions. She indicated for David to rise from his chair and proceed towards the door, which he did and she followed. There was no resistance to this order from Lorna; the detectives observed in silence as they exited the interview room. They had come to an abrupt halt at a verbal wall. They looked at their watches in unison; David's apartment had been entered and various linked surveillance equipment had been secreted in locales within the apartment. They gave each other the perfunctory high-five as the door closed on Lorna. The interview had been successful for two reasons; first David was not the epicentre of the interview Lorna was. Secondly the interview was the optimum time to enter David Fisher's apartment. The interview had yielded unexpected results from Lorna and David, and the forthcoming data from the surveillance equipment would be a treasure trove of information that could not be secured anywhere else in London.

    Lorna had been using David Fisher's apartment when he had left London for the peace and tranquillity of Broughty Ferry, for meetings with a coterie of Russian dissidents and businessmen that had one thing in common they hated Putin and funnelled millions of dollars back to Russia fomenting protest groups to gather in public places to voice their disaffection with Putin which would be transmitted all around the world. Was it a coincidence or just sheer bad luck that some of the businessmen of questionable characteristics decided to commit suicide after having a few drinks and a shower at their expanding new built mansions in the Surrey countryside? Then the long drawn out process of a Fatal Accident Inquiry dragged on for a morale sapping interminable timeline, while the expected benefactors and recipients of the deceased; fought as Russian gangsters do for the assets that ran into millions of pounds. Those in the know let them squabble over these frivolous assets with their guns and knives; the close confidants of the recently deceased knew the Bitcoin passwords would quickly reclaim the multimillion fortune without anyone knowing; thus the civil war began of mistrust, that ended in violence and rancour. Some of the violence continued in other countries, private jets were tracked fleeing the United Kingdom, it was not too difficult to secure the flight plans in exchange for a financial benefit if this was not tempting enough, minds would be altered to review their original decision when the family pet disappeared and in the early morning the owner would find the deceased pet on the bonnet of their expensive car beheaded.

    Lorna's ebullience ebbed more than it flowed as they ;left the car park of the police station, David was animated she barely heard him as she was concerned about her triumphant exit; with precise hindsight she demurred it was in fact a disaster; but decided to treat these two emotions as imposters. Her muddled thoughts were clearing and David's words echoed clarity; he was making good points and praising her for abruptly ending the interview. He placed his hand on her shoulder and brought her to an immediate halt she was surprised at the intensity of his voice as he thanked her over and over again. She put her finger to her lips and took his hand and pulled him towards the waiting taxi. David was impressed that she had ordered the taxi, hence her repeatedly glancing at her watch. David's assessment was understandable but wrong, Lorna had a more important thing on her mind. However, she would explain this to him after the task was completed to her satisfaction. He opened the taxi door for her and she instructed the driver to take them to David's apartment. She let David chatter and explain how he was more relaxed in Dundee/ Broughty Ferry. She was well aware of his lifestyle and difficulty with the moronic behaviour of GI Joe; she had concern deleting his video of him from her mind. Some light laughter expunged the serious situation she was now embroiled in. However, that would wait until she was completely sure her thoughts were indeed correct, if so she was prepared to act and David would be the unwitting accomplice. She had accepted David's invitation to have dinner at the Iron Duke pub and a few drinks; if this relaxed David he may let his guard down and in confidence reveal his plan for the immediate future. Pavel had used him as a pawn sending him to New York and completing his business with Jonathon Gove; it was anticipated they would have consumed copious amounts of alcohol, and be in the company of two intelligent attractive women. Pavel was no fool; his plan and the executing of it was not left to chance or any unforeseen circumstance. Jonathon was an ardent jogger come hail or shine he would unfailingly complete his well-worn route in Central Park, and his religious stop at the same bench to sit and greedily drink all the contents from his water bottle. The execution of Jonathon Gove was witnessed from a sky scraper overshadowing Central Park and relayed to Pavel immediately. Now it was in Lorna's hands to convince him that his future was in New York as the fulcrum of Pavel's extensive assets. The accommodation would be for David to choose from various luxury apartments, and of course the salary would be competitive. Pavel was generous as well as ruthless if the incumbent deviated from tried and trusted methods; as the former incumbent realised far too late; when he was encouraged to throw himself from his newly-acquired apartment with his wife present.

   Lorna would segue New York into the conversation as it would eradicate psychologically remove the horrific experience when his colleague and friend Jonathon Gove was murdered, and at the same times evoke warm pleasant memories of the brief but loving relationship with Gwen. In Grove Road Broughty Ferry when David had called her and told her of the pressures of the police frequenting his door and the recurring guilt he felt following the deaths of Jonathon Gove and Gwen; he felt overwhelmed by grief and sadness. When David broke down into tears; Lorna was sympathetic but paradoxically she was delighted, as she would use these tragic personal events to manoeuvre him back to New York to be Pavel's top executive managing his financial investments and affairs. The occasion had landed on her lap. She would sift through all the benefits of expunging the crushing thoughts of New York, but she would advise him to seek a job in his field there, knowingly that Pavel would offer him the lucrative position in New York, and she could advise him to split some time back in Broughty Ferry for a few months at a time; Pavel would agree to this. The Iron Duke dinner would trigger thoughts of another colleague who was deceased; Michael Ogilvie; this was turning into a job lot of physiological tragic events; there would never be a case study like this ever she concluded; or hoped, but who can be confident of history never repeating itself? However, she would not ruminate about this unlikely event occurring. David was returning to his normal self, at the dinner tonight she would limit her professional input unless absolutely necessary; she would use her professional nous to guide the conversation back to the tried and trusted route to lubricate the agreement to return to his career and in a challenging economical environment; the Big Apple. The small talk in the taxi ended as the taxi drew up outside the red mansion block. For all the tragic events that had occurred in his brief time, she couldn't help notice the smile as he eyed the mansion block; no signs of fear or trepidation, he was more mentally hardened than she anticipated. She was concerned.

***

The message on the EncroChat phone was an order not a request. He had let the feeling of confidence morph into complacency; the message removed any doubt. In France he was settled to some degree; but events change the mood; he had taken every security measure possible to avoid detection; however the message was clear; they have you marked down as deceased from next Thursday. A further message would be sent when this information was more precise. Fuck! What was he to do? The message came later that evening; return to the UK. No way was he going to adhere to this command; he would rather take his chances in France than in the UK; there would be no altering his decision. However, after a restless sleep his view had altered and not for the better. Driving through the rain in the unattractive car with the window wipers at full pelt had a calming effect on his cluttered thought process. It was an offer he couldn't refuse; kill or be killed. He chose unremarkably the former. His sins had caught up with him and he had to agree to the penance; on his phone a montage of his various

Airbnb apartments and his myriad of debit cards transactions under aliases and his statements added to his discomfort. The person that was to be removed from society did not come with any explanation, however, after the task was completed his debt would be eradicated and he could live his life without fear once again. He had circumvented a plethora of business deals with shady characters in darkened rooms; but these businessmen were environmentally friendly and declined to supply any paperwork; kill or be killed was enough for him to accede to their demands however unsavoury. There would be no monetary bonus for completing the murder. A life for a life; his life spared and his victim's ended. His demeanour as he approached Dieppe was ambivalent; returning to the United Kingdom for the final time before his return to France where he felt less threatened and of course in the winter the South of France had its attraction. He had never been to Newhaven but that was the route he had been advised to take. Once aboard the ferry he would receive further instructions they didn't make clear whether it would be by EncroChat or orally on board. He had played potential victim bingo in his mind who the real victim would be; some of these rum characters he would take sadistic pleasure in removing; due to their abrupt business methods of extracting money or forcing contracts to be signed.

 The rain became heavier as he followed the signs for the route to the ferry; no visible tension was etched on his tanned face; his small travel bag was all he would need for the brief return to the United Kingdom; he asked himself a rhetorical question; when the task was completed and he was offered a safe haven in the UK would he accept this generous offer? No he shouted out loud; Never ever. The process was efficient driving the car onto the Ferry; imagine having to use this mode of transport on a regular basis? The thought sent a shiver up his spine. 4 hours plus meant he would not be bored; he would purchase a snack, coffee and read his newspaper and wait on the message who he had agreed to remove from this earth. The ferry was busy he took great comfort in that; his well-being was enhanced he settled in to take in the task ahead periodically glancing at his phone, he had never had any thoughts of returning to the UK; but here he was returning under duress, but what else could he have done? He was inclined to look to the future which when the task was complete he was free to live his life as he chose. He was having difficulty with this concept; but that was the choice; the only sensible choice. The nagging concern was this journey was one way only, it was part of his cover story UK citizen returning to see friends and family then return at a unknown future date; nothing complicated or sinister about that, He accepted his cognisant and erudite explanation with good grace; he had mastered mindfulness to a great measure. The couple in their forties seemed to be under pressure their mournful expressions signified to him that they were experiencing some personal cataclysmic event .or were smuggling contraband; he had become a well-seasoned body language expert through the years; or that was his immodest opinion; which to be fair he had been proven correct on the majority of occasions. He sipped the coffee which he expected to be truly awful; but the greatest coffee critic concurred that it was excellent and cheap, normally strangers to each other.

The EncroChat subtly pinged; the photograph was High Definition; he chortled this would be a pleasure not a predicament; his mood was heightened; he ordered a cognac the only thing missing was his favourite cigar when he was a wild and obnoxious city trader. Another message complimented the photograph; the time, method and date would follow. They are teasers. His victim bingo was no way near his choice but this wild card pleased him more. Simon Corndale felt good returning to London albeit in a more economical, crude and unsophisticated mode of transport.

***

Lord Alexander was enjoying the trappings of the nobility; no pecuniary concerns, no feeling of despair when waking up in the morning after a pattern of broken sleep; his only feeling was that he was a rebel without a pause in every waking moment in bringing down the entitled establishment who dined out regularly on the backs of the desperate and poverty stricken electorate; now he was a member of the Establishment and he was far from eradicating the parasites from the inside; To assuage this hypocritical thought he vowed to modify his vocal outrage to subtle suggestions. There was never a sliver of doubt about his envious lifestyle was enjoyable; and he comforted himself by reminding his critics that he believed in Santa Claus at one time. His views changed when facts changed; he was even erroneous with the facts to himself. He was off the booze and his physical shape and mental health had improved remarkably all down to that chance meeting with Lorna, Fate and circumstances had offered him a second chance and he accepted it with good grace and thankfulness. He shivered where would he be now if the chance meeting had not taken place? He refused to explore the avenues he would have taken and the state he would have been in, The tea filled whisky bottle was the reminder where he was now and where he had come from; life lessons were all around his plush apartment; limited editions adorned his walls and the smile grew wider; not so long in the dark times his walls were adorned with embossed wallpaper bought at B&Q at a discounted rate.

Lorna had encouraged him to sit down and reflect where his life was in the moment and to trawl through the many unhappy experiences he had experienced, Reflect, reflect was her mantra. There was very little time to meet former socialist MPs for lunch at the low market pubs with fundamental but nutritious menus; dining in the House of Lords was inexpensive and the cuts of meat were from the finest herds; which came from a Lord's farm. You scratch my back was the norm in the House of Lords; many favours were offered and favours reciprocated on a regular basis in the dining areas. He was the eager apprentice when he arrived in the House of Lords but he listened and observed; this did not go unnoticed from the influential small cabal of Lords who had informants everywhere. Now he was part of the cabal and there was no shame or heaven forbid of being a class traitor. Those views which he once held so dearly were dropped before you could say expenses. He had relinquished his outdated ideology and embraced more sensible and lucrative principals which were not set in stone. He took comfort from having an open mind; laws were changed through negotiation rather than confrontation. Another sound bite which Lorna had installed in him; she had influenced every aspect of his political and personal life. He had raised the nation's epidemic of mental illness that was sweeping the country with a powerful and evocative speech; the media were clamouring for interviews and the phalanx of mental health charities were concurring with every aspect of his speech. He gave very few speeches in the House of Lords but when he did the red benches were filled to capacity. It was generally forgotten or forgiven when he was a red tooth and nail socialist he described 'the red benches as the blood of the workers that the fat arsed Lords and Ladies sat on every day to undermine the working conditions of working people; then fall asleep on' However change had come swift for the newly ennobled Lord; he was flexible with his principals and he adapted smoothly to the practices of the House of Lords. This was the crème de crème compared to the House of Commons; things could be achieved here for the working people of the United Kingdom rather than the corrupt cesspit of the House of Commons

  Pavel had chosen mentors for him in the House of Lords; very influential individuals; they would have no difficulty eliciting suggestions to him, They would also help persuade the unpersuadable to be persuaded through cognisant arguments and overseas trips to observe how climate change was affecting poorer countries. Lord Alexander was an affable and charming individual albeit with a caveat; if he had not been imbibing. And of course he knew where his sourdough bread was buttered. He was instructed to exit and wait at his front door where his prearranged taxi would take him to a newly-built mansion in Surrey to meet Pavel. He wanted Lord Alexander to meet someone who had been impressed by his environmental achievements and he had influence in the EU; that was the cryptic message, the completed message would've ended, 'and it would be of a financial advantage to you.' All legal and above board of course; he was in the grey area that never blended into black; in fact it actually blended into green; greenbacks. He glanced at the old stationmasters' clock unlike the trains it had never lost time

***

GI Joe had tried to put his impending disciplinary hearing to the rear of his worries; however, it was a futile exercise, his Police Federation representative was not too disappointed to pass on a mutually consented proposal from senior management; go gently into that good night, and you retain your pension and a medical discharge; PTSD from his heroic time fighting in Afghanistan. The Police Federation representative had to stifle a laugh considering his insipid battle with the drug emaciated youths from the Hilltown that had inflicted more psychological damage than the feared and ruthless Taliban. He had three weeks to accept or face the wrath of the conscious biased disciplinary panel. They had let it be known he would be dismissed without any pension rights and criminal proceedings would be initiated against him. And David Fisher would be there in person to give inculpatory evidence against him.

The cold whipping wind on the Law(Hill) made him think more clearly how to extricate himself from the disciplinary hearing; if it took place he faced a future devoid of money and prestige; he had convinced himself without any cerebral reason he would be an inspector in a few years time; an optimistic view from a deranged individual.

He glanced at his watch, he was late, the rain started to lightly hit his face, no one was here at this unearthly hour, he heard the car changing gear, at last he was here, there would be no rehearsed suggestion, once he heard his proposal his problem would be over. The car reversed into the parking space, it was clear the occupant would not be leaving the comfort of his car; probably not taxed he thought to himself. He flicked the cigarette into the wind, and made his way over to the car, the occupant smiled at his obvious discomfort; something big was going to be asked from him, The bounty in exchange would be beneficial to him. The early rise annoyance had diminished he opened the door for GI Joe. 'Okay, what's on your mind?' The words flowed, and the shock on the hardened criminal's face had GI Joe luxuriating on his shock and awe strategy. It was quite simple really; if the criminal did not carry out his instructions; he would either be killed or spend the next decade at least incarcerated. GI Joe would ensure it would be the former. To reinforce his view he pulled out his EncroChat phone; and passed it to the fear ridden criminal; encrypted messages were read with fear and impending doom, and not to mention the far reaching consequences; he didn't need to hear from GI Joe who the identities of the group chat; all were identified as a noun and an adjective. But GI Joe identified each and every individual in the group. How loose they had become in their conversations; how much drugs were being transported from location to location, and the boasting of how many millions they had made from previous deals. It would be a futile exercise to ask GI Joe how he came into the possession of the encrypted EncroChat phone and the method that he had identified everyone in the group chat. He had always treated GI Joe as a joke; now the landscape was changing before his eyes; he had been conned all along by GI Joe for two years. He handed the EncroChat phone back to GI Joe, opened the window for air closed it again and turned to the grinning police officer. 'OK, there is no doubt you have done your homework, I'm in trouble, how much money do you want, in exchange for the phone?' GI Joe leant back against the car door, contempt barely disguised. 'Do you think this is about money?' He was genuinely surprised at this. 'So what do you want from me, if it isn't money?' 'I need your esoteric skill.' He was toying with the uneducated erstwhile pupil of St. Michaels, he didn't understand'. 'He opened the phone again. A lifeless body with a shot to the head in a leafy copse stared out at him. 'Not a good idea to murder someone, even a fellow dealer and share amongst your friends, proof that you had carried out their orders, and the bank details they had deposited your fee into this bank account; your bank account.' His will to live was fading; the embarrassment of posting the lifeless victim from his phone to the rest of the cartel was insanely stupid. 'What do you want me to do, to make things right, I'll do anything...' 'You have no choice; I want you to arrange a meeting with all four of them, in an outside environment; then kill them.' He could not believe what he was hearing; but he had to be sanguine about the situation. Killing did not cause him any anxiety he had killed before if the situation arose. If he attempted to warn the intended victims; they would kill him, once he had told them of the EncroChat phone he had seen with his own eyes and it was a police officer who showed it to him, he wouldn't make it out of Glasgow, they would think, rightly that he was entrapping them. GI Joe glanced at his watch, he enjoyed the flow of money in the past from him; but in the early hours of a windy rainy day on the Law, it would be the best day of his life. 'I'll be in touch where and when you'll extinguish your business partners. They would do the same to you in a heartbeat.' He opened the door and made his way to the Law monument, saluted and made his way towards the descending path into the darkness.

 The businessman/dealer was embarrassed how GI Joe had played him for a fool; GI Joe was just a plod that he slipped cash to for advanced information of imminent raids; he paid him peanuts; after all he was his monkey. Little did he know he was a former intelligence officer in Afghanistan, colleagues would argue with justification that GI Joe was not imbued with intelligence and surely this was an oxymoron? While GI Joe lacked social skills and self awareness according to his colleagues; this was a front not to draw attention to himself. He was a natural thespian, but had a voracious appetite for money; he had served his country with distinction but little financial reward. The police force was his route to greater riches; this was an optimistic forecast that came to a shuddering halt after his encounter with the disaffected youths on Alexander Street on the Hilltown; his carefully nurtured reputation came crashing down the same time he was attacked by the feral youths. Hand to hand combat was not for him. His careful elevated potential move from a modest constable to an Inspector in a few years embarrassed him, but he had thought carefully out of normal ambition; the rapid promotion was not for him after the embarrassing debacle on the Hilltown; and with hindsight it was fate giving him a second chance. He was part of the muscle team when the drug squad would raid a prominent dealer's house in Ardler who seemed to have carte blanche to continue his vile but lucrative trade; of course the media crew would be there to record another raid to reassure the viewers that Dundee was no safe haven for dealers. Whatever.

It was long suspected that the ever-changing drug squad mislaid cash and drugs; this was put down as a clerical error; no big deal. GI Joe was acquired to go into the main bedroom and not let anyone enter apart from the identified drug squad member; they all rushed in and the occupant was in the lounge enjoying a joint; he went to the designated bedroom and stood at the open door; his eyes caught the phone charging; he instinctively took the phone beside the other phone that was charging; his instinct had alerted him to seize it; it was locked; this didn't perturb him; he returned to the door while the cacophony of various voices filled the air with demands. The house was searched and drugs and cash were removed from secreted locations from the detached house. The individuals in the drug squad were supercilious to the uniformed officers present and they didn't try to disguise their overt disdain for them Thus began the odyssey to locate his former colleague and alumni of Oxford University; Crispy. He had his own software development company in Madrid but sold out to a global company. It took him months to locate him; Crispy was genuinely delighted to hear from him and invited him over; GI Joe explained he was due time off and he would be over once his leave of absence was granted. He would meet him in the cafe they had both frequented when they were on leave behind the Plaza Mayor. When they met GI Joe explained in bullet point conversation his career and the fortuitous find of the phone that was locked; Crispy never asked why he wanted it unlocked and the information released. Crispy wrongly assumed GI Joe was an undercover drug dealer or drug officer and he couldn't release the phone to the relevant department as they had been compromised. GI Joe had the phone in a bag; Crispy had no inclination that he wouldn't be able to unlock and release the information;

Interpol had come to him for assistance and were so grateful that they awarded his small specialist company a multi-million euro contract. Of course this information was never shared with GI Joe; after a few bottles of beer they were both relaxed; however GI Joe became less exuberant and slowly limited his conversation; Crispy sensed this and told him that he would have all the information released and explained to him in a matter of days, and he was confident identities and locations also. Thus was the verbal adrenalin shot he needed; the real GI Joe character emerged with gusto; he knew once he had the identities it would be drug dealers in Dundee and from major cities in the UK and abroad, A treasure trove of information that could be traded for gold. He had the plan in his head how to convince the dealers that it would be in their interests to accede to his reasonable demands; if not someone would be selected and used as an example to comply or face the consequences.

While GI Joe slept soundly in Crispy's apartment; Crispy had his ear buds in and worked through the night with the floor to ceiling windows slightly ajar to allow the cool night air to touch his face. Crispy got by on only four hours' sleep. GI Joe never politely enquired if he was making progress after each evening had been completed by Crispy; he had total confidence in his skill and perseverance. He would work through the night until eight am coffee was his only companion. When GI Joe surfaced he would serve him croissants and coffee, have a chat; nothing about the phone, then retire to bed and surface about noon, shower and amaze GI Joe how life enthused throughout his body and no irritability in his voice.

They walked for hours around Madrid and visited art galleries and museums; perfect foil with their curious minds and solutions to extant problems. GI Joe did not surprise Crispy with his knowledge of the Spanish Civil war; seeing the various locales brought his knowledge up to a more humane understanding of how the people of Madrid had suffered. On the third day GI Joe was becoming pensive as the self imposed deadline approached he had faith in Crispy laying out the relevant information extracted from the SIM card from the EncroChat phone; he had to rescind more adventurous guesses that caused him to awaken from his slumber. Eventually he was woken from his fractured sleep and welcomed the sight on sunlight on the wall and the noise of traffic. He rose slowly sat at the edge of the bed and vigorously rubbed his face and made his way into the lounge; Crispy was on his laptop, he looked up at the anxiety riven erstwhile comrade and pointed to the recently poured coffee on the opposite side of the table; GI Joe's worry laden face was becalmed. 'Is it done?' Crispy let out a gentle laugh; 'Oh ye of little faith?' GI Joe moved quickly to his chair at the table sat down and turned over the single A4 sheet of paper; his mood was enhanced immediately when he had seen the lonely A4 sheet; nothing too technical and just bullet points. He lifted the mug of coffee and devoured the information; the SIM card was KPN (Dutch Company) which allowed roaming on UK networks; this information alone filled him with optimism, Crispy had identified eight individuals from their infantile code names (noun and adjective) he named them and their addresses; two from the Dundee area two from Glasgow and the others from the Wirral area. Crispy had examined the communications between the group; photographs of money drugs, firearms and villas in Spain. Numerous boasting of murders completed; drug transactions completed and approved drug deals. He had written a footnote it was acerbic. 'None of these gentlemen could have any lineage to Albert Einstein I can state with the utmost confidence.'

   While reading this GI Joe was formulating a feasible plan in his head how he could use this information to his financial advantage. Boy these guys were thick! He turned over the page and glanced at the grinning Crispy. 'Now rather than me asking questions which you have already anticipated, just tell me everything I need to know.' Crispy removed his glasses still smiling,

'As always you're way ahead of the curve...as you are well aware these characters are dealers in drugs, and in securing guns, and are not immune to boasting of their wealth, deals and where these deals have taken place and of future deals and sometimes killings. Now why would people openly do this? For example, these fellows come into contact with the police, can you imagine they have been arrested for one reason or another, and the police access their phones? So why do they do this with the utmost confidence? Simple really, they believe that they have encrypted phones to carry out their drug deals etc, and may I say with the utmost confidence; the longer they carry out their deals, collect money and deposit money; arrange assassinations etc, the longer it goes on the more confident they become and more complacent they also become, hence the photographs of them with money and drugs, and of course showing off their villas. Utter madness. Now I do not want to know what is your business with these characters, obviously to trace money to certain off shore accounts and locations of stash houses; but I would caution you with this; do what you have to do very soon; it is my settled view that it is Interpol that have created EncroChat to get these dumb bastards to conduct business through

EncroChat for a number of years; whilst Interpol and no doubt intelligence services; collate all the information of deals completed and where the money is. Then sometime in the near future Boom! Carry out raids simultaneously throughout Europe; once the criminals are arrested and shown their communications with each other, they will turn each other in; guaranteed.'

GI Joe sat in awe of his erstwhile comrade; he couldn't wish for any more information However, he had a pertinent question to ask and that would be it. 'As you can imagine, I am very thankful for your cerebral assessment, but are you telling me that no local drug squad in the UK will have knowledge of EncroChat just Interpol?' 'You have answered your own question; I would wager that Europol if they are involved at all, they would be on the peripheral and at the latter stage of the investigations. As for any police force in the UK, undoubtedly no, because of leaks,' Everyday is certainly a school day mused GI Joe. When would Interpol contact the various police forces in the UK was anyone's guess, what was abundantly clear, time was of the essence he had to fine-tune his plan and act decisively; there was no hint of doubt. Crispin had come through with flying colours once again. Time to pack and make their way to the airport; his nascent strategy to extort money from Einstein's relatives was updating regularly in his mind. No one would inhibit him from completing his task.

***

In The Shard Pavel is patiently waiting on a text message from Lorna he is always drawn to the vast window with the panoramic view of London; he could sit by his large desk and be immersed into the zeitgeist of the amazing view, but he was more comfortable standing with a cup of coffee admiring his plethora of expensive properties that he could easily point out to Lorna or other wealthy individuals, however, he was not part of the Instagram generation, in the shadows he felt more powerful and safe.

The expensive coffee machine was gurgling, he was delighted to hear the sound; Lorna had used her psychotherapist skills to cultivate the seed in David Fisher to take up the position in New York; however the two New York detectives were the impediment in the financial ointment. He was ambivalent about his safety in London as well, he had read the online theories about the sudden deaths of influential and sworn enemies of Putin who were diminishing by the year He would be offered an alternative to be based in New York; he would be able to work from his home in Broughty Ferry for at least three months of the year. This would be put to him and he would run this past Lorna who would congratulate him on negotiating such a brilliant contract.

The text came through she was in the lift on her way to the apartment/office. He poured the coffee the barely audible sound of the elevator had reached its destination. The silent opening of the door; then she stepped out, looking radiant as per usual, he would impart information to her that would elevate her mind, body and soul. She came to the window and sipped her coffee while intending to update him on David Fisher's state of mind and whether he was lagging in ambition to move to New York and make Pavel rich by acquiring assets that would not raise any concerns from hedge funds. Steady as she goes was Pavel's byword. Too many Wall Street traders were high on their opinions of themselves and their honed skills and cocaine in outpacing market returns.

However, David Fisher would be the bulwark to damage their portfolios and bullet proof reputations. There would be a fintech company that had developed an app that was highly profitable in currency trading and was rumoured to be listing the following year on the NASDAQ, however, various advisors were waiting in the wings to bring the company from being private to public share ownership, of course the hedge funds would be offered a discounted share price if they agreed to purchase millions of shares, up to twenty percent. From this minority of shares, sold at a discounted price the owners would earn over $200 million. Pavel was the seed financier behind the fledgling fintech company and he had it written into the contract that it would be listed on the NASDAQ within four years; this day had come. David Fisher would be his guardian, and would be fomenting interest from big corporate entities to wealthy individuals who were acting as a proxy for hedge funds,

However, Lorna would be rewarded for her uncomplaining endurance in cultivating professional relationships; Pavel invited her to sit at the table. 'Now is the time to place your fitness centres in the market; there will be much interest, this will make you a multi-millionaire, however, you will invest at least forty percent of your profit in a new fintech company that will be listed on the NASDAQ, I am confident to predict you will more than double your investment, and can draw down the profits after a year; you will form a company and base it in Jersey to avoid punitive taxes; there are funds in London that are desperate to buy companies like yours outright, then after few years put the company on the FTSE so they can realise their profits. You will benefit twice; by selling to a private equity company, then the proceeds will be invested in the new fintech company.' Lorna was not expecting this; however she remained calm while absorbing this news. 'How soon do you think the company will be offered to private equity companies?' 'As we speak there are representatives of a myriad of private equity companies and global hedge funds formulating bids, you may recall when the insurance and surveyors came and inspected all the gyms to update their records? That was to collate all the information into the prospectus for a few trusted and not so trusted insiders who want to be the broker to earn exorbitant fees. There is a shortlist; they will be invited to submit sealed bids; which will be compromised, which will increase the value of your company. All is in hand Lorna.' 'All I can offer is my thanks Pavel, you never seem to amaze me, I can never predict your next move, again all I can say is thanks,' He raised himself from the chair and gestured for her to follow him to the window. She followed, surely no more surprises?

He raised his right arm and pointed to the newly constructed apartment building where celebrities had purchased multi-million pound apartments. 'You own a three bedroom apartment on the top floor with private roof garden. Now how has David Fisher reacted to the news....?'

***

GI Joe sat outside the Ship Inn, the construction workers were going about their tasks with enthusiasm; unlike the police and justice systems. He was on sick leave due to 'work related stress' the 'stress' was cunningly disguised in his demeanour; this was a man who had no qualms with the world or personal woes, he sipped the expensive coffee while manoeuvring the croissant to his eager mouth; a few construction workers had recognised him as he had given them advice on a civil matter that they hadn't asked for, thanked him but returned the advice with hostile invective; alas trying to impress the female officer came to nought, GI Joe guessed correctly that he was the subject of their laughter; on this rare occasion he was correct; with casual contempt for his admirers he consumed the croissant in a slow erotic manner; their laughter gained decibels. He returned to a more serious matter, the EncroChat dealers. He had the place, location and time where the dealers would meet their fate; he had placed cameras in the location and monitored them daily; there would be no change of mind from the executioner every scenario had been assessed and any problem met with a solution.

Previously he had walked the length of the Esplanade after the ground had been broken to install the foundations on an inclement day; at first he had congratulated himself on deciding the deceased dismembered dealers' bodies would be within the foundations then covering them with concrete; however, his impromptu plan was easier and simpler. And they would never be found. He had checked the weather the unending heavy rain had ceased. He couldn't have asked for more ideal weather; the meeting was on; no suspicion would be raised at the location; a property owned by the dealer; who was converting into luxury apartments in the west end of the city; body bags were also in the basement; once killed they would be allocated a body bag after been stripped of personal affects and clothing.

They would arrive by different modes of public transport; this did not come with unanimous agreement, but the cover story of why this had to be agreed melted any suspicion. Someone was leaking information, he wouldn't even send the message by EncroChat, as imagined this had caused anxiety and paranoia to break out within the group; who were not bosom buddies, being Celtic and Rangers supporters didn't inculcate friendship; they tolerated each other; the only common cause was to make money. It was the sustained heavy rain that had made him think of the locale to dispose of the bodies; no dismemberment would be required; cleaner and quicker to transport them. He had frequently checked the weather; heavy rain and wind no more.

The instructions had been uttered once on the Law, there were no questions from the assassin; he was impressed; he didn't ask about disposal; he would be texted where to bring the bodies for disposal; and was cautioned he would be monitored; any deviation from the instructions would result in him being placed in the extra body bag; a sober reminder to adhere to the brief instructions. Now it was one pm, the fun would be commencing shortly; he watched on his phone the tense meeting begin with each victim sat at the table as the assassin went to get the paperwork to explain how the group had become compromised; after returning from the filing cabinet he pulled out the Glock with silencer and shot each one in the head, six seconds; he checked their pulse on their necks all dead, He left them where they fell on the floor or slumped at the table, coffee still steaming; none spilled. His army skills had never left him. GI Joe smiled as they were all dispatched rapidly; then stripped of personal items including their burner phones. The audio and visual content was first class. However, there would be no champagne cork popped just yet, he sent the message to his burner phone the post code. The builder's van was fitted with a tracker; which would be easily removed. It would take fifteen minutes to reach the location; he could imagine the stress levels he would be experiencing with bodies in the back under the tarpaulin; two minutes from the location; he texted the location, Birkhill cemetery, where burials were halted due to the incessant rain; burials would resume tomorrow, but today no heavy rain was falling, the mini-excavators were left in situ only covered with blue waterproof sheets; he was an experienced builder he could pick any of the six graves that had been dug; excavate them deeper and dump the bodies; cover them with earth and his task was complete; there would be no need for any pious homily. He wore the supplied Council uniform and completed his task in forty-five minutes. Once the last body was interred he returned the mini-excavator to its original location. The observing GI Joe removed himself from his car to hand over the EncroChat phone to him as agreed. All through the burial process the assassin was not disappointed in the removal of his fellow dealers; he was the dominant person now and wouldn't have to worry about being 'removed' from the group. GI Joe approached him dressed in the Council uniform with the EncroChat phone being waved to him as he covered the excavator with the waterproof sheet; his eyes sparkled as he anticipated the EncroChat phone, GI Joe silently handed over the EncroChat phone, then pulled out the handgun and shot him twice in the head. He had dug his own grave; he had been texted 'excavate another grave I've got the missing dealer who had absconded from Castle Huntly; a known C.I, (confidential informant) in the boot.' He removed the personal effects and burner phone then dumped him in the grave, covered him with earth, then put the wooden boards over the grave; as the recently deceased had done. Excavator parked alongside the others, the builders' van was torched; the sun was emerging from the leaden sky. Now a few hours later he was enjoying coffee outside the Ship Inn, if only the construction workers openly mocking him only knew. He lifted his coffee cup to acknowledge their pejorative laughter.

***

He was now in London, there were no feelings of misty nostalgia, he was here to complete a deletion of another human being. He felt neither nervous nor an attack of conscience, London was experiencing a knife crime epidemic, the police were concentrating on the less affluent areas of London where the knife crime showed no signs of abating; sad for the victims and their grieving families but it made his task less stressful. A night in an Airbnb in a prestigious address not unfamiliar to him, no one would be there to greet him, he was texted the code for the digital door pad. Being known to the victim would make his task easier. Tomorrow after his task was completed he would return by ferry to France, the long drive would help him evaluate his life once more.

The victim would be relieved of his watch and packets of cocaine would be left adjacent to the body; the police would come to the obvious conclusion it was a drug deal that had went wrong in an unlit car park next to a crime ridden council estate. That would be the conclusion of the police; however, that was the final act; but the murder would have taken place in the victim's house, and then the body dumped in the car park where there was no CCTV, and there were numerous CCTV blind spots en-route. However, he would text him saying he had broken down in the car park, could you get here quickly? He was calm and fully focused it would be killing two birds with one stone; or in this occasion a bullet. He was shortly to return money from an investment, this would be the perfect reason for the meeting; the victim would not suspect an ulterior motive. The police would examine the phone and assume this car park meeting because of a broken down car was code from the dealer.

  He had slept well, and now was the time to go to the car park, his car would be parked a few streets behind the car park in the council estate. The dark night sky had been the starting gun to commence his murderous odyssey; it was not too far from his Airbnb.. This time tomorrow he would be back in his adopted country safe, sound and content. He pulled into the street with strewn old vehicles on either side of the pot holed road, his old car blended in perfectly. He parked and turned the engine off; and texted of his bad luck with the expensive car, could you pick me up? The reply was instant; he knew where the pub car park was; stay in your car, it's quite a lively area. He removed the snub nosed pistol from under the passenger seat. When he held the gun, his demeanour changed from utter calmness to apprehension; this was a shock, but it must be the holding of the gun that triggered him. He scanned the empty street for dog walkers or gangs of teenagers; two were killed the previous month; however there didn't seem to be a police presence. He waited on the text arriving; at last the ping came; he had arrived at the car park. He went through the scenario once again in his head; after the smiling and informal greeting he would pull out the gun and shoot him twice in the head from close range. He took off the silencer, and screwed it back onto the gun, why he did this he didn't know, but it made him feel better. Having a viscerally dislike for the victim definitely helped him; and the message 'kill or be killed' made up his mind for him. He opened the car door and stepped into the cold damp evening air, every step towards the car park drained confidence from him which alarmed him; he tried to ignore the gloomy car park that lay fifty metres in front of him, as he studied the car's dipped lights through the trees from the street, he gathered his thoughts, he couldn't back down now. He gripped the gun in his overcoat pocket for reassurance, he heard a car door open and close; then footsteps on the gravel, he was comforted by the sudden halt, and would say he had managed to start the car, but the car engine had stopped again, he was in the adjoining street; yes, brilliant cover story. He entered the car park, a few cars and vans were there; he walked towards the victim, who had his back turned, and looked towards the entrance of the car park. He then heard rushing footsteps behind him; he turned quickly around to face a gun inches from his face; the unmistakable crack of a gun had been fired twice. He hit the ground in a crumpled heap, drug packets were placed in his warm hands. His phone removed. The female New York detective joined her colleague at the waiting car.

***

David Fisher was keen to return to the sedentary lifestyle he enjoyed in his kitchen in Grove Road; he was not keen to return to New York; however, he would comply with Lorna's suggestion that it would emancipate his closed mind; this was an unexpected barb to his fragile ego. He would take her to his favourite and nearby pub the Iron Duke in the evening for dinner and tell her of his plans for the future. He was on the flight to Dundee in the morning; the taxi was prearranged to transport him from the small airport to Grove Road. His dad was texting him about the news that the Royal Bank of Scotland was intending to close the branch in Brook Street. This was a genuine shock to the local community that would hit the elderly community that were not comfortable with online banking. He would make a few discreet phone calls to the old money millionaire class that still lived in the Ferry; the reason for the closure was the customer base had declined over the years; not according to his dad it hadn't; then he went on to rant against the former socialist MSP who had discovered love and a wealthy industrial family who were overtly Conservative. Funny that. She had been replaced with an ineffective fairly invisible individual; who was apparently 'upset' at the branch closure. There was a rumour that her criticism would be tempered as she had a substantial mortgage with the bank. However, if the bank closure were to happen this could be an unexpected business opportunity. If the building were to be sold on the open market, he was supremely confident that his new company that he would form would be successful in securing the purchase. He would sell it on immediately to a London buyer; Pavel.

Lorna on the other hand had a financial problem on her mind; she had to use her personal charm and professionalism to assure David that moving to New York would increase his world view and bring more responsibility which he thrived on. When David signed the contract with the London lawyer; she could relax, not completely but definitely relax. The Iron Duke was familiar with her in her previous life working in Canary Wharf for the global bank. She had spent a many a boisterous evening there, before moving onto a club.

The newspapers were filled with another apparent suicide of an exiled Russian oligarch who had previously contacted Pavel and others regarding the sale of his billion dollar assets and along with his newly-built mansion in Surrey as he was moving to Tel Aviv as his mother was ailing. Pavel knew that he was invited to bid for his portfolio only because other interested parties were made aware that he was interested in securing all of the assets; the price would rocket. Pavel was insulted; he declined and word came from brokers that the assets were tainted by 'financial irregularities' this was a blow to the soon to depart oligarch; that he committed suicide; unlucky for him but fortuitous for Pavel; who purchased the assets at a deeply discounted price; he would keep hold of them, and when David was settled in New York he would divide up the assets into bite size chunks then sell them on to various hedge funds in New York for an eye-watering profit. This was the reason Lorna had to convince David Fisher to locate to New York.

David Fisher was the unintended recipient of the deceased oligarch's burgeoning highly-valued portfolio of assets that he would slice and dice to maximise the price of the assets. This was not unfamiliar to David. Pavel had a few hedge fund managers that would bid higher than normal to create a frenzy auction amongst the less experienced hedge fund managers that they would be intoxicated with the insider trading gossip that would be filling their ego driver vacuous craniums. They would pay a premium (overpay) but over a short period of time would wipe out their losses. David Fisher could anticipate where the market was heading; and New York was the place to maximise assets; and include non-performing assets amongst the lucrative assets that would be split into affordable packages. After this David would return to London or Dundee, that was the plan, however Lorna could utilise David's mercurial talent to her and David's personal benefit. She would refrain from informing Pavel of this strategy for the moment this was her ruminating in the taxi en-route to the Iron Duke; it had been a journey with Pavel, however it was time to travel solo once again through life. She would break the news to Pavel when David had completed the sale of the assets in New York and had returned to the United Kingdom. But for now she would ride the waves of good fortune; how would David react to the death of the oligarch? He would not be aware of the assets he would offer to the market on behalf of Pavel, had once belonged to the unfortunate oligarch he had met briefly. And knowing David he would not voice any concerns if he did; he would treat Pavel's good fortune as being in the right place at the unfortunate time. Lorna was pleased how the assets could be divvied up and repackaged, but she was not the only one to remark that the oligarch seemed to be in good spirits as they left his mansion.

Edwina was also an interested spectator of another suicide of another Russian oligarch; she was in the Iron Duke pub awaiting Lorna. Her presence with David at his apartment block had intrigued her. She had established her identity by processing her image through the Facial Recognition Data Base; this did not raise any suspicions as there were thousands of images seeking confirmation of identities every hour of the day. The evening in the Iron Duke was uneventful; however, the data base did not disclose any red flags; successful City trader, misuse of recreational drugs (cocaine) sought therapy (successful) reinvented herself as a Venture Capitalist; who had bought out ailing companies turned them around successfully; then sold them for profit; presently sole owner of gyms. Edwina had a latent admiration for her; as she had come from a financial background herself (accountancy) she knew how many barriers that had to be surmounted. As she sat at the rear of the bar observing them, there was nothing ostentatious about her attire; Smart jacket and matching trousers, it was plainly a business meeting of some sort rather than a romantic liaison; maybe David Fisher was proposing to invest in her gyms and maybe expanding her brand, or he may be proposing to buy her out, then sell off the gyms individually?

Edwina's befriending of Lena the member of staff in the Iron Duke was an investment that had reaped information dividends. Lena had forwarded David Fisher's booking of a table to Edwina, and she made sure that she would have an uncluttered view of them. Edwina had come in earlier and asked Lena to attach a small indiscreet microphone to the underside of the table, her single ear bud picked up every word, she returned a few hours later. To say she was shocked and also alarmed when Lorna suggested that he return to New York to repackage assets and sell them in New York alarmed Edwina; not for the financial implications but for his well-being; she could only imagine the trauma that he had suffered with the death of his colleague in Central Park, then the murder of his American partner in his apartment; he may have a relapse.

Lorna had retrieved from her small case what looked like a contract that the audio confirmed was relating to his new position in New York; he studied the four page document for a few minutes, his grin grew larger, he was satisfied that was very clear There were few questions regarding the contents of the contract in which he commented it was very clear, and there would be no need to peruse it when he returned to Dundee in the morning. Lorna was relieved as she studied her face as he scrawled his signature across each page. Her task had been completed and all there was to talk about was his impending return to Dundee. He had declared without any encouragement that he was not intending to sell or rent out his apartment, and then the conversation turned dark; he was troubled that the murder of Gwen had went quiet as if it had been shelved, there had not been any further contact from the police, and he had been thinking of the events in New York when Jonathon Gove was murdered in Central Park and Gwen's apparently motiveless murder in his apartment, do you think they were linked? This caused Edwina to halt the fork from reaching her open mouth. She wondered when he would bring this up, had he been advised to keep his thoughts and concerns to himself and refrain from discussing it with anyone as these were 'live' inquiries. She continued to consume her meal in a leisurely fashion; Lorna had replied that as she was his therapist she advised him to avoid thinking or blaming himself in a tenuous way as that was not conducive in maintaining good mental health and he was completely free from any guilt, although it was natural for him to try and blame himself. When Edwina heard that Lorna was a therapist of some kind, she was shocked as this was not recorded in the Facial Recognition Data Base which was diligently up to date. Could the reason that her profession was not on the data base as it was simply not true? And if this was the case, why was she lying? Her appetite waned when she heard this and she was losing concentration, she may have missed part of the conversation but it was recording on her Smartphone

Lena was quietly polishing glasses behind the bar while observing the three of them she was collating information not just for Edwina; she had more than one financial beneficiary. In the discreet corner of the bar/restaurant out of sight sat the two New York detectives listening in to Lorna and David's conversation; they just needed the date when he would fly to New York; they looked at each other Lena had served them well as she passed on details of the microphone that she had attached to the underside of the table. In New York the final part of the jigsaw would finally fall into place and too be brutally honest they were starting to feel under pressure themselves; the bustle of London did not protect them as the cacophony of noise that wrapped around them as a protective blanket in New York. However a time consuming and meticulous plan may need modified if an event was not taken into consideration.

***

Sitting in the Post Office bar a regular watering hole for detectives who thought they blended in with the clientele, were mistaken, they were all easily identifiable even though their attire was similar to other hipster males. GI Joe was becoming impatient with the Police Federation representative not advising him that he was running late. His eyes intermittently returned to the entrance; he had to temper his overt anger, after all he was looking for his assistance that would mutually benefit all parties; an optimistic assumption. It was late afternoon and meals were being delivered to the tables by the harassed staff member, another member of staff seemed to take some pleasure from her discomfort.

GI Joe was an avid student of human behaviour; in his opinion. He made his way to the bar in which four young males had recognised him, they did not welcome him at the bar, and in contempt turned their backs on him, two well-known drug dealers; unsuccessful he thought to himself. He ordered his coffee and returned to his seat, picked up his newspaper and peered over the newspaper as if he was observing them; he was chuckling at their discomfort; they had a workman's bag at their feet; they moved together to block his view of the bag which contained cannabis. They went into a huddled conversation that GI Joe was observing them, their eyes studied the clientele; they couldn't identify any other detectives, they made an executive decision to vacate the premises with the bag, He made sure that they all knew he was watching them; and pulled out his phone and mimicked he was texting, and after he had stopped texting he looked furtively out the window and towards the door as if a raid was imminent They nearly crushed each other as they sped towards the exit; this bizarre action drew attention from the other patrons and comment. He watched them gather pace as they ran towards Brook Street; this was his good deed for today disrupting the drug trade even off duty.

  He glanced at his fake Rolex, he was running thirty minutes late; he pulled out his phone to text him, but he came through the door with a smile on his face; he had been drinking. GI Joe against his instinct ordered a double measure of Bell's whisky for him, and returned to the table, the short walk to the bar mitigated his seething anger towards him. He placed the whisky in front of him; his smile disappeared and was replaced with a disapproving frown. 'What's wrong?' 'There is no ice, did you forget?' He took the drink and returned to the bar, and placed a couple of ice cubes in the double measure. 'Here we go...now I have a proposal for you that will satisfy all parties...' The rep held up his hand in a dismissive fashion; he consumed the drink and handed the empty glass to him, 'Do you want another double?' He nodded. Once more he returned to the bar like a good little boy; 'Here we go...now as I was saying...? 'Hold your horses, whatever your proposal, this proposal negotiated by me, will knock yours into the River Tay. Do you want to hear it, or do you want to continue with your proposal?'

  Now this was an unexpected positive development; his internal anger was no longer boiling up to the surface ready to vent. 'No you go on.' He downed the whisky and returned the glass to him, he took it with good grace and returned to the bar with the familiar order, and trekked back to the table; anger on standby. 'Here we are, now go on and continue ...please.' He pulled out from his jacket a contract and placed it on the table face down and placed his pen on it. This was bullshit thought GI Joe, but if it is good as his shit acting conveys, he'll accept. But he won't return to the bar until the contract is explained and perused then signed. 'It's a NDA do you know what that means?' 'It's a Non Disclosure Document. How much are they offering?' He was excited now; the finish line was in view and he was stretching his lead. 'Good, I'm glad you understand, and I don't know what you've got on somebody high up; but it's an unbelievable offer, and its netto.' Fuck me; it must be that good if the offer is net of tax. 'Well how much is it?' 'See for yourself.' He turned the paper over to the rear page; experience had taught him all the relevant details were repeated there with the signature space directly underneath and countersigned by the Police Federation Representative. And he had already signed it; £150,000 plus full pension. He wanted to order champagne; he was totally mystified why this life changing sum and full pension had been offered. He would not argue. 'And I have more good news for you; I have an appointment in town with their solicitor; he will send you a copy of the agreement and the date the money will be in your account in five days. He downed the whisky stood up and left the bar. GI Joe had another plan in mind to put to his rep; £50k and he'll resign. Now that he had surpassed this figure, he was delighted, however, with the bank details of the drug cartel in his possession; he would be returning to Madrid to put a lucrative proposal to Crispy, a life changing proposal; however this was dependent on the money accumulated in the various deceased bank accounts. Their bank accounts would have in excess of £150k. He was talking millions of pounds.

The burnt out van would not cause any eyebrows to elevate; the area where it was set alight was a stolen car graveyard, frequented by the parochial educationally challenged youths; the police would not diverge from trivial events such as this, they had more pressing matters to pursue such as moving plant pots in Broughty Ferry.

GI Joe had the perfect cover to leave the police and enjoy the dealers' ill-gotten gains; his imminent departure with PTSD being the reason, due to his heroic service fighting the Taliban, had ominously left mental scars on him and he was no longer fit for duty; all being told his experience on the Hilltown had a more life changing effect on him than fighting the Taliban, although he kept this to himself, for obvious reasons. However, he had a bright future to look forward to and in a sunnier climate; he had learned from Crispy that the Dutch and French intelligence services software that gave them a back door into the EncroChat could only get in after two months had elapsed after a message had been sent. Thus the recent communication with the dealers' cartel would remain encrypted and of course they were recently deleted from society, however they all had a decent burial. He would relax for the next couple of days then book a holiday for a week in Madrid; nothing suspicious in getting away to Madrid, then moving south where the climate was warmer for another week. He would contact Crispy advising him of his forthcoming visit to Madrid. There would be no need to be verbose of his visit to Madrid; Crispy would figure it out that it was connected to the EncroChat, however, he would not envisage that there were millions waiting for him at the click of links on his supercomputer; he may be an Uber wealthy individual, but he would not turn down the proposed bounty from him. Of course GI Joe needed his technical expertise to activate the dealers' accounts and transfer the money into a new account that would of course be in an alias of GI Joe's name. He had to thank David Fisher for these unimagined riches and all because of a plant pot; who would have thought? And to think he would have been be prepared to inhibit David Fisher from appearing as a hostile witness at his disciplinary hearing; even committing the ultimate sanction. But he was no longer the focus of his anger, this was a sliding doors moment, all the dark clouds had been chased away by good fortune and the exit from the police was rapid and of a financial benefit to him, and of course 'netto'. But this was peanuts to what Crispy would recover and divert from the dealers' no doubt linked bank accounts; and he would be able to guide him how to disguise this money which would become his very soon. It would take months before any serious concerns were raised about the dealers' sudden disappearance. However, the social media 'experts' would offer their theories some plausible and specious but the more outlandish would be prominent. One thing for certain the paranoia amongst their friends and families and international dealers would be ultimately immeasurable. And of course the missing dealers would be spotted in various cities throughout Europe and South America; there would be sporadic repercussions from the more excitable dealers who had been left out of pocket; real and imagined double-crossing incidents from the past would occupy their minds and resurface and where were the missing millions? The 'grieving' families left behind would be under surveillance from police and the dealers' former 'business partners'. There would be outbursts of violence from the warring families from time to time was never in doubt, and Spain would be the epicentre of death for some unfortunate individual who openly accused 'someone of being behind their disappearance.' Going by the scuttle buck there were a few high-living solicitors in Dundee who would be drawing their blinds earlier; they had acted for the local incommunicado dealer in property transactions; the family members would be upset of the legal ramifications of 'a missing person' and the legal timescale it took for them to ask the court to declare him dead. This procedure was in vogue in Glasgow and Liverpool; a time consuming process. There would be violent ramifications from drug wholesalers to the indigenous dealer who hawked the drug through the deprived areas of Dundee where there were many; the drugs were the recipients escape from life's troubles and reality; they deemed they had no future. County Line Dealers were making their way to Dundee from London and Liverpool as it was seen as a lucrative market. They booked themselves into an Airbnb in an affluent area as cover while selling their wares to sentient local dealers for cash who would then sell the drugs onto a myriad of dealers then return down south after completing their transactions; unsurpassed capitalism but where there are winners there were imminent and future losers who paid with cash and sometimes their unfulfilled lives; to be replaced with another willing recipient. Another would die and be replaced; the pernicious vicious circle of life keeps turning.

***

The last flight from London City airport was approaching Dundee, he smiled as the plane circled once more as it prepared to land; the cheerful bright lights masked the underbelly of a city in social decline, however, it was his city and he was fiercely proud of it, even though he had harboured his exit strategy when he worked for Dundee city council; his ambition had been enhanced as he had seen unqualified employees being elevated to positions in which they had little or zero experience; chumocracy at work in plain sight. However, this distasteful practice was the catalyst for him to start fraudulent practices which netted him an abundance of funds that went straight into his fictitious accounts; his eyes were drawn to the recently constructed apartments courtesy of Michael Ogilvie near the prestigious V&A design museum.

Lorna had been able to convince him to return to New York to manage Pavel's considerable portfolio, he had many doubts about returning due to the deaths of Jonathon Gove and his fleeting partner Gwen; as Lorna had pointed out there would be bittersweet memories of them and locations in New York.

Disembarking from the small plane he felt the cold wind on his face, his taxi should be there waiting for him, and in fifteen minutes he would be back home, safe and secure in the knowledge that he had cooperated with the police and answered all their questions up to a point. He had travelled light and made a speedy exit from the airport, the taxi was waiting and he entered into the warmth of the taxi's rear seat, took out his phone and activated his heating and lighting from the app on his phone; it's a pity he couldn't activate the kettle he mused. The short journey to Grove Road went quickly by, and the reassuring soft lights from his lounge were welcome, he had to visit his dad tomorrow to see him and patiently agree with him about the political class which he had an unhealthy obsession with, due to their frivolous personal spending habits. He was without doubt old school when constituents had respect for politicians; unlike today where the actual voting was in decline. But he had taught him the value of money and installed a relentless work ethic and ambition that was still burning within him. But tonight he would metaphorically kick off his expensive leather shoes and heat his feet beside the coal effect gas fire, which perpetually reminded him of the replacement of the coal fire with a two bar electric fire he had in Kirkton when he was growing up, it was funny how his mind would remember the 'good old days' which they were certainly not as far as he was concerned. He had accumulated millions of pounds through education and relying on his instinct; he did not follow the herd he followed financial data and knew when to liquidate assets, and of course he had insiders who advised when good financial results were masking underlying financial turbulence. His city 'friends' were well-rewarded not with money but his intrinsic financial market knowledge, quid pro quo society socialism for the capitalists. However, it had worked well for both sides so who was he to argue? It was amazing when the funds dropped into his business account how his concerns faded. It was a pointless exercise to explain how rudimentary his job was to his blinkered dad. He tipped the quiet taxi driver £10 on top of his fare; he had welcomed the comforting silence from the airport to Grove Road, without fail the curtain twitchers would welcome his return. He felt the warmth greet him as he turned the key and pushed open the original heavy stiff black door; which he pointed out to a neighbour when he had just moved in and who had not been impressed by the depressing colour; that it was paint from Downing Street; she was taken aback by this revelation and asked if he had any spare paint left? Alas he had none, and intercepted her next question which make was it? His reply was the paint was supplied in an unbranded container. He removed his shoes and placed them alongside the skirting board in the hall, and snuggled his slippers on and made his way into the warm lounge, then and closed the blinds; now he felt relaxed. He retreated from the lounge to the main bedroom removed his clothes and slipped into sweat pants and a warm hoody He returned to the lounge and ignited the gas fire admiring the realistic flames licking around the imitation coal; he had never been failed to impress at the thought and design that went into this fire. He avoided his obligatory act of pressing the remote for the TV to burst into life; Lorna had advised removing shoes first then change into comfortable leisure attire check emails whilst sipping a non caffeine coffee; which he found very difficult to adhere to as he was hyperactive and chores took longer to complete.. However, she was the professional and he had immense respect for her; she had pulled him from the dark abyss of depression in days gone by; which he would never return to, he went from the lounge to the kitchen to boil the kettle rather than use the complicated coffee machine; he lifted up the kettle and immediately stopped; it was warm.

***

They observed him leaving the taxi and both noticed the smile of someone who was glad to be home, It was time to return to the hotel in

Barnhill, the Woodlands hotel. They acquiesced they had made a monumental mistake in not killing him in London; they had ample time and opportunities, and of course motive. However, after monitoring the conversation between Lorna and David Fisher in the Iron Duke, it would be easier to remove him in their own backyard; New York. The bounty on his head surprised them; they never asked or questioned why it was so high. They had the press release for David Fisher's murder in London he was the financial advisor/consultant that had acted for the oligarch that had committed suicide. The statement would be brief and short on detail; social media 'experts' would inflame outlandish conspiracy theories.

However as David Fisher was returning to New York that would make their undertaking easier to complete; his death would only be in the minds of the public for a matter of hours; a street robbery would be the theory for the public to chew on. They would be departing in the morning for the return to New York confident that the impending death of David Fisher would be tragic but treated in a token manner, which was how people in New York lived and some tragically died.

They were in the midst of moving off but a restaurant home delivery employee on a pathetic bicycle was struggling up the incline of Grove Road, they couldn't hide their disdain why couldn't the delivery person get a better job; he wanted to pull out in front of the struggling delivery person as their fitness proved they had not worn the famous yellow jersey on the Tour de France; the comments that passed between them were unflattering about how out of condition and so slow that he took his colleague's advice to let the out of condition delivery person pass. While this caused him to be annoyed, overt anger replaced the vicious banter. The bicycle stopped alongside their car, the gloved hand was held up to apologise and the laden bag was carefully removed from the person's back and various meals were carefully placed on the pavement. He was annoyed at where the delivery employee had stopped and now he was looking at various homes to determine where the address would be for the meals. He exploded into a tirade of anger littered with expletives; the delivery driver grabbed the bicycle from the road in an angry way and placed it against the stone wall of the house, and rumbled impatiently through his bag once more; then he instantly turned towards him and fired a shot at the female and then turned the gun on her startled colleague. The silencer did its work; he admired his handiwork; then casually replaced the gun in the bag and rode his bicycle to the top of Grove Road and nonchalantly secured the bicycle into the van. He did not remove the helmet until he had returned the van that he had 'borrowed' from the building site on Strathern Road and returned the bicycle to the workmen's container where various tools where kept. He removed the helmet and returned it to the bicycle's handle bars. A nice evening work completed. He was unaware that they were New York detectives; but he would be shocked to the core when he opened his laptop in a few hours; then the news would fill him with fear. He assumed they were dealers of some kind; New York detectives assassinated would be international news; and the local plods would not be able to do their cursory investigation. The National Crime Agency would be elbowing the local detectives out of the way. He had been used as a patsy by an anonymous rogue drug squad senior detective or so he had thought and they had shared the spoils of deceased dealers' hidden assets in the past. When the news broke he had serious doubts that he had a future...on this earth. The tariff for removing 'them' was £50k; he never asked who they were or why they had to be removed. He assumed rightly that the burner phone that was activated to contact him would have been disposed of before the hit was completed. He was correct. When the news broke that one male and one female were found shot dead in a quiet Broughty Ferry road social media went into meltdown it was a cuckolded spouse that had murdered them; it was a drug deal that had gone awry; the theories lifted any anxiety from him; until the news broke that they were two New York detectives. At first he laughed out loud as did others; they all came to the same conclusion; why would two New York detectives be in Broughty Ferry? Too fantastic too be true, the laughter dissipated as the news was confirmed that the two deceased were indeed New York detectives. Holy Fuck! He couldn't believe what he had done, and all for a miserly £50k! He would not have completed this murderous task for £500k! He had been used by his unknown handler. He now had serious doubt that his paymaster was a corrupt drug squad detective. He spent hours on Facebook going through the plethora of posts for a sliver of information; it was all wild speculation some theories entertaining but undoubtedly untrue. What the fuck had he done? He had consumed the beer in his fridge that had lay untouched for months; annoyingly the beer had not elevated his mood or suppressed his anxiety. There was no way he could turn back time; the money for completing similar tasks would placed in his locked outside cupboard on his shared landing as an Amazon package; then the ultimate insult; would he even be paid and if not what could he do? Sometimes he wished he was back on the Hilltown scrapping with emaciated junkies.

***

Edwina was already on the plane from London City Airport to Dundee; her wish to return to Dundee had been answered but in unfortunate circumstances. She did not realise that her department was so secretive; all she was told was there could be a 'tenuous' connection of the assassination of the New York detectives and the death of her colleague, (Armstrong) as they had been cooperating on a matter that could not be discussed at this moment in time. Really..? She was being sent up to Dundee to unofficially supplement the international investigation and covertly forage for information on the deaths of the New York detectives; she would not be part of the official investigation she was repeatedly told. The FBI /CIA would be conducting their own independent investigation and would not be sharing or requesting information from the Scottish Police/National Crime Agency. She was to work in the shadows and collate information. What disturbed her, David Fisher was never mentioned. She found that strange, after his entire house had been under surveillance and two New York detectives were murdered metres from his house. She had to dig out more information about David Fisher, wherever he goes the grim reaper follows without fail; she privately hoped he was not considering holidaying in Benidorm next November; she smiled at her mawkish humour. She had booked the same apartment in Beach Crescent Broughty Ferry; she was at ease with the serene location and the walking routes on her doorstep, and of course Grove Road was only a short walk away. She would try to suppress who had returned her umbrella that she had left behind in the Ship Inn and left it on the mat outside her door; however *that* stare from the detective or ex-detective that had unsettled her was not always dormant in her subconscious. She went under the modus operandi that the she would also be under surveillance; she hoped this would not be the case but this was hope over expectation.

  On the plane the pilot infrequently announced how many minutes they were from Dundee, her fears were minimised; her confidence was growing that she would be able to discern fact from fiction why the New York detectives were assassinated; then the suppressed theory that she did not want to see the light of day could not be ignored; were they assassinated in Grove Road to bring David Fisher into the investigation; and would they request his extradition to New York? That would suit the UK Government which was coming under pressure to admit that Russian Oligarchs were committing suicide at an alarming rate in London and the wealthy suburbs. This was her hunch, and if her fear became reality David Fisher could be coerced into admitting various crimes from the favourite laundering money and wire fraud or the favourite catch all; RICO. (Racketeer Influenced and Corrupt Organizations) this would be her realistic outcome that the D.O.J. (Department of Justice) would pursue and the compliant UK Government would nod its vacuous head and wag its tail.

  David Fisher would have concluded that he had made the correct decision to leave the bloodbath of London for the leafy suburb/ picturesque fishing village/open prison for the wealthy; Broughty Ferry. He could never have imagined two New York detectives would be slain in their car by a professional assassin metres from his house, and the media would be going door to door asking the neighbours if they were shocked and other inane questions; there would be long concealed make-up applied to various visages in anticipation of the knock on the door and an apparently surprised glamorous woman would answer...hmmm.

Would David Fisher stay put or vacate his house, and if so where would he go? She could guarantee that he would not be having a shave and a haircut anticipating being on a news bulletin. The National Crime Agency would be made aware that David Fisher was a person of interest; so he would be either excluded from a home visit or be the first to be interviewed; she would not roll the dice on this quandary. The plane was circling Dundee 'international' airport according to the pilot that had the passengers in fits of giggles; she must admit this brought a wry smile. The serene bandstand on Magdalene Green gave her a warm at peace feeling as her eyes were fixed on it. She would definitely have a stroll around Magdalene Green and the bandstand beseeching her to visit it. She would.

Her phoned pinged with a text message; her taxi was waiting; another positive example of Dundee compared to the London fascist taxi drivers that were increasingly bombarding their unwanted political views upon unfortunate passengers. If only they knew what she knew? London was far away in distance and erased from her thoughts now; she was determined to reach an empirical conclusion that even the Eton boys could not challenge; she thought of Armstrong and his overt contempt for these privileged Prima donnas from another age. Getting away from London was always on her mind. She felt that the Economic Crime Unit was losing its focus and investigative skills; individuals were being promoted not because of talent or innate skill but through diversity and cronyism. She was not the only one of the Economic Crime Unit who felt this way. She had been approached by disillusioned and confidence sapped colleagues that investigations were taking far too long to complete; and some cases were surprisingly shelved midway through the investigations when arrests were imminent. She was actively perusing and formulating a plan to set up as a consultant in the lucrative private sector, she had made the overtures to the brightest and dynamic colleagues and they were with her all the way. Some had told her separately that they felt that the investigations which would lead to arrests and were confident of convictions were being influenced by politics to curtail their investigations. She did not offer an opinion but agreed silently.

Edwina frequently used to toss and turn in her bed in the early hours and think the same that the Economic Crime Unit had been at worst infiltrated or benignly influenced by foreign government(s) influence. Now her worst fears were being independently verified by various lucid and intelligent colleagues. Edwina was reluctant to air her most damming fear; that one of the foreign governments could be the United States; her fear if she raised that she would be sidelined and removed from the sharp end of investigations to a less dynamic role. Was it too much of a coincidence that her colleague Armstrong was killed accidently and he had been in contact but was less than enthusiastic to share information with the deceased New York detectives? And of course them being assassinated in Broughty Ferry in the road where David Fisher lived? No one would bring this up at any update meeting, and she certainly would not offer her reservoir of theories because she valued her career better to be silent than brave or stupid. She left the mundane meeting with the corrosive thought that maybe they were testing her to voice information that she had painstakingly accumulated and when it was heard she would be removed from future update meetings?

The information dossier that she failed to share with her superiors and withheld information from Armstrong; specifically regarding the deceased New York detectives having coffee with David Fisher and his now murdered partner Gwen in the Carlyle hotel in New York; and now there was only David Fisher left that could consume coffee. David Fisher was he involved intentionally or otherwise, and she was determined to solidify her theory with empirical evidence. She was in two minds to set up a whiteboard and link the various characters that were connected to the deceased as she instinctively knew the apartment in Beach Crescent would be wired with surveillance equipment, she could not be seen looking for the hidden equipment as that would clarify to the silent observers that she knew she was under surveillance and they had been exposed. And their next action would be her being humiliated by being suspended? Would her clothes be found in a neat pile on the beach and she would end up in the nearby River Tay and her body being swept into the fury of the North Sea, and being washed ashore on a deserted beach in a far away land? These were thoughts that could not be ignored; better to explore them in the comfort of daylight than the all consuming fear of the silent darkness.

The plane had a bumpy landing which alarmed her but did not raise any concerns amongst the returning locals who continued their loud excited chatter, and they burst out into loud spontaneous clapping when the plane came to a dignified halt. She refrained from joining in, but smiled. The plane emptied its passengers and she was through security and into her waiting taxi in ten minutes. Darkness was descending when the taxi entered Broughty Ferry, the warm relaxed feeling was replaced with disappointment when the scaffolding that ensconced the modern glass and brick apartment block came into view; she had to be philosophical it would only be for maintenance surely? She paid the driver not taking her eyes from the building, her apartment had the lounge lamps shining proudly but the remaining apartments were empty and in darkness; the slow burn of concern enveloped her; walking towards the apartment block with a degree of apprehension, she had to be stoic, she could be under surveillance and did not wish to display any obvious discomfort. She felt like JFK as he entered the Dealey Plaza; a perfect scenario to isolate and corner an intended victim of malice and murder. Her instinct and training were ringing alarm bells and waving red flags in and out of her head; she had to expect the unexpected in the apartment building. She instinctually turned around the taxi driver was staring at her and speaking into his phone; then suddenly screeched away.

***

David Fisher sat at his kitchen table both hands wrapped around his mug of coffee, he was anything but naive; who had been in his kitchen and what was the purpose of their entrance? He was totally unaware that the perpetrators were outside lifeless in their car virtually outside his home; karma came swift and brutal, in a matter of departing the murder scene the bodies would be discovered by the perennial dog walker. While David Fisher was musing the purpose of the expert break-in, Grove Road was descending into a mass of humanity and police cars and ambulances were arriving at high-speed with wailing sirens. He was one of the few residents that were ignorant of the international news event playing out live outside his home. He was shaken out of his depressive state by the sudden constant ringing of his doorbell. He wearily made his way to the front door; he heard the cacophony of sirens before he opened the front door; expectant to see an excitable neighbour saying there had been a kitchen fire of some kind; however he was met with the sight of the two youthful detectives from Jersey. He was neither relieved nor disturbed by their presence. While they were introducing themselves...again, David looked over their shoulders to witness the police load the car onto a low-loader. The police were setting up and cordoning off the crime scene.
'What's happened here?'
'Be best to explain everything inside David, away from the media.'
'Sure come inside.' He let them pass him and they went straight into the kitchen. Should he explain to them that when he arrived back into Grove Road, via a taxi about twenty minutes ago, he noticed the kettle was warm, or should he omit this from their forthcoming questions?
He switched on the kettle. 'No coffee for us David, we can't afford to be seen here, we won't be long, it's pretty straightforward, the two detectives you had met in New York were shot dead in their car as you have confirmed about twenty minutes ago, the taxi driver will confirm as will

any video doorbells, they have suspected links to the mafia; and we suspect they were over here to kill you. We lost track of them in London, we were wrongly informed they were returning to the airport and onwards to New York. That's obvious that didn't happen as we are all now aware.'
David was experiencing an adrenalin rush and became less anxious and more lucid. 'Mafia?' Kill me? Are you sure?'
'There is no doubt, And the New York detectives were behind several murders in New York, they had the perfect cover, the victim would feel secure when the detectives asked to meet the victim in a secluded area, and after extracting the information that they required; they would shoot the victim. They would feed a reporter with the background of the victim who would be painted as someone who had borrowed money from the mafia or was in the midst of a drug deal that went wrong.'
'Why would they want to kill me, all my business transactions are above board, what would be the reason to kill me. I don't understand?'
'That's where we are at, we simply don't know. All we can say is the obvious, have you been threatened or has someone attempted to blackmail you? Hence the two detectives were up here to murder you.'
'I've been lucky no one has tried to extract money from me for any reason. I cannot in all honesty think of a reason why someone or the mafia would want me dead; all my business deals are in order as you will find out when you go through the multitude of business contracts,'
'You can understand our concern for you, and I don't wish to go through the amount of people you have come into contact with have all been killed or murdered. We also think you would be better staying put in this house as the mafia would not return here; too much in the media glare.'

He was pleased to hear this. And to be brutally honest the two detectives could no longer return to this well for more money as extortionists repeatedly do. It was no stretch of the imagination that they *had* been in his house; had a coffee waited outside in their car on him arriving home, and then after a few minutes talk their way into his home and kill him. Whoever killed them had saved his life inadvertently or was it a carefully coordinated plan? Either way, he was still breathing; and they were not. Today had been a good day for him and a bad day for the New York detectives. 'If there are any developments we will keep in touch. Someone is looking after you.' They smiled, told him to stay where he was and made their way towards the front door. When he heard the reassuring closure of the old door; he felt exhilarated.

He resisted the urge to meander casually into the lounge and view the carnage and media scrum in Grove Road. There was no empty feeling of despair or hopelessness lingering that his blackmailers were no longer functioning. Quite the opposite in fact. When they extracted the money from him in New York, it did not take a genius to work out that the mafia were involved; the deceased detectives would need a tech person to set up bank accounts in another country and collate all personal information certified by the regulator who may be persuaded to take a cursory relaxed view of foreign deposits of large sums of money. The last time he had seen so many police officers in Grove Road was because he had moved a plant pot without his neighbour's permission. He laughed at this ridiculous comparison, but truthfully he did not feel any sorry or sense of loss because of the violent deaths of the two New York detectives.

He opened the laptop to continue his work; there was money to be made and his appetite had not waned. New York would be a welcome distraction from the executions of the New York detectives; it would only be a matter of time before the New York media were knocking on doors in Grove Road. His meeting with Lorna and her reason to return to New York was an unexpected bonus of removing him from the bloodbath in Grove Road. When his business in New York was completed he would return to his recently purchased larger home in Broughty Ferry, and the work that was required to gut the dated kitchen and bathroom and replace an area of the roof would be completed while he was in New York and his dad would take care of this, and keep him up to date how the work was progressing. London would be off his radar until he was advised from the police that it was safe to return, but he had no intention of returning...yet.

***

GI Joe had made up his mind to vacate the flat he was renting; things had changed beyond his wildest nightmares, he would give the landlord one month's notice saying he was going to live abroad; his fee he suspected would not be left in the shared cupboard as agreed; he was concerned that instead of the money being left in an Amazon package, the messenger would leave a bullet in his head. Flights and accommodation had been booked for Madrid; he would politely decline Crispy's hospitality on this occasion after he had completed the money transfers from the various dealers' accounts into his new one under an alias; he would not be hanging about. The New York detectives' deaths did not trouble his conscience, he had seen more harrowing incidents in Afghanistan in the Helmond Province, but it was the nagging thought, were the New York detectives connected to the deceased dealers' accounts in some bizarre way? His early morning sweat was connected to this definitive thought, there had to be a connection, and he was confident if it was left to the Serious Organised Crime Squad that stone would lay unturned. Three cheers for bureaucratic incompetence.

In the meantime he would look for a rental property in southern Spain on a golf course, near an airport and mountains where he could venture and breathe the cool air and clear his mind. Crispy would take care of the personal details in securing an apartment.

He was glued to his laptop for information, theory or reason from the police why the New York detectives were in Dundee and Broughty Ferry. He didn't have to wait too long; 'a source close to the investigation has suggested the New York detectives were under investigation as allegedly being connected to organised crime in New York, and they had been followed from London (where they were investigating a financial crime alongside their counterparts in the Economic Crime Unit) to Dundee and executed'.

He was exulted to read this in the Press Association release which was syndicated in all the newspapers and on the news channels. He felt much better and agreed with the source as it made sense. This investigation would be soon over in Dundee and the FBI would be making inquiries in New York.

Life would return to normal and he could hang up his gun for good. He came to terms that he had been used and abused in completing this contract, and he had some sympathy for his paymaster, if he had explained who they were he knew he would turn it down, this wasn't the run of mill low-level drug dealer. Had he been premature in giving up his lease on this flat? He shook his head, no it was time to move on and out of Dundee for pastures new and to live the life he wished for. Spain was the ideal country great weather, reasonable priced accommodation and great food; man cannot live on mince and tatties alone. In a sick matter of fate if the New York detectives executions were not the usual scumbags he disposed of and would not for a second make him think of leaving his flat and living in Spain; this catastrophic event had changed his life.

An ominous impatient series of knocks were hammering on his door; he nervously squinted through the peep hole; it was an Amazon driver, he nervously opened the door slowly. 'Package for you mate.' He took a photograph of the package and requested a signature, then left hurriedly. He eagerly took the package to the small dining table and opened it; it contained vacuumed sealed packs of Euros of various high denominations. How did his paymaster know he was going abroad?

***

In London, Lorna was taking more than a passing interest in the deaths of the New York detectives in Grove Road where David Fisher resides. He would be more malleable and enthusiastic in returning to New York; it would remove him from the carnage outside his home for starters. She was intrigued similar to the populace why were they *really* in Grove Road? It was fortunate for her that this violent episode while unfortunate for the New York detectives; was a wind of fortune for her and David Fisher. She had planned to inform Pavel that she would be returning to her vocation as a psychotherapist this was not true, she was contemplating another business venture on her own and now was the time to go their separate ways.

London's crime rate and influx of immigrants were having a debilitating affect on her mental health; the underground which she frequented Monday to Friday in the evenings were returning to the days when muggers lay in wait for single women outside the underground station; she had used her martial arts training to prevent an attack on a young woman. She left the assailant crumpled on the wet pavement calling for someone to get the police; irony with a sense of humour she didn't hang around because there would be a chance she would be charged with assault.

Pavel had the utmost respect for David Fisher; he knew that the respect was reciprocated without anything expected in return apart from a hefty bonus for increasing the value of his assets. Pavel had done his homework on Lorna and her patients, David had been a patient of Lorna's and they had formed a laconic intimate relationship, if the business relationship with Lorna soured in any way he would forward the dates and times of the romantic liaisons she had had with David, which when confronted she would have the choice of resigning from being a practicing psychotherapist immediately or appearing in front of the disciplinary panel with the glare of the media reporting the accusations. He hoped he would not have to use this information as leverage, but he would not hesitate while going about his daily business and act shocked at these malicious allegations became public..

Pavel came to the same conclusion as Lorna, the deaths of the New York detectives in David Fisher's road was not an impediment to his return to take up the post in New York it was an incentive. His information from New York was copper-fastened; they were corrupt and were there to 'take out' his newly-appointed 'finance guy' in Dundee to cause chaos with his investments in New York. Pavel had gone through a trusted third-party to confirm this *after* their deaths were reported on the multitude of news channels. GI Joe had been the perfect recruit to assassinate them. When he was in Afghanistan he realised there was a business opportunity courtesy of the Taliban, they were destroying poppy fields to eradicate them being turned into heroin which was creating addiction in Kabul at an alarming rate; and disposing of the pure heroin However, GI Joe and an American contractor (mercenary) who was GI Joe's babysitter on night time incursions suggested that they could make millions by taking the heroin back into the UK where it would be sold in bulk to a contact in the UK. This was GI Joe's last tour, he had to make plans for his future, this scheme with the importation of heroin would supplement his meagre army pension; he was in and he had figured out how to transport the heroin with him on the direct plane journey to the UK. The contractor listened intently to his plan; he couldn't fault it, he would arrange someone purporting to be an engineer in a van to pick up mechanical parts (which had the heroin secreted in the casing) that had to be refurbished and transported from the airport when the plane landed in the early hours of the morning. The security had been privatised; the immigrant security guards were paid the minimum wage they were quick but not thorough in checking the cases; as long as it had a barcode on the wooden case it would be loaded onto the waiting vehicles They didn't relish the cold early mornings on a freezing windswept airfield .When the heroin arrived at the wholesalers it was parcelled out to various parts of the UK including Dundee where it had anxious 'customers' awaiting their delivery.

An 'Amazon' package stuffed with cash would be dropped off in a safe place. Keep it simple was his motto. And thus the lucrative business friendship was initiated. He was advised not to tell or boast and to be incognito when spending the money which would arrive in intermittent tranches on the same date every month for six months. He advised him to travel to Edinburgh and deposit the money in a certain bank and he would be advised by text on his burner phone that an account in Panama had been set up with name and password. The account would be opened by someone on his behalf. Sounds good to me thought GI Joe. The plane landed in the south of England at the quiet military airfield everything was checked hurriedly, GI Joe had a letter waiting for him that his application to join Police Scotland had been successful. It would be the perfect cover; act the eccentric former dense squaddie, as far as possible from an importer of heroin purchased from the Taliban and sold on to satisfy the cravings of addicts in Dundee and beyond. He had a business plan already, secure a mortgage purchase a property in Broughty Ferry and rent it out, and then rent a property for himself.. He would be at this address when the American contractor would sporadically offer him lucrative assignments. However, that was then but this is now. The American contractor left the war zones that were sporadically but mainly unreported in the press; he was still a gun for hire but wore a suit rather than battle fatigues.

GI Joe had removed a few unsavoury individuals from this world; and in some cases was their undertaker; as evidenced at Birkhill cemetery. Of course he argued with himself on rare occasions that he was acting in the public interest; that these dealers were a scourge on the younger generation without a trace of hubris but he was heavily rewarded for his public service, and he had been an importer of heroin. His former American business partner was the go to guy for removing corrupt dictators in Africa; if it went wrong the American government could tell their citizens that the US government were not involved it was a private company not the US army. They would omit that they had advised or encouraged who the next dictator should be, and of course help in bringing democracy to the benighted nation, it was helpful if there were bountiful reserves of oil and gas.

 GI Joe had declined the offer in leading the indigenous army to remove the dictator peacefully and giving him the choice of departing by private jet to a new country with his family and some treasure or let him be executed by the army. This contract was laced with difficulties and danger; the money guaranteed would not change his lifestyle as he had more than enough; however; his maxim resurfaced; you can't have enough knowledge or money.

 However, he had his pride and he tried to avoid a fall. The rare foray into removing local malcontents from society for an impressive tariff; he was loath to refuse, but after the executions of the New York detectives he modified and curtailed immediately some out of hours leisure pursuits (assassinations). He was clever enough to meander through life at his pace with riches he had accumulated however the dealers' bank accounts that Crispy had emptied were now coalesced in a singular bank account in Panama. Crispy would move the millions periodically to other safe havens. When he was over the shock he confessed he had felt exhilarated at the enormity of his action, but his decision to move to Spain not on a permanent basis was a welcome by-product of his action. The fee paid in Euros still troubled him; he had booked the flights to Madrid *after* the hit on the detectives; however, he had booked flights over to Madrid in order to see Crispy about the EncroChat phone. Thus his Laptop must have malware of some kind in it; that was the logical reason, but in truth what was there to worry about if he was going to be a victim of malice so be it. He was becoming weary of the speculation online regarding the seedier sides of the male deceased detective; gambling and hookers were his nocturnal choice of activities; they burn through money at an alarming rate. However, the female detective was apparently clear as a sewage plant; she was behind money laundering schemes and the architect of numerous murders; she was the brain while he was the brawn.

 It had occurred to him while he was understandably preoccupied of the fallout of the deaths of the New York detectives he had not counted the money in the Amazon package. He could no longer sate his urge to count out the money. He did and it was more than expected when he converted the daily exchange rate; £55K. Definitely cheap at the price he could not estimate the cost this service would have cost to exercise in New York; upwards of $500k he suspected, he had been sent the crumbs while the benefactor had enjoyed a feast, and at his expense. The night was casting its encapsulating shadow in his lounge, he moved from the table after replacing the Euros back in the trainer box, he switched on the lamp beside the leather sofa, and also the lamp beside the single chair. He was calm now and he had made decisions that he prayed he would not regret; the millions from the dealers' accounts did not excite him bizarrely though that may sound. He could not eradicate any future violent comeback in revenge for the assassinations of the corrupt New York Detectives from intermittently crossing his mind. The only other person that would be aware of who the assassin was his comrade the American contractor; however, he had a similar mindset; kill or be killed; if it came down to protecting oneself.

***

She rose wearily from the Queen size bed, rubbed her eyes slowly, it had been a long night of broken sleep; she had been spooked by the demeanour of the taxi driver and being the only resident in the apartment block. She yawned and wearily made her way to the shower where she hoped once again the powerful shower would stimulate her body and calm her turbulent mind. Ten minutes had passed and she felt enthusiasm return, her plan was in her head before she stepped out of the shower; she would have a coffee and venture out and up to Grove Road, in all honesty she did not expect to see much difference in the sedate area of Broughty Ferry, but there could be something that would trigger her and aid her cursory sweep of the area. In the lounge she gazed over the Tay towards Tentsmuir with coffee mug intently held in both hands. This was a different world from London; she may return in the future or maybe not. She placed the empty mug at her feet and pulled up a chair and peered through the telescope towards Tentsmuir then towards Tayport and continued up to the Tay road bridge she was not looking for anything in particular it helped her mind slow down with the numerous questions racing through it. Now she was tempted to have a croissant; but she had to make hay while the rain that was threatening and meander through the busy streets on her journey to Grove Road. She had returned to her mischievous self and was tempted to wave and say goodbye to her malevolent unknown observers. It had occurred to her that Armstrong's death may not be purely coincidental and could be linked to the New York detectives deaths amongst others, but fundamentally David Fisher was the key to unlocking the mystery to so many deaths; but why she didn't know, but he was like a death virus so many people friends, colleagues and in this case his lover, their lives came to an abrupt end.

She pulled her pink beanie hat tightly over her head, and her eyes caught the troubled broody clouds amble in from the North Sea in the direction of Broughty Ferry; the wind was gaining speed and it would not be too long before the expanding dark clouds unleashed heavy rain. Looking in the direction of the Ship Inn she decided to follow the beach and onwards to Douglas Terrace even though the wind would be prominent there. Her optimism had returned and the impending inclement weather had no impact on her mental health. She ventured forth fortified by expectation and confidence that she would discover whether David Fisher was an unfortunate individual that his colleagues and friends were acting in unprofessional and criminal matters and therefore he was unaware of. Or he had manipulated them into financial transactions that he knew were criminal and was rewarded for this. She had the folder with the names and transactions of the people he had come in contact with and the lucrative transactions that they had been involved in; after concluding these transactions they then had been a victim of foul play or a twist of fate. Her professional opinion as a forensic accountant and a detective were unanimous; they were murdered or *assisted* in taking their own lives. However, opinion is a galaxy away from fact, and that was her focus to gather facts rather than circumstantial evidence. Then on the other hand she could be manipulated by unknown person(s) into fixating that David Fisher was the criminal mastermind behind their deaths. She had five days to gather information from her own inquiries but social media for all its faults and there were many, sometimes a diamond could be harvested. Her past experience guided her to this; people want to feel worthwhile and valued; the nuggets came from unfulfilled serving or retired police officers posting under an alias or information had been shared with friends.

American female reporters were experts at extracting information with a healthy budget and expense account; their friendly attitude made them be noticed and local detectives from the Serious Organised Crime Taskforce would be helpful; the detective would be invited to have dinner with them and unlimited alcohol would be consumed but not by the reporter; the male ego was easily inflated by kind words delivered with a gazing smile and an American accent, information was delivered 'off the record' while replenishing his malt whisky at an impressive rate; then she would replace her smile with a frown, she was aware of that segment of information; slightly embarrassed he would release information that had not been in the media. When that reservoir had been drained she would signal to   her colleague sitting at the bar and he would call her; she would profusely apologise and thank the detective and leave the table in a hurry and inform him that she had to go to Edinburgh to meet with a source of the Scottish Government. She stood up and shook his hand then departed up stairs to her room. Satisfied with the collated information and impressed how easy it was to extract information she would file her report in an hour and it would be in the New York newspapers the following morning then aired on cable news channels which would be highlighting the exclusive report under 'Breaking News'.

In London Pavel watched the perennial news reports unfold from his comfortable chair, intermittently moving his attention to the opening bell of the New York Stock Exchange (NYSE) he was a master architect in stock manipulation; he had eight 'market movers' on Wall Street and four in London, they were unaware of the others' role in increasing or decreasing a newly listed stock. He would through a well-respected third-party advise the 'market movers' that the shares would rise or fall on their debut; millions would be gained or lost on the first day. The shares would rise by a minimum of twenty percent; after this locked in profit, information would be released that there were outstanding issues with the stock (however minor) this caused a panic, Pavel had his twenty percent profit safeguarded, and when the shares dropped ten percent his funds overseen by David Fisher who would purchase the shares from desperate hedge funds looking to cut their losses. In the last thirty minutes of trading the beleaguered stock would steady then rise in value; Pavel's fund had gained over $150 million dollars at the end of the trading day. David Fisher had earned a bonus in excess of a million dollars and a percentage of the yearly profit of the myriad of investment funds under his sole control; David Fisher thrived on the responsibility and being in unilateral control.

This achievement unleashed a torrent of endorphins that the purest of cocaine could not bring. After the successful day's trading of hundreds of millions of dollars/ pounds of shares and then studying the real time value of his trading with the profit margin for the day in percentage and actual profit in monetary terms he would mentally work out his bonus. He would sometimes stare at the profit he had made for the various funds and the increased value he had accrued for them and see *his* profit in comparison to the funds and feel that he had been short-changed, then his council scheme mentality would shout at him, 'are you fucking kidding me? £1.4 million for sitting on your arse tapping keys on your laptop and after tax you're left with a measly £700,000 plus, how the fuck do you survive?' He stood at the worktop next to the coffee machine (a waste of money according to his dad) embarrassed at his feeling of entitlement, when less than a mile away in Douglas some individual or family were really going through extreme financial hardship.

The coffee brought him to his senses he shut the laptop down, and sat at the kitchen table, he had an epiphany; he opened the laptop and went on Facebook, he looked up his childhood friends, some were doing well, and remained loyal to their roots and resided in Kirkton, some had been dealt unfortunate
cards; he studied their posts, fridges, televisions and washing machines had come to the end of their natural lives; they didn't mention energy costs, they must be struggling. He would replace the worn out household goods and give them money, but his difficulty was getting the money to them without revealing his identity. One of his friends had climbed up the social economic ladder and ran his own construction business, which was in the Coldside area of Dundee; he would contact him and meet him at his office or for a coffee after explaining his concern for their childhood friends. He called him and they arranged to meet with the conversation ending 'no one must know who the benefactor was.' He could trust Freddie, the thought of him complaining about *only earning £1.4.million for a day's work* was expunged. Freddie supplied him with their addresses, he went onto the electrical wholesaler's (Currys) website which was the most competitive and then called to speak to the sales manager. he was looking for a discount and he would pay now. The sales manager was puzzled at the various addresses; reluctantly he told her that they were childhood friends that were experiencing difficulties; she was humbled at this as she had experienced the kindness of strangers and knew that they would be overwhelmed. Of course he asked her to keep this to herself, and she pledged that would remain the case. She had a gentle voice, he asked her if her life was going well, she said it was, no complaints; she hurriedly ended the conversation as she was being called to the shop floor. Not a problem, he returned to the laptop entered the promotional code that the woman had supplied and paid for the items. The following day he met Freddie and gave him the six envelopes with their names on them the envelopes contained £1000 (Freddie didn't ask how much money was in the envelopes).That would alleviate some way in making their lives less stressful. Then he pulled out another envelope with the name Shelley it contained a thank you card and also £1000. Freddie was not surprised at this generosity; when they were children David had shared sweets with others who had nothing for their playtime snack. The conversation between two successful businessmen never broached how well each other was doing; they enjoyed talking about their bittersweet memories of their childhoods which would be classed as poverty ridden and disadvantaged today. They described their childhoods as tough and learning about life. After their short meeting Freddie drove up to the Currys superstore, he parked his Tesla and his eyes searched over the vast floor space. a few

sales assistants were hovering about, he couldn't see Shelley, he was about to ask a sales assistant if she could contact her when she appeared pulling a trolley with various electrical items on them; he paused and decided to wait till she had completed her journey to the front door, then returned with the trolley into the warehouse section. 'Hi, I'm sorry to interfere in your busy schedule ...'

'That's okay; do you need information about something?'

'No, you had a conversation with my pal, and he has asked me to give you a thank you card, he was very impressed with your empathy.' Instantly she knew who he was talking about, and felt emotionally overwhelmed that someone would take time to buy a card for her. He handed her the envelope with her name on it, and smiled and walked away. She had the card in her hands, should she open it here or in the locker room? The latter was her decision, in the locker room she looked around no one was here, she carefully opened the card, inside were £50 notes, she sat down, took the notes out and placed them beside her on the bench, and read the card. 'Thanks Shelley.' Short and sweet. She picked up the fresh notes and counted them; a £1000. Her prayers had been answered her car was going in for its MOT tomorrow; her day off. The pre-mot examination had estimated repairs about £250-300; the surplus money would fill her fridge freezer and add £100 to her pre paid gas meter. Life could not get any better. The young working couple next door like others were suffering from low-pay and rising prices and had a frugal lifestyle, if the MOT estimate is true, she would slip £100 through their letterbox late at night.

***

Lorna had been summoned to meet at Pavel's recently purchased top floor new apartment in 'Red Square' mansion block, it was in need of renovation and he wanted to discuss with her the revised timetable of David Fisher's appointment in New York; it had been brought forward because of an urgent matter; she needed to inform David that he would be starting work in New York in five days. He would be kept busy studying certain investments that were not performing as he had been told. This alarmed Lorna, the previous incumbent in New York had suddenly flung himself from an apartment block due to discrepancies in the portfolio he managed for Pavel. Now was not the appropriate time to inform him of her new path in life; she had served him well, it was not about dissatisfaction with her salary; her remuneration could not be surpassed from any other financial institution, but in her defence she had made him money and there would be no feeling of guilt when she furnished him with the details after she handed him her resignation letter which was in her large purse.

That morning had not been the time or even the place to discuss verbally with Pavel of the reason. She had spoken to David, about the rescheduling of the move to New York, and told him the reason why. His response was nonchalant agreement, and he added with various competing news outlets becoming a nuisance to the residents and the Scottish newspapers which were competing with social media influencers who were knocking on doors and countering any official narrative, why the New York detectives were over in Broughty Ferry and the *real* reason they were in Broughty Ferry. However, the social media influencers would only reveal *the truth* behind a pay wall. Departing to New York ahead of the planned date was welcome.

Pavel wanted him down in London to meet him at his new apartment where he would hand him the file with his instructions; he wanted Lorna to be present incase there was any reluctance and to also witness him sign another letter that had a 'golden hello' bonus that was activated on his first day at his office in New York; she concluded it would be in the millions. In the present day Bull market this was not unusual.

From a personal point, this would be the ideal opportunity to inform him of her resignation and David would inadvertently be a witness to hear her resign verbally and witness her hand Pavel her resignation letter. Then she would profusely thank him, and drive David to Heathrow airport and discuss her future investments with him, although he would be in a state of shock with her sudden resignation; however, she knew what made him tick psychologically as she had diagnosed him and helped alleviate a personal crisis when he had mental health problems, and of course Pavel had been a patient and she knew that the brutal regime that he had been a participant of in Russia, this brutality shaped him to value human life less than money. She had become disillusioned with the ruthless race for riches under the free market and human beings trampled on if they got in their way. However, Pavel's ideology went further and eliminated colleagues or business acquaintances as the rule not the exception. Her training as a psychotherapist had signposted her to the imbued esoteric trait that when an individual was of no use to him or his various companies that the proxy respected businessmen had overseen; death followed.

***

David Fisher's cutting comment was embedded in his brain, when he had visited his house unofficially but still wearing his uniform, he now with hindsight wish he had kept the comment to himself; he was a figure of fun in the laughing eyes of his colleagues. He wished he could erase their laughter and hurtful comments; his plan was to get one over on him and make him feel he was doing him a favour; but this offer was dismissed, with barbed comments. The casual comment aired while he was standing on his doorstep apparently admiring the sheen of the black gloss paint, and an invitation into his home to iron out any mistaken or threatening comments were dismissed in a matter of a few seconds. David Fisher was not expecting any apology for any misunderstandings on GI Joe's part. He had work to do what was the purpose of this visit?

The lame smile irritated David Fisher and the word salad that erupted from GI Joe's mouth at a stuttering speed. He was not making any progress and had only accomplished making him irritable. He looked at gathering clouds and commented that it looked as though it was going to rain and supplemented this amazing observation that his DNA had indicated he was twenty-five percent Cherokee. David Fisher eager to return to his burgeoning workload looked at the sky with a smile and his anger subsided; 'and seventy-five percent chimpanzee'. And thus the cerebral conversation ended.

Walking down the once disputed path, he was humiliated; his plan to assuage David Fisher and hopefully withdraw the complaint lay in tatters. He had been super confident using his brooding charm and they would end up shaking hands. When he returned to the station, he repeated chapter and verse of his disappointing encounter with 'an official complainer'. The reluctant recipient of this 'confidential' information found it difficult to contain his astonishment of this unofficial visit, if he complains again; he would have difficulty in rebutting the contents of the complaint. Was he really that dumb, that he thought this was a good idea, did he not think of the downsides? GI Joe had not expected this unsympathetic response and the seriousness if another official complaint was lodged; did he not consider that this second complaint would make the first complaint more plausible?

GI Joe's demeanour was awkward and he was shredding confidence, but he would throw in another part of the conversation.

'Well, what if he was trying to intimidate me?'

'Was he, and remember *you* went to his house uninvited and on your own, which is not a good look is it? And how did he intimidate you, what height are you six foot four inches and have seen active service against the Taliban.'

'Well he didn't physically intimidate he's quite small actually/'

'So he's closer to a midget than a giant?'

'I suppose that's fair comment, but it was what he said to me that could've set off my PTSD.'

'You can't keep on playing that PTSD card...and what did he say to you that could or might have set off your PTSD?'

'We were casually speaking about the weather, and I said just to break the ice, it looks like rain, and somehow mentioned that my DNA was twenty-five percent Cherokee...'

'...and then he laughed?'

'No, no he then went on and said that the remaining seventy-five percent must be chimpanzee...'

His confidant burst out laughing, and so did his silent colleagues who had been listening in silence from the lockers behind them. 'Now, come on, that is funny!'

Suddenly a banana was thrown from the other side of the lockers where they had been silent and held towels over their mouths tightly to stop laughter emitting listening to this conversation; now the towels were removed and wrapped around their heads and they emerged from either side as if they were the Taliban, GI Joe had humiliated himself by his own comical words. If it were anyone else the colleagues would have unanimously agreed it was a wind-up, and a good one at that. He came to the executive decision it was an unwise decision to offer a peace offering to David Fisher; but he convinced himself that it was done in good faith. He left humiliated and would have a few sleepless nights dreading that look from the sergeant that a further complaint had been lodged and he was suspended, and to seek advice from his Police Federation representative. Tomorrow he would expect bananas to be left for him, and other offensive items. However, this cataclysmic 'confidential' conversation brought him to his senses, and added to the litany of the growing list of personality defects; which in essence would exclude him from being an assassin. He would have meticulously designed a violent way to debilitate David Fisher, but there was no need now as he would jeopardise his freedom and bring unwanted attention, which in turn would upset the American contractor. Life had to become structured and modest, he hoped the answer lay in the south of Spain maybe he would have an epiphany while exploring the rugged countryside, valleys and appealing mountains.   However, the humiliation was embedded in him; he couldn't look at bananas in the supermarket never mind consume them. When he was relaxed and his mind was calm he often laughed at his self imposed boycott of bananas; but these were rare periods of levity; his thoughts never returned to the brutal slaying of the New York detectives in sleepy Grove Road; it always returned to the chimpanzee jibe, and that jibe was an everyday occurrence from unsympathetic colleagues until he was suspended and officially pensioned off from Police Scotland. He hoped time would erode his thirst for revenge against David Fisher; he couldn't help being thin-skinned about a comical remark, as opposed to the much admired battled hardened personality that grew within him in Afghanistan, which led to the by product of a fledgling business opportunity courtesy of the American contractor; who he had listened to intently and without comment and was struck with his advice on a new career in the police. 'The most successful drug dealers are police officers or police officers with inside knowledge where stash houses are and who the wholesalers were.' He took the facts onboard and thus another personality was born, and the side hustle began, his colleagues could not keep operational drug raids quiet, names and locations were casually talked about in the locker room; he was a human sponge who did not need to write the names or locations down, nor did he ask any questions; he played the fool with embellished tales of heroism in Afghanistan, which did not make a favourable impression on his bored colleagues.

He rarely was invited to nights out with his colleagues who were meeting up with experienced drug squad officers, who had a subterranean opinion of their uniformed colleagues and an elevated opinion of themselves. The uniformed police officers seemed to be in awe of their esteemed colleagues apart from GI Joe; he thought they were boorish and bombastic, and could not hold their unimpressive amount of alcohol nor retain future 'intelligence led operational raids'. However, he was able to identify who the real kingmakers were amongst the drug squad; it wasn't the cadre who were letting their hair down with abandon and buying the uniformed drinks from corporate credit cards. He chuckled to himself how unfit they looked with the smart casual designer clothes, and guessed their reaction if they knew they had a rogue police officer amongst them who was an importer of heroin? He listened as his colleagues extracted the urine from him and mocking laughter came from the drug squad; he just smiled and slowly sipped his lager, this was an evening where he learned much and disclosed little.

The information regarding future raids on premises within the city's deprived housing schemes would make headlines and be the main news item on the evening televised news channels; this was a cynical exercise in public relations now called optics (how would the public view this) the police would be proudly telling the news reporters the next day 'that the dealers of misery were never going to win. And would be hunted down, imprisoned and assets forfeited'. Whatever. The dealer would be a low-level dealer who was not unaccustomed to being incarcerated for a few years; it would be great to meet up with former inmates; much akin to a much anticipated school reunion. Some of the more enterprising dealers would spend their time well by learning a new language; Spanish was popular for some reason. The victorious raid would have a beneficial side-effect for the uniformed officers they would be invited to another night out with the celebrating drug officers. GI Joe first inclination was to decline the invitation as it would be a reproduction of the first gathering, accompanied by the same mocking repertoire aimed at him; however, he relented some diamond may surface from the coal of information from the inebriated drug officer or officers. He was far from optimistic this would be the case, but he would have a fixed grin and grow a thicker skin. The evening moved along in a more mature fashion, alcohol was being consumed, but certain drug squad officers were concerned that some dealer from Dundee and other dealers outwith the city boundaries had 'disappeared from the face of the earth.' Imagine that, mused GI Joe, now he was relaxed as he listened intently; one of his colleagues who mentioned that the chatter that there was a C.I. (criminal informant) amongst them, and the dealers had all been probably tortured to extract information and then murdered; this was unofficial of course, so keep quiet he told the engrossed group of police officers. Good luck with that, thought GI Joe. The reason and only reason that two of the normally exuberant drug squad were subdued and looked worried was not that the dealers were missing and the respective families having to come to terms with their deaths with no bodies to bury; and a financial stream no longer there to advance their lifestyle; some would be downsizing from affluent areas, others it didn't matter at all; they might take this unfortunate turn of events to pursue a meaningful and fulfilling life. The gossip from the officers was that 'the drug squad officers had cultivated a productive relationship that produced a treasure trove of information from one or more of the missing dealers'. That may be the case but they had left out a salient matter; they were being paid in exchange for the dealer(s) to carry out their unlawful business without interference from the drug squad; there was a caveat though, they had to throw the drug squad officers a bone now and then; some low-life street dealer where the risk of arrest and prison was treated as an occupational hazard. And if there was an internal disagreement or financial dispute some big fish near the top of the chain would be set up by the financially dissatisfied dealer. GI Joe had seen some of the conversations on the dead dealer's EncroChat phone and Crispy walked him though the childlike codes that they were conversing. The subdued drug squad officers had an EncroChat phone and were worried who had the dealer's EncroChat phone and would they be able to distinguish them from dealers?

  He was glad he had attended this night out to celebrate another 'intelligence led operation' which was in itself laughable; the majority in the street were well-aware that there was a guy dealing. Some were concerned but the majority concluded it was like a social service; handy if they need gear. However, the more he listened intently to his colleague convey that the dealers were dead, and he said in hushed tones that the normally animated detectives were sitting at the table in silence compared to their boisterous colleagues identified that they were the 'two little pigs that needed feeding' that were on the EncroChat phone that GI Joe was now the custodian. The cost of the two little pigs' feed was £25k. Whether this was for each 'pig' was of no relevance, over a six month period the cost of the feed totalled £100k. He could only imagine the scenarios that were swimming and bulleting through their heads. Had the dealer revealed their identities during torture? And will they be blackmailed by the dealers seeking information about imminent intelligence led operations? Would their lifestyles be materially affected? You better fucking believe it, thought GI Joe. Judging by their worry etched faces they will be dreading or welcoming a text message on their EncroChat phone. He couldn't recall if the 'feed' was delivered to an established safe pick-up point or an off-shore bank account; either way was secure and had little disadvantage.. But they would be on a diet from now. He felt a sense of satisfaction in glancing at their morose faces, and their colleagues being angrily rebuffed from their table that was adorned with untouched drinks bought by the 'corporate credit card.'

GI Joe appeared to listen to his colleague who imparted the information from various drug squad officers; he disguised his interest in the conversation with utter contempt for them. If the dealers' were aware of the 'two little pigs' they would extract as much information as possible then see their two assets evolve into liabilities, and then would dispose of them. He could only imagine which method they would choose; but his instinct would be the two little piggies would be taken to market.

***

The information that Pavel received was disappointing but not unexpected; his instinct had to date never let him down, but he was still disappointed. Lorna was preparing to jump ship on him and also Lord Alexander Marr who was a political asset who had expensive tastes but was worth every rouble, euro, Pound or dollar. And in respect so had Lorna. Never dwell on success too long but never ignore the warning signs; he was rigid in adhering to this infallible doctrine. His concern was how would Lord Alexander Marr react to her terminating their relationship? Would he return to his disastrous former life of alcohol abuse and God forbid a relapse into purchasing and consuming cocaine which would evolve into violence? The consequence of releasing sensitive information regarding Pavel's business transactions; and how certain Lords, Ladies and influential MPs were incentivised to implement without too much scrutiny under the guise of green, environmental or medicinal expedience were devastating. He hoped the anonymous email he opened was inflated with a litany of misguided and malicious information; however, his instinct indicated that Lorna's demeanour had gradually changed from bringing him numerous business propositions; to mention on occasion that she was feeling mentally drained and physically exhausted. He would have to pursue a path of flattery with words, deeds and financial incentives. Lord Marr had achieved so much with words than a gun could; it was simpler in Russia to persuade a competitor with a gun at their head to refrain from continuing their business; and no onerous lawyers' fees. However, in London he had to shed these unorthodox methods and cultivate political lobbyists who cost the earth but identified political figures who were not allergic to acting as a consultant to smooth matters in a dignified and expeditious manner in exchange for 'expenses'.

Lord Alexander was a willing participant and his charm and intellect allowed Pavel to dispense with the lobbyists whose fees were astronomical. He had former parliamentarians who now had careers in the E.U. which was a lobbyist's paradise; the information Lord Alexander had extracted from them was incalculable. Medicinal cannabis would over the next few years become available over the counter at licensed pharmacists and online. This was already a billion dollar market, and the United Kingdom was the epicentre of growing cannabis and exporting to the rest of the world. The E.U. would be the next market and very few companies would be licensed; Pavel's had seen the future and his companies had secured the licences at an inflated cost. However, when the E.U. legalised medicinal cannabis the shares in his companies would increase overnight. He would install Lorna as CEO of mergers and acquisitions at a seven figure salary with the trappings of a private jet at her disposal. Surely this would banish any thoughts of leaving? He did not want to explore the sanctions he would be compelled to take against her if she did not acquiesce to his generous offer. But that bridge had not even been built never mind crossed. She was not aware of it but Lorna was the legal owner of Pavel's apartment, she would receive the documents when she was installed as the CEO, she was here to primarily design the apartment for herself; however this was before he had received the email with Lorna's future exit plan he would at the moment accept that she would not decline his offer.

***

Edwina had been strolling in Grove Road after the car and bodies had been removed; the street returned to the quiet enclave for polite society. A number of 'experts' on social media ignored the assassinations and forecast 'Broughty Ferry would see a rapid decline in property prices, and it was well-known that Broughty Ferry was the epicentre of financial crime for decades and drugs had become a more lucrative career.' If that was the case she would seriously consider buying a property in this 'crime ridden cesspit' as another 'expert' had posted but refused to say where he lived when challenged. But she had more serious matters on her mind; the police had doorbell footage of an unidentified person on a bicycle peddling up the steep incline; privately it was agreed this was the assassin who had donned a perfect disguise; and had used a suppressor (silencer) carrying out a text book execution. At least at the moment there was only one person involved; while there was no actual footage of the execution it was compelling. Had the assassin been met at the top of the road by another accomplice in a vehicle (van) bicycle loaded in; job complete. This was the theory as there was no footage of the bicycle or assassin from door bells or CCTV cameras. Discreet enquiries from a multitude of take-way outlets drew a blank; no orders for Grove Road or surrounding areas were taken. This had been delivered in an email overnight from London to her; armed with this information she decided to wander up to Grove Road for no other reason than to see if something would make her curious and study the photo of the 'man on the bicycle'; as he had passed the video door bell. She would re-enact accurately the execution in her mind and the time it had taken to complete. She was passing the house where the footage of the assassin had been captured on the video door bell and where the car had been. She looked at the stopwatch on her Smartphone twenty seconds to reach the car; ten seconds to fire the shots; gather the empty shells from the ground ten-fifteen seconds, an accomplished contract killer, there was no doubt. Contract completed in less than a minute. She walked briskly to the summit of Grove Road she looked at the stopwatch one minute twenty seconds. The assassin on a bicycle would have taken maximum thirty seconds; bicycle thrown in van, then assassin walks away to his vehicle or joins his accomplice in the van; quietly but deadly efficient. She was no further forward on whom the assassin was or who had ordered the 'hits'. Her past experience had guided her to study similar assassinations in Europe and in the United States; she would be surprised if the assassin had flew to Scotland from the United States under a false passport, it would be someone from London, probably Albanian, But this was all etched in her mind in pencil and could be erased as more information became available. The New York detectives had carried out hits for the American mafia; it was established that there had been 'cooperation' with the Albanian mafia in the past.

London was where the ever increasing members of the Albanian mafia had congregated and set up fiefdoms. Intelligence reports stated that they were muscling in on drug abuse hotspots in the UK. There had been a number of drug dealers reported missing from London, Liverpool and Dundee. Unlike friends and relatives who clung onto the sliver of hope that they were sunning themselves in various countries ranging from Spain, Mexico and Brazil; however the report made it abundantly clear they were all dead. Edwina was in a bind should she follow the intelligence report's conclusion or was it moving her away from the deaths of the New York detectives, and if she concurred where did it leave David Fisher in all of this? Was the internal security service avoiding conflating the deaths of the New York detectives, and for what advantage or reason? For all its faults social media was a font of conspiracy theories but sometimes a post would be brief and to the point regarding the matter in hand. She studied local Facebook pages from London, Liverpool and Dundee and noted several posts that were similar that had been posted on all of the cities' Facebook pages, nothing heart stopping but breadcrumbs that may lead her to a crack in the door that she could peer through and clarify her inner thoughts. As she cast her eyes down the steep decline from the top of Grove Road, she noticed David Fisher was placing traffic cones outside his home; very interesting, she ambled over to the pavement on the opposite side and made her way down Grove Road observing David Fisher return to his home in a hurry he was animated and returned to the pavement outside his home, he was facing down the road in anticipation, she heard the heavy loud engine first then saw the large removal van emerge into her view. Where was he going, and was this a spontaneous move initiated by the murders on the opposite side of the road or a planned move? He would not be returning to live here that she was certain of; he had strongly been advised that there was no advantage to returning to London and there was no need, except in exceptional circumstances; signing contracts that needed him there in person and then returning to Dundee on the next plane home. He had made it clear he was returning to Scotland on a permanent basis. The security services did not have to outline to him of the 'live' danger to life and limb.

    She took out her phone from her pocket and noted the name of the local removal company and contact number. David Fisher seemed anxious and repeatedly glanced at his watch, continuing down Grove Road, satisfied with her information gathering exercise, she was distracted by a car parked on the opposite side of the road, there were two occupants; male, they looked relaxed as the driver placed his hand up to hide part of his face, she entered the registration number into the DVLA website; no information, regarding the MOT, it was a spooks car or the police, not local. She couldn't continue, she pretended she had received a call and glanced at her watch and did an about turn and made her way back up Grove Road, she needed to ascertain if the occupants of the car were there to follow the removal van or were they there to protect David Fisher? Was David Fisher aware of this, and if so was it unilaterally connected to her original question; the assassination of the New York detectives? Her phone pinged 'get yourself out of Grove Road immediately!'

***

David Fisher continued the conversation on his phone while directing the removal crew what items of furniture would be staying and the furniture that would be going to his new address a short distance away. Lorna did not have to persuade him that meeting her at Pavel's newly purchased top floor apartment in 'Red Square' would be to his advantage she apologised for calling at an inconvenient time, as he hadn't mentioned that he was moving house but was not selling up; she heard sporadically him return to his native Dundee vernacular when talking to the removers. The schedule would be to meet at Pavel's sign documents, and then she would drive him to Heathrow. After completing the call with David, she rescheduled her diary to accommodate her long goodbye with Pavel. As the days turned into darkness, her confidence ebbed and flowed, regarding Pavel's potential reaction to the news that she was burnt out and needed to take a new direction to help her recuperate and bring her oscillating mental health back to calmness. Of course she had rehearsed her lines if he was to react badly to her leaving; but she hoped that he would fully understand the reasons that she had written in the letter that she would hand over personally to him. David being present would inhibit Pavel from erupting or so she hoped. Her future would not be controlled by Pavel, she was independently wealthy, and was of independent of mind, she would not be psychological bullied by him or accede to any subtle concerns for her wellbeing now or in the future. She was professionally equipped to counter any psychologically or physical pressure. Or so she thought.

***

He did not know whether to laugh or cry. It had made news first in London and then worldwide; "a man had been shot dead after he had fired a number of shots at armed police officers as they forced their way into his home via a battering ram (Big Red Key) to arrest then question him in connection to the deaths of the New York detectives in Dundee. It is believed that the suspect was an Albanian national and had been a person of interest". GI Joe knew that this was patently untrue; but a mixture of relief and puzzlement encapsulated his thoughts; relief that the case was closed but bewildered how the connection to the Albanian had been linked so quickly. He had to sit down and think about the chronological speed of events. Kettle on, he opened the coffee jar, put two heaped teaspoons in, followed by milk, kettle boiled he poured the water in stirring furiously; he would leave the coffee for two minutes. He pulled the sofa towards the window to stare at the azure sky, feet up on the coffee table. Calmness and laser focus slowed his rapid heartbeat down, he had unravelled his chaotic thoughts and ambivalence about the bolt from the blue regarding the

Albanian national being the only suspect and now shot dead after he had aimed a volley of shots at the police as they were forcing their way into his home at five am. The smile that had been in hibernation slowly emerged; all had fell into place. After he had completed the 'exercise' on Grove Road, and he parked the van in the exact place in the grounds of the large detached villa on Strathern Road that was being extensively renovated, he walked the short distance to Dawson Park where he had parked his car, threw his bag into the boot then drove home. He showered, put on fresh clothes and placed his clothes in a black bag that he had worn as the inconspicuous takeaway delivery guy. The gun lay on the worktop he professionally cleaned it and dropped it into a freezer bag, looked through his peep hole opened the door and entered the numbers into the combination lock then placed the gun in the designated Amazon return bag; went back into his flat removed the disposable gloves and dropped them into the kitchen bin.

He perused his thoughts forensically and chronologically from the executing of the New York detectives, to him, loading the bicycle into and returning the van; showered and cleaned the gun, he went out for lunch in Broughty Ferry, then returned home, before entering his flat he checked the landing cupboard the Amazon return package had been collected, another wave of anxiety dissipated.

The Albanian would have been texted a rival Albanian gang were on their way to kill him and forfeit the money and drugs, the text was sent as the police formed a line ready to use their battering ram to knock down the door. The Albanian would look at the text hear the battering of his door, run down the stairs firing through the door, the police returned fire. Surprisingly it would be revealed that the house contained drugs, substantial amounts of cash in holdalls and a gun. Later the gun and remaining bullet in the chamber of the gun matched the bullets removed from the New York detectives during the autopsy. He couldn't help admiring the intricate planning and details that went into locating the professional assassin and fortunately he would not be held to account. Case closed.

GI Joe's conscience rarely troubled him, but he was slightly annoyed that some foreign assassin would be pimped up how he was an individual that made his way up to Dundee undetected apparently while he was under observation; the police admitted there had been 'gaps' in their surveillance as they didn't want to alert him, thus they withdrew from their observation post for a few days. Amazing.

However, he had to admire the 'spooks' behind this elimination of the 'assassin' they had probably had someone 'observing' the successful police operation as it happened in real-time. Then casually departed the scene to return to their imposing building (MI6) overlooking the Thames, and watched their narrative being delivered by the much respected journalist who was educated at Cambridge and embedded in the BBC. The newspapers would be filled page to page how they had been tracking this Albanian for months, and of course social media would be awash at how professional MI6 carried out the deletion of this terrorist or was it another secret branch of government the Deep State? Well in America that was the theory and it was endorsed by ex-Generals who came across as rabid conspiracy theorists. The light of suspicion had never been shone on him in any way or connection to the deaths of the now labelled 'dirty cops' which were now accepted to be connected to the New York mafia. He could go about his mundane life sometimes interspersed with random romantic liaisons with women who were bored with life and their partners. Soon he would be settled in Spain with a settled mind and an optimistic view of his future. He wondered if he was still the butt of his ex-police colleagues' jokes. He was.

***

CHAPTER SIX

Sitting on the bench in Dawson Park trying to make sense of the two male occupants in the Audi estate in Grove Road and the stark text message that pinged on her phone, ordering her to leave Grove Road immediately was the language that Armstrong conveyed over the years, complete with exclamation mark, she was alarmed and connected the message with the two occupants in the Audi didn't have her best interest at heart, in the oasis of peace, she was thinking rationally and was dissecting the theories that were at the foremost of her mind. First of all they were there to monitor David Fisher's movements and or keep him from harm, her thoughts were suspended when the text message was read return to London, and an attachment of the news that police had shot and killed an Albanian who was suspected of executing the New York detectives. She watched the BBC video, a sense of self satisfaction, her theory that an Albanian would have had the contract to remove the New York detectives surprised her not. Was this the reason for the get out of Grove Road, and in fact the two males were there to protect her, and did one of them send the text? She had to think this through over a cup of coffee. She rose slowly from the bench, reluctantly she was slowly being drawn to the sedate pace of life apart from the mafia hit job carried out by an Albanian in Grove Road; she had to stifle laughter at the absurdity of life and death. She would avoid Grove Road incase her theory that the two occupants were not of a benevolent nature; better to be safe than sorry. She would continue her odyssey to Beach Crescent via Strathern Road then take a pit stop at a random coffee shop in which there were many in Brook Street to service the inmates of the open prison for the wealthy. As she ambled down Strathern Road in a buoyant mood , she noticed the black Audi emerge slowly from the junction, it was occupied by two males, and was heading in her direction, her hands tensed up, she decided to cross the road, the car was not slowing down, a young mother pushing a baby in an old fashioned pram was on the opposite pavement and had stopped to pick up the discarded dummy teat that was thrown from the pram, the car was not far away although she could not identify the occupants, she ran over the road to pick up the teat for the distressed young mother, she glanced at the occupants as the car passed her; they took no interest in her, she picked up the teat, rinsed it with her bottle of water then handed it over to the young mother, who accepted it with alacrity and thanked her, the tension melted away. Chatting to the woman she kept her eyes on the black Audi as it thankfully disappeared into the distance. She told the young woman that she was an artist and was on holiday and she was planning to stop at a cafe for a coffee, Anne was delighted to hear this and accepted this unexpected invitation. Edwina was distressed to hear that Anne was having a difficult time at work, as she was suffering from post natal depression, but could not afford to take too much time off, as she was a self-employed free lance journalist. Her mum was retired but she did not wish to burden her mum with her child. She was going to see the doctor tomorrow and hoped he would prescribe pills to calm her down, and get her back to normal. Edwina persuaded her to take the baby to her mum's; she pretended she had been in the same situation; she could learn through her experience; that's all she needed to hear, a neutral advising her to accept her mum's kind offer. The worry and perplexed face slowly dissipated and she had become more talkative. They were nearing the junction at Claypotts Road, Edwina was anticipating an hour spent chatting and hearing her life story; the baby had been very quiet and obviously sleeping; it was decided that they would go to Jolly's for a coffee, as there were plenty of space inside and out. They were near the bus stop, Anne had said she would text her mum to tell her that she would take up her offer, her phone was in her small bag, she took out a gun and Edwina was frozen, then two shots were fired into her head, the Audi estate, silently pulled up beside 'Anne' and the prone Edwina, she removed Edwina's phone this had a treasure trove of videos including David Fisher and his now deceased partner Gail having coffee with the corrupt New York detectives in the hotel in New York. One of the occupants emerged and picked up slid the pram into the rear. Anne opened the back door took a lit cigarette from the driver, then the car moved off.

***

David Fisher looked around the near empty flat various memories arrived and departed quickly especially the sad ones. He was ambivalent whether to sell Grove Road or lease it out; but he knew the truth was that he didn't want to sell it because living here had been the best period of his life; his mansion block apartment was more opulent but this place had a hold on him. His dad was thriving 'advising' the various contractors that were working on his recently purchased house not flat. While the house was getting refurbished he would be over in New York organising and relinquishing deals that had not been as profitable as Pavel had been advised; for the first four weeks he would be examining certain transactions that Pavel was not entirely happy with. This was code for unauthorised sales of assets that had been sold and the proceeds were obligatory ring fenced but had been transferred into another unidentified account. In layman's language someone was embezzling or sending part of the vast profits to an account that was not connected to Pavel's plethora of bank accounts worth billions of dollars. His taxi pinged on his phone that it was outside to take him to Dundee Airport for his flight to London, he would spend a few days at his apartment a USB file would be given to him by Pavel with the highlighted documents that contained all the financial transactions that had been identified as 'causing concern'. He would skim through the files in his apartment to distinguish if it was a sophisticated fraud or if it was conceived and carried out by a Russian accountant; it would be that obvious. Meeting Lorna at Pavel's new apartment was going to be the highlight of his short trip to London, and of course Pavel who would very clearly tell him of his concerns; if he were to unearth some fraudulent transactions when he skimmed through the files in his London apartment he would not burden Pavel with the distressing discovery; he wanted to have a pleasant working period in New York; and he needed to visit where his colleague, friend and neighbour (Jonathon Gove) had been shot dead on the bench in Central Park. He was in a difficulty whether to mention this to Lorna; and was it a good idea? He felt compelled to go there for what reason he did not understand. Lorna would either agree then reveal the reason why. Or on the other hand if she in her gentle but persuasive manner suggest that it would not free him from any perceived guilt; he would still go to Central Park and lay a small bunch of flowers, knowing someone would remove them in a few minutes and make better use of them,

    He did not want to turn around to look at his home as he closed the gate as the taxi driver took his case without prompting and placed it in the boot. Settled in the back seat, he examined his emails. He texted Lorna advising that he had left his 'crib' and was on his way to the airport, he was looking forward to meeting her in a few hours time. She texted back immediately, she would meet him on arrival at the airport. He felt a rush of happiness knowing this, it would not be too long before he was in his apartment, the driver did a u-turn in Grove Road and told him that police and an ambulance were on their way to a bad car accident on Strathern Road, so they would leave by Dundee Road for the ten minute journey to the airport. He was looking at the majestic river Tay with a feeling of sadness, he would not be ensconced in New York for too long, but the sporadic feeling of melancholy was awakened from its dormant compartment in his mind. The taxi driver commented that the car crash must be serious as there was a convoy of police cars with blue lights heading in the direction; he opined that there must be something more serious; David agreed. He was a man of few words but thought more than he talked; an asset in his profession. His mind was on other things at this moment in time; New York would be more pleasant and hopefully bring him to terms and remove the illogical guilt of the murder of his friend.

The taxi driver caustically commented on the new build flats not far from the V &A that they were passing on Riverside Drive were very expensive and the vast majority were purchased by Edinburgh and London property companies as they were renting them out to visitors to Dundee which was trying and achieving to become an attractive city for tourists because of its rich heritage. He gazed at the smart expensive apartment block, and wondered why he had been left a number of them by Michael Ogilvie, he mused why didn't this good fortune not come his way when he was on an average salary? The flats did not mean too much to him he had millions in various banks and investments in tax sheltered countries all legal of course. It would take some time for Michael Ogilvie's financial bequests to become official; once it was all dispersed as he had bequeathed he would visit the apartments, but not until then. The taxi pulled up outside the airport, he handed the driver £20, they got out of the taxi, the driver removed his case from the boot and handed him his suitcase, he returned to the taxi, and started the engine, he smiled at David and said 'enjoy New York'. He was stunned at this; how did he know that he was going to New York? The melancholy grew, his face went to chalk white, as the taxi drove away he could not take his eyes from it, was he becoming paranoid, had he mentioned New York as he was texting Lorna? And did the taxi driver commence small talk about the Riverside apartments because he was aware that he was the fortunate recipient of multiple apartments. He entered the airport building and scanned the passengers that were waiting to board the same flight as him, then he suddenly looked behind him, he felt he was under malevolent observation, he felt nauseous, he had gone over in his mind whether he had mentioned New York and he was of the firm opinion that he had not. The flight was boarding, he picked up his suitcase, he smiled and exhaled heavily, on the handle were labels with his flight number and destination New York that he had printed off after he had checked-in online.

***

Pavel placed the letter that had been signed legally gifting the apartment to Lorna; the most expensive incentive to alter Lorna's preferred decision. He did not require her signature; he would give her the letter after she had agreed to continue their business relationship; if she declined, the letter that she was not aware of would be ripped up and immediate unrefined action would be taken against her, It was just another business decision that he had taken when no amount of gold could change someone's mind; more fool them. He gazed around the flat, the kitchen and bathroom had been ripped out ready for Lorna's input; no expense would be spared, she had exquisite taste. The lounge and bedrooms were empty all the dated furniture and carpets were discarded into the skip below; if any scavengers were attracted to the contents of the skip he was indifferent.

Pavel was not prone to nostalgia; it was a brutal and poverty stricken childhood, When you don't have money it's tough to eke out a living, but when you have an unlimited money supply you invent problems in your head that was the salient advice Lorna had seared into his conscious when he was in therapy and couldn't understand he had everything that money could buy apart from happiness, he couldn't recall the last time he laughed. And her wise words were never far away when problems did arise. No longer was it acceptable to settle a business disagreement at the end of a gun. Nigel was the legal 'gun' to settle disputes in a timely manner, he left all the details with him and he would 'encourage' the other side to settle quickly, and quietly. Unbeknown to Pavel, when Nigel's letters and legal consequences were ignored he would arrange to have dinner on the understanding that Pavel's company was willing to settle on their terms, he would bring the paperwork to be signed after they had completed the routine pleasantries. Nigel assumed correctly that the protagonist would be uncorking the champagne and boasting to the tight Whatsapp group that Nigel was no longer at the top of his game; 'there was a new sheriff in town'. Nigel was sent this message from a former colleague that he had dug him out of a legal catastrophe that would have ended his lucrative career. He had become lazy and boastful; the opposite of Nigel's advice when he had left on good terms from Nigel's practice.

This information was useful but it was of no legal advantage to him, as the night wore on, the meal and drinks were consumed, Nigel brought out the paperwork, the 'victor' of the negotiations started to read the four pages in the document binder and his eyebrows rose above his horn rimmed spectacles, Nigel just stared intently at him, he caught the eye of the waiter who brought over the customary Krug champagne, Nigel pulled out his pen and sat it in front of him. 'I can't sign this; my clients will be seriously disadvantaged'. Nigel took out his phone and read out the boastful messages he had sent to the Whatsapp group. 'You can't blackmail me, with betraying client confidentiality; a misdemeanour not a hanging offence'. Nigel then read out a list of clients that had committed suicide; that were inexplicably Russian or lawyers that had engaged on Russian clients' behalf. He then advised him to study the clientele at the next table. They were of undefined nationality but were brutes that there was no doubt. Nigel told him to pour the champagne, the role of the defeated lawyer to express that there was no malice. Nigel gently pushed the trolley that contained the ice bucket which contained champagne and an enormous amount of ice towards him.

'Leave the champagne, and dig your fingers into the ice.... deeply'. With the eyes of the next table upon him he obeyed and was horrified what his fingers had discovered; he withdrew his fingers and poured champagne out for the victor. Nigel did not taunt him; he waited on the champagne filling his glass and told him to fill his own glass. Then Nigel told him to sign the documents, there was no resistance, then Nigel asked him for his phone and handed it to the shaven head occupant of the nearby table to take a number of photographs of Nigel overlooking his reluctant victim sign the papers, Nigel examined the photographs and typed in the accompanied message 'All done and dusted' with a thumbs up emoji. Nigel stood behind him as he sent the photos to his Whatsapp group;

once delivered he stood up and left the table with the document binder, and forthcoming invoice for dinner to his crestfallen dinner companion, no threats were delivered, the waiter came to the table and withdrew the small trolley that contained the bucket of ice, champagne and submerged gun from the table. Nigel consumed the champagne wished him well and left.

  His boastful adversary accepted he had been too confident and had underestimated Nigel, but he took some solace in he had defeated him on legal grounds, but when you are up against naked violence and certain death, it would be best to quaff the champagne and live to fight another day. He would not entertain any messages from his fawning admirers asking how much money he had made from this once in a lifetime deal; for two reasons, Nigel would hear about it and leak certain details to his inside man in the Whatsapp group, or had he someone hack into the group? which was not at all implausible about the actual terms of the documents he had signed making him look foolish. And the second; how long before he had an accident or committed suicide?

  Pavel was delighted but not surprised that Nigel had managed against the clock to persuade the abrasive lawyer to sign the documents at such a late stage, he had doubts that the dinner would end in a resounding victory for him, saving many millions and years arguing his case in court. Two Russian oligarchs suing each other in London brought unwelcome attention and shone an unsympathetic light on the methods that the two oligarchs would go to, to achieve victory and heap humiliation on their opponent. Pavel would rather have fate intervene and his opponent would suddenly change their mind and agree to Pavel's interpretation of a particular clause in the legal document at the final meeting before assets were transferred and monies exchanged. Or bad luck would befall them; their money would be frozen by the UK government, courtesy of Lord

Alexander Marr who whispered to someone influential that the person was no longer of a benefit to London or the economy, Lord Marr was a gatherer of information when he was on his fact finding trips abroad, he was advised that it would benefit him in the future if he was able to ascertain certain matters regarding an individual who was willing to trade political information for a British passport. No money was offered by the UK government or requested by Lord Marr who had gave up his socialist principles when he experienced how members of the Establishment lived their lives and how many doors opened that benefited him socially and financially.

So late in life he had discovered keep your head down, and omit his outrageous allegations that he was prone to air under parliamentary privilege usually against Russian oligarchs. And not forgetting Lorna who had took him under her wing and convinced him to give up alcohol and drugs, and he had never experienced such kindness before that 'chance meeting' in the local hostelry near parliament, where former comrades and adversaries subjected him to cutting remarks and mocked him mercilessly; how times had changed, he was more influential than they could ever imagined, he knew how to play the political game more than the experienced MPs and Members of the House of Lords, now he could forgive his former comrades who had entered parliament as fire breathers and were now lounging on the leather seats in the House of Lords picking up a daily allowance of in excess of £300 a day. Giving up the booze and drugs helped him adjust his eyesight to focus on where the influential people met and had lunch. Lorna was able to assist him where these locales were.

After meeting with Nigel at his office, he was alarmed to learn that Nigel had drifted into persuasion by subtle threats that resulted in the documents being signed. He had learned this courtesy of Lord Alexander Marr via Lorna. This was intolerable; Nigel could plainly see how bypassing the legal and civilised methods documents would be agreed in a timely manner. He did not raise this disturbing news with Nigel, he put into place a Polish lawyer that Pavel would fund so that he could shadow Nigel, then when Nigel was satisfied he would return to open an office in Strasbourg to lobby the EU politicians to legalise medicinal cannabis for EU citizens and of course boost tax revenues from the cultivators of cannabis, namely the pharmaceutical companies.

Nigel who was avaricious as well as egotistical was hearing inside information, and the Polish lawyer inadvertently passed on tips that Pavel had paid millions to an insider in a pharmaceutical company that they had formulated a prototype drug that could slow down dementia, it had been successfully administered under strict independent doctors and the results were promising. Nigel purchased a tranche of shares in the company. After a year the Polish lawyer had been a keen student of Nigel's methods, he had learned all that was required of him; Nigel arranged a surprise farewell party for him, while he was in the midst of organising the new office in Strasbourg. Pavel would have an impromptu meeting with his Polish lawyer and was disappointed that Nigel was billing him for services that did not materialise as he had done with other rich clients who lived in London or in Cyprus or split their time in both locations, Pavel came to the decision that it was time to come to a parting of the ways; he would not formally inform him, events would surpass any legal formalities; satisfied that all his companies that Nigel oversaw would pass any rigorous scrutiny from the legal authorities and police forensic accountants; it was time for Nigel to make his Maker, And he hoped he did, after the visit to the luxury flat where he met an untimely gruesome death.

   David Fisher's world was being inexorably linked to the deaths of friends and colleagues, he had to return to Broughty Ferry, and on reflection the irritable visits from the police on numerous occasions regarding the heinous offence of moving a plant pot, momentarily was escapism from the deaths that were occurring on a frequent occurrence in London. Then the murders of the New York detectives in Grove Road close to his house made London a safe sanctuary even though he had left London for his personal safety. New York would be the safest place for him at the moment; who would've thought that? When Lorna picked him up from London City airport, her face was ashen, she kept repeating that things were getting out of hand and she didn't feel safe. Now when David heard this he was alarmed, what was she talking about? She was no longer the ice maiden she was talking in staggered sentences and he had to advise her of the speed limit. At traffic lights she turned round to him.
'How can you be so calm?'
'About what? I don't know what you are referring to.'
'The woman who was shot in Strathern Road, near your house surely you must have heard?'
Now it made perfect sense when the taxi driver had said there had been a car accident, then the fleet of police cars that sped past them on the way to Strathern Road. He mentioned it must be something more serious, and now it was a woman had been shot dead! 'No Lorna, the taxi driver said it was a car accident so we had to take an alternative route, then we saw police cars pass us, going at speed.
Who was the woman? And I know this will sound stupid was her death connected to the New York detectives?' She took a series of deep breathes as the traffic lights changed, now she was aware that he was oblivious of the mayhem that had occurred not far from his home, she started to process

this information in a calm and professional manner. Should she explain to him now or wait till they were in his apartment settled and all would be revealed over a cup of coffee in a calm manner? He was overcome by a bout of anxiety at her sudden silence. 'Do you have information that my life is in danger'. She didn't expect him to come out with that comment. 'It would be best to explain or explore what I think is going on and what I know what is going on.' He accepted this with good grace; he noticed she had a plastic bag with various foodstuffs and milk. They continued the journey to his apartment in unnerving silence. He would swap this apartment and all his riches for his previous position as a humdrum Information Technology officer with Dundee City Council instantly. He was looking out the window in a daze, how can this life that he had cherished be so miserable? He used to mock those multi-millionaires, who went into therapy, but he had taken that road himself and now agreed with them; they like him, had climbed to the top of the mountain but were disappointed with the view.

He had felt so low during those days, but reluctantly sought help, and Lorna was his saviour, she made sense of his low moods, and understood when self-made men and women achieve all their goals then face a world that does not bring happiness as they anticipated. She had suggested that he look up his friends on Facebook and examine their posts and compare their lives with his, and ascertain if they were any happier? She did not offer the answer, he had to explore and come to a conclusion by himself. His conclusion this minute would be they were happy if not content with their mundane lives. The car pulled up outside the apartment block, her mood had lifted, while his low mood continued. She handed him the grocery bag.
'Are you glad to be home?'
'This is not home...' He continued to the security door, and placed the fob on the sensor. He then smiled. One of the workmen that helped refurbish his apartment, 'seconded' the security apparatus including fobs from Dundee City Council, she noticed a smile replace the sadness on his face.
'I'm so glad you're feeling better David.'
'I'm not really, I was just looking at the security system and thinking about my friends that came down and refurbished my apartment and other jobs; they all loved it down here.' They made their way to his apartment, their steps echoing up the marble stair case, they walked in silence, but were in a relaxed frame of mind, he turned the key, he had activated the heating from the app at Dundee airport; the warmth of the apartment lifted his mood. She took off her coat and went to the kitchen filled the kettle and joined David at the table he was on his laptop voraciously reading about the woman who had been shot dead approximately at the time he was waiting for the taxi. He would be anticipating a visit from the police and or security

services, to clarify the reason why he had left Dundee at the same time the woman was shot dead; going on from the previous deaths it would not shock him; woman shot dead in adjoining street from his, and he buggers off to London, nothing suspicious about that is there?

'Don't overthink things David, over the next few days things will become clearer' She was saying this to herself as well. The unidentified woman shot dead had to be connected in some way to David Fisher and axiomatic to her. Pavel was looming in her thoughts also. 'Fuck me!' he shouted out loud,

'I don't need to wait a few days to find out who she was or the reason she was in Broughty Ferry. She's been named and she was a forensic accountant with the Economic Crime Unit.' He turned the laptop around so she could read the story for herself, he left the table to make them coffee, He poured the water in the mugs stirring furiously; this is all going to come back to me, he thought. The Economic Crime Unit in Broughty Ferry, then a glimmer of hope, entered his head calming him for a minute or two, she was shot dead in Strathern Road; there were a few foreign nationals that had moved into the salubrious Strathern Road, could be tax evasion, yes, that would make more sense, his dad had went on a rant about them a few years ago, he smiled and took the coffee and his theory over to the table to explain to Lorna, who had a furrowed brow. She took the mug from him as he joined her at the table; he looked at her she was not in total harmony with this specious theory. 'I can assure you that the woman's death and leaking of the details indicates to me that this is connected to you, and the New York detectives. Of course there is a slight chance that she was up in Broughty Ferry for the reason that you state, but I can't see it.' He was crestfallen hearing this, but in his heart he knew she was probably correct. 'Okay, I accept what you are saying do you think it was the Albanians that had shot her?' Was this the time to come clean with him up to a point, and if she did, what were the consequences if he rejected what she said? 'I'm not sure but whoever did shoot her had to silence her, and she must've had information that was toxic.'

'What do you mean toxic?'

'No one kills a government agent without considering the consequences; and two New York detectives as well, even though they were proven to be venal. And you have benefited from their deaths.' He placed the coffee mug on the coaster in a state of shock as he processed what she had just said. 'You'll have to explain that to me Lorna, I know what you just uttered but I'm in shock, benefitted? You must mean financially, I can assure that is not the case.'

She sipped her coffee as she sat in silence staring at him, he found this unnerving. 'No, you're wrong you benefitted that there is no doubt, not

financially, but vicariously by the New York detectives being killed, if it wasn't for the assassins or assassin they would've killed you. Surely that must have crossed your mind?' He looked at her and felt a great weight had been lifted. 'Yes I did think that, but I didn't want to think that, I was running away from reality on this occasion.'
'Good I'm glad you have got that out, but that raises another question, were they murdered to protect you and why?' She lifted up her mug and waited on his answer. 'I can't for the life of me think of a reason.' 'C'mon now David, don't delude yourself you are an intelligent man.' He was not enamoured by this scolding. 'You're the expert you tell me.' She shook her head. 'You have to be honest with me and yourself, you as well as I know the answer, unless I've got this completely wrong, which I don't.' He felt his neck warm under his collar, she was right but still hoped she was wide of the mark. 'Why would someone murder two New York detectives outside my home, to protect me? It must be because I am Pavel's financial advisor and manage his high-performing investment portfolios, is that correct?'
 She looked at him with bursting pride. 'Of course that is the reason, there is nothing unlawful or any accusations of suspected money laundering in your purchasing or disposing of assets owned by Pavel's off-shore or UK managed funds. I suspect that you have managed his assets far better than expected and Pavel's competitors or political opponents are disheartened at your professional and successful results.'
'I can't see the problem, my results are paid on a basic salary and bonus for exceeding expected results, it's not an uncompetitive contract, it's quite common in the City.'
'No, no, you misunderstand me, Pavel is very happy with your performance, it's his enemies home and abroad that see you as his wealth producer; that's the reason they wanted you dead'. He wasn't stupid he knew that was the case all along, yet had no fear going to New York. Sometimes it paid dividends financially and emotionally playing a thirty watt light bulb. 'Now, I understand so unknown Albanians inadvertently saved my life?'
'Not inadvertently, let me explain....'

***

 Pavel stood in the moonlit filled lounge bereft of furniture; not many lights shone in Red Square, the majority of apartments were unoccupied for most of the year, and some changed hands at inflated prices without anyone staying a night in them; money laundering; crude if not simple method. He knew some of the oligarchs who had earned their millions by murder and extortion in Moscow; these were unsophisticated street thugs in bespoke Savile Row suits, which the tailors delighted in offering their bespoke service. However, when there was a sporadic bout of violence between the warring oligarchs that spilled onto the affluent London streets, Pavel assisted through his willing intermediary Lord Alexander Marr who passed apposite information to the police which ultimately removed the loathsome oligarchs from their homes in London; the oligarchs would flee London in their private jets to Cyprus to avoid being arrested and ultimately remanded in prison for many months then deported. They would be tipped off that the police and Border Patrol officers would be making early morning arrests. Sometimes this information was erroneous but had served its sole purpose to rid London of bloodshed and when they had left they would not be permitted to return; their assets would be frozen including their multimillion pound apartments in London. They would be offered a choice; sell your assets and houses within a narrow time frame and never return. If they employed a K.C. to challenge this decision it would cost a fortune in legal fees and years to reach court. Pavel could assist by offering cash for their apartments to finance their new boring lifestyles in Cyprus. Then once the purchase was completed he would sell the newly acquired property at an inflated price to a newly arrived oligarch and help him settle in. David Fisher was the intermediary who met the potential buyer at the apartment.

If Lorna knew that this apartment had come into his ownership via this method that could make her queasy, but when she had researched the previous owner it would be listed as an off-shore company with no identities listed; all legal and common practice. It had taken many years to trace assets that had been stolen from Mother Russia but his endeavour and patience had been profitable for Russia and himself, and some of these respected oligarchs would never see Russia again nor their unlawful acquired assets. He had immersed himself into the London political class through Lord Alexander Marr; you do not need an interpreter to adjust or influence government policy; money is the universal language.

He would be returning to Moscow for good in a few months' time, his mission had been nearly completed; his female successor would be fully acquainted in the flexible practices of the City of London and the lobbyists that pulled the strings in their favour. David Fisher had been an exception to the financial investment managers that he had previously employed to act on his behalf, he was honest. Lorna would be well-rewarded for her patience and business acumen, and would be able to assist Pavel's successor; hence the gift of this soon to be refurbished apartment, and if she wished to sell it after a year, the profit would be guaranteed as it would be an off-shore company that would purchase it. How would she able to turn this offer down? He opened the balcony doors to take in the night air and the panoramic view with iconic buildings jostling for his eyes' attention. The cigar was lit; he had self satisfaction infused throughout his body and mind. He would not shed any tears when he was on the plane to Moscow; London had never impressed him nor had the full blooded capitalist system that raged through every minute of the day. The political system was all smoke and mirrors parliament was teeming with careerists who had their eyes on the House of Lords when they had served their political masters in the City; their constituents were left out of their thoughts until election time. There were no real opposition parties, they all rubbed against each other and rarely fell out. There were only four percent of former manual workers in parliament; it was gender and diversity Members of Parliament now. He studied the deserted streets and pavements, it was the perfect location, quiet and crime free, however less than a mile away the streets were classed as no go areas, street crime was rampant, and police rarely intervened. In Moscow the police were robust and direct; he missed the authoritarian police in Moscow; in London civilisation was collapsing in full view of the public and the rule of law was being eroded in broad daylight. He looked forward in anticipation on looking out of the plane's window at the receding skyline of London and Canary wharf. He sucked on the cigar for the last time and tossed the cigar onto the deserted pavement below, he watched the lit cigar hit the newly painted railings and roll towards the street. He leant on the balcony; it was so quiet and unnerving. He was grabbed by the waist, and casually tossed over the balcony to land on the spiked railings, and screamed out in excruciating pain. The deserted street could offer him no comfort from the slow painful lingering death. 'Hello, I'd like to report a man has jumped or fell out from a balcony...' The operator found it hard to understand the Russian or Eastern European accent, and the caller did not wish to disclose their mobile number or name, and after establishing that the address was confirmed, the call was abruptly ended. Lorna removed the SIM card from the burner phone and left the apartment and exited the building at the rear entrance into darkness.

***

David Fisher was feeling relaxed as he removed his feet from the table, a habit that was difficult to break. Tomorrow he would be on the flight to New York, the meeting with Pavel had been postponed the documents that Pavel wished him to study had been sent by encrypted e-mail. There were less than he had anticipated, the sale of assets and money that should have been sent to the company's bank account had been deposited in an escrow account that the company on occasion had used, it would not cause him too much difficulty to establish the reason why. He would use his time on the plane to establish why the money was in this account. Pavel knew about the escrow account, but was circumspect how long the funds would stay in the escrow account before being transferred to the company's main account in the British Virgin Islands. He had informed David that he would be residing in the company's newly-acquired Fifth Ave apartment, Lorna had told him that she would be accompanying him to New York and would help him settle in to the apartment and bring over documents from the main office for him to study; she was of the opinion someone had been less than honest with the company's finances.

Enjoying a cold beer feet up watching the news channel, the obligatory breaking news banner made him remove his feet from the table and lean forward, "A Russian businessman has reportedly fell from a top floor apartment in Belgravia,,, details are still coming in." The media cameras were outside the apartment block and a large blue tarpaulin cover hung over the railings, on the pavement a large tent was being erected, it was obvious that the body had not been recovered. Was he so glad he was leaving all this death behind, he switched his attention to his laptop, social media citizen journalists would be there in their droves and were not reticent in giving out their views without any evidence. He was not disappointed that the vloggers had revealed it was a Russian but they had no name, and he had either fell or was tossed over the balcony. Again they were correct in their assessment as they broadcast live from outside the apartment block. Then one of the vloggers came out and stated it was Pavel. She had said that her information was correct and stated with supreme confidence that he had many business interests in London. He was stunned when he had heard this, but hoped she was wrong. He would not call Lorna incase her information was incorrect, if it was correct should he continue onward to his business in New York? He finished his beer and retrieved another from the fridge; this could not get any worse. Then his feverish imagination was replacing rational thoughts in his head; was Pavel's death in any way linked to their mutual lawyer's (Nigel) death. He sat at the table sipping the beer riveted to his laptop with multiple live feeds from Facebook TikTok and a feed from the local news channel, the live comments were confirming it was Pavel, again, they could be the vlogger's friends just posting to add credibility to their scoop. No media channel had confirmed the identity of the victim apart from the deceased was male and Russian. His phone vibrated on the table it was Lorna, she was in the Iron Duke pub, and asked if he had seen the reports on social media? His heart sank. He asked is it Pavel and she said it was, then casually put her grief aside to advise their schedule flight to New York was still on. He was stunned and relieved that New York was still on, but bewildered that she was in the Iron Duke pub, he was about to ask this when she invited him down, he didn't need to be asked again. He went to the wardrobe and placed his casual jacket on then the thoughts were exploding in his head, was he murdered or did he jump? And how did Lorna know it was Pavel? He placed trainers on and switched on all of the lights in the apartment, why he did this he wasn't sure. He made his way to the front door feeling uneasy, the Iron Duke was the place that would settle his chaotic mind down, and Lorna would indulge him when he asked a multitude of questions, the trainers did not make a sound as he descended the marble stairs, the cold air and short walk would hopefully make him receptive to logical explanations that would be forthcoming from Lorna, she was a straight shooter, and would not resile from ignoring uncomfortable truths and how to reconcile them with difficult choices or solutions

Lord Alexander had been helpful supplying information to assist in expanding Pavel's business empire and initiating legislation regarding medicinal cannabis; a multi-billion pound business, however, it was time for her to break free; she had her story in her head about leaving the UK for a short period of time, and hoped the infrequent communication between them would lead to a mutual uncoupling of their relationship.

David would be easily to manipulate into concurring with her explanation of her theory why Pavel had threw himself over the balcony onto spiked railings which would not bring his life to an end instantly. Meeting David in the crowded pub and wearing a bright red dress would firm up her alibi if the police conducted a comprehensive investigation, but she doubted that they would, it would be a cursory investigation and few stones would be upturned. Pavel was a unobtrusive business partner, he let her run and acquire businesses with little interference as long as the acquisitions were profitable and could be sold quickly, but she had foreseen the day when she had to break free and make her own future, early on she had established that this termination of her contract would not involve given a written four weeks' notice. When he had advised that he had purchased a top floor apartment in Belgravia the stars had all aligned for her. It was no coincidence that the spate of suicides had an ominous connection; Pavel. He had not used his manicured hands to carry out the foul deeds, but he was the architect but not the executioner. All the deceased businesses had been purchased or sold by the multitude of business partners of Pavel, some were oblivious of the methodology and reasons behind purchases and sales unexpectedly that came their way. However purchasing companies for a discounted price could not be ignored. They were naive that this opportunity was engineered by Pavel, and on prima facie evidence he was just disposing of their assets as the shareholders required capital to pay their guarantors which was a company coincidently owned by Pavel, based in Jersey. Her eyes were fixed on the door awaiting his entrance, she had her story ready to unfold to him, she could not seem to be visibly upset as she was a professional psychotherapist, this unfortunate death was the consequences of outside pressures He came in through the door and he sought her out in the crowded bar, he was wearing multicoloured trainers an unexpected bonus, the patrons of the bar would notice them and remember him, same with her wearing a bright red dress; alibis in abundance, even though there were CCTV in discreet locations. On her phone Pavel had called her about the meeting in his new apartment; again this was another fact that would bring the investigation to a shuddering halt. Her wine was barely touched as he sat at the table bursting with questions but took a deep breath and let Lorna explain.

'Are you comfortable? I will give my assessment with the sparse information that I have collated thus far from social media, and compare it to the first hand information that I have that no one else does.'

He looked at her trying to assess whether this would be of benefit to either of them. She continued.

'Pavel had called me about the apartment purchase which was unusual, he then without elaborating told me he was under pressure from business rivals, and felt unsafe. I arranged a meeting with him for next week where he could unburden his fears, I told him to contact the police immediately if he felt his life was in danger; that was yesterday. I think he could not see a way out and purposely leapt over the balcony aiming for the railings. Why would he do that you may ask, this could be in defiance of his tormentors. When people are under pressure they wilt.' David took a long drink from his frosted glass, trying to expunge the leap from the apartment onto the spiked railings.

'What a horrible death, I just can't think why he would do that, and all to send a defiant sign to his enemies. That is bizarre, but the Russians have different standards to us; it would not surprise me. You will have to notify the police about the phone call. And will that affect our business in New York?'

'I've already contacted the police and told them of the content of the phone call, I have also told them of our trip to New York on business, I said if you wish me to cancel the trip, that's fine. They said no need to cancel they have my mobile number if they wish to speak to me again.' He was visibly relieved to learn that New York trip was still on. Then he laughed out loud.

'What's so amusing?' He sipped his beer, would it be so crass and unfeeling to mention the thought that crossed his mind? 'No, I'm very sorry for laughing, I was just thinking that the police have said just carry on with your business, and they have not established whether it was suicide or murder, but I moved a neighbour's plant pot to cut my grass, and I was visited regarding this serious matter four times!' She looked at him he was an observer of life's ridiculous moments, and he was correct.

'Contrast and compare is a good trait to have David. And that does not mean you have no empathy for Pavel quite the opposite I think.'

'Pavel came to my rescue when the Merchant bank was ordered by the government to stop lending while there was a pending investigation into alleged money laundering. This was to be the last tranche of money; millions of pounds for the fitting out of the office block, then Nigel my lawyer worked his magic once again and no doubt to his financial advantage, by explaining my predicament to Pavel, long story short, I got a better rate of interest on my loan, and compensation from the merchant bank when the investigation came to nothing; it was a malicious rumour. Pavel saved my business.'

Lorna listened intently to this, David was one of many people who had their future funding frozen from Merchant banks, and similar to others Nigel came up trumps with a better financial package with reduced terms. David was due to complete the loan term in six months' time, if heaven forbid he had an accident the office building would be security for the loan; Pavel would be able to force the sale of the office within ninety days to recoup the loan plus interest paid at a daily rate of eight percent. Pavel could not afford to lose David Fisher, maybe after completing the forensic examination of the books in New York but not before then. If the New York detectives killed David Fisher *after* he had completed his financial audit in New York, he would have taken ownership of the commercial building that the global bank had signed a fifteen year lease; a quirk of good fortune. There was no question that she would or could tell David that this fairy godfather had him in his sights courtesy of Nigel for some time. As with the others that had been felled by misfortune, Pavel had manipulated Nigel through stroking of his ego and filling his coffers; but Nigel had come to the end of his efficacy he needed to be let go without severance pay.

Currently Lorna mused, how would David's fragile ego process and cope with this information? He was talking and smiling but his words were faint, as she imagined after eliciting this information, that she would supplement this by informing him that Gwen his brief partner did not meet David by chance? He would of course ask her to explain. She would then tell him, that Gwen and her family had invested millions of dollars in a share scam in which Pavel was the genius behind the scheme, with the help of financial journalists who had great respect on Wall Street. They had been the 'insiders' of the scheme and had put their wallets where their opinions were, they had invested heavily and one particular favourite journalist was advised by text to sell immediately recouping an impressive profit; however when there was a stampede for the exit Pavel's compatriots in the Russian Mafia had exited first before informing the journalist. Gwen and her family like thousands of single investors were left with worthless shares when the fund was liquidated. Some hedge funds had been advised by the journalist to sell immediately, When the dust had settled the hedge funds who had sold their share holding were shut down, they enthusiastically revealed the name of the journalist who called the head broker and told him to 'liquidate all assets in this fund immediately.' No explanation was asked or required; he did as instructed, and the whole fund started to lose value very quickly, but he had reaped millions of dollars in profit in a matter of minutes. Unfortunately the SEC (Security Exchange Commission) was a dollar short and a day late in locating the 'missing' journalist. Pavel had it on good authority that he would never be found, Unfortunately for Pavel he was not informed that the 'missing' journalist had been contacted by Gwen when she had seen shares being sold in quick succession, Gwen had seen this movie before when a new company came to the market, shares would be sold to create a panic the share value would plummet, then miraculously within hours a hedge fund would Hoover up the rapidly declining shares, and there would be a impulsive upturn in the market and the shares would appreciate in value.

How Gwen rued her judgement, her eyes fixed on her screen and disappointed as the shares dropped and settled and declined eighty percent of their first day of trading on the open market. She, similar to other experienced traders had been robbed of their family's savings. Through her contacts in the SEC, she was told it was a Russian financier in London that was the brain behind the inception and liquidation of the fund, through proxy traders throughout the western and far-east worlds. Her planned odyssey was to secure a position in London, and through networking eventually reveal who the fraudulent Russian financier was. David was just subterfuge so she could subtly enquire who had been stung by the fraudulent 'pump and dump' scheme. Her thirst for knowledge of the Russian financier resulted in her knocking over tables and chairs instead of dancing around them intelligently. Her name was passed onto the New York detectives; David was at work when they came calling. Lucky him.

Edwina from the Economic Crime Unit was suspicious of her colleague Armstrong that maybe he was not working for the best interests of Economic Crime Unit her fears multiplied when she realised the apartment in Beach Crescent was under surveillance inside and out, however, *sometimes* he was acting in her best interests, it was he who had contacted a former colleague a retired detective in Dundee to warn her somehow that she was in danger, (he had noticed she had left the umbrella in the Ship Inn and left it at her door) although the opposite seemed the logical conclusion.

She had observed the New York detectives have coffee with David Fisher and his partner in the New York hotel, it was apparent that they were delivering news that was not helpful and caused them to become visibly uncomfortable. She could not share this information with Armstrong incase this lead to him pulling her off the case. Armstrong after meeting with the New York detectives in London was wary of their explanation that they were in London to assist the Economic Crime Unit, he was suspicious of their insipid explanation and contemplated maybe they had through their own observations or informants in the hotel that Edwina's presence in the hotel had been noted, Armstrong would regret venting his exasperation at the New York detectives as he was leaving the office by sarcastically mentioning did they enjoy having coffee with David Fisher and Gwen Russo in a New York hotel? Armstrong was correct in this assumption, the young waiter who had spent the night with Edwina relayed his suspicions to the New York detectives, Armstrong and Edwina's stay on this Earth would be brought to a premature conclusion. In summary they were correct to have had their suspicions of each other. The New York detectives aim was to eliminate David Fisher *and* Edwina, when Pavel was informed that the New York detectives were travelling to Dundee to interview POI (Person of Interest) that could only be David Fisher. David Fisher still had to audit the sales of assets in New York, these detectives were linked to the New York mafia, where their investments had been wiped out from the pump and dump scheme orchestrated by Pavel through a myriad of shell and off-shore companies; they would not be interviewing David Fisher that was for sure. Edwina's whereabouts were readily known to them, they would enter her flat and wait on her return, no questions would be asked, she would be forced to the floor, and be injected with a drug that an autopsy would reveal the cause of death as a cardiac arrest, she would be found in her running attire slumped at the table. No one would be looking under her unshaven armpit for a sign of a needle being inserted at the autopsy. However Pavel was not a man who put too much detail into planned assassinations, he supplied the photographs, finance and the person would be contacted with the information, who was the assassin or who had supplied the finance was of no interest to the participants; it was custom and practice to Pavel. The contracts to remove the New York detectives and Edwina were commissioned to different assassins, it would be quickly established and leaked to veteran journalists that it was the Albanian mafia who were behind the assassinations, a cigarette (Viceroy favoured by Albanians) with DNA was found near the body of Edwina in shrubs near the bus stop at the junction of Strathern road and Claypotts road.

The professional diners that met on a regular basis at The Ivy were the perfect unaware financial consultants to launder the New York mafia's ill-gotten gains from the pump and dump share scam that Pavel had convinced the New York mafia to participate in; of course some were prone to retaining some of the profits; when the money was reinvested with David Fisher, Pavel's associates would identify the financial consultants who were laundering the stolen New York mafia's money; one by one they were all identified and removed except David Fisher; when he had completed his task for Pavel, the New York mafia would learn that Pavel's assets in New York were to be audited; they would then take their revenge on Pavel by removing David Fisher. There had never been a misappropriation of Pavel's funds for David to uncover it was all a ruse to get him to New York; he would pass on David Fisher's arrival and residence in New York through a third- party and the mafia would terminate David Fisher. No bonus would be accredited to David Fisher's company.

THE END

Printed in Great Britain
by Amazon